"**C**an't you return home?"

"No, my family would be shamed," Mariyah said. "I am dirty now, and my face full of scars. No, it is best if I stay lost."

"Mariyah, you are not dirty. There is nothing unclean about you. I hope you know that," Abby said, struggling to keep her voice from breaking.

Mariyah smiled, her scar pulling at her skin. "*Shukria,*" she said.

Abby blinked back the tears that lined her eyes. "You have a beautiful smile," she said, her voice trembling. "Your scars can't change that."

"I learning to smile, to be happy," Mariyah said. "Someday, *inshallah,* I go all the way home, and then I really smile."

Praise for *Lipstick in Afghanistan*

Also by Roberta Gately

Lipstick in Afghanistan

The Bracelet

Roberta Gately

G

Gallery Books

New York   London   Toronto   Sydney   New Delhi

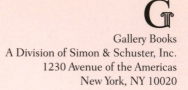

Gallery Books
A Division of Simon & Schuster, Inc.
1230 Avenue of the Americas
New York, NY 10020

First Gallery Books trade paperback edition November 2012

GALLERY BOOKS and colophon are registered trademarks of Simon & Schuster, Inc.

For information about special discounts for bulk purchases, please contact Simon & Schuster Special Sales at 1-866-506-1949 or business@simonandschuster.com.

The Simon & Schuster Speakers Bureau can bring authors to your live event. For more information or to book an event contact the Simon & Schuster Speakers Bureau at 1-866-248-3049 or visit our website at www.simonspeakers.com.

Designed by Davina Mock-Maniscalco

Manufactured in the United States of America

10 9 8 7 6 5 4 3 2 1

Library of Congress Cataloging-in-Publication Data
Gately, Roberta.
The bracelet / Roberta Gately.—1st Gallery Books trade paperback ed.
p. cm.
1. Human trafficking—Pakistan—Fiction. 2. Humanitarian assistance—Fiction. 3. Investigative reporting—Fiction. 4. War casualties—Fiction. I. Title.
PS3607.A78836B73 2012
813'.6—dc23
2012006865

ISBN 978-1-4516-6912-1
ISBN 978-1-4516-6913-8 (ebook)

*For Dennis Lucyniak, who will live forever
in the hearts of the people he touched.*

Acknowledgments

My deepest gratitude goes first to my incredible agents, Judy Hansen and Cynthia Manson, whose advice and vision have guided me through every step. I will be forever grateful for their wisdom and their wonderful friendship.

To Louise Burke and her extraordinary team at Simon & Schuster/Gallery, including Jen Bergstrom, an enormous thank-you. That team includes my wonderfully insightful editor, Abby Zidle, who not only makes me a better writer, she makes me laugh out loud in the process. To her dauntless assistant, Parisa Zolfaghari, thank you for your rapid response to everything. And endless thanks to the people who take my words and magically craft a beautiful book—Lisa Keim, Lisa Litwack, Carole Schwindeller, Regina Starace, Davina Mock, and Steve Boldt.

To Lauren Kuczala, my thanks again for your dazzling attention to detail. To the many book clubs, libraries, and groups that have invited me to speak, I am enormously grateful for your support, and to Suzanne Dana, Laurie Craparotta, and the

Marine wives and families of Camp Lejeune, boundless thanks for inviting me to your Ball and into your lives and homes.

As always, to my family and friends, thank you for your support, your laughter, and your willingness to read page after page of first drafts.

The Bracelet

Prologue

A silvery haze shrouded the streets of Geneva when Abby set out on her early-morning run. The sky was still dark, the air still crisp with the night's last breeze, as she stepped from her hotel into the quiet of the street. The doorman tipped his hat in greeting.

"*Bonjour,* Miss Monroe. Another run?"

"Morning, Claude. My last one here in Geneva. Tomorrow, I'm off to Pakistan."

"Ah, good luck, miss. Enjoy your run."

Abby waved as she glanced at her watch and eased into her morning routine. Since this would be her last run, she wanted it to be her best. Tomorrow, she'd board a flight to Dubai and, from there, head to a UN program in northern Pakistan.

"No running there," she'd been warned. "Too dangerous. Probably no time for it anyway."

Abby would be evaluating an immunization program for UNICEF. It would be her first overseas assignment, and she wanted to make a great impression, show that she could do this kind of work, that she was capable and professional.

Geneva was deadly quiet this Sunday morning, and she ran in solitude, no cars or noise or people about just yet. The sun was just creeping over the horizon, the city still struggling to shake off the night's long sleep. The streets and the scenery faded from her view as she focused all her energies on pushing forward, step after step. With every footfall, her legs throbbed, and her heart pounded. She wanted to stop, but in a day or a week or a month, she'd ache for the misery she felt now, so she picked up her pace, willing her muscles to remember this final sprint.

Abby's legs ached with the exertion but she pushed harder, thrusting her arms out grabbing the air. She felt her breathing ease as she crested a small hill and coasted on a level surface. Here the street narrowed as she passed the graceful old UN buildings. The government buildings that had loomed large in the shadowy morning light soon gave way to quiet residential streets bordered by trees, hedges, and privacy gates.

She turned her attention back to the road, wishing she'd brought her iPod. Running to the sounds of her own panting was a distraction. She turned back toward the hotel and found herself running along a wider street lined with high-rise office buildings. The street, framed by the buildings, was deserted and utterly quiet this Sunday morning. Steam seeped from the buildings' grates and rose lazily before evaporating in the morning air. Abby inhaled deeply. This indefinable time, the hour between night and day, was her favorite time to run at home. Everything was so peaceful, and that was especially true here in Geneva. Lost in the steady cadence of her footfalls, Abby savored the way her body moved and felt.

Suddenly, voices raised in anger broke through the morning hush. Abby, her senses alert, came to a full stop. She looked around, but caught here in a street of soaring office towers, she saw only blank walls of granite and steel. She hesitated, the voices rising again, an urgency spiking the sounds, and she realized they were coming from somewhere above her. She looked up, and there, framed at the edge of a fourth-floor balcony, a man had a woman pinned, her back bent over the railing.

Abby's hands flew to her mouth. She was frozen to the spot, unable to move.

Suddenly the man leaned in to the woman. Was he kissing her? Abby couldn't tell. No, she thought, they're struggling. The woman pulled the man's eyeglasses from his face, and the man exploded in anger, reaching for the woman's neck. Just then the woman let out a piercing scream, and even from the street Abby could feel her terror. She looked around, desperate for help, for someone to stop whatever was happening. But this was a business district and the streets were empty, no buses or delivery trucks, not even a dog walker in sight. The woman screamed again, her arms flailing at the man. Was she pushing him away? With a twist, the woman seemed to free herself from his grasp.

A gout of steam from a sidewalk grate stung Abby's eyes, and she blinked away tears. When she opened her eyes, she gasped in horror—the woman was plunging through the air.

Everything seemed to happen then in slow motion, and Abby's heart pounded as she watched helplessly. The woman would fall directly onto concrete—there was no padding, no soft ground, nothing to break her fall. Panicked and helpless, Abby heard her own scream, but it was lost in the sudden whoosh of air as the woman hurtled past and landed just in front of her with a sickening thud.

Abby was paralyzed. She closed her eyes and tried to rub away the image, but when she opened them, the woman's body was lying at an impossible angle, her neck twisted and broken. Abby edged closer and bent to the shattered form. She leaned over the body, and though her hands trembled wildly, she felt the woman's neck, checking instinctively for a pulse. Of course there was none. The woman's olive skin was laced with cuts and bruises, and blood seeped out from beneath her head. Abby reached her hand gently under the woman's head and felt a large depression—her skull was shattered. Bits of gray matter leaked onto the street. The woman had landed on her back, her arms thrown out, her legs broken and bent, her face still contorted in fear, blood oozing from her ears and nose. One bloody wrist was adorned by thin, brightly colored bangles, and the other bore an ornate and intricately jeweled cuff bracelet. In her hand, she clutched a pair of splintered and shattered eyeglasses, the wire cutting into her skin. The woman's long black hair, splattered now with blood, spilled around her, framing her face. Her clothes, loose and colorful like so many of the exotic dresses Abby had seen at the UN, were stippled with blood. Abby leaned over the woman's chest and listened for any breath sounds. But there was nothing. She was dead, already beyond CPR.

Abby sat back on her heels and tried to think of what to do. She was a pediatric nurse, but she knew traumatic death when she saw it. The woman's bracelet sparkled in the streetlight's glow, and though Abby wanted to look away, she found herself riveted by the flashing gems.

"You!" A menacing voice cut through the quiet, and Abby looked up to see the man who'd thrown the woman. He was leaning far over the balcony, his hands planted firmly on the ledge. He teetered there for only an instant. "Don't move!" he shouted, and Abby rose and stepped away from the body.

"You!" he called again. "Stay there—I'm coming down!"

Abby's heart thumped wildly, and her eyes scanned the street. Surely, someone had heard the commotion, but the street remained empty, making the quiet seem all the more sinister.

Where was everyone? She had to get help. She stepped back and looked warily around. Should she run? Should she hide? She couldn't think. There wasn't time. She wouldn't get far out in the open. She hurriedly looked for a place to hide. A row of full, unclipped hedges bordered the building just to her left, and she pushed her way through them to a spot low against the wall. She crouched low, pressed against the granite, willing herself to be invisible.

She huddled and waited, and then he appeared in the doorway, looking around, his head twitching as his eyes scanned the street. Abby watched as he bent over the body, pulling at something on the woman. Suddenly he stood and turned. Abby pushed herself against the old building and watched through the tiny gaps in the lush shrubbery. She tried to memorize the details of him—his slight build, the soft woolen sweater in a charcoal hue, the thinning gray hair. The man hesitated, then walked right toward the hedges where Abby hid. She held her breath and her thoughts raced. Did he see her? Surely he could hear the pounding of her heart. The street was still empty, Geneva was not yet awake. Even if she screamed, no one would hear her cries for help.

His footsteps drew closer. She held her breath and prayed for the pounding in her heart to stop. . . .

Abby crouched lower and watched as, inexplicably, he walked right past the shrub where she cowered. *He hadn't seen her after all*. She listened as his footsteps faded and moved away. Abby squinted and kept him in her line of sight as he peered up and down the street, searching, she was certain, for her. He reached into his pocket and pulled out a cell phone, furiously punching in numbers. He turned then, and almost facing her, he spoke into the phone, his tone urgent and forceful.

"*Allez, allez!*" he barked. "*Tu comprends?*" He scratched at his head, his eyes locking then on the body in the street, and almost in response his voice rose, a swelling anger evident in his tone. "*Immédiatement!*" he shouted, turning abruptly. Abby watched as he headed back to the building, his footsteps fading, his silhouette lost in a sudden surge of steam from the grates. He disappeared into the building from which he'd just emerged.

Abby didn't hesitate. This might be her only chance to escape, and she sprang to her feet, pushing through the hedges before taking flight, running madly through the streets and back to her hotel. After what seemed an eternity, she spied the smiling Claude at the door. Panting, she almost fell into him.

"Oh, miss, slow down. You've had a good run?"

"Oh, Claude, call the police!" Abby gasped for air. "Something terrible's happened."

Chapter 1

Abby woke with a start and bolted upright, throwing her arms out for protection, but nothing was there, only lightweight covers, which fell away. She wiped her hand across her sweating brow and rose quickly, but a sudden dizziness caused her to stumble, and she sat back heavily. Inhaling deeply, she tried to get her bearings, but the sound of footsteps outside the door made her freeze.

"Who is it?" she whispered, but the footsteps faded, and a heavy silence settled in their place.

A dull throbbing erupted in her brain, and her hands trembled as she tried to rub away the goose bumps on her bare arms.

She took a deep breath and looked around, trying to push away the fog of confusion that had settled in her thoughts. Streaming sunlight fell on a rickety wooden chair and the familiar suitcase it held.

Pakistan.

She was in Pakistan. The UN staff house. She'd arrived yesterday from Dubai. She'd been sleeping, though fitfully.

Sighing with relief, she rubbed at her eyes, still gummy with sleep. Had it only been forty-eight hours since her run in Geneva? She shuddered at the memory of the woman falling to her death. Though the police had initially seemed concerned and had taken her back through the streets, they'd quickly grown weary of Abby's failure to find the body, and they'd raised their brows in disbelief.

"I was certain this was the street," Abby said. "But—"

"Why are you confused, miss?" the younger policeman had interrupted her. "This is such an important detail. Was she thrown? Did she fall? Which was it? And where is she now? Bodies don't just disappear."

His rapid-fire questions and her failure to find the body had only fueled Abby's growing alarm. Her eyes scanned the streets, but the same monotonous buildings, all granite and steel, had loomed above her, one building, one street, indistinguishable from the next. And without the body as a landmark, she'd felt her certainty fading. "One more time," she'd pleaded. "There *was* a woman. I'm not making this up."

A growing panic had nipped at her thoughts. Which road *had* it been? Perhaps it was the next street, she'd said. The police had taken her down one street and then another, filled now with cars and people, but there was nothing to see, no body, no blood or tissue in the street. Finally they'd driven her back to the hotel, derisive smirks playing at their lips.

"Get some sleep, miss, and you'll forget this," the younger policeman said, impatience dripping from his words.

"But—" she tried to protest, but the second policeman spoke up.

"Be sure to call us if you see the body again." He broke into a wide grin that was almost a sneer.

But she'd neither slept nor forgotten. Even now she could clearly remember, in crisp detail, the woman's olive skin, her thick black hair, and the bracelet that had sparkled almost obscenely on her shattered wrist. Abby could see too the face of the man as he'd searched for her in the street, and she shivered at the recollection.

On her overnight in Dubai, unable to sleep, and drenched in sweat despite the air-conditioning, she'd dialed the hotel operator and made a call to Emily, her best friend in Boston. Abby had forgotten the time difference until she heard Emily's voice, heavy with sleep.

"Oh, Em, I'm sorry to wake you. It's early morning here, and I was desperate to talk, to tell someone."

"What's wrong?" Emily said, the sleep suddenly gone from her voice.

"I . . . oh, jeez. This will sound crazy, but I saw a woman fall from a balcony in Geneva, and, well—I don't think she just fell. I think I may have witnessed a murder. My heart is pounding just telling you about it."

Abby's story spilled out quickly—the eerie quiet of Geneva, the arguing voices, the woman hurtling through the air to her death. "She wore this beautiful jeweled cuff, and I remember it so clearly. The thing is, I'm not sure if she fell or if the man threw her." Abby paused, but Emily was silent.

"Em? Are you there?"

"Where *are* you?"

Abby heard the concern in Emily's voice. "Dubai, I'm in the airport hotel. I came in last night from Geneva. I fly out to Pakistan later today. I just had to hear your voice. My hands are shaking." Abby made a fist to quiet the tremors. "I reported it to the police, Em, and they took me back, but the body was gone." She swallowed hard. "I know how it sounds, and I know the police thought I was a little bit off, but I am one hundred percent certain that I saw a woman fall to her death. I just don't know if she was thrown or if she fell."

"Why are you so worried now?"

"The man who was with her, he came looking for me in the street, and when I came back with the police, she was gone, just gone. I just . . ." Abby hesitated, hoping that Emily would say something reassuring. Instead, the line was quiet, and Abby thought she might have lost the connection. "Em, are you there?"

"I am. I'm just trying to understand what you're telling me."

"Oh, Christ, you don't believe me either?"

Emily sighed heavily. "It isn't that, but, well, you're sure she was dead? I mean, maybe she *did* fall, and the man you saw was looking for help, and not for you. Otherwise, your story does sound a little crazy. Bodies don't just disappear, right?"

"I don't know," Abby almost whispered. "Maybe he did call for help. I just don't know."

"You don't think you might have imagined it?"

Exasperated, Abby snapped back, "No, I didn't imagine it."

"I love you, Ab, but you do have a tendency to be dramatic, and with everything going on in your life . . . well, it seems, I don't know, maybe you're making more of this than there is. You probably saw a jumper or maybe a woman who slipped and fell. Maybe an ambulance just came and took her to a hospital." Emily paused, letting her words sink in. "As horrible as it must have been, the whole incident has probably been magnified by your malaria medicine. You've read about the awful side effects of Lariam—nightmares, dizziness, breakdowns—and those are just the known effects. And on top of that, you're on your way to Pakistan, of all places. Maybe this is a sign. Just come home."

Abby took a deep breath. "Emily, come on. I'm not coming home, not yet at least. And I don't think I've been especially dramatic. I just can't shake this feeling that I saw a murder."

"Abby, take a deep breath and think about this. You've had one blow after another—you were laid off, Eric left you, you're on your way to a strange country, and you're on Lariam. I mean, come on. The only mystery here is why you haven't booked a flight home."

Abby hesitated. "Maybe you're right. Not about coming home, but everything else."

"Try not to dwell on what happened." Emily's voice was tinged with worry. "It was probably a terrible accident, but there's nothing you can do about it now. Just let it go and get on with things."

Abby drummed her fingers on the desk. "You're probably right, Em. I just had to tell someone, it makes it less scary. It *was* awful seeing that poor woman on the street, but it's over."

"I still wish you'd just come home," Em had said.

Abby stood and stretched, and tried to erase the image of the dead woman from her mind. She exhaled loudly and saw the woman's bracelet again in her mind—a beautiful diamond cuff shot through with rubies and sapphires and sparkling garnets. It had sparkled so—

A knock on the door interrupted her thoughts. "I'll be right out," she said, the threads of her memory slipping away.

Abby's room in the Pakistan staff house had an adjoining

bath, and she headed in. The little room was dark and she clicked on the light just as a bevy of cockroaches scurried away. She groaned and stepped carefully around the collection of larger bugs that lingered in the tiny space. Though she'd occasionally spied roaches in her apartment on Beacon Hill, they were nothing like these enormous insects. She peeled off her nightgown, then turned on the shower and stepped in, turning her face into the spray of tepid water. Maybe a shower would wash it all away. She'd come to Pakistan to do just that, and she planned to make it work.

She'd been a new nursing graduate in New Orleans when Hurricane Katrina struck, devastating her hospital and her future there. Within days, her hospital, drowning in six feet of stagnant water, had closed forever, and New Orleans, drowning in a sea of looters and rot and misery, seemed a place to escape. She and Emily had headed to Boston, where Abby had found her dream job—in a pediatric clinic where she was in charge of immunizations. She kept track of which babies needed which vaccines, and she managed the records and logged the vaccines. She and Emily squeezed into an impossibly small apartment on Beacon Hill, and just when she thought life couldn't get any more perfect, she'd met Eric, a six-foot-tall intern who thought more of himself than he probably should have, and maybe Abby should have known better, but she hadn't, and she'd fallen head over heels in love.

After three years together, her heart had still fluttered at the sight of him, and when he told her he loved her, she was certain her life was set—perfect job, perfect life. She glided on air for the next three years, sure he'd ask her to marry him, but he didn't. And when Emily became engaged, Eric almost seemed to wither at the news. He'd mumbled something unintelligible and changed the subject. Abby had shrugged her shoulders. He was just overworked. That was it. And she didn't bring it up again.

When the recession hit and cuts were made, her hospital slashed jobs, and hers was one of the first to be eliminated. Eric had barely blinked. "Forget about that job," he'd said, but what she heard was *I'll take care of you.* The layoff, she thought, might turn out to be a blessing in disguise, a chance for them to get closer. Eric had accepted a fellowship in Oregon, and Abby just assumed she'd be traveling there with him, making a new life together. Instead, within weeks of her layoff, and just days after her thirtieth birthday, Eric, the man she loved beyond all common sense, had—well, he'd *dumped* her—by e-mail no less. Said he needed space so he'd be moving to Oregon alone. Abby's dreams had dissolved into nothing. In a heartbeat, everything was gone. No job, no boyfriend, and thirtieth birthday alone. Her birthday horoscope—"This is the year you find true love"—served only to mock her misery.

With her perfect life in tatters, she took to her bed, where she devoured Godiva chocolates and guzzled Grey Goose until neither her stomach nor her dwindling finances could support her misery.

Abby knew full well her self-pity couldn't last forever, and after a full day and night of decadent melancholy, her throat scratchy and her head pounding, she'd picked herself up, thrown out the candy wrappers, and piled the empty bottles in the recycling bin, certain that the garbagemen would be clucking their tongues.

She was desperate to leave Boston and her wretched life far behind, and her parents, newly retired and moving to a retirement community in Florida, had tried to convince her to join them. "Abby, we'd love to have you move with us," her mother had cooed. "The three of us again, just like when you were little."

Abby had winced at the thought. "I love you and Dad," she'd replied, "but I'm thirty years old, Mom. I need to figure this out on my own."

"I know, sweetheart, but you'll always have a place here," her mother had said.

But Abby wanted to make her own place in the world, and with Emily getting married and Eric gone, she'd have to stand up and do something for herself. She'd stumbled across this United Nations position online, a six-month assignment that seemed custom-made for her—vaccine statistics—and she'd decided it couldn't hurt to apply. The confusing application process seemed designed to weed out the less determined applicants, but Abby had persisted, doggedly filling out the tedious paperwork. Still, no one was more surprised than she when she'd been offered the post. Perhaps it was the pay, a stipend really—$500 a month with room and board here in the UN house—that had thinned out the interested applicants. Or perhaps it was the area—Peshawar, in Pakistan—"unstable security situation" was how the ad had euphemistically put it.

Emily had cringed at the news. "Pakistan?" she'd moaned. "God, Abby, why not just stay and get another job here? Why do you have to go halfway around the world to find yourself?"

"It's not that I'm trying to find *myself*," she'd replied. "I just want to find where I fit in."

"Which brings me back to *why Pakistan*?" Emily was nothing if not persistent. "You're jumping into this. *Stay*. Figure things out here."

"I have to stop relying on everyone else, Em. I'm going, so stop trying to talk me out of it."

And now here Abby was—in *Pakistan,* a place she couldn't even have found on a map not so long ago—on a UN assignment. This could be the adventure of a lifetime, she thought.

This place that was so far out of her comfort zone could be just what she needed.

Abby turned off the water, the rush of air on her damp skin bringing her back to the present. She stepped out of the shower and quickly toweled off. Here in Pakistan, the desperate heat should have dictated what she'd wear, but, instead, the delicate cultural balance of this Muslim nation had influenced her wardrobe. Women here, she'd been told, did not show skin. No shorts, no sleeveless shirts, nothing that might offend. She pulled on a long cotton skirt and blouse, and already she could feel beads of perspiration running down her back.

Abby's hair, the color of wheat, hung in waves to her shoulders, and she ran her fingers through the still-damp strands before shaking them into place. She wiped away the fog from the mirror and studied her reflection. For the first time in a month, her brown eyes were not rimmed with the red of her tears, and she smiled as she applied a thin stroke of eyeliner and a coating of clear lip gloss. Pakistan, she thought, is going to be way better than Oregon. She tucked her feet into sensible Nikes, missing her designer sandals. Too late to think about that now, she reminded herself, probably no chance to wear them here anyway. She was beginning her new life, and this was her first day.

She grabbed her work bag and, pulling open the door, stepped into the dim hallway . . . where she almost ran into a squat, scowling woman.

"Sorry, I didn't see you," Abby apologized. The woman, dressed in the local garb of long dress and loose pants, wore a scarf tied around her head and clutched a broom. "I'm Abby, the new UN staffer." She smiled to herself—she liked the sound of that, *UN staffer*.

The woman nodded, unspeaking, and Abby, thinking perhaps she'd spoken too quickly, repeated her introduction slowly and enunciated every syllable, hoping that the woman might understand. Instead, as though she'd just wrapped her lips around a bitter fruit, the woman's face crinkled into a scowl.

"I'm not deaf," she said, a British edge to her voice. "I heard you the first time. I'm Hana, the housekeeper and cook. She's waiting for you in there." Hana looked over her shoulder, nodding her head to the room at the far end of the hallway.

Embarrassed, Abby stuck out her hand. "Sorry, Hana. Nice to meet you. I guess I'll see you later."

Hana shrugged her shoulders and turned back to her broom, tapping it against the floor as she worked.

Abby pulled back her hand, swallowing her disappointment at Hana's unpleasantness. She gathered her courage and headed toward the stream of light at the end of the hallway.

Chapter 2

Abby peered into the dining room and saw a large window flooding the room with morning light, and a young woman sitting at a long table, intent on the pile of papers before her. "Good morning," Abby said, stepping into the room.

The woman looked up, and Abby stepped back. With her olive skin and lush black hair, she was almost identical to the dead woman in Geneva. Abby exhaled and tried to steady herself. It's over, she chided herself. Let it go.

The woman smiled broadly and jumped from her seat. "Come in, good morning." She rushed forward and took Abby's hands in her own. "It's good to meet you, Abby," she said, her voice almost breathless. "I was coming back to knock again. I'm sorry no one was here to meet you last night." She spoke quickly, her words piling on top of one another, and Abby leaned forward, straining to hear.

"I am Najeela, the administrative assistant for this office," she said, smiling the wide smile of someone trying hard to be liked. "I am so happy you are here. I just know we will be great friends." She squeezed Abby's hands in both of hers and leaned in to plant a kiss on each of her cheeks. "Welcome."

The knot of worry that had built up in Abby's stomach unraveled. She smiled and watched as the energetic Najeela pulled out a chair and motioned for her to sit. Najeela was about Abby's height, a full five foot six, and she shook her long hair away from her face. Her olive skin was smooth and dewy and her brown eyes had a hint of green. A long red scarf was draped over her shoulders, and like Hana, she wore a large dress over balloonlike pants.

Abby slid into the seat. "I'm happy to be here, Najeela, and excited about my position."

Najeela took her seat across from Abby. "Oh, good. I'm sorry that I couldn't meet you last night when you arrived, but it was late and I had to be at home with my parents. Were you able to settle in?"

"I was. Thank you. My room is lovely and having my own bathroom is more than I expected."

"I'm glad you like it. Did you sleep well?"

Fragments of the dream she'd had floated in Abby's mind. "I . . . I did." Not wanting the events in Geneva to intrude on her day, she changed the subject. "But I never did get to see any of the city last night. It was so dark when I arrived, and the car brought me straight here. Will we be able to go out today?"

"Ah, but of course. There is so much for you to see—the city, the refugee camp, so, yes, of course we will go."

"Your clothes and scarf, Najeela," Abby said, looking down at her own skirt. "I have large pants and long skirts, but I'd like to get some local clothes."

Najeela looked her over. "I wish we could shop for real clothes, for the latest Western styles, but I suppose we should get you some local pants and long-sleeved shirts and maybe a scarf. But, do not worry. Peshawar is a city, and people will know you are foreign. As long as you are covered, you will be fine."

Abby nodded, still uncertain in this new place.

"Please, make yourself comfortable and have something to eat." Najeela seemed to sense Abby's discomfort. "If you'd like something cooked, I can have Hana prepare it."

"Oh, no, please," Abby pleaded. "I've bothered Hana enough already. Coffee and toast are fine."

Abby watched as Najeela spooned instant coffee into a cup and poured steaming water over it. "Milk?" she asked, passing her the cup.

Abby shook her head. "I take mine black, thanks, but I have to say I don't know how you can drink hot coffee here." Abby sighed, noticing how already the morning's heat had seeped into the room.

Najeela laughed. "You will adjust to this. In Peshawar, the electricity is not always so reliable. It comes and goes. We do have a generator, but we save it for the office computers and the phone, and only for the air conditioner when the heat is just too much to bear. We kept it on last night for you." Najeela wiped her scarf across her face. "There is often no escape from the heat, and maybe that is better. Soon, you will not even notice it."

Najeela had a lilting speech, a hint of French mixed with something Abby couldn't quite identify.

"Hana has put out fresh bread and jam for breakfast."

Najeela pushed the jam and bread to Abby. "Help yourself. Though the bread is not a crusty French baguette, it is good."

Abby reached for the jam as a cluster of flies swarmed over her cup of coffee and the small container of milk that Najeela had set down. Abby swatted them away and laid her hand protectively over the cup. The flies buzzed in earnest, settling on the back of her hand. When she shook them off, they settled back on her cup. It seemed a hopeless game of cat and mouse and the flies were winning.

Najeela watched and smiled. "They are awful," she said with a loud sigh. "But it is best if you get used to them. They aren't going anywhere."

Abby shrugged and swatted one last time before she lifted the cup to her lips and drank the steaming coffee. She watched as Najeela lifted the lid on the jam and slid a spoon into the gooey confection. A buzzing swarm alighted on the spoon, and Najeela indifferently shrugged them away. When she spread the jam on a piece of bread, one fly struggled in the jam until Najeela plucked him out.

"Disgusting," she muttered, pushing the jar away. "Come," she said, rising from her seat. "Bring your coffee, we can eat later. I'll show you around, and then we can get you started in the office."

Najeela led Abby back down the long, dimly lit hallway. "This is a one-story house, and the rooms are all off this central hallway." She opened a large double door and peered in. "This is the parlor. I'm not sure why, but no one ever uses it."

Abby poked her head in and understood why. The furniture was obviously antique and very ornate, lots of heavy velvet and delicate wood. She didn't think she'd spend much time in there either. The main entrance was just beyond the parlor, and the imposing front door was framed by full-length, frosted-glass windowpanes on either side. Not a very practical house, Abby thought. Najeela pointed out two other unused bedrooms along the hallway.

"Sometimes," Najeela said, "there are more staff living here, but with the trouble, it is only you."

"Is that the *unstable security* situation the UN mentioned?"

"It is. If you ask me, it's much ado about nothing, but those words keep some people away. I'm so glad you weren't frightened off."

"The UN assured me that they keep a close watch on the situation, and if there is trouble, they said they'd send me someplace else."

Najeela frowned. "We'll have to avoid trouble so that you can stay right here with me."

Reassured by Najeela's matter-of-fact tone, Abby smiled and turned her attention back to the tour.

When they passed the kitchen, a large room filled with cabinets and a gleaming table, Abby spied Hana bent over the sink, furiously scrubbing dishes. Najeela leaned in. "Hana, please clean the dining room. We are finished with breakfast." Hana turned and gave them both a long stare. "And the jam . . . ," Najeela continued. "Please throw it out and remember to cover the food." Hana bent back to the sink.

Abby cringed at Najeela's sharp tone. "Does my being here add to her work?" she asked. "She just seemed so unhappy this morning. I mean, if I've done something to offend her, I'd like to make amends."

"Don't let her bother you. That's just her way."

"But I'd like to be her friend."

Najeela's mouth opened wide. "Really? I think it's best not to befriend the staff. Most of them are illiterate and very different from you and me. It's probably wise to keep your distance."

Najeela stepped into a room at the rear of the house. "Here we are. Welcome to your office."

The office, tucked at the back of the house, was tiny. Two worn wooden desks pushed against the wall held bulky desktop computers. An old metal filing cabinet filled the space in between, and a lone metal chair with a cushioned seat sat in the center of the room. The single window was propped open with a piece of wood, allowing sunlight and warm air to stream in, but a musty scent hovered in the room. Abby peeked out—there was no view, just a glimpse of the high, white fence that ran about the periphery of the house.

"In there"—Najeela pointed at the filing cabinet—"are the vaccination reports and statistics. You'll need to spend some time going over those numbers so you'll understand what you need to report. Did they explain that to you? Does it make sense?"

"I think so. I guess I'll have to look through everything, but in Geneva, they went over the paperwork and statistics, so I think I'll be okay."

Najeela reached into her pocket for a key and unlocked the cabinet and the drawers in one desk. "I moved your blank reports and papers here to this desk." She pointed to the one she'd unlocked before slipping the key back into her pocket.

"Will I need the key?"

"No, no. It's best if you keep it open. That way you can work anytime you like."

"Okay. What about the other desk? Is it locked?"

"Yes, but I think you'll need only the one desk. Otherwise you'll work too hard, and I . . ." Najeela dropped her voice to a whisper though Hana was all the way down the hall. "I use that desk for my own things."

"Will you be working in here with me?"

Najeela giggled. "I'm the administrator for this suboffice,

and there isn't much for me to do. I mostly go to meetings and listen to dull men speak about their dull plans."

Abby smiled. "I've never thought of the UN as dull."

"Wait till you've been here awhile."

Abby relaxed. She hadn't expected Najeela to be so friendly and open and, well, so like herself in many ways. She'd expected a very foreign woman, not this ebullient person who acted more like a girlfriend than a colleague. Abby sat in the chair and listened as it creaked and groaned. This room had been unoccupied for a while, she supposed. She clicked the computer to life. "If you'll show me where I can find the documents and files in this computer, I'll get started."

Najeela leaned in and typed *UN Vaccination Program,* and the old monitor exploded with an endless list of files and folders.

"This is everything, Abby, everything the UN orientation group showed you in Geneva—it should all look familiar to you. So, spend some time going over the files to be sure you have what you need, and then we'll go out. I'll take you to see the city and the refugee camp and maybe we can shop as well."

"Is there Internet access? I'd like to e-mail my mom and a friend or two so they'll know I arrived safely."

Najeela leaned in and pointed out the Internet icon. "Just click here, and you'll be connected."

Relieved that she'd be able to keep in touch with Emily and her parents, Abby nodded, eager to get started on her work. She bent to the computer screen, a pile of reports in her lap, and began to read and record the numbers. Before long the heat of the day seeped into the room. The trickle of sweat that had gathered on the back of her neck when she'd first sat was now a veritable flood of moisture running along her back. A quick look around confirmed that her little office had no air conditioner, not even a fan. Though she'd grown up in the soupy heat of New Orleans, air-conditioning had always taken away the sting, but here in the UN house, Abby would have to get used to sticky shirts and hair plastered to her neck. She could already see that in this room at least, the stifling heat enveloped everything. She decided against shutting the window—at least it offered some fresh air.

Abby spent the next two hours huddled over the computer, checking objectives and target numbers, and finally she smiled to herself. "*Now* I see," she said out loud. She stood and stretched. The time had flown, and she was stiff and hot. She clicked into the Internet and typed quick messages to her mom and Emily. That out of the way, she went in search of Najeela.

"I'm ready for a break," she announced, wiping the beads of sweat from her brow.

Najeela smiled. "Let's have a cold drink," she said, her voice bubbling with enthusiasm. "Is Coca-Cola good for you?"

Abby nodded in reply. Her throat was parched.

Once Abby had guzzled down the bottle of Coke, Najeela summoned the car and driver. "Ready, Abby?"

Abby grabbed her bag and met Najeela at the door. A small, wiry man wearing an oversize shirt and the same big balloon pants as Hana and Najeela appeared and bowed to Abby. "Miss," he said softly. "I am Mohammed, your driver."

Abby smiled and bowed in return. "Mohammed, we met last night, I think. You picked me up at the airport?"

A gentle smile creased Mohammed's face. "I am thinking maybe you too tired, maybe you forget."

"No, I remember you. It's good to see you again." Abby and Najeela settled themselves in the backseat, and Mohammed guided the car out of the long driveway, through the gate, and into the street.

"This area," said Najeela, "is University Town. The UN and most of the aid groups have offices and homes here."

The homes and offices were hidden behind high stucco walls, all painted white and all bearing engraved business signs announcing just who resided there. Abby read as they drove. She saw the offices for UNICEF, the World Health Organization, the International Rescue Committee, and the Red Cross—though here it was called the Red Crescent.

They turned a corner and drove smack into the middle of a chaotic, dizzying scene. The narrow street heaved with a crush of veiled women, pitiful beggars, wobbly pushcarts and rickshaws, donkeys, even a camel. The men all wore pajama suits—oversize shirts and the same billowy pants the women wore under their dresses and veils. Music blasted from everywhere—the sounds of lilting Indian flutes and guitars and singers with high-pitched voices mingled with the braying of donkeys, the tooting of rickshaws, and the honking of cars. The noise was earsplitting.

Along the edges of the road, crowded storefronts spilled their wares—bolts of cloth, gleaming silver teakettles, and burlap sacks filled with rice and sugar. Abby watched as harried vendors bargained with sharp-tongued customers. Everywhere, power lines and antennas looped precariously through the air connecting crumbling archaic buildings to the modern world. The frantic scene was spellbinding—not even Mardi Gras had been this packed.

"This is the bazaar," Najeela said. "Here you can buy anything you might need—even blood for transfusion."

Abby looked skeptically at Najeela and pulled herself forward, craning to get a better look. Then she spied the large sign: BLOOD TRANSFUSIONS AND DONOR BAGS AVAILABLE HERE. Abby's mouth fell open. "Wow, you weren't kidding." She wished Emily were here to see this.

Najeela laughed. "Peshawar is not like Boston or Paris. If you are sick here and in need of blood, you must get it yourself. Only a very few hospitals provide blood."

"I'll have to stay well."

Abby watched as the car squeezed through the narrow streets, people and animals walking in a crush alongside. Little girls wearing head scarves and little boys wearing grown-up scowls pushed up close, peering into the car. The car glided along the street before finally pulling out onto a wide boulevard, where it picked up speed.

"The camp is just beyond the main city," Najeela said, touching Abby's hand. "We are almost there." Soon thereafter, the car pulled into an area surrounded by a high, white fence. A sign painted there read SAFAR REFUGEE CAMP. "*Safar*," Najeela announced, "means 'journey,' and for the people here, this place is a stop on their journey home."

The car pulled into the camp, depositing its two occupants. "Wait here, please," Najeela directed Mohammed. She and Abby stepped out of the car and onto the camp's main road. The sun's glare sliced through the morning sky, flooding everything in its path. Abby squinted. The bright blue sky was utterly cloudless; the sun was so intense that the heat seemed to tuck itself into every corner. She drew her sleeve across her sweat-stained face. The air here was thick and soupy and not unlike New Orleans before Hurricane Katrina blew through. Abby shivered at the memory and hoped that wasn't an omen.

Najeela walked up the dirt and gravel path with an enviable spring to her step. Abby hurried to keep up.

"This is your first refugee camp, yes?" Najeela asked.

Abby nodded and tried to take it all in. An endless sea of dusty tents spread to every corner of the camp. Some were held up by sticks, some were tethered to the ground with long ropes, and some were covered with heavy plastic tarpaulins. Scattered in between were small brick-and-plaster buildings, offices maybe. People, mostly women and children, milled about.

It was an image of pure desolation. Abby supposed New Orleans hadn't been so different after Katrina, but she'd lived north of the city, and she hadn't seen it except for the images that had flickered across her television screen. A tiny twinge of guilt touched her. She should have stayed after the hurricane. She could have helped. She sighed heavily. This time, she'd stay, no matter what.

Najeela seemed to sense Abby's trepidation. "In a very short time, you'll get used to this, to the sights and the scents here, but it is overwhelming when you first see it. On my first visit, I fell quite ill with the sight of it." Najeela paused and looked around. "I thought I could never come back, but I have trained my eyes to look away from the sadness." She turned, and as if to emphasize that, she looked away and smiled broadly. "And now that we are here, you can see why we need you."

Abby took a deep breath and nodded. That much seemed clear.

Najeela turned back to the road and her tour. "This camp has been running for over twenty years. I don't think anyone thought it would still be needed." She pointed down the long road. "You know that we still have refugees from Afghanistan, and now some Pakistanis as well. Flooding has forced thousands upon thousands of Pakistanis into Peshawar. That crisis, coupled with the lingering presence of thousands of Afghan refugees, means that vaccinations are a priority. The UN keeps track of and administers the vaccines. Everyone has to be vaccinated. Did you know that an outbreak of measles can wipe out a camp in weeks?"

Abby nodded.

Najeela giggled. "I've just memorized those statistics. How did I sound?"

"Impressive, Najeela. You were definitely convincing." Abby turned her attention back to the primitive road that wound through the camp's center, rows and rows of tents stretching out on either side. The terrain was desolate—just dirt sprinkled between the tents and huts. Abby's shoulders sagged as she looked around. She hadn't imagined that a place could be so sad, so filled with misery. Barefoot children in threadbare shirts and pants watched her warily.

Abby smiled. "Hello," she called out. A few children giggled in reply and ran off. "There are so many children here. Is that usual or is it the floods?"

"This is the area for separated children, for those children whose parents have been killed or are lost."

"Oh," Abby sighed, "poor kids. Who takes care of them?"

"The UN does, and the staff here search for their families. UNICEF has an office—well, a tent, really—where they work with the Red Crescent to reunite lost children with their families, and to protect those children who are alone. They keep files and photos of the children here and of those who are still lost so that people might come or reconnect and provide information. It is a complicated situation."

"What will happen to them?"

"The staff here will try to place them with family or people from their own villages, but that can be risky. It's the hardest part of the UN's mission—caring for the lost children. They are easy prey for the evil ones. At least here, they are safe."

"Evil ones?" Abby asked. "That sounds ominous."

"It does, doesn't it? We won't speak of such things today."

When Abby turned her attention back to the road, she saw women clad in the full covering of the burka, the tentlike garment that she'd seen in photos. They walked in small clusters through the camp. "Do they have to wear that?" Abby asked, motioning to a woman nearby.

"If they were in their own villages, they would probably wear only the head scarf, but here in the camp, there is no privacy to speak of. They are without the high walls that shield them from the outside. So here, the burka is their wall, their security from prying eyes." Najeela sighed heavily and smoothed her hair. "At least that is what they believe. I think the burka is primitive. Come, enough of that." She turned off the road toward a thatch-roofed, plaster building. "This is the Immunization Clinic. Two days a week, UNICEF vaccinates the children. It's closed today, but this is where you'll come to pick up your reports and statistics. You can help out if you'd like. It will help you to get used to everything."

Abby nodded and peered into the darkness of the small space. "I'm looking forward to being here when it's open." She smiled. "Vaccines and clinics—the stuff I know, makes me feel that I can help, not just with statistics, but with these poor people."

Najeela took Abby's hand and squeezed. "But they are not so poor—they are *here* and they are taken care of. Come, we've seen enough for today. This place is too sad for you, I think."

"I . . ." Abby started to say that she wanted to see more, but already Najeela was dashing away. I guess it is awfully sad, Abby thought. Everything here was sad, the sheer numbers of people and the unrelenting misery, all of it more pitiful than anything else she'd ever seen.

Chapter 3

Abby followed Najeela to the car, where a flushed Moham-med stood waiting in the full glare of the sun. "Oh, Mohammed," Abby said, "you look so hot. Wasn't there any spot of shade?"

He didn't answer and simply looked at Najeela. "It's impor-tant that he watch the car," Najeela said as she turned and slid into the backseat. Abby followed, grateful for the bit of shade the car offered.

"I don't know about you," Najeela said, her tone petulant, "but I'm hungry. Let's go to the Pearl for lunch." She spoke curtly to Mohammed in Urdu, then turned to Abby. "The Pearl Continental is Peshawar's finest hotel. We can have a civilized lunch, even a glass of wine if you'd like."

Abby could only nod in reply. Her mind was still on the camp, the lost children, and the sheer misery of the place. Tucked inside the comfort of the air-conditioned car, she found it almost unreal. She closed her eyes. "You were right, Najeela. The misery in Safar is almost too much to absorb." She paused. "I can't even imagine how difficult life is for those people."

Najeela patted Abby's hand. "The villages they came from really weren't so different from this place—dusty roads and mud houses." Najeela flashed a smile. "But enough of refugees today. You need a good lunch, Abby, and you'll feel better."

And just like that, Najeela steered the conversation away from the refugees. It was, Abby supposed, a kind of defense mechanism. If you thought about it too much, you probably couldn't work here.

As the car pulled away from the camp, it was surrounded by a large group of beggars, their faces peering in, eyes open wide, noses pressed to the windows, their hands held out. Abby sat forward and fished through her bag for money.

"No, no!" Najeela exclaimed, her voice loud. She pulled Abby away from the window. "Mohammed, speed up please."

"But I have some change," Abby pleaded, "and these people look so desperate."

"They are desperate for your money, Abby. Many of them are professional beggars. See that woman." Najeela pointed to a legless woman who sat atop a wheeled platform, a child at her breast. "She likely had her legs amputated to help increase her income, and her baby—she will likely do something terrible to maim him, to make him more sympathetic."

"Oh, Najeela, you can't be serious." Abby was unable to hide the irritation that had welled up in her voice. "That woman has no legs. Good God, I don't think she did that to herself."

A frown creased Najeela's face. "Suit yourself, but please don't give them money when you are with me."

Abby sat back, defeated, and Najeela, seeming to sense that she'd gone too far, gripped Abby's hand. "I know it seems cruel, but trust me, handing out money only makes the situation here worse."

Abby, dazed and speechless at Najeela's point of view, could only nod in reply. The car ground to a stop, and when Abby gazed out, she saw a group of young men glaring angrily at her and Najeela. A small shiver ran up her spine. "What's that all about?" Abby asked, nudging Najeela.

"Oh, they're probably radicals. You know—fundamentalists. Pay them no mind. They're angry that women can do things on their own." Najeela shook her head and turned away from the window. "Maybe, if you're not too tired, we can shop after lunch," she said, her tone suddenly happy as if the beggars and the angry young men had never happened.

Abby opened her mouth to speak, to say, *Not today,* but Najeela piped in. "Here we are," announcing their arrival. Abby's mouth fell open. The hotel was ornate and gracious and, well . . . beautiful. Surrounded by lush green lawns, it seemed to have been plunked down in the midst of misery and squalor by some cosmic mistake. Abby followed Najeela through the lobby to the restaurant, a quiet, elegant place. They could have been at the Ritz in Boston. Maybe this was why those young men had seemed so angry. It was rich women they didn't like, and they could peg Najeela a mile away.

"How many?" the man asked Najeela.

"Two," she replied, holding up her fingers as if unsure he would understand her words. They followed the man, who led them to a table near the back. Najeela sat facing the large room. "I like to see who comes in," she said, picking up the menu. "I'll order, if that's okay? The kebabs and biryani rice are wonderful. Yes?"

Abby nodded. She *was* hungry. Maybe Najeela was right— all she needed was a good meal.

When the food came, Abby inhaled the fragrant aroma of the spices. Though she'd never been much of a cook and had no idea what she was eating, she did know that it was delicious, filled with spices and seasonings she'd never able to identify. "Hmm," she muttered in between bites, "you were right, Najeela. This is really good."

"I knew this is what you needed. A little piece of civilization and all is right with the world, yes?"

"Well, I don't know about that, but I was famished."

Najeela picked delicately at her meal. "May I ask about you? Is your boyfriend in Boston?"

Abby cringed at the question. Eric was the last person she wanted to think about or speak about. "Well, I don't have a boyfriend, at least not now." She bent to her meal, hoping that might end Najeela's line of questioning, but Najeela was intent on her probe.

"Ah, but you did have someone? You're so pretty, Abby, with your buttery hair and pale skin. You must be very popular."

Abby laughed. "I actually thought I'd be engaged by now, but things didn't work out, so here I am."

"Tell me about him," Najeela murmured.

Abby felt her heart beat faster at the mere thought of Eric. She shook off the still-raw memory and looked at Najeela.

"My last boyfriend was Eric," she said, hating the sound of his name, hating that he was here smack in the middle of her new life. Najeela's eyes sparkled at the hint of a romantic tale, but Abby, eager to steer the conversation away from herself, added quickly, "But that's finished now."

"But what of the others?" Najeela leaned in. "In America, women have many boyfriends, yes?"

"Oh, Najeela, I don't want to talk about old boyfriends, not today."

"One more, Abby, just tell me about one more. I've only had one boyfriend. I envy you your freedom to have as many as you'd like."

Abby laughed. "Believe me, it's not as exciting as it sounds to you, and I've really only had two serious boyfriends."

A pout sprang to Najeela's lips. "Still more than me."

"All right," Abby murmured, "one more." She folded her arms. "In college, I was engaged." She stroked the spot on her finger where her diamond had once been. "I broke it off when he decided to leave school. I was younger then and much more impatient, and I thought he was just lazy."

Najeela frowned. "Where is he now, this lazy one?"

"Not where I expected—he's very successful these days, he's a well-known attorney in Louisiana. And no one would describe him as lazy."

"Is he wealthy?" Najeela asked, her eyes wide.

"I suppose so."

"Then you must take him back."

Abby laughed. "I don't think he'd take me back. Besides, he has a wife and children now. I only told you about him to show that I am the queen of poor judgment where men are concerned. So, that's it. Enough about me. What about you? You said you have a boyfriend?"

Najeela's face flushed pink through her olive skin. "Oh, I do have someone, but he is my secret, at least for now."

"Your secret? After the secrets I just spilled to you? It's only fair to tell me more."

Najeela pushed her plate away. "I would love to tell you, Abby, but first, you must swear to keep my confidence."

Abby stopped eating. Najeela was suddenly so serious. "Of course I will."

"I am in love and I hope to marry this man, but my father would not approve because he is European. You see, though I am technically an Afghan refugee, I've never set foot inside that country, and to tell you the truth, I have no desire to do so." She settled herself back in her seat. "My parents were well-off, and they escaped from Afghanistan to Paris during the Soviet invasion. I was born in Paris and went to school there. I expected to spend my life wandering around Europe, but after your soldiers liberated Afghanistan, my father was determined to return, to become a diplomat, and perhaps someday to be president."

Abby's eyes grew wide. "President?"

"That's not so far-reaching as it might sound. Hamid Karzai is my father's friend, and my father would like nothing more than to follow him into office."

"Wow," Abby said, impressed more than she thought possible.

"Well, for me, it is not such good news. I am expected to wear the veil, and as a dutiful Afghan daughter to go joyfully into an arranged marriage."

"Oh, no." Abby reached out to give Najeela's hand a squeeze. "Surely you can speak with him?"

"No, I can't, at least not yet."

Abby sighed. "Men are always the cause of our troubles, aren't they? We should work on that, you and I."

Najeela smiled. "I am so glad you are here, a new friend, a good friend. And what of your last man—Eric, you called him? Will you someday reunite and marry, do you think?"

Abby's mind flooded with memories of Eric. She swallowed the hard lump in her throat. "No. There's no chance. It's done." Her voice was firm, her resolve to rid herself of Eric less so.

"Ah, then you need to meet someone new. And I may have just the man for you. A journalist is coming to do a story on the UN for a big American newspaper. He's won some big prize, the . . . Pulitzer, I think. Does that sound familiar?" Najeela smiled, seeming quite pleased with her news. "Anyway, the UN wants him to write about you. I don't have all the details, but he'll be here in a few days, I think."

Abby groaned. She wanted to object, but she'd only just arrived. It was too soon to assert herself, and besides, maybe the journalist wouldn't come at all, and if he did, he'd probably want even less to do with her than she did with him. Eager to guide the conversation away from herself and now this reporter, Abby asked, "What of your boyfriend? Where is he?"

Najeela smiled. "Ah, Lars—he is my favorite subject, the reason I smile, and the reason I breathe. But, alas, he is in Switzerland where he has an office. He has one in Paris as well." Najeela spoke quickly, hardly taking a breath between sentences. "He is the most wonderful man, I think, in the whole world. He is very well respected—why, even the UN loves him! He donates generously, and in return they have given him permanent diplomatic status." Najeela's fingers toyed with her scarf. "Can you tell that I am in love?" She dropped her voice to a conspiratorial whisper. "Someday soon, he and I will tell my parents and the world that we are in love and intend to marry, but for now, for the sake of my father's honor, I must be silent."

For all of her seeming intolerance to the plight of the beggars, and even Hana and Mohammed, Najeela, Abby thought, was much like her—a young woman just hoping that her dreams worked out.

"Perhaps soon, you will come for dinner with my family. It would be good for them to see that women are capable on their own."

Abby smiled. "I don't know, Najeela. If I'm your example, you might be in trouble."

"They will like you very much, just as I do. My mother, especially. She is a professor at the Medical College, a respected teacher by day, but in the evening she becomes another subservient Afghan wife, veil and all. And my father, a quiet and distinguished diplomat at the UN, becomes a veritable beast at home. He rules with an iron fist and demands absolute submission from my mother and I."

"Oh, Najeela, I'm sure he loves you."

"He does. They both do. That much is certain, but the truth is I am a source of great sadness for them both. You see, I am an only child, a daughter in a nation where only sons matter."

"But you must matter to them, and I'm sure they're proud of you. Look at you—here, working for the UN."

"I am here in Pakistan, the last place on earth I want to be, only because it makes my father appear to be forward-thinking. The same for my mother and her job. He would like nothing better than to lock us both up at home, but he wants to appear a man of the future." Najeela sat forward. "What of you, Abby? Surely Pakistan wasn't in *your* plans?"

Abby nodded. Pakistan hadn't been in her vocabulary, never mind her plans. She'd never even heard of the place until bin Laden's death. But things had changed, she was here now, and her old bucket list would need readjusting. She'd already had to erase *married by twenty-five, honeymoon in Paris,* and *two children by thirty.* She had to agree with Najeela. Pakistan was the last place on earth she'd ever expected to be.

Abby placed her hand over Najeela's. "You know what? We're both here now. Let's make the most of it. I want to see the world and live an exciting life, and this is my first stop. It may not be Paris, but I am with the UN."

"Oh Abby, you are my good friend already." Najeela smiled widely, her sadness evaporating as quickly as the heat of the green tea that sat before them. "Come," she said, folding her napkin and resting it on the table. "Let's shop. We can find some beautiful clothes for you today."

Abby smiled. No use in resisting. Najeela seemed the type of woman who always got her way.

Chapter 4

Abby's first week flew by in a haze of vaccine statistics and UN reports. She spent her days huddled in front of the computer compiling and analyzing numbers of vaccinations administered at the camp, then cross-checking those numbers with expected UN outcomes. The work was almost mind-numbing, leaving her to wonder if Najeela was right after all—this UN post did seem dull, not the exciting work she'd somehow envisioned. She hadn't even been back to the clinic at Safar. She'd left the house and her little office only once, and that was to accompany Najeela to the main UN office for introductions. There, she'd met Najeela's father, a quiet, almost obsequious man. He'd bowed slightly when he met Abby, and she'd smiled in reply, remembering Najeela's description of his ghastly behavior at home.

He seemed mousy almost, not at all the tyrant Najeela had described. His mild manner reminded her of her own father, a retired dentist, who'd never raised his voice or even his brows at Abby. She'd been the only child, a change-of-life baby born to already aging parents who'd doted on her. When she'd called her parents to say she was going to Pakistan, she could almost see her mother's eyes glazing over. "Pakistan?" she'd said, her voice muffled and distant. "Doesn't the UN have anything for you in New York, dear?"

Abby had chuckled. "No, Mom, they don't. But this job in Pakistan will be good for me," she said, trying to convince herself it was the right move after a string of questionable decisions. "It will give me a chance to see the world, and who knows? Maybe the UN will like me well enough to find something for me in New York."

Her mother had sighed so heavily, the phone crackled with static.

But the truth was, Abby had taken the position to save herself, to get out of Boston, to get away from everything. Now she was determined to make the most of it. The only sticking point so far were the events in Geneva, and the unrelenting images—the hideous fall, the twisted body, the frightening man, the dazzling cuff bracelet—that still haunted Abby's days as well as her nights. And always the questions at the back of her mind—she'd seen something, that much was certain, but had it been a murder or an accident? And either way, where had the body disappeared to?

Determined to put it all behind her, Abby shook the images off and chewed away the last bits of her nail polish. For the next five and a half months, there'd be no manicures, no hairdresser either, not to mention no television, no malls. On the other hand, she thought with a wry grin, she could buy blood if she needed it. If she kept her sense of humor, she'd get through this, and without the distractions of home she could devote herself entirely to her job and the UN.

That said, Abby still faced some predicaments here. Hana, for one, remained as prickly as ever. Her shoulders sagged deeper and her scowl intensified as the days wore on. She had the posture of someone expecting bad news, someone prepared for the worst. At a loss what to do, Abby turned to Najeela.

"Her son is missing, like the children you saw at Safar." Najeela delivered the news matter-of-factly, as if announcing the price of bread.

"Missing? How do you mean?"

"Well, *missing* is probably not the correct term. *Sold* is the appropriate word, I guess." Najeela folded her arms across her chest. "Her husband," she said, "sold the boy to an Arab who came through Pakistan in search of future camel jockeys. Hana's husband sold him without consulting her, and she's been in mourning since."

"Camel jockey?"

"It's precisely that. Rich Arabs buy young boys to ride on the backs of camels. In the West, you race horses. In the East, many race camels."

Abby couldn't quite make sense of it. "But where is her boy now? Why can't she just get him back?"

"Her husband died," Najeela replied, her words flat and emotionless. "He was the only one who knew where the boy was sent."

Abby wanted to shake Najeela, to make her feel something, but she seemed incapable, at least where Hana was concerned. "When did her husband die?" Abby asked, her voice soft.

"Last year. He was hit by a truck. But they said he'd been drinking, his own fault really."

"So, she has no way of knowing where her child is? Can't we . . . can't the UN do something to help?"

"No, this sort of thing happens. The children, usually refugee children, disappear. He may be in Saudi Arabia or Kuwait by now, but there's no way to find him. Her only hope will be if the boy finds her, but if he's illiterate as she is, he's probably lost to her forever."

"Oh, Jesus," Abby murmured, suddenly seeing in her mind the set of Hana's shoulders and her relentless frown. She *was* waiting for bad news. "What about the UNICEF tent where the pictures of the missing are posted? Can Hana post a picture of her son?"

"She may have already." Najeela sat back and folded her arms. "I know you won't let go of this, that it troubles you more than it should. So, let's take action to clear your mind. Would you like to ask her or just go to the tent to see for yourself?"

Abby felt her own shoulders relax. Najeela was just busy, not as uncaring as she sometimes seemed. "Well, I'd like to go to the camp today anyway. Can you get away to join me and show me around the tent?"

"Of course. I'll go to the UN office later. Come, get your things."

Abby headed back along the hallway, passing a hunched-over Hana in the kitchen. Abby paused, wondering if she should stop and tell Hana that she knew, that she understood, but she swallowed the urge and hurried on to her room to get her bag and notebooks.

The car crawled along Peshawar's congested streets, the clamorous sounds of the city muted behind the car's heavy windows. Najeela leaned back. "I wish we were in Paris, don't you? I could really show you around, Abby. Promise me that you'll come with me after your assignment here. I think I could convince my father that you would be a perfect chaperone."

"Paris is definitely on my list." Abby smiled in spite of herself. She needed to throw herself into this new life—no Eric, no crowded commuter train, no lines at the bank, nothing to sidetrack her from what mattered.

Once at the camp, Najeela breezed through the front gate, waving and smiling as though she were at a party. Abby followed dutifully and quietly, even her footfalls silent as they trudged along the camp's main road before arriving at a collection of large tents that almost looked like buildings.

"This tent"—Najeela motioned to a large tent with the UN logo on the side—"is the Protection Tent."

"What does that mean?" Abby asked, intrigued.

"Remember, last week you asked about the lost children? Well, in times of war, children and women are easy prey for people who would exploit them, use them for bad things."

"Bad things?"

"The women and even children are taken, they say—I have no personal knowledge of this—but it is said they are taken for sex. I *know*," Najeela said in response to Abby's horrified expression, "it is terrible. Here in the tent, they try to track those who are missing. Families can put up pictures and information so that if someone comes in and knows where that person is, they can inform the family. Come"—Najeela lifted the front flap of the tent—"in here you can see the pictures and read the stories for yourself."

Abby stepped into the tent, and once she'd blinked away the remnants of the sun's glare, her gaze was drawn to the large poster boards that lined every available space. There were hundreds, maybe even thousands, of pictures of women and children, all missing. Abby's heart sank; there was so much misfortune here. She began to read the short bits of information that accompanied most pictures. A photo of a smiling young girl drew her. She had long, dark eyelashes and a head of shiny black hair. Abby smiled at the photo as she read—she could almost feel this child's energy. She was six years old and had disappeared almost two years ago from a small village just beyond Peshawar. Abby pointed at the picture and turned to Najeela. "Two years, she's been gone two years? Does anyone search for these children?"

"No, there is no funding for a search. The hope is that people will come in and recognize a woman or child. Sometimes, the woman has run away, the children too. Things are not always as they seem."

Abby frowned. "Where would they run to? There's nothing here."

"Ah, more than one woman has run away to marry someone other than the one her family has chosen. I've thought of it myself. People do what they have to do. Some of these women here on the wall probably hired themselves out as maids in Europe or Kuwait, and then they just seem to disappear."

"But what of the children? They wouldn't run away. Look at this little face. She's a baby."

"I know that it is terrible to see. I'm not trying to minimize the tragedy, just to explain it."

"I'm sorry, Najeela. I didn't mean to sound accusing." Abby turned back to the wall and continued to look at the faces of the missing. There were hundreds of photos of women, some partially hidden by veils, but all were young and all were pretty. The stories under the pictures told little—first and last names, and the village or camp from which they'd disappeared. As unnerving as it was, Abby couldn't pull herself away, and she continued along the wall, peering closely at the photos until they blurred together, an endless wall of misery.

"Is Hana's boy here?" Abby asked, pointing to the wall of photos.

"I don't know, though I suppose he is." Najeela shrugged. "There are so many photos, it might be impossible to find him here. We can ask Hana if you'd like."

Abby felt her shoulders slump. "I don't think I want to do that just yet. Maybe when she gets to know me better."

"Well then, enough in here. Come with me," Najeela said as she exited the tent. "The Immunization Clinic should be open, and you can have a look."

After a short walk, they arrived at the clinic, already filled with screeching babies and howling children, and mothers trying to hold them tight while staff administered the vaccines.

Abby stood at the doorway and peered in. The space was small and smelled of dirt, sweat, and baby tears. The lone lightbulb sizzled, throwing off more heat than light. Abby smiled at the primitive scene. "A clinic is a clinic," she said, squeezing through the crowd.

Najeela stopped at the desk and introduced Abby to the staff. "Simi," she said to the woman who had been busy registering patients, "Abby is the nurse the UN has sent to do the reports, but perhaps she can help here?"

Simi, a sturdy woman with a veil pulled tight across her forehead, smiled. *"Salaam aleikum,"* she said as she stood and came around to meet Abby. "I am Simi, and I speak some English. Welcome. Would you like to see the clinic?"

Abby nodded. "Thank you, Simi."

Simi placed her pen on the desk. "This area"—she pointed to the desk—"is where we register the patients." She turned and pointed to a thin woman who sat hunched over the desk, furiously writing. "She is Mariyah. She and I register and keep track of the patients. And these two"—Simi gestured toward two others who were busy administering the vaccines—"are our nurses, Shoma and Nasreen." The nurses paused only long enough to smile at Abby before bending to their work. "You see we are very busy," Simi said. "Do you want to see how we work? Have a look at everything?"

"It's very nice to meet all of you, and I'd love to have a look around," Abby said as she watched, spellbound by the familiar hum and rhythm of the clinic, but already, with Simi at Abby's side, a long line had formed at the desk. "But it's too busy today, I think. I've interrupted you, and now this." She pointed to the line that snaked through the door. "I'd like to come back and spend the day, if that's okay?"

Simi smiled and nodded. "Please to come, Abby. Whenever you wish."

"Come, Abby, we should be going," Najeela said, standing at the doorway swatting at the flies that filled the small space. "You can return another time."

Abby nodded absentmindedly, reluctant to pull herself away. It was reassuring to be in a busy clinic again. "I'll see you soon, Simi."

Simi nodded. *"Khoda khafez,"* she said as she returned to her work.

Back at the UN house, Abby found Hana in the kitchen nursing a cup of tea.

"Excuse me," Abby said, thinking maybe she'd ask about Hana's missing son. She leaned in so Hana would hear. "Are you busy?"

Hana thumped her teacup down and looked up. "What is it?" Her voice dripped with barely concealed exasperation.

Suddenly, Abby was nervous. She couldn't intrude on Hana's sadness, at least not yet. Perhaps in time, Abby thought, perhaps in time. "Umm, nothing, sorry to bother you. I just wanted you to know that I'm back."

Hana heaved a sigh and rolled her eyes, before she finally nodded in acknowledgment.

Chapter 5

The delicate olive-skinned hand seemed to be waving, but it was the bracelet that drew Abby's eyes—the sparkling diamond cuff dotted with intricate gems. Flowers and stars of sapphires and rubies, and one large star—an especially bright garnet—sparkled in the streetlight's glow. The light danced over the jewels—the sapphire flower seeming almost to come to life, the diamonds glistening and casting their own hypnotic glow.

Abby's eyes were focused on the bracelet when suddenly the man she'd seen on the balcony approached, his footfalls silent this time. She froze, a chill running through her veins. Abby backed away from the body, her eyes fixed firmly on the man. He was taller than she'd thought he'd be, his body slighter, his hair thinner, but *it was his eyes that made her heart go cold. Nestled in a bed of doughy flesh, they seemed dead, somehow empty of life.*

A scream rose in her throat only to be drowned out by the sound of a whirring motor.

Abby sat upright and looked around in terror. She was in bed.

Bed.

Oh, God, she'd been sleeping . . . the damn dream again. The dull pounding in her head dimmed to an echo, and then she realized that the sound of the heaving motor was real. She looked up. The ceiling fan had come to life, whirring and clicking—someone had turned on the generator. The hum of the generator had interrupted the morning quiet. Abby rose and hurriedly threw on a dress before stepping into the hallway to find Najeela. The generator was never on this early. Something must be up.

A man's voice wafted out from the dining room, and Abby stopped, remembering that Najeela had told her the reporter would be arriving today.

Abby's pout ripened into a frown at the thought, and she turned toward the dining room, almost tripping over a breathless Najeela.

"He's here," Najeela whispered. "You're not ready?"

"I didn't think he'd be here so early. I'll hurry. Can you speak with him until I come?"

"I'd rather not, Abby. It makes me nervous being around a foreign man."

Abby sighed and let her arms fall to her sides. "I wish you'd let him interview *you*. You have to admit, you'd make a far more interesting subject. You know—a woman straddling both worlds, traditional Afghan and modern European. Now that would appeal to readers."

Najeela smiled sweetly. "I don't think it would be proper for me, and my father would surely be angry."

"But I thought you wanted to take a stand, show him who you want to be."

"It's not an easy process, Abby. He is my father, and I must show respect. I cannot appear to be so impudent. If he knew of Lars and my true intentions, he would arrange to marry me off tomorrow. I would never see the man I love again."

Abby reached out and squeezed Najeela's hand. "I'm sorry. I was being selfish. I'll do it. It'll be dull as hell, but of course I'll do it."

Najeela giggled. "I love the way you speak, Abby. You can always make me smile."

Abby nodded and raced through her shower and pulled a light cotton shirt over her head. She pulled on her loose pants and opened the door, taking a deep breath before she strode into the dining room as the reporter, writing in a small notebook, leaned down to retrieve something from his duffel bag on the floor. He turned at the sound of her footsteps, and Abby saw right away that he was disheveled even for this place. He wore a baseball cap, threadbare T-shirt, and jeans, and Abby wondered if there'd been some mistake. Surely a Pulitzer Prize–winning journalist would arrive with at least a bit of fanfare, or at least dressed better than this.

Abby looked down, kicking at the fraying rug under her feet. Was it too late to sneak away, put this meeting off till later? But she was already in the room, he'd seen her and he was upon her in an instant. He smiled and stood, holding out his hand.

"I'm Nick."

Abby studied his face. With his square jaw, deep brown eyes, and easy grin, he was, she thought, handsome in a rugged kind of way, in a way that Eric was not. Eric had been more polished, he'd taken great care with his appearance, and Abby had often joked that he spent more time on his morning face than she did.

She put aside her memories and turned her attention back to her guest. "You must be the reporter." She pushed a stray hair back from her face. She smiled weakly and looked up just as he let out a long, low whistle.

"They didn't tell me I'd be interviewing a beautiful young thing."

Abby cringed and backed away.

"I didn't get your name."

"Abby Monroe," she said, trying to hide the sudden dislike she felt for this stranger.

"Not the New York stock market Monroes?" he said, his smile fading. "Beautiful *and* rich, huh?"

"No," Abby replied, her voice sharp. "I'm one of the middle-class Louisiana-bayou Monroes."

"Sorry." He smiled sheepishly as he pulled the baseball cap from his head. His chestnut-colored hair was tousled and he ran his fingers through it. "My mistake, though not about your beauty." He offered his hand again, and Abby spied a small, color-ful tattoo on his wrist. The burst of color was red maybe, but too small and smudged to identify. "Nick Sinclair, *New York Times*." His voice was deep, his shoulders broad, and his handshake strong. If she'd met him on the street, she'd have guessed him to be a truck driver, a regular guy, not some smart-ass reporter.

She half smiled and released his hand. She wasn't letting her guard down just yet. "Nice to meet you," she said, hoping her voice didn't sound as wary as she still felt. He leaned in and she inhaled the sharp, bitter scent of stale cigarettes and old whiskey. "Come on, you must want to freshen up after your trip. I'll show you where the washroom is."

"I'm fine—just took a shower at my hotel and donned my finest writing clothes. I'd like to talk, if you don't mind."

Abby opened her mouth; she wanted to suggest that they speak another time—she hadn't even had her coffee. But already it seemed too late to do that. She slid into a seat across from Nick.

"All right, I guess we can get started." She forced a smile.

"So, tell me about yourself," he said, pulling a fresh notebook from his bag.

"Tell you what? I'm not sure what you're looking for."

"Well, I could write a story about an American beauty in Pakistan, but there's got to be more."

Abby felt the color rise in her cheeks. His frequent use of the word *beautiful* didn't feel like a compliment so much as a put-down, as if he didn't think she had a brain.

Nick seemed not to notice her growing discomfort. "I know a little bit about you, but maybe you can fill in the blanks for me. For starters, why are you *here*?"

Abby crossed her legs and sat back. "Just so we're on a level playing field, why don't you tell me what you 'know' about me?"

Nick's upper lip curled. "Well, I know your name, I know you're a nurse, and now I know you're not from New York City, but there's got to be a bigger story." He paused, his pen hovering over the paper. "I mean really—why did an attractive young woman come to a place like Peshawar?"

Hana came bustling in carrying a large tray. She eyed Abby and then Nick before turning to Nick. "Coffee?" Nick nodded without glancing up. Hana made a show of pouring a steaming cup of coffee and pushing it to Nick. "Cream and sugar?"

"None," he replied, leaning over his notes.

Hana smiled and set out a tray of sweet rolls.

Abby watched, perplexed. She'd been here for weeks and

had never seen the disagreeable Hana smile, and here she was playing to Nick, who hadn't even noticed her beyond the arrival of his coffee.

Hana finally turned her attention to Abby. "Coffee's there, help yourself," she said as she left.

Nick smiled, and Abby was sure he was mocking her with that Cheshire-cat grin. He may have won Hana over, but she wasn't going to fall so easily, and she definitely wasn't going to fall prey to his stupid questions. She sat forward and poured her own cup of coffee, the aroma strong. She took a sip before speaking.

"I'm going to be honest. I'm not really prepared to be your subject or your guide through the UN program here. There's absolutely nothing interesting about me, and I just got here myself. On top of that, I'm no expert on Peshawar." She tugged at her hair, pushing it into place. "Besides, I have lots of my own work to do, none of it very exciting. This is my first UN job, and I'm still learning the ropes. I'm cross-checking proposals and grants, and hopefully I'll be working in the Immunization Clinic. And though it's important work, even you can see there's nothing sensational or noteworthy there."

She looked up to see disapproval etched into his face, and his eyes had crinkled into a long frown. "I can see you're going to be a tough nut to crack, so why don't you let me be the judge of what is and isn't noteworthy. This is, after all"—he tapped his pen against his notebook—"what I do for a living, and believe it or not, I'm damned good at it. And to tell you the truth, I don't have all day. Can we just cut to the chase and get started?"

His show of irritation fueled her own. "I'm not even sure why you're here in Peshawar. I mean, why not go to Afghanistan and see what's going on there?"

Nick stopped and dropped his pen onto the table. "We're just not getting off to a very good start, are we? We seem to be at odds here."

Abby folded her arms across her chest. "It seems that way."

"Okay, I'll take a minute to humor you, and to tell you what you don't seem to know, and that is that Peshawar is a damn interesting place these days. Wedged between Afghanistan and India, Pakistan is the miserable international stepchild, largely ignored by the world unless leaders need access to its fractious neighbors. And bin Laden hiding out here didn't help their image any. Pakistan gets the leftovers of world aid, at least that's how they see it, and as a result, it's a country filled with anger and distrust and hatred of anything American. On top of that, these days, it really is the gateway to Afghanistan, the port of entry for terrorists, journalists, even aid workers." He paused as if to let his words sink in. "I'm here to do a serious piece on the UN, and *they* decided I should do a sidebar story on an aid worker, which brings me to you, though I confess I'm mystified about why they'd send a new aid worker here, of all places."

Abby looked away, trying to hide her resentment bubbling within. He obviously thought she was an idiot, though admittedly, he knew a hell of a lot more about Pakistan than she did. She was *here* only because this was the job that was available to her. It could have been Timbuktu and she would have gone. She exhaled loudly, trying to rein in her instant dislike of this guy. "Well, let's try again," she said.

"All right, I'm here to write about you." Nick smiled. "You know—tell me what it's like for an American in this turbulent, dangerous place."

Abby flinched at his words. "I've actually had that discussion with the UN, but if it's so turbulent and dangerous, wouldn't your story make life that much more dangerous for me? I'm trying to just get my work done, and you want to tell the world I'm here? No way."

"Don't worry, the story won't be printed till you're long gone. You have to admit, it'll make for edge-of-the-seat reading."

"Don't hold your breath. There's nothing edge of the seat about my days here." What a jerk, she thought.

"I'm not holding my breath, but no matter how dull you try to be, I can write a compelling story. So, back to the beginning. Why *are* you here? Peshawar's not exactly every young woman's dream destination, is it?"

"I . . . I . . . well, I guess . . ." Suddenly, she was nervous. She didn't want to say that she had a history of running, that she'd been running from nothing and from everything all at once. Wasn't that precisely what she'd done in the hideous aftermath of Katrina? Instead of staying to help, she and Emily had booked the first available flight to Boston, a city loaded with hospitals and jobs. And when things hadn't worked out with Eric, she'd run again. She swallowed the dry lump in her throat. She didn't want to say that maybe just this once she'd been desperate to stand on her own, to find her own way, and so for the first time that morning, she just kept quiet.

Nick seemed to sense her hesitation. "Boyfriend trouble, huh?" He winked. "I mean, isn't that the most likely reason for a pretty young nurse to come *here*?"

Abby tried to count to ten, to take a deep breath, to hold her breath, anything to quell the growing impatience she felt, and her voice was stiff when she answered, "I was laid off. I needed a job, and this looked as good as anything."

Nick chuckled. "Now I know you're kidding. This terrorist hot spot really seemed like a good place?"

Abby folded her arms. "It did. Still does, as a matter of fact." She felt herself closing down. She didn't want to speak with him, not right now, maybe never. She didn't know which of them had dug themselves in deeper, but either way, she was finished with this interview.

"Yeah, well, I can see already how you're not exactly an appealing subject, but this is what I'm gonna write about. Okay with you?"

Was this guy for real? Abby thought as she stood and pushed her chair back from the table. "Are you . . . ?" Abby paused, remembering her promise to Najeela. "Listen, I don't want to be rude—"

"Well, you're doing a great job of it so far."

"I'm no match for you," she said, her voice and her anger rising. "And let's face it, it's obvious that you know more about this place than I do. You don't need to trail me about. And besides, I just, well, I don't especially want anyone writing about me."

"Well, good, since it's not really about you. You're just the conduit, get it? This is a story about the refugees."

God, what an ass, she thought, biting her tongue. The UN would surely let her go if they got wind she was smart-mouthed to the big-shot reporter. She tried to take a slow, deep breath. "Then why do you need to interview me?"

"I'll let you in on a little secret. Your story, or lack of one, is safe with me. I'm not really here to write about you, but the UN wanted to showcase an aid worker, and I needed to get my visa and permission from the UN to get in here."

"Why not just write about the refugees then? That seems a more interesting piece anyway."

"I will write about them, but Americans like to read about Americans. Human interest gets them every time."

Abby crossed her arms and stood firm. "I think maybe you don't really know what readers want. Why not just help refugees?"

"I *am* here to help the refuges—just not in the usual way."

"Can you just get to the point?" she asked, her words dripping with sarcasm.

"I am here for the refugees. I'm as committed to helping

them as you are. There's just something else I'm working on, and being here is the best way to do that."

Abby shook her head. "I don't have a clue what you're talking about."

"You don't have to, and you don't have to help me either. Just let me hang around and I promise I'll stay out of your way. I'll even do a great fluff piece on you." He held out his hand. "Truce?"

Abby hesitated. "As long as you're not hanging over my shoulder, we'll get on fine. If you want to call that a truce, then you have one." She fixed him with a steely gaze, hoping that he knew she meant business. Nick dropped his hand. She didn't much like him, but she wondered if she'd gone too far. She'd never been so prickly before. She shook her head; it was the combination of everything that had happened recently, and that woman's death in Geneva. All of it just made her suspicious and quick to anger. She had to get a grip. She looked up, about to apologize when she heard Nick mutter, "Jeez, get over yourself."

"Jerk," she spat, as she turned on her heel and stormed off.

Najeela caught up with her halfway down the hall. "I heard. It didn't go so well, no?"

"Sorry, Najeela. I don't know why I'm so touchy."

"Not to worry," Najeela said just as they heard the front door slam. "He'll be back. They always are." She took Abby's hand. "I'm sorry that you didn't like him." Najeela's voice was soothing. "Just put it all out of your mind. I'll find a good man for you."

Abby bristled at the thought. A man was the last thing she needed.

Chapter 6

Six days after his first appearance, Nick returned. Abby groaned when she heard his voice in the hall. Najeela had yet to arrive so Hana plodded to Abby's office to announce his arrival. "The reporter is here," Hana said with a hint of a smile, her lips curling upward. "Says he's looking for you."

Abby saw her carefully planned day dissolve with the news. "Tell him . . ." she started to say just as Nick appeared in the doorway.

She stiffened at the sight of him and restrained her desire to tell him to get lost.

"Two things," he said. "First, I'm sorry about last week.

Sometimes I get carried away with my work, and I come on stronger than I should."

"I guess you do. Apology accepted," she said reluctantly. But if he thought she'd reciprocate, he had another think coming.

"Glad that's out of the way," he said. "I'm here on my way to the camp, to Safar. Thought I'd see if you might be interested in joining me?"

Abby hesitated. She'd been impatient to get back to the camp, but Najeela had the car most days. "UN work," she always said, leaving Abby to work alone in the house. She'd felt confined, isolated almost, and Nick's appearance, much as she detested him, presented her with the perfect opportunity to get back there, maybe arrange a work schedule with Simi in the clinic.

"I do need to go back," she said. "Sure, why not? Just let me get my stuff." She was almost giddy with delight to be getting out, but she wouldn't let him see that. In her room, she grabbed her bag and, almost as an afterthought, checked her reflection in the mirror. She ran her fingers through her hair and swiped a line of clear gloss over her lips before heading to the front of the house in search of Nick.

"He's outside," Hana said as though reading her mind.

Nick was behind the wheel of a rusting hulk of a sedan. Abby pulled open the door and cringed at the loud creaking sound. "Love your car," she said, inhaling the musty scent of old smoke and stale sweat.

"Hey, my expense account will only go so far," he said, easing the car onto the main road. "Not gonna spend big on wheels when there's all that scotch to buy." He winked.

Abby turned and looked out at the passing street.

"Well, I'm still glad to be out. There's only the one car, and Najeela has dibs. I think too with all the street riots the UN is just as happy to keep me in the office."

"Could be," he said. "Were you here for the demonstrations two weeks ago?"

Abby nodded. "I wasn't out, but I heard about them."

"You have to be careful. I mean, I don't think you should even be here, but it's not my call."

Abby rolled her eyes. Here we go, she thought.

The car wound through the crowded streets to Safar, where Nick pulled in and parked. "You've been here, right?"

"Two quick visits," she answered.

"Just want to be sure you can find your way around. I'm gonna walk around and have a look." He leaned back and pulled out his backpack, settling it onto his shoulder. "I'll find you later."

Abby strode to the Immunization Clinic and poked her head inside. The rooms were quiet and dark. "Anyone here? Simi?" she called out, but her voice echoed in the empty space. Damn, she hadn't even thought to ask which two days the clinic opened. Well, she thought, at least it gave her a chance to explore and maybe return to the Protection Tent.

She turned and headed back through the camp, passing rows and rows of raggedy tents, some covered with tarpaulins, some taped together. Tiny children, maybe the same ones she'd seen on her first visit, giggled and waved when they saw her. Abby smiled in turn, and when she spied the now familiar Protection Tent, she stepped inside. Out of the sun's glare, she blinked to adjust her eyes. There, squatting before a row of pictures placed at the lowest edge of the poster board, she saw Nick. He was scribbling furiously into his notebook, looking up every now and then before bending to his writing again. Abby watched as he stood and moved to the next row of pictures, intent on the subjects. Somehow, from this vantage point, he didn't seem like such a jerk, and Abby moved to his side.

"This is a sad place, isn't it?" she asked.

Nick seemed startled to be interrupted. He rose quickly. "What? Yeah, yeah, sorry. I was reading." He pointed to the pictures. "And having a look at Hana's boy. You know she put his picture here?"

"She told you about him?" Abby asked incredulously. He'd only just met Hana. How in the world did he get that out of her? Hana had hardly acknowledged Abby's existence, yet she'd shared her tragedy with Nick?

"She did." Nick looked away. "She's pretty desperate to find him. Sad story."

"Which is he?" Abby asked, looking around at the rows and rows of pictures.

Nick turned back and pointed to a picture taped low on the wall. Abby bent down and peered closely at the black-and-white photo of the smiling boy. He was small and thin with a head of untidy, thick black hair. He'd looked directly into the camera when the picture was taken, giving the impression that he was looking right back at Abby. She touched the picture and gently stroked the glossy paper cheek. "Sweet child," she said, a hint of sadness in her voice. She leaned back on her heels and looked up at Nick. "This tent is filled with these pictures, these stories. Well, I guess you know that." She rose to stand beside him.

"This is compelling stuff, isn't it?"

"Not to bring up old arguments, but isn't this what you should be writing about?"

Nick chuckled. "And here I thought you were just another pretty face."

Oh, jeez, here we go again, Abby thought. "I'm going to look around in here. Let me know when you're ready to leave," she said, bending down again to inspect the picture of Hana's son.

She was just as glad to be out of Nick's line of fire. There was just no way to have a civilized conversation with him.

Abby leaned in closer to the wall and read the small bit of information posted with Hana's picture: *Malik Khan, age 7 years—disappeared 1 year ago, may be a camel jockey in one of the Arab nations. If you have information, please contact Hana Khan.* Beneath that, someone had printed the address of the UN house. Abby sighed. Malik seemed so real here, not just a story, but a real boy whose disappearance had broken his mother's heart.

Most pictures had achingly similar messages. One scribbled under the picture of a beautiful young woman read, *Jehan, age 16 years, disappeared from the village of Darra.* A rustle of movement from somewhere behind her startled Abby.

"She's beautiful, and probably sold already." Nick shook his head.

Abby had been so absorbed in the photos, she hadn't noticed Nick standing next to her until he'd spoken.

"Sold?" she asked.

"Probably kidnapped, or maybe sold by her family and now probably sold yet again into the trade."

Abby was perplexed. "I don't understand."

"Human trafficking," he said, his voice almost angry. "Most of these people have been kidnapped or sold or worse."

Abby's stomach churned. "What could be worse?"

"Well, off the top of my head, I'd say murder."

Murder. A fleeting image of the woman in Geneva nipped at her thoughts. "I . . ." She caught herself. She couldn't tell him about the woman in Geneva, not now at least. He'd have a field day with her story and the missing body.

"What?"

"Nothing," she said.

"Come on, let's get out of here. Time for lunch—and the *New York Times* is buying." He slipped his hand under her elbow and guided her back to the car.

Abby, absorbed again in the pictures, bristled slightly at his touch, but she didn't pull away. Once in the car, she sat quietly, mulling over the pictures and Nick's comments—*human trafficking, murder.* God, could that really be happening here?

"Why so quiet? Finally speechless in the face of my charms?"

"God, no," Abby groaned. "I just want to hear more—the trafficking and the murders."

Nick leaned on the car's horn, setting an unwitting dog howling. "Jesus, this place is too damn crowded. Sorry about that. You asked a question. Trafficking is the world's dirty little secret. We don't even know the exact numbers, but somewhere between seven hundred thousand and four million people are victims each year. For some inexplicable reason, we never talk about it and rarely write about it. We just ignore it."

"Why?"

Nick shrugged. "Not sure, to tell you the truth. Maybe it's just not appealing enough or maybe the victims aren't white enough. Either way, the result is the same. It doesn't get attention."

"What is *it* exactly?"

"Trafficking?"

Abby nodded.

"Trafficking is today's equivalent of slavery. Women, and sometimes children, in miserable situations or terrible poverty are kidnapped outright or sold or they're promised safe passage to, say, Kuwait, where they are told they'll be placed in good jobs. But once they reach their destination, they find themselves living as virtual slaves—often sex slaves in brothels. They're sold again and again. They're trapped and voiceless. They're invisible to everyday people."

"How are they—how is this—invisible?"

"Ever get a manicure at one of those little salons, the ones run by Asians? Well, the quiet woman polishing your nails may have been forced into that job, and at night she may be forced into prostitution. They're invisible, Abby, that's why traffickers choose them. They're refugees—desperate to survive, desperate to get through another day. In Boston or New York, they're the timid servants, and workers. They're right under your nose, and you barely notice them."

Abby felt her shoulders sag. Could she have been so close to someone like that and not known? "Why wouldn't they speak up?"

"Why would they? And just who would they tell? They don't know if you're a good guy or if you're part of their misery. If they open up, they could be killed."

Abby stiffened at his words.

"These women, girls mostly, were desperate to leave wherever it was they were, and they believed, or maybe their families believed, some creep's promises." He paused and turned to Abby. "So they go quietly, happily even—smuggled across borders until they get where they're going, and then they're told, 'You have no papers, and you owe thousands upon thousands of dollars to the bastard who helped you escape.' They have to work it off, they're told, but their debt only grows because now they need room and board and clothes, and so it goes on and on. There's just no way out. It's a never-ending bondage of debt."

"Why can't they go to the police?"

"They have no papers, they're illegal. They'll be arrested, or at least they think so. And on top of that, they're afraid to report the abuse, afraid their families will be shamed and may not take them home. And maybe it was their own family that sold them to begin with. For so many, there's just no escape, and the traffickers know it. And the victims don't even speak the language of the place they've been shipped to. The reasons are endless."

Abby shook her head. "Jesus, that's awful. Can I ask why you're writing about me when there's this tragedy to write about?"

"You can ask, but I'm not saying, at least not yet."

Abby smiled. He was as distrustful of her as she was of him. At least they had that in common. "Fair enough," she said.

"I do have to ask that you repeat none of this to the Afghan princess. Deal?"

"Who's the Afghan princess?"

"Najeela, and you have to promise."

"Najeela? She's no princess. You're wrong about her."

"I don't think so, and I always trust my gut. I'd just like your word that you'll keep your lovely mouth shut."

What a jerk, Abby thought. Just when she thought he might actually be a human being.

"You promise?" His voice was insistent.

Abby nodded and sighed.

Nick guided the car through the maze of Peshawar's streets to a quiet side street where a smiling policeman waved him into a spot right by a high privacy wall. Abby recognized the buildings. This was University Town, her own UN house just down the street.

"The American Club," Nick said. "I thought maybe you'd like to have lunch here, among friendly expats. Whaddaya say?"

"Hot dogs?"

"Yes, even beer or something stronger. Whatever you need, the American Club has it."

Abby relaxed. It would be a nice change from her never-ending diet of rice and toast, Hana's specialties. "I'm game," she said, alighting from the car and joining Nick at the gate. He showed his ID and they were ushered into a house that, at least from the outside, was not so different, although maybe larger, from her own UN staff house. On either side of the entry hall were dining rooms, and the air was filled with the comforting clatter of silverware and glasses mingling with the soothing hum of American voices raised in conversation.

"Let's go upstairs," Nick said, leading the way. "The bar's there. There's food too, but the bar is where everything happens, and where you hear everything you need to hear in Pakistan."

Nick steered her along the narrow, dim stairway, and at the top an old-fashioned pub beckoned. The smell of burgers and fries and beer filled the air, and Abby hadn't realized until just then how much she missed home. She inhaled deeply and took a seat at a corner table alongside Nick. He turned, and an unexpected smile draped his lips.

"A little slice of home," he said, his eyes scanning the room. "A place like this helps to take the edge off when you just can't stomach the misery another minute."

"Does it get to you?" Abby asked. "The trafficking and everything?"

Nick nodded. "Hell, yes. I'm not the ogre you think I am," he said softly. "I'm as passionate about helping as you are."

Abby heaved a sigh. Maybe he wasn't so bad after all. Maybe they'd just got off to a bad start. "I don't think you're an ogre, Nick. A royal pain in the ass, maybe."

Nick's eyes crinkled with laughter as he picked up the menu.

Abby ordered both a cheeseburger and a hot dog and swallowed them down with the coldest, best-tasting beer she'd ever had. Nick's food order was almost demure—a chicken salad.

"I'm saving myself for the liquor," he said, ordering a double scotch straight up. "Don't want to fill up on the food and miss the best part of the club." He winked, and Abby laughed. It wasn't so long ago she'd been filling up on vodka.

"Great atmosphere, huh?" Nick looked around the dark room. Only three others, all men, huddled deep in conversation, shared the room with them.

It looked like an average bar to Abby. It even had an old dartboard on one wall, but she nodded to keep the peace.

"At one time, this place was the center of the expat universe. Still is, in a way," he said. "Twenty years ago, if you were a serious journalist or spy or aid worker or even a mercenary, this was the only place to be. It was the most exciting place in the world."

"Really? Why?"

"You're probably too young to remember, but during the Soviet invasion of Afghanistan, the Soviets had trained missiles on this club, and even on Green's Hotel, where I'm staying, so naturally everyone who was anyone hung out at those two places. It was like thumbing your nose at a superpower—and how often does anyone get to do that?" Folding his arms, he smiled smugly.

"Were you here?" she asked, trying to figure out how old he was.

"Hell, no, I was in high school, but my uncle was here, and I heard his stories. Even as a kid, I was desperate to get here. Look around, it's still a place of intrigue—of spies and journalists and even a few terrorists. It's like starring in a spy novel."

Abby laughed. "You do have an imagination."

"You don't believe me? Peshawar is filled with spies and ne'er-do-wells. Trust me. Hell, there used to be a patio out there filled with tables and chairs." He pointed to what looked like a rooftop deck. "But it's off-limits now, too easy for a sniper to pick you off. This is exciting stuff."

"If you're so fascinated with this, why not just write a spy novel?"

"Are you kidding? Real life is far more interesting, thank you." He threw back the last of his scotch and fished a $20 bill from his pocket. "Let's go while I can still drive."

"I can walk."

"Not in Peshawar, you can't. Let's go."

At the house, Nick turned to Abby. "Remember—not a word to the princess."

"Please—don't call her that."

Nick groaned. "I only call 'em as I see 'em, but I'll try. And remember—not a word, and that includes our trip to the club."

"The club is a secret too?"

"Best to keep it one. In this place, it's almost impossible to tell the good guys from the bad, so at least for now, just zip it around Najeela."

Ass, she thought, though she nodded yes politely.

Chapter 7

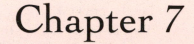

Najeela finally appeared at the house three days after Nick's last visit. "Have you seen the reporter?" she asked.

"I have," Abby replied, a frown on her lips.

"You don't much like Nick, do you?" Najeela's fingers played with her necklace as she spoke.

"We seem to be like oil and water. There's just something about him." Abby shrugged. "You're right that we'll never be best friends."

Najeela touched Abby's shoulder. "Then if you don't like him, I won't like him either."

"I don't know if that's fair," Abby said, laughing.

Najeela smiled. "Well, that's what girlfriends do, I'm sure. Anyway, I think that you're in need of an outing, yes?" She paused, waiting for Abby to respond.

"I'm in need of an outing for work, that's what I'm in need of. I have so much to do, the reports will be piling up, and I'd still like to get back to the clinic when it's open. And while you're here, I need to tell you that I have to have access to the car." There, Abby thought, she'd finally said it. Without the car, she couldn't get to the clinic, couldn't get their statistics, and couldn't do her job, never mind that without the car she was stuck here like a prisoner, no television, no music, nothing. "I can't do my job without the car."

Najeela looked contrite. "You're right, Abby. I guess I'm not used to sharing, but I promise, I'll ask Daddy for his car. Better?"

Abby nodded, glad of the freedom a car would give her.

"I have an invitation for you," Najeela said, clasping her hands together. "From my mother. She wants you to come for dinner. Please say you'll come. Perhaps my uncle will strike your fancy."

Abby groaned. "I'm not really interested in meeting anyone just now, but I'd love to come for dinner."

"It's settled then. My parents will be very happy. Tomorrow is good?"

Abby nodded in reply.

Late afternoon the following day, Hana knocked on Abby's door. "Your car is here," she said before her footsteps shuffled away. Abby ran her hands over her new Pakistani *shalwar kameez* and draped a scarf across her shoulders as she'd seen Najeela do so many times. She ran her fingers through her shoulder-length hair and drew a thin line of black kohl under her eyes. She stood back from the mirror and looked again. The black liner made her brown eyes stand out just as Najeela had said. Not bad, she thought, and smiled at her reflection. A fleeting thought of Eric raced through her mind and she chased it away. She thought of him less and less, now lost in the daily routine of her position. Perhaps soon he'd be a painless, distant memory—a romantic bullet dodged.

She stepped into the hallway and called, "Hana, I'm going. See you later." She heard Hana's grunt in reply and wondered again why Hana so disliked her. Hana had somehow bonded with Nick, but still avoided Abby like the plague. Well, there was nothing to be done about it tonight. Najeela's car was waiting.

Abby stepped into the courtyard to find a gleaming black Mercedes parked in the driveway. She let out a low whistle and turned as the uniformed chauffeur opened the rear door and motioned her inside. As the car pulled into traffic, Abby gazed through the deeply tinted windows at the passing streets. The car left University Town and turned into the posh, tree-lined streets of Hyatabad, the wealthy enclave that was home to diplomats and entrepreneurs. The villas, as Najeela called them, were all hidden behind high, ivy-draped walls and large flowering trees, and Abby was hypnotized by the sudden display of wealth in such an impoverished city.

Before long, the car stopped for a large gate to be drawn open, and it was waved in to a long driveway. A house, a mansion really, stood before them, and Abby, her eyes wide, was escorted to the door, where a smiling Najeela stood.

"Oh, Abby, I'm so happy to see you." She kissed Abby on both cheeks. "Come in, my family's waiting."

Abby suddenly felt nervous and out of place. The floors were covered in luxurious Persian carpets, and the tables held intricately sculpted statues. Above the entryway hung a sparkling chandelier, and Abby felt her mouth drop open when she spied what could only be a genuine Renoir on the wall. Najeela, sensing Abby's anxiety, took her hand and led her down a long corridor past a curving staircase and into a large room lined with books and overstuffed chairs. "Have a seat," she said. "I'll tell them you're here."

Abby sat on the edge of a lushly upholstered chair and picked nervously at her fingernails. Within minutes, she heard footsteps and stood up, her hands tugging at the ends of her scarf.

Najeela appeared with her father at her side, looking a little more bent and a little thinner than the day Abby had first met him. He removed his wire-rimmed eyeglasses and placed them in the front pocket of the dark suit he wore. He held out his hand and took Abby's, his grip so slight, Abby's hand slipped from his. "Ahh, Abby, so very good to see you again. Please sit," he said, motioning with his hand.

Abby sat and folded her hands demurely in her lap. Suddenly, she wasn't sure how to behave. She'd never been around people who lived this way.

"This is my wife, Dr. Siddiqui." Najeela's mother, plump and dressed in traditional clothes with a veil draped over her head, smiled and nodded. Abby smiled in return.

"And this scoundrel," Mr. Siddiqui announced, turning as a heavyset man dressed in traditional large pants and oversize shirt entered the room, "is my brother, Imtiaz."

Najeela joined Imtiaz and quickly kissed his cheek. Out of the corner of her eye, Abby saw Najeela's father frown, but Najeela seemed not to notice or perhaps not to care.

"This is *Uncle* Imtiaz," she said, her arm draped loosely across his back.

Her father's frown deepened, and Abby's gaze slid to the

henna stain that colored the sparse head of hair and full beard of Uncle Imtiaz. He rubbed at the paunch that pulled his shirt tight and held his hand out to Abby. When she slipped her hand in his, he bent to her and kissed it, the wetness of his lips settling onto her skin. Abby resisted the urge to wipe her hand, and instead she smiled. "Nice to meet you, Uncle Imtiaz." She hoped her smile would hide her growing revulsion.

"*Uncle* makes me sound so old. You may call me Haji," he said, leering now.

Abby squirmed in her seat. "Haji? Is that your name as well?"

"He's made the Haj," Najeela said, "the pilgrimage to Mecca. For the rest of his life people will refer to him as Haji, a sign of respect for his pilgrimage."

Imtiaz stroked his beard. "But for you—perhaps you should just call me Imtiaz. That suits me, I think."

Abby only nodded and looked to Najeela, her eyes pleading for rescue.

"Uncle is a farmer and exporter, a true Afghan." Najeela smiled widely at Imtiaz, and Abby shuddered. "He still has a home in Kabul, and his farms in Helmand and Spin Boldak in Kandahar, but he travels the world for his business. I saw him often during my school days in Switzerland."

Imtiaz smiled a smile that made Abby's skin crawl. "Don't give away all of my secrets, dear Najeela," he said.

"Ah, enough chatter, I think," Najeela's father said, rising from his seat. "Are you ready for dinner, Abby? I believe that all is ready."

Beast or not, Abby liked him.

The dinner was sumptuous and filled with Afghan specialties—salad, plain yogurt with cucumbers, lentil soup, grilled lamb, rice with beans and raisins.

Finally, Imtiaz was quiet except for the loud slurping noises he made as he ate. Abby devoured everything in sight, and when dessert appeared—small sugary cakes covered with rich frosting and layers of velvety ice cream—she gobbled those down as well.

"Ah, Abby," Mr. Siddiqui said, "you have a healthy appetite. Would you like another serving?" He pushed the dessert plate in her direction and motioned to the little cakes.

"Oh, God, no," she replied. "I've eaten enough to last me a month."

"Tea then?"

Abby nodded, and he poured tea into a delicate porcelain cup and pushed it to her. "It is good to finally sit with you, Abby. Najeela speaks of you every evening. She has found a good friend, we believe." He gazed at his wife, who only nodded shyly in reply. "And though we are pleased that she has a friend, it is our hope that Najeela will someday soon agree to marry, and then perhaps she'll make a life with her family in Afghanistan." He paused as if considering that thought. "Can you believe that my charming Afghan daughter has never even set foot inside Afghanistan? She has never breathed in the crisp air of the Hindu Kush nor tasted the sweet melons of Herat. It breaks my heart." He shook his head sadly, and his eyes seemed to fill with tears.

Abby sipped at her tea and looked away, uncomfortable with Mr. Siddiqui's show of emotion. It was then she noticed that Uncle Imtiaz was watching her closely. His black eyes, set in a doughy wad of flesh, seemed locked on her every move. She wriggled in her chair as if that might free her from his line of sight.

She looked at her watch. "Oh my." She pushed back her chair. "I had no idea it was so late. I'm sure Najeela can tell you we start our days early. I hate to end this evening, but I must be going."

Abby caught Najeela's grateful smile before she lifted her napkin to cover her face. "Ah, yes," she replied, her voice muffled by the napkin. "It is late. Abby's right. It is time to say good night."

The family walked Abby to the door, where Imtiaz took her hand once more and planted yet another disgustingly wet kiss there. This time, avoiding Imtiaz's gaze, she pulled away abruptly.

"Good night, all, thank you so much for dinner. Najeela, I'll see you tomorrow."

The Siddiquis' limousine was summoned, and once Abby had settled herself into the private rear seat, she breathed a sigh of relief, glad to be away from that leering old goat of an uncle.

The next morning, Najeela appeared earlier than usual. "Everyone loved you, Abby."

"Your parents are very nice."

Najeela responded with a scowl. "My mother, yes. My father, not so much as you might think."

"Oh, come on," Abby said. "It must be difficult for him, away from the country he so obviously loves."

"If he loved his country so much, he would never have left. Dear Uncle Imtiaz has never left—well, except for business and to see me."

Abby couldn't help but roll her eyes, but Najeela seemed not to notice.

"My father and Imtiaz are at odds. They are brothers in name only. My father hates that Imtiaz has made a very good living with his farming and export business. It was Uncle Imtiaz after all who supported us during our years of exile. He's the one who paid my school tuition, and my father resents him for that. He says that Uncle's farming of poppies is illegal, and his export business is nothing but a smuggling operation." Najeela pursed her lips and pouted. "My father is ungrateful, that's what he is."

Abby's mouth fell open. At the height of the war in Afghanistan, she'd seen a news report about the poppy farms and opium exporting, and the US attempts to eradicate them. It somehow didn't come as a surprise that Imtiaz was involved. It confirmed her suspicions—the man was a creep and a criminal. Abby cringed at the thought of him.

"Can you tell that I adore Uncle Imtiaz? Did I tell you," Najeela said, her voice gushing with affection, "that it was Uncle Imtiaz who introduced me to my beloved?" She smiled at the memory. "I was in Paris, and Uncle Imtiaz needed to get papers delivered to his business partner. He asked me to make the delivery, and the recipient was none other than my dear Lars. It is Uncle who is now *my* messenger, delivering gifts from my secret lover to me." She smiled dreamily. "I don't know what I'd do without him."

"I don't know what I'd do *with* him," Abby muttered, wondering why her friend was so blind to Imtiaz's dark side.

"What?"

"It's your father you should respect, isn't it? Your uncle is, well—an uncle."

"I do respect my father. I'm here, aren't I?" Najeela asked testily. "But, it is my uncle who really cares for me. He knows that I am in love, and dear man that he is, he has kept my secret to himself, so now I keep all of his." She smiled slyly, and Abby wondered what kind of secrets the fat old uncle might have.

"But enough of me," Najeela said. "What about you? Are you ready to move on from Eric?"

Hearing his name made Abby wish she'd never told Najeela her story. She wanted his name erased from her memory. "I'm doing my best."

"Well, my uncle liked you very much. Perhaps you'd like to see him again?"

Abby felt her stomach churn at the thought of being close to Uncle Imtiaz again. "Hmm, I'm going to concentrate on work for now, but I'll keep him in mind."

She buried her head in a new UNICEF vaccination handbook, hoping that would be the end of *that* conversation.

Chapter 8

Abby reached out for the bracelet, the diamonds and precious stones lying cold and hard against the woman's soft, bloodied skin. She should have been nauseated, but she wasn't, and her mind registered the strangeness of that. She bent low and leaned in close, touching the woman's face, her skin still warm with life. She checked again for signs of life, but the woman was dead.

Abby sat back on her heels, sadness overwhelming her. Suddenly, and silently, the man from the balcony appeared. He stood and stared. Abby froze, but only for an instant. This time she knew what to do, and she turned and ran, her arms pumping wildly, her heart thumping in her chest, but her footfalls were slow and choppy, she just couldn't run. She looked at her feet and willed them to move, but she seemed stuck in quicksand. Oh, God, she could feel him behind her, he was going to catch up.

Tangled in her sheets, her skin slick with sweat, her heart racing, she sat up quickly. Not again, she thought. A jackhammer went off in her head, and she closed her eyes in an effort to silence it.

God, she wanted to tell someone. She looked at her watch and tried to calculate the time difference between Pakistan and Boston. What was it—nine hours, ten hours? Either way, too late to call—Emily was either getting ready to work the night shift or just getting to sleep. Maybe it was just as well. Emily didn't want to hear the story again. Abby rose quickly. Geneva was behind her. She couldn't let it affect her like this.

When Nick arrived later that morning, Abby moaned to herself. Tired as she was, he was the last person in the world she felt like seeing. "Morning, Nick. What brings you here?"

"You. Thought maybe we could do that interview."

Abby rubbed at her eyes. "Sorry, not today," she said, offering no excuses.

Nick was unperturbed. "No offense intended, but you look like hell."

Abby frowned in reply. "Thanks so much, just what I wanted to hear."

"Don't take that the wrong way," Nick said quickly. "You just look as though you haven't slept in a week."

"I feel as though I haven't. I've been having nightmares." Oh, damn, she thought too late, she didn't want to tell him about that. "Maybe from the Lariam," she added quickly. "Ever happen to you?"

"God, why do you take that stuff? You're a nurse, you must

know the side effects are horrific, and vivid nightmares are the reason most people throw it out. Hell, it's even said to be a hallucinogenic. I'd rather take a chance on malaria than take that damn pill."

"Hallucinogenic? Makes my nightmares seem minor. I'm not sure what to do."

"Get a mosquito net if you're worried, but I think in Peshawar, malaria is the least of your worries."

"Why is it the least of my worries?" Abby was perplexed. Speaking with Nick seemed always an effort in cryptic communication.

"The riots."

Abby was even more confused.

Nick seemed to sense that. "You haven't been out, I take it?"

"Not today, yesterday either."

"Where's Najeela?"

"Home, I guess, or on UN business. She hasn't been here in a few days."

"She's no fool. The riots have increased in intensity—loud, angry, armed mobs. I suppose they haven't come to University Town yet, but I'm willing to bet they will."

Abby rose from her desk. "The demonstrations—is that what you mean? Are they still demonstrating?"

"They have definitely moved from demonstrating to rioting. Haven't you read the newspaper?"

Abby shook her head. She hated to admit that. She didn't want to confirm his initial impression that she was too green to be here. "Why are they rioting?"

"Because they can, that's why. Peshawar is part of what's known as the lawless North-West Frontier Province. It's administered by tribal law, though these days government soldiers and police are here trying to get a handle on things. The danger is that these protesters have easy access to rocket launchers and missiles. A riot here is liable to explode, literally. You need to stay inside. They'll be looking for Americans, and with your light hair and pale skin, you'd be targeted in a millisecond."

"I guess this is what the UN meant by 'unstable security situation'?"

"'Unstable'? That's the understatement of the century. Didn't the UN elaborate on what they meant by 'unstable security'?"

"They did. They said that Pakistan had always been unstable, and that it was worse since bin Laden's death. But they also said they had plenty of foreign staff in-country, and they kept a close eye on things, and if trouble developed, they'd move me to a safer post. So, you see," she said, rubbing the sleep from her eyes, "I'm not as naive as you think, but I do hope they don't move me. I feel as though I'm just getting used to things."

"Believe it or not, I wasn't going to say that you're naive. I think you can never plan for this stuff. It just happens." Nick strode to the doorway. "Not to change the subject, but is Hana here? Any chance I can get some coffee?"

"I'm sure she'll get some for you."

"So—back to the interview. How about it?"

"Not today. Between the nightmares and my headache, I'm at my wit's end."

Nick moved closer, concern in his eyes. "I can see that. Want to tell me about it?"

Abby wasn't especially keen on sharing the episode in Geneva with Nick. "Not really, it's just a nightmare, but it's so vivid, so real, I invariably wake up terrified." She looked at him, ready for a smart remark.

"Why don't you write it down? Might help you sort it out. Make it seem less scary."

"Thanks, Nick," Abby said, finally looking away. "And thanks for not making fun of it."

"Hey, I'd never question someone else's dreams. My own"—he smiled—"now that's another story."

Abby led Nick back along the hallway to the kitchen, where Hana was at the sink scrubbing dishes. When she saw Nick, she smiled and quickly wiped her hands on her dress. Abby had never seen her move so quickly.

"Hana," Nick said, genuine concern in his voice, "that can't be good for your hands. Have Najeela get you a dishwasher."

"It's not so bad, and someone's got to do it." Hana looked accusingly at Abby.

"If it's not too much trouble, could I get some coffee? With the riots, there's nothing downtown."

"Have a seat in the dining room," Hana said. "I'll make you a nice breakfast."

"No need, coffee's fine."

"Are you going to spend the day here?" Abby asked, leading him into the dining room.

"If you don't mind."

Abby resisted the urge to tell him she didn't want him hanging around and instead smiled. "Knock yourself out, but there's only the one computer, and I'm using it at the moment."

"Fine with me." He sank into his seat. "But, before you run back to work, sit with me awhile. Tell me what you've been up to."

"Is this for your article?"

"Maybe—or maybe just an innocent, friendly question."

"Well, my answer will prove how boring I am. I worked on my statistics, that's it. Haven't even been back to the Immunization Clinic since I last saw you, and though I hope to have the car this week, I haven't done anything. My only outing was dinner with Najeela's family."

"Whoa, how was that?"

"Nice. They're wealthy I think, or at least her uncle is. They live in a beautiful mansion in Hyatabad."

Hana came in then carrying a small tray with Nick's coffee and slices of cake. She looked straight at Nick when she spoke. "If you need anything, let me know."

"How do you manage that?" Abby asked once Hana had left the room. "She barely acknowledges me."

"Doesn't mean anything." Nick bit into the cake. "I've talked to her about her son, told her I'll do my best to find him. That's all. Don't change the subject. Tell me about dinner."

"Not much to tell. Her parents are lovely, but her uncle is, well, he's something else."

"What'd he do?"

"He didn't *do* anything. It's more the feeling he gave me. He's creepy, and he's probably a criminal too. He's a poppy farmer and exporter with farms in Helmand and Spin Boldak, and before you say it, I've seen the news reports about the opium business. Anyway, it seems he doesn't get along with Najeela's father, but I guess they tolerate him since they need his money."

"What's his name?" Nick asked as he polished off the last of the cake.

"Imtiaz." Abby felt her skin crawl at the mention of his name.

Nick seemed to sit up straighter. "Imtiaz Siddiqui?"

"Well, his brother's last name is Siddiqui so I suppose that's him."

"Holy shit." Excitement dripped from Nick's words. "You've met him? Do you know who he is?"

"I bet you're going to tell me," Abby replied wryly.

"He's *the biggest* poppy farmer and opium exporter in Afghanistan. There's just no catching him. He plays both sides— supports the Taliban and Al Qaeda, and just to hedge his bets, he supports Karzai. He's even pushing his brother to run for president once Karzai steps down." Nick pushed a shock of unruly hair back from his forehead. "I'd give anything to meet that bastard, see what makes him tick. He's rumored to be involved in human trafficking these days too, and why not? Easy money selling and smuggling these invisible people, and something to fall back on if the poppy business dries up."

Nick got up and paced around the room. "This is really big, Abby, *really* big."

"I couldn't stand him. He's arrogant and, well, just gross."

"Don't tell me—he came on to you, right?"

"How'd you know?"

"I know his type. Shit, I can't believe you met him. Any chance I could meet him?"

"Are you kidding? I hope I never see him again, but even if I did, if he's as bad as you say, and I don't doubt you in this, what do you think the chances are he'll speak with a reporter from the *New York Times*?"

"Hmm." Nick scratched his head. "What does Najeela think of him?"

"She loves him."

Nick rolled his eyes.

Abby felt a tiny bubble of anger for her friend. "I agree he's a total creep, but he is her uncle. It doesn't mean she's evil. Jeez, you don't trust anyone."

"A lifetime of experience, Abby, all thirty-four years, and I'm usually right. Matter of fact, I can't think of when I was last wrong."

Abby stood and turned for the door. "I'm going back to work. Hang around if you'd like. Just let me know when you leave."

"I will, and remember—deep-six the Lariam. I bet your nightmares will come to an end."

"Believe it or not, I'm going to take your advice."

"Smart girl," Nick said.

Chapter 9

Abby took Nick's advice to heart and packed her Lariam away. To hedge her bets, she didn't throw it out, but as if to prove him right, her days and nights were quiet—no nightmares, no haunting images of the woman hurtling through the air. She hated to even think it, but it seemed he was right.

Three days into her dream-free life, Abby signed into her e-mail to find a message from Eric in her Inbox. Her heart raced a little at the sight of his name. In the subject line, he'd written—*I love you*. Abby took a deep breath. Should she even open it? Her index finger hovered over the DELETE button as she remembered his last e-mail telling her he was "moving on." You bastard, she thought. She'd have given anything to see a message from him just a few weeks ago, but already the hold he'd had on her heart was slipping. Abby was making a new life, at least she was trying, and there was no room for him here. Still, she thought, it couldn't hurt to just read what he'd written. She took a deep breath and clicked on Eric's message.

Dear Abby,

I expect that this e-mail will be a surprise, although if you're not using your old e-mail address, I suppose you'll never see it. I wish we could speak but I'll have to settle for writing this e-mail and hoping for a reply.

I've moved to Oregon and started my fellowship. I've done everything I thought I needed to do to make my life and my future perfect. But there's a big hole in my plans and it's you. You belong here with me. I don't know why I needed to move to Oregon without you, but it was a big mistake. I am so lonely without you. I hear someone laughing and I look for you. I see a couple embracing and I long for you. I miss you, I miss us. I miss it all.

I am sorry that I said good-bye in an e-mail. If I could take back my words, I would.

I know that you're with the UN in Pakistan and I'm so proud of you. I hope you'll reply to this e-mail and I hope you'll take me back. My life is dreary without you.

I miss you and I love you.

Eric

Abby read the e-mail over and over and felt her resolve to forget Eric slipping away. Tears stung her eyes, and she wiped them away with her hand. She reminded herself that he'd let her down more than she'd ever thought possible. She knew what she should do, and her index finger floated over the DELETE button. But she couldn't quite bring herself to do it, and she hesitated for only an instant before finally clicking print. It wouldn't hurt to keep it in her notebook and have a look every now and then. Closing her e-mail, she began to write her vaccine report.

That night, Abby woke with a start, pulling wildly at the sheets that had entangled her legs. Her nightmare had returned, and this time she woke not in the bright, forgiving hue of morning light, but in the full, deep, dark of night. She sat upright, her fear somehow washed away by her overriding need to write it all down. She leaned over and snapped on the bedside light, cursing when it failed to work. The damn electricity was off again, and no generator either. Abby swung her legs over the side of the bed, her fingers searching for her flashlight. When her hand found the cool metal cylinder, she smiled, relieved. She wanted, no, she *needed,* to write this down. If she wrote it out, the threads of her memory wouldn't unravel with time, and the details of the woman's fall would remain as clear and crisp six months from now as they were tonight.

Abby reached for her pen and notebook and began to write, and once she was finished, she sat back and read her account of the woman's plunge to her death. Should she erase that line, she wondered, about the bracelet mesmerizing her? She hesitated before deciding. It was the truth, even if it did sound a bit peculiar to be so riveted by a bracelet on a dead woman.

She felt a kind of relief to have written it out, and she laid the notebook on her bedside table before she burrowed back under the sheets. Maybe she could sleep again tonight.

*   *   *

It was almost seven thirty when Abby woke, feeling better than she had in weeks. It was, she thought, because she'd written the details in her notebook. She reached for the little book and read the words again. Seeing her words, her descriptions, on paper was comforting. It made it seem tangible, more than just wild imaginings. She wasn't sure yet what she'd do with her notes, but she slipped the notebook into her nightstand drawer.

She was feeling refreshed and eager for company when she opened the door to the hallway, but the house was quiet. She peered into the kitchen, where Hana sat reading a newspaper. A newspaper? Hadn't Najeela said Hana was illiterate?

"Morning, Hana," Abby greeted her.

Hana looked up, and—would wonders never cease?—she didn't frown. Instead, she hastily folded the newspaper and motioned to the coffeepot. "Help yourself. Want some breakfast?"

Abby's stomach growled in response. "I'd love something, but don't go to any trouble, whatever you have is fine." She sat down across from Hana.

Hana pulled herself away from the table. "You can't eat in here. If Miss Najeela comes, we'll both be in for it."

"Oh, come on," Abby pleaded, but Hana shook her head.

Abby carried her cup to the dining room and sat in silence, wondering if Najeela would be in today at all. She looked at her watch—just eight o'clock. At home, she'd already have been up for hours, having risen at the crack of dawn to catch the crosstown bus, and once at work, she'd have grabbed a quick cup of coffee and a doughnut. But here in Peshawar, life was upside down. She slept in, worked from the house, and someone else got her coffee. Things that should have been a treat really weren't, and she found herself wishing she could take a bus to the clinic, get her own coffee, and munch on a doughnut. She sighed. None of that was going to happen here.

Lost in her thoughts, she didn't notice Hana arriving with a plate of scrambled eggs and toast until she'd cleared her throat loudly and pointed to the food. Abby sat straighter. "Can you sit with me at least? I'd love the company, and if Najeela comes, we'll hear the car from here."

"No thanks," Hana replied over her shoulder as she headed back to the kitchen.

Abby, tired of the solitude, ate quickly and headed to her small office, where she sat and typed out a few reports and looked at her watch again. Nine thirty already. The house was still quiet; even Hana dusted soundlessly today. It figured: the first time she wanted company, Nick probably wouldn't show. She wandered through the empty rooms, and peering through the front window, she spied Mohammed and the precious car. Najeela had kept her promise, and now Abby had a way back to the camp. She pulled open the door and stepped outside. Mohammed jumped to attention.

"Morning, miss."

"Morning, Mohammed. Can you take me to the camp?"

He smiled. "Yes, yes." He opened the passenger door.

"Let me get my things." Abby hurried back to the house. She grabbed her bag and last week's clinic report from her desk and said a quick good-bye to Hana before climbing into the car.

Mohammed navigated the now familiar route with ease, and as they arrived at the camp, Abby let herself out of the car and turned back to face him. "It's just too hot here in the sun, so let's have different rules today. Don't stay right here, just find some shade or go relax somewhere." She looked at her watch. "And come back for me in two hours. Is that okay?"

"I'll stay here," Mohammed said, and Abby headed for the Immunization Clinic. When she stepped inside, the heat of the small space felt as though it might squeeze the breath out of her, and she paused. Though the crowd had thinned considerably since her last visit, the heat had grown thicker. Swiping at the beads of perspiration that had already formed on her brow, Abby headed toward Simi, working intently at the desk.

"Good morning," she said.

Simi looked up and smiled. "Ah, good morning. It is good to see you. I was just finishing up the numbers for you." She tapped her pen on the papers spread out on the desk.

Abby smiled. "That's good, but why is it so empty here? Oh, no, did I get the day wrong?"

"No, no. Today the food rations are distributed. Mothers and children will be there, waiting in line, worried that if they show up too late, the rations will be finished."

"Is that common? That people miss out and don't get anything?"

"It is. The food rations are less now than at any other time, and there is always the chance that the supplies will be finished before the line is done." Simi stood and stretched and wiped her scarf over the dampness on her face. "It is too hot in here." She readjusted her scarf to cover the stray hairs that peeked out. Her hair, Abby saw, was streaked with bits of gray, and though her face was unlined, she had the unmistakable look of someone older, someone who'd seen disappointment more than once, and who fully expected to see it again.

She seemed to sense Abby's gaze and smiled. "Come." She held out her hand to Abby. "Without the crowd of patients, you can see how the clinic is organized."

Abby nodded and followed. The entire clinic was housed in this one small room, maybe twelve by sixteen, made smaller by a canvas curtain that cut through the center to create a separate area. The first section held the registration desk and the same bare lightbulb Abby had noticed on her first visit. Though it gave off a hazy glow, it only added to the heat collecting in the small space. Simi lifted the curtain and gestured for Abby to step through. A slight woman, clipboard in hand, stood in the far corner, hunched over a box of supplies. Abby could just make out her face, her milky-chocolate skin, her delicate features, a black braid peeking out of layers of the bright yellow fabric that draped her head. Abby tried to remember if she'd met her.

"Mariyah," said Simi, "come and see Abby."

Her head down and almost buried in the bright yellow scarf she wore, the woman, a slight limp to her step, approached.

"You remember Mariyah," Simi said. "She was at the desk with me when you came to meet us."

"Ah, yes." Abby remembered the thin woman who'd sat hunched over her work. "Hello, Mariyah." Abby offered her hand.

When Mariyah raised her head, Abby saw the jagged, ropey scar that cut through her face. Abby recoiled at the sight, her hand frozen in midair. She took a deep breath, hoping that Mariyah hadn't noticed her shock. But Mariyah, she saw with relief, had kept her gaze locked firmly on the ground.

"Hello," Abby said again, her voice gentler this time. "Nice to meet you." She reached out, and Mariyah slipped her own delicate hand into Abby's. Her fingers, long and tapered, were covered with rock-hard calluses, the hands of a worker. She raised her chin, and Abby saw the full extent of the scar. Mariyah had been sliced from ear to ear, and her upper lip had been cut clean through, leaving her face contorted into a permanent frown. Her eyes, a deep, smoky black, sparkled against her light brown skin, a touch of unexpected beauty on her disfigured face. Abby locked her gaze onto Mariyah's eyes.

"Mariyah," Simi said, "is from a small village north of Peshawar."

Mariyah nodded and adjusted her head covering. Abby squeezed Mariyah's hand and felt the small tremor that had settled there. "Hello, Mariyah," she said softly, hoping to ease the woman's obvious anxiety, and her own as well. Mariyah's rows of colorful bangles jangled on her wrist, and she slipped her hand from Abby's to silence them. She nodded again and turned back to her work. She hadn't said a word, and Abby wondered if the wounds had stolen her voice as well as her smile. Abby wanted to say something to somehow provide comfort, but her horror at the sight of Mariyah's scars had left her speechless.

Embarrassed at her ineptness, Abby turned to Simi. "She doesn't travel every day from the north, does she?" Abby asked, hoping to get more information. "I thought the staff was local."

Simi nodded. "Well, we are. The three of us," she said, motioning to the two nurses, "are from Peshawar. Mariyah is on a special UN program, and she is living here in Peshawar now." Simi didn't offer any more information, and it seemed rude to ask. "Come," Simi said, "let's finish seeing everything."

She led Abby to the opposite side of the room. This area was packed with stacks of paper, boxes of syringes and needles, a refrigerator to hold the vaccines, and a small generator to keep it working. A baby wailed, and Abby saw then the remaining patients lined up, anxiously awaiting their shots. The nurses, Shoma and Nasreen, were just finishing up with their injections, and Abby watched as the last of the patients drifted out.

"Hello," Shoma called. "You like?" She waved her hand around the clinic.

"I do," Abby said, "although the space is a little tight." She straightened a pile of boxes and looked around. "I'm sorry that everyone is gone, but I'll be back again to help."

Shoma giggled and pointed to Nasreen. "No English." Shoma turned and whispered to Nasreen.

Abby smiled. "No Urdu." She pointed to herself and watched as the two laughed in reply.

"I guess I'll go. The clinic is open on Tuesday and Thursday, yes?" Abby asked, stepping outside.

Simi stopped at the entrance, angling her head as if listening, and then Abby caught it too—a low rumble, thunder almost, gaining speed and coming closer. Sharp bursts of gunfire broke through the racket, adding to the chaos swirling closer. Abby gulped in a deep breath and inhaled the sharp scent of something burning. What the hell was going on? She turned questioningly and spied Mohammed sprinting toward her.

"Go back inside, miss," he said urgently.

"What is it?" Abby asked, her mouth suddenly dry.

"There are demonstrations just beyond the camp. They're burning an American flag. They won't come into the camp. Just stay inside." He pushed her toward the doorway. "We won't leave until they're gone."

Abby stumbled, and Simi steadied her, propelling her to the rear of the clinic. "Stay here," Simi said, pulling the canvas curtain across the room. The two nurses, along with Mariyah and Simi, huddled in the front area, and Abby could just make out their fretful whispers. Abby could still hear the thunderous shouts, and she sank into a rickety wooden chair, her heart pounding, her eyes darting to the doorway, still visible through the canvas. "'Unstable security situation,' my ass," she said aloud. Despite the warnings and the demonstrations in the city center, she'd never actually expected to be caught in the middle of some kind of street riot. But here she was, and it was her own fault—she'd jumped at this position.

She drew in a slow, deep breath and chewed on her fingernails, the glow from the lightbulb adding to the stifling heat and the tension in the small space. She reached up and pulled the tiny chain, and the room went dark. At least they wouldn't see her so easily if they did get in.

"Are you all right?" she heard Simi ask.

"I am," she whispered, though she knew that she wasn't. Shit, wouldn't Nick love to hear this? She sighed and listened as the rumble of the crowd grew fainter and more distant, then all but died away. The whole thing hadn't taken more than twenty minutes, but it had felt like an eternity.

Simi lifted the canvas and peered in. "It's quiet now, and Mohammed is here. Are you ready?"

"It's over?" Abby asked, peering through the doorway.

"It is," Simi replied. "Don't let the demonstrations bother you. There is always one group or another making trouble."

Abby forced a smile. "I'm not sure that's a comforting thought."

"You're safe here," Simi said. "You can't let this kind of thing trouble you. It is just young men with nothing better to do. Without jobs, they stir up trouble. When things improve here, when there are jobs again, there will be no time for this nonsense. You understand?"

Abby nodded. Simi's commonsense response was the perfect antidote to the afternoon's events.

"You will come again?" Simi asked.

Abby turned. "Yes," she said softly. "As long as there's a car for me, I'll be back this week."

"*Khoda khafez*, Abby." Simi smiled and stood at the entrance watching as Abby walked to Mohammed, standing nearby.

"You are good, miss?" Mohammed asked.

"I am. But I was scared. Not for long, but I was scared."

"Don't worry, miss," Mohammed said, opening the car's rear door. "I will take care of you."

Abby slid into the seat. "Thank you, Mohammed." She

leaned forward. "I believe you will, and I hope you'll be able to bring me back this Thursday?" Mohammed nodded, and Abby found herself smiling and looking forward to Thursday.

Back at the house, the driveway was occupied by a long, black limousine, similar to the one that had ferried her to Najeela's house for dinner. Abby squeezed around it and headed for the front door, where she was almost knocked over by Najeela, who hurried, almost ran, from the house. She looked up, startled to see Abby. "Back so soon?"

"I am. My work was finished, but there was some kind of riot nearby. Is that a problem often?"

Najeela seemed preoccupied. "Sorry for the rush, but I'm meeting my uncle. I'll see you tomorrow."

Abby wondered if she'd heard a word Abby had said. "But . . ." She wanted to talk about the day's chaos. Instead, she watched as Najeela slid into the limousine. Abby shrugged and waved, but already the car had pulled out into the street.

So much for sharing news of surviving her first riot. She couldn't e-mail anyone about it—they'd just worry and insist she go home. She couldn't tell Nick—he'd just say he'd told her so. But she did find herself wishing he'd stop by. A drink at the American Club would be the perfect remedy for her post-riot nerves. She exhaled slowly and headed into the house, her footsteps echoing in the long hallway. It was quieter than usual. No banging pots and pans, no running water, no sounds at all.

"Hana?" Abby called into the silence, but there was no answer. She poked her head into the empty kitchen and peered into the dining room, then the office, but the house was empty.

She opened the door to her room and stepped inside, dropping her bag on the bed. When she turned, her leg hit the open drawer on her nightstand. She rubbed at the soreness and moved to open the curtains. In the flood of daylight that streamed in, she turned back and surveyed the room. Everything was just as she'd left it except for the nightstand drawer, which hung open, her notebook lying undisturbed. Could she have left the drawer open? It wasn't like her, but she'd been in a hurry. She sighed and shut the drawer.

It was odd, but the whole day had been off, and maybe she was just getting forgetful. She headed to the office to get started on her day's reports.

Chapter 10

Abby opened her eyes wide and sat straight up.

"Abby, are you still asleep? The car is waiting." She recognized Najeela's voice, and she closed her eyes to help ease the dull pounding that had started up in her head. Jesus, that damn dream again. She reached for her bottle of Motrin and swallowed two capsules without water. What day was it? Thursday, she thought. She was going to the clinic. It must be Mohammed who was waiting.

"Sorry, Najeela, I'll be right out," she said as she headed for the shower.

Abby rushed through her shower and took one long gulp of

instant coffee before running out the door and heading to the clinic. Mohammed wove through the maze of cars, bicycles, and rickshaws that filled the streets, and they arrived at the clinic in record time.

"I'm here for the day," Abby said. "I'm not sure if you should go back to the house or stay here. What do you think?"

"I think, miss, I'll stay right here. I want to be sure you are not alone."

"Mohammed, thank you. And thank you too for the other day."

Mohammed looked away shyly.

Abby hurried to the clinic, arriving just as the first patients of the day began to form a line at the door. She squeezed through the growing queue and greeted Simi. "Good morning, Simi," Abby said breezily. "I'm hoping that I can help out today. I see there's a line already, and since I don't speak the languages of either Afghanistan or Pakistan, I thought I could give shots."

"Good morning to you," Simi said. "You have been sent from Allah today, I think. Nasreen is not here today, so you can help Shoma." Simi showed Abby the registration card with the patient's name, age, and vaccination record. "This section"—she pointed to the card's heading—"tells you which vaccine the patient will receive today. You see—measles, polio, it's right there—in English and Urdu, and once you've given the vaccine, initial it here." Simi turned and gestured to a table off to the side. "Shoma has already started organizing for the day. The syringes and vials you'll require are there. You just need to have a look and take what you need."

"Okay, that sounds easy enough." Abby nodded to Shoma. "*Salaam aleikum*, Shoma." Shoma giggled and called the first patient. Abby watched the procedure, then called a patient. It wasn't so different from home, except that these babies didn't offer up the same plump arms for vaccines. Instead, their tiny, shriveled limbs seemed too frail to hold a needle, and Abby hesitated, her hand trembling. The patients seemed to sense Abby's reluctance, and they looked questioningly at Shoma, who mumbled soothingly to them in Urdu.

Abby took a deep breath and plunged the vaccine into the first baby's arm. He wailed in reply, and Abby smiled. Some things were the same everywhere. Before long she was engrossed in the rhythm of the clinic, and though she couldn't speak their language, she could nod and smile. Still, she wanted to say something so she wouldn't seem so foreign.

"Simi," she called, "how do I say 'it's okay'?"

"*Acha*," Simi answered. "Just say *acha*."

Abby smiled and motioned for the next mother to step up. "*Acha,*" she said soothingly, stroking the baby's head. She held the tiny arm and, in one quick movement, administered the vaccine. The baby whimpered, his large eyes following Abby. "*Acha,*" she said again, kissing his cheek. She watched as the tiny woman clutched her baby close, and an idea began to form in Abby's mind. Why not document this, she thought, the sadness, the frailty, the people behind the numbers?

"I wonder if I could put this in my reports," she said, turning to Simi. "Document more than just the statistics, describe these babies and their mothers and everything here."

"You should," Simi said. "Numbers don't tell everything."

Abby smiled. Simi was right—numbers didn't tell everything, especially in a place like this. Suddenly the prospect of writing reports didn't seem so boring or dull. She might actually be able to make a difference with what she reported. "Will you ask this woman where she's from?"

Simi approached the woman as she swaddled her doe-eyed baby in a large shawl. The two spoke haltingly, the refugee turning to smile shyly at Abby. "She is from Afghanistan," Simi reported. "Just beyond Kandahar, but the Taliban are there now, and the workers with the vaccines have left. Her first baby died because there were no vaccines."

"Please tell her I'm sorry for her loss." Abby moved closer and touched the woman's arm. "Does she live here in the camp now?"

"Yes," Simi said. "She and her sister and their children live here."

The woman from Afghanistan finished wrapping her baby and nodded at Abby. *"Khoda khafez,"* she whispered as she hurried from the clinic.

Abby quickly jotted down the woman's story. "Simi, can we add a small space on the vaccine card for background? You know—where someone's from, why she's here in the camp. What do you think?"

Simi smiled. "I think it's very good. No one's ever asked before. The UN people just collect the numbers."

"Then it's settled," Abby said. "It's about time someone collected the stories, shake things up a bit."

She turned then to the next patient, a tiny woman struggling to hold her howling baby. Abby leaned in. *"Acha,"* she whispered to the wriggling child, who stopped long enough to take in the face of this stranger before he began to cry again. Abby quickly vaccinated and then soothed this baby before turning to the next, and the next. Her mind was spinning with the possibilities, and the hours flew. When the line finally thinned, Abby glanced at her watch—one o'clock already. She stretched and stepped into the registration area.

Mariyah sat hunched over the registration desk. *"Salaam aleikum,* Mariyah," Abby called. Mariyah raised her gaze, her brown eyes flashing, and she nodded quickly before bending back to her pencils and registration cards. Abby hesitated. She wanted to approach her, to make a connection, but instead she turned away, looking for Simi, and saw her just as she came into the clinic.

"I've been to the kitchen for tea," she said breathlessly. "It will be quieter now. Most come in the morning before the day's chores are upon them."

"It's been so busy. How many have we seen today? Do you know?"

Simi picked up the registration ledger, then leaned over Mariyah and counted her numbers. She wrote both numbers down and sat and added. "Ninety-eight," she said proudly.

"That's more than usual, right?"

"A few more than we would have," Simi replied. "It is good you were here."

"Good for me too. I'm going to head back to the house, but I'll try to come next week. And tonight," Abby added, smiling, "I'll add some of today's background stories to my report. Thank you, Simi. And Mariyah and Shoma, thank you as well. *Shukria*, thank you."

Abby arrived home to an ebullient Najeela. Though Abby had seen her quickly that morning, she hadn't had a chance yet to tell her about the riots.

"Oh, Abby!" Najeela exclaimed, cutting into Abby's thoughts.

"You seem especially happy today," Abby said. "Is there news from your boyfriend?"

"Ah, there is always news," Najeela said. "You have worked very long today already, yes?"

"I guess so, but it felt so good to do some real nursing. I didn't even notice, especially after the trouble earlier this week."

"What trouble?"

"Riots, demonstrations just outside of Safar."

"But you are fine?"

Abby nodded. "I'm trying to think of it as an adventure."

"Oh, no," Najeela said softly. "The UN will not be happy. They may decide the trouble here is too much and send you home." Her face crumpled into a long frown. "What will I do without you?"

"The UN hasn't mentioned it yet, have they? Although home sounds good to me, I'm pretty sure I'm here to stay."

Najeela smiled. "Let's go out then," she whispered. "We can celebrate that you're staying, and we can do some shopping and have dinner."

Images of Uncle Imtiaz danced in Abby's head. "Oh, I still have my reports to finish. I have so much to do."

"Oh, you do not." Najeela pouted. "I need a friendly ear. Please say yes. We can go to the Pearl. Yes? We have hardly seen one another. I want to look at fabric for my wedding dress. I know I'm not officially engaged, but it will happen soon and I want to be ready. I've decided I want to look like Kate, the new princess."

Abby laughed and felt her resistance melting. "Princess?" she said suddenly, remembering Nick's nickname for Najeela. "You want to be a princess?"

"Of course. I want to live happily ever after, don't you?"

"No way. I loved the royal wedding, but that's not the happily ever after I'm looking for."

Najeela's brows furrowed. "But you want to be married, no?"

Abby nodded. "I do, someday, but I don't have any interest in being a princess."

Najeela sighed. "Any word from Eric?"

Abby could almost hear the rustle of the folded page as

she'd pressed it between the pages of her notebook, and she opened her mouth to share the news of Eric's e-mail, but Najeela, she thought, would try to persuade her to take him back. She closed her mouth and shook her head.

Najeela placed her hand on Abby's. "Do not be sad. It will work out for you, Abby. I just know it. And, I confess I still have hopes that you might find Uncle Imtiaz to your liking."

Abby felt her stomach churn at the mention of Uncle Imtiaz. She knew she had to nip this talk in the bud. "Listen, Najeela, I don't mean to be impolite, but the truth is, I'm just not interested in older men."

Najeela's lips puckered. "Oh, Abby, an older man will always take care of you." She paused as if trying to understand Abby's point of view. "Otherwise, you'll be settling for someone you don't even like. Which reminds me, I forgot to tell you that reporter, Nick, was looking for you."

"When?" Abby asked too quickly. She felt curiously disappointed to have missed him, though she couldn't say for sure why. She barely knew him. Maybe it was just that he was an American, an instant friend in a strange land. Could he have heard about the riots? Was he checking on her? "Was he here today?"

"Hmm, I'm not sure. The days run into one another, but maybe it was yesterday. But, well, it doesn't matter, does it?" Najeela didn't wait for an answer. "Come, let's go."

She pulled open the front door and called for Mohammed. Abby picked up her bag and followed.

At the sound of Najeela's voice, Mohammed snapped to attention. "Yes, miss," he said, hurrying to open the rear passenger doors.

They drove through the now familiar city streets, and when the car passed the American Club, Abby peered through the window hoping to catch a glimpse of Nick, but there was no sign of him or his rusting old sedan. She sat back against the cushioned seat and wondered where he was. Underneath that tough exterior, he probably wasn't a bad guy, she thought. He was attractive in a bad-boy kind of way. She smiled—*what* was she thinking? He wasn't even her type. She'd always gone for the brainy, quiet guys, but where had that got her? Alone at thirty. What was that statistic she'd heard on *Oprah*? A woman over thirty, or maybe it was forty, was more likely to be attacked by a terrorist than to be married? And that seemed not so unlikely given where she was.

She heaved a sigh and pushed herself forward in her seat, finally noticing that Najeela had been chatting happily about her wedding. Abby caught only snatches of the one-sided conversation—*rings, dress, wedding trip*—words that had been in Abby's vocabulary not so long ago, but seemed so foreign now.

The car stopped at a fancy tailor shop in the University district, and Abby sat forward, her hand on the door handle.

Najeela patted Abby's back. "Wait for the driver to open the door, Abby. That's his job." Najeela smiled sweetly when Mohammed opened the door. Abby slid out and smiled at Mohammed. "Thank you, Mohammed," she said, rolling her eyes at Najeela's back.

Inside the tailor's shop, they were ushered to comfortable seats, and the shopkeeper, obsequious to a fault, jumped at each of Najeela's requests. "I'm very interested in this gown," she said, pulling a large, colorful picture of Kate Middleton from her bag. "But it's a little plain for me. Could you add ruffles here?" She pointed to the hem, and the tailor nodded vigorously. He pushed a table in front of Najeela before disappearing into the back.

Najeela turned to Abby. "You will be in my wedding, won't you?" she asked earnestly. Abby nodded. "Oh, good, then we can ask to look at fabric for your dress. I liked that Pippa girl's dress, but not in white. I think only the bride should be in white. Don't you agree?" Najeela spoke so hurriedly, Abby could barely keep up.

When the tailor reappeared carrying bolts and bolts of fabric, Najeela sat forward and looked closely at each swatch he placed before her. She ran her fingers dreamily over the cloth, then pulled her hand abruptly away and frowned. "No, no, these are too heavy. I want the fabric to be light and lacy. Do you know what I mean? Do you have that?"

The old man nodded and scurried to the back once again.

Najeela leaned toward Abby and whispered, "We won't stay long. I know that this must upset you."

"Najeela, it doesn't. I promise. Take your time. I'm not pining for Eric, I promise you." Instead, Abby's thoughts had wandered to Nick. She wondered if he was researching his secret story. She almost wished she were with him sharing a beer at the club. He did have a way, there was no denying that.

"But you look so sad," Najeela said, her words interrupting Abby's imaginings.

Abby caught herself and smiled. "I'm not sad, and I don't miss Eric. I was just daydreaming. Sorry."

The tailor returned, his arms laden with more heavy bolts of fabric. Najeela barely looked at them before rejecting them all as not quite what she was looking for. "Do you carry tiaras?"

Abby had to cover her mouth with her hand to smother a laugh. Najeela, intent on finding the perfect fabric, seemed not to notice Abby's shaking shoulders.

The tailor shook his head. "Sorry, miss, no, but I can order one for you."

"No. I think Paris is where we should be shopping." Najeela turned to Abby. "Don't you agree?"

Abby nodded and held back the laughter that was percolating on her lips.

"Blue, Abby, or maybe lilac. One of those shades is best, I think, for your dress. It will make your brown eyes stand out. What do you say?"

"You're the bride, Najeela. You get to make all the decisions, including the colors. I'll wear whatever you say."

Najeela tucked her arm into Abby's. "You are my first true friend, Abby. My very first."

Abby felt a pang of guilt at having a secret chuckle at Najeela's expense. She *did* like Najeela, who, despite being petulant and pouty and sometimes a pain in the ass, was also infectiously bubbly and almost childlike in her belief in happily ever after. Najeela was so different from Emily, her best friend in Boston. Emily was quick-witted, sarcastic, a damn fine ER nurse, and a long-legged beauty who had little patience with self-absorbed people. She and Eric had never gotten along. Emily had dismissed him as a "lightweight" the moment she'd met him, but she'd held her tongue and tolerated him for Abby's sake. Nick, on the other hand, was just the kind of guy that Em liked—straightforward, no-nonsense, a regular guy. God, Abby missed hanging out with her. She sighed. Maybe she'd send an e-mail later.

Najeela and Abby arrived at the Pearl in the late afternoon, long after the lunch crush had left, and before the dinner crowd appeared. The restaurant was empty, and Najeela led the way to a table at the rear. "We'll sit here," she announced to the surprised waiter, who hurriedly filled glasses with water and set the table before handing them both menus. Najeela ordered for both of them again.

Abby took a long sip of her water and turned to Najeela. "You've met Mariyah?"

Najeela, looking puzzled, shook her head. "I don't think so. Who is she?"

Abby tried to hide her exasperation. "She works at the clinic, the woman with the scar?"

"Oh, yes." A frown creased Najeela's usually smooth forehead. "Oh, yes, I know that one. I've seen that scar." She shuddered. "Awful."

"Awful for her, I'd guess. Do you know her story? I know it's none of my business, but she seems so sad, and she must have suffered terribly."

Najeela sat straight, her back tight against the seatback. "Abby, of course it's your business. Everything that happens in the clinic is your business, but I admit all I know is that she's in a special UN program. They were very hush-hush about her. They wouldn't tell me anything, though I expect if you pressed the matter, you could learn her story."

Abby shook her head. "I wouldn't ask. It's none of my business. I just thought maybe you knew something."

"No, but if you learn the story, you must tell me. It must be just terrible."

Abby nodded, thinking if she learned the secret, she wouldn't tell anyone.

"We should speak of happy things today, don't you think? And, well, I have something to show you." Najeela's voice was almost a purr. She pulled a folded newspaper from her bag. "My dear Lars is in the newspaper, a wonderful story about the good work he does. Here, see for yourself how handsome he is." She pushed the newspaper toward Abby, who took the paper just as the food arrived.

Making room for the plates, Abby placed the paper on the seat beside her, and they both turned to the food, eating with relish. Najeela had ordered the kebabs and biryani rice that they'd shared on their first visit, and Abby savored every bite. She wondered if Mariyah, with those scars around her mouth, had a problem eating.

Abby had eaten her fill when Najeela looked at her watch and exclaimed it was time to go. She motioned to the waiter and signed the check. "I'll meet you by the car. I just want to run to the powder room."

Abby smiled. "I'll see you outside." She gathered her bag and noticed the newspaper Najeela had handed her lying untouched on the seat beside her. She folded it and slipped it into her bag. She'd have a look later.

Back at the house, Najeela said her good-byes. "Thank you for coming with me today. It makes me so happy to think about my wedding." She planted a friendly kiss on Abby's cheek. "You are an angel, Abby." Najeela headed back to the front door. "I'll see you tomorrow."

Abby headed to her office and logged in, excited for once at the prospect of working on her reports. Today, she'd include the new section, the refugees' stories, and she knew it would make her reports come alive. If she could persuade someone on the other end to see beyond the numbers to the people who lived or died here in the camp, maybe the UN officials would see how desperate the conditions at Safar were. Maybe they could increase funding, staffing—or finally help search for some of those missing children in the Protection Tent.

Abby fished through her bag for a pen, and her hands glided over the newspaper at the bottom. Damn, she thought, pushing the paper out of the way and zipping her bag. Tomorrow, she thought. She'd remind herself tomorrow to give the paper back to Najeela.

Chapter 11

At the house, Abby was often alone. She hadn't expected to live such a solitary life, but that solitude, she thought, had helped her slide into an easy routine. During work hours, she huddled over her reports with a renewed enthusiasm, determined to bring the clinic to life on paper. But with the clinic open only two days a week, she still faced great gaps of empty time. She should have been doing so much more, she thought. And her evenings—well, they were empty. The solitude gave her time to brood over the woman in Geneva and her own failure to find the body. That brooding, she thought, eventually led to nightmares. It was a miserable cycle with no way out.

Days after her lunch with Najeela, Abby jerked awake one morning, her hand on the alarm, her body slick with sweat from yet another nightmare. She could still see the bloodied body of the woman sprawled on the street, broken eyeglasses clutched in her hand, and the flashing diamond cuff on her wrist.

She sighed and stood up, pressing her fingers into her forehead. A shower, she thought, stepping into her bathroom, that was what she needed. Refreshed by the warm water, the dream fading, her mind turned to coffee, and she opened her door and stepped into the hall.

The house was quiet. Najeela hadn't been in since their lunch at the Pearl, and that was days ago. Mohammed and the car hadn't been back either, despite Najeela's promise not to leave Abby without transportation. She hated the isolation here. She couldn't go out for a walk or a run, and even if the car was here, she couldn't drive. She was trapped, a veritable prisoner whose comings and goings were dictated by Najeela's whims. Not even Nick had been around. She heaved a long sigh and wished that he'd show up.

Hana arrived just as Abby poured herself another cup of coffee. At the housekeeper's questioning glance, Abby smiled. "I thought it would be okay with you if I made breakfast for myself. I've already cleaned up. The water"—she raised her own cup to emphasize her words—"is still hot if you'd like tea."

Hana nodded, and Abby headed to her office. She sat at her computer and booted it up, the soft whir the only sound in the house. Just as she began to compile her statistics, she heard the front door slam shut, followed by the sound of Najeela's heels clicking down the hall. She whirled into the room, happiness oozing from her smile.

"Good morning, Abby," she whispered excitedly. "I want to show you something." She opened her hand, revealing a diamond-and-sapphire necklace that shimmered in the morning light, twirling and sparkling as Najeela lifted it for Abby to admire.

"It's beautiful," Abby said, reaching to touch the necklace. The diamonds and sapphires were familiar somehow, their sparkle and shimmer, the almost hypnotic glow. Her gaze narrowed, and she peered closely at the gems—in cut and clarity, they were eerily similar to those of the bracelet on the woman in Geneva. She closed her eyes. She didn't want to think about that today.

"There's more," Najeela said, oblivious to the stunned look on Abby's face. Najeela turned and closed the office door before she slid a key from her pocket and inserted it into the top drawer of the second desk. Her eyes grew wide as she slid the drawer out. "See," she said, her voice soft and filled with a child-like wonder. Abby leaned in and saw the source of Najeela's happiness. The drawer was filled with jewelry, and even to Abby's amateur inspection, it was apparent that these jewels were real. Earrings, necklaces, and rings sparkled as brightly as the bracelet in her dream.

"Are these—"

"I told you he loves me," Najeela interrupted, her eyes aglow. "He sends me these so I'll know just how much." Her fingers sifted through the jewelry until she pulled out a pearl necklace, a large sapphire hanging in the center. "This one was the first one he gave me. Is it not just the most beautiful thing you've ever seen?"

Abby reached out and ran her fingers along the cool, glistening pearls. "They're lovely. Why don't you wear them? Why keep them locked away and hidden?"

"I must hide them. My father would kill me if he knew." Najeela draped the necklace around her neck. "But, oh, how I love to see it, to hold it close to my skin, and I know that someday soon I will be able to show these to anyone I choose. But for now, they are my secret, and now yours as well. I am so happy that you are my friend, and I am able to share this secret with you. Would you like to wear something? Maybe these earrings?" Najeela pulled out a pair of sparkling diamond studs.

Instinctively Abby fingered her own thin, gold hoop earrings. "They're beautiful, but, well, I've never been much for jewelry. Although I guess I did expect a diamond ring on my finger by now." She held up her unadorned left hand for emphasis.

"Oh, Abby, do not be sad. You will meet the man you're intended to marry. I just know it." Najeela pushed Abby's hair back from her face and smiled. "You are a beautiful girl, my friend. You will make a good match."

Abby couldn't help but smile in reply. "You are so good for me, Najeela, always so happy."

"I am happy because I have met the man I will marry, and I am certain that we will convince my parents that he is the one for me. Like you, it is the waiting that is difficult for me, but my fiancé has told me that soon we will announce ourselves to my family." Najeela cupped the diamond earrings in her hands, her fingers caressing the precious stones. She lifted her gaze from the jewelry to Abby once again and turned, her face flushed, her eyes shining. "I hope that you and I can travel to Paris soon."

"I hope so too," Abby said.

Heavy footsteps sounded in the hall, and both Abby and Najeela turned. "It's that reporter," Najeela whispered, stuffing her jewelry back into the drawer. "Will you go out to him so that he doesn't come in here?" Najeela turned back to the drawer. "I don't want him to see this."

Abby nodded and headed into the hall, meeting Nick just as he arrived at the office door. "Hey, good to see you," she said.

Nick turned and looked back down the hall. "Just checking. For a minute there, I was sure you were speaking to someone else. Good to see you too," he said wryly.

"Come on. Want some coffee?"

"Forgive my skepticism, but I have to ask—it's *good* to see me?"

Abby smiled. "Sometimes I *am* happy to see you. Believe it or not."

"Oh, right, and this is one of those times. Well, I'll take advantage—I'd love some coffee. Two sugars."

Abby forced herself to smile. "Be right back." She entered the kitchen. "Hana, any more hot water? Nick's here, and he's looking for coffee."

Hana smiled. "Tell him I'll be right there."

Abby took a deep breath and walked to the dining room. Though she almost couldn't believe it herself, she really was glad to see Nick, and today she wouldn't start an argument—she'd be friendly even.

"So what's up?"

Nick sat sprawled across a chair. "Not me, that's for sure. Scotch got the better of me last night at the club. I'm desperate for coffee. Is it coming?"

"Hana's fixing it. She'll take care of you."

"Sit with me, will you? I need to ask you a favor."

"Not the article again?" Abby asked, sliding into a seat across the table.

"No, well, not entirely, not yours at least. I've learned there's a house, a kind of safe house, for trafficking victims, here in Peshawar." He sat up straighter, engrossed in his own words. "I don't have all the details yet, but the program rehabilitates these victims, teaches them skills so they can work, and provides therapy so they can get over the trauma."

"Wow, great lead for a story on trafficking victims. Are you going to follow up? Write something?"

"I'd like to, but here's where the favor comes in. The reality is they won't talk to me alone. I'm a man, the source of most of their problems. I need a woman with me." He focused his gaze on her. "I need you, Abby. Please. I'd like to look into this."

"Today just might be your lucky day, Nick. I'd actually like to hear more about this trafficking, and if I do go, you'll owe me a favor. Sounds like a win-win for me." Abby smiled. "You going today?"

Nick nodded. "I thought I'd head to the camp, to the Protection Tent. I know a woman who works there. Well, *know* is a stretch, but I've met her, and I think she'll help me out. Can you come?"

Abby didn't even have to think it over—the answer slipped from her lips before the question was out of Nick's mouth. "Count me in. Let me tell Najeela and get my stuff."

Nick put his hand up. "Slow down, will ya? I didn't expect such an easy sell, and I'd still like that coffee."

"I'll get my stuff. Your coffee, I'm sure, will be here in a snap."

Abby stepped to the doorway of the office, and Najeela looked up. "Is he gone yet?" she whispered.

"Not yet, but soon. I'm going with him to the camp. You don't mind, do you?"

Najeela hesitated and seemed to force the limp smile that draped her lips. "No, of course you should go, Abby. I'll see you later."

"Thanks, Najeela. I'll finish my report tonight."

Najeela nodded as Abby hurried to her room to collect her

bag. She saw her notebook, filled now with her description of the incident in Geneva, and she considered bringing it to share the details with Nick. She picked it up and paused. No, not yet. It could wait. She placed it back in her nightstand and slid the drawer shut.

Nick was drinking his coffee and finishing up toast. He looked up. "That was quick, but I'm ready." He stood and gulped down the last bit of coffee. "Let's go."

Once at the camp, Abby headed to the clinic. "I know the clinic's closed. I just want to have a look."

"Fine with me. I'll tag along if you don't mind."

Abby took her time getting to the clinic. She wanted to fully experience this place. It seemed she was always in a hurry when she was here, and she never knew what it was to really *be* here. Emily had written asking what everything was like, and Abby realized that although she could describe the rows and rows of tents, the line of patients at the clinic, and the unrelenting sunshine, she didn't know what things were like for the people forced to live here. She inhaled deeply.

Nick grimaced. "Most visitors choose to hold their breath in a place like this. They want to get it over with, but not you, huh?"

"I haven't been here that often, and I don't want to be just a visitor. I'd like to really feel it, if you know what I mean. I've added a section for refugee stories to my reports to underline what the numbers really mean. But maybe I can write something about the camp too. You know, tell what it's like here." Abby slowed her pace to match the sun's demands. On her left, she noticed again the long rows of scraggly tents that seemed to spread on forever, and to her right, the rocky path that wound through the camp. Veiled women with babies and children in tow shuffled along the paths. She didn't think she'd ever get used to this, to the smell and the sights, but she wanted to try.

"Take a deep whiff of the place then. Tell me what you learn."

Abby closed her eyes and tried to blot out the sounds of children shrieking, and dogs barking. She inhaled deeply through her nostrils, pausing before she exhaled. "It's an evocative smell, spices and sweat and something else I'm not sure of, but it's a hopeless kind of scent that just lingers. It makes me think of disease and starvation and fear. I suppose that's because I know what's here." She opened her eyes and looked straight at Nick. "Close your eyes. Can't you smell it? Can't you feel it?"

"When you describe it like that, I can. You're poetic. I might even use that description."

Abby smiled. "Always a writer, huh?"

"Abby, you're a nurse. My guess is you came here to save the world. I came here to save myself, at least my professional self. If I don't pound out one hell of a story, I'll be chasing celebrities for the *Enquirer*."

Abby couldn't hold back her laughter. "God, you're dramatic. I mean, you won the Pulitzer, right?"

"Yeah, I did, but a writer is only as good as his last story, and I haven't had anything good in at least two years. Pulitzer or not, the *Times* wants compelling stories, not fluff."

"Fluff—wasn't that what you planned to write about me?"

Nick raised his brows. "I was trying to get out of the hole I'd dug myself into. Don't hold that against me."

"I won't, especially when there's so much else to hold against you."

"Aww, hell, that hurts. You must have noticed I'm trying."

Abby smiled. "Which brings me to just why *are* you trying?"

He was nervous, she thought, the way she was when she liked someone new.

"You don't miss much, Abby. I need your help, and I'm smart enough to know that I won't get it if I'm a jerk." He smiled. "I'm really not a bad guy once you get to know me."

It occurred to Abby that he probably wasn't, and that maybe Nick and she were more alike than she cared to admit. He was honest enough to confess that he'd landed here to save himself, and hadn't that been her aim as well? Not that she'd share that information with him—not now at any rate. She studied his face and thought, not for the first time, that he was surprisingly handsome. With his chiseled features and deep brown eyes— well, there was no doubt about it. And he seemed not to be aware of that the way some men are. He just seemed comfortable with who he was, and that was appealing, though Abby reminded herself that she was definitely not interested in any man, period. At least not now.

She crossed her arms and caught herself too late. She'd been looking—no, staring—at Nick, and he'd been looking right back. Her mind scrambled trying to pick up the thread of conversation they'd been having—something about his not being a bad guy. That was it, she thought.

"No, you're not bad, I guess. I think my friend Emily would like you."

Nick raised his brows. "Really? Well, you'll have to tell me more about Emily, but what about you? What do you think?"

Abby smiled. "Jury's still out."

"I'll win you over. You know that, don't you?"

Abby smiled and shook her head. "Time will tell."

"Back to business. We might as well get this show on the road." Nick headed in the direction of the Protection Tent, the sun's glare bearing down on them.

"God, is it always so hot and sunny here?" Abby swiped her hand across her forehead. "Doesn't it ever rain?"

Nick wiped the beads of sweat that had gathered on his brow. "There is a rainy season—March, I think, but don't quote me on that." Nick lifted the flap of the tent for Abby. "That woman I told you about, I want to ask her if she might be able to get me in touch with a few victims of trafficking. Turns out she's part of the team involved there. I just want to check and see if she's in today."

Nick walked to the center, where an older woman, her face almost fully hidden by her veil, was working on a pile of photos. Nick leaned in and said something. Abby couldn't make out what the woman was saying in reply, but she shook her head as she spoke. Nick returned, his brow creased in disappointment.

"Not here today. Damn, I keep missing her. That woman told me where she lives. Want to come with me, see if she's there?"

"Sure." The statistics Abby had to write up could wait. She hadn't seen much of Peshawar. This could be interesting.

They set off in Nick's rusting old sedan. "We're not going to University Town or anyplace remotely nice. We're headed to the slums where most of the locals live."

They drove along a road lined with canals filled with stagnant, muddy water. "Not mud," Nick said, watching Abby's face as they drove. "Open sewers. And this"—he rolled down the window—"is the real smell of misery. It's the smell of rotting food and rotting lives." He turned to Abby. "Makes the refugee camp seem grand, doesn't it?"

Abby held her breath. She hadn't ever seen anything like this. The houses, crumbling mud-and-plaster homes that bore long, dusty cracks, lined the narrow paths. Screeching children played on heaps of steaming garbage, oblivious to the smells and sights.

"I had no idea things were so tough here," Abby said. "The woman who works in the camp lives *here*?"

"That's what I was told, and it makes sense. If she lives here, she knows what this is like, and you can see for yourself"—he slowed the car—"these people are invisible. No one in the world that we come from pays much attention to people in places like this. And that makes them easy to kidnap or even talk into leaving. This is the kind of place that people are desperate to leave, and not even their families will notice, at least not for long. And the sad truth is—many of these girls and women are sold by their own families. Women here have value on the open market but not so much at home."

"Jesus, Nick, their own families?"

"Don't be so quick to judge. They're living their own miserable lives, struggling to find food and keep a roof over their own heads. They're powerless too. I'm not excusing them, I'm just saying not everything's black-and-white." He rolled his window up and eased the car to the side of the road. "I think we should just walk from here. And a little advice—if you have anything of value, take it with you."

Abby hoisted her backpack onto her shoulder and stepped out. The stench was overpowering, and she opened her mouth to breathe. Her feet sank into a pile of squishy garbage, and she felt her stomach lurch. The taste of bile filled her mouth. "This place is pretty awful, huh?" She pulled her feet free of the oozing slime, relieved she hadn't brought her designer sandals after all.

"There are places like this all over the world," Nick said.

"This bad?"

"Hey, sometimes worse. In Nairobi and Mumbai, the slums

would make your hair curl, and yet some of the world's kindest people live in those hellholes."

Abby looked around and saw that a small crowd had gathered. People glared at them with barely concealed hostility. She stopped and wondered if they should maybe leave. "Nick?"

"Keep walking, and stay next to me." He dropped his voice to a whisper. "I wanted to ask for my friend, but I think it's better if you ask. Say you're a nurse at the camp and you're looking for Zara Hussein. Okay?"

Abby nodded and smiled at the next woman she saw. The woman puckered her brow and beckoned Abby with her finger.

Abby walked to her side. "You speak English?"

The woman responded by rolling her head side to side.

Abby smiled. "A little?"

A long wrinkle creased the woman's forehead. This woman, Abby thought, didn't have a clue as to what she was saying, but she forged ahead anyway.

"I'm a nurse at Safar, and I'm looking for . . ." Abby suddenly realized she'd forgotten the woman's name, and she turned to Nick.

"Zara Hussein," he whispered.

Abby repeated the name, and the woman's droopy eyes opened wide. She pulled her veil forward on her head and touched her hand to her chest. *"Beti,"* she said, suddenly smiling. "Come."

Abby and Nick fell in behind the woman and tramped along the narrow path. The children stopped playing and watched before falling in step behind them. A few curious women joined the group, and by the time they arrived at a small plaster house, they'd acquired a crowd behind them.

The woman turned and threw her arm out. *"Burro,"* she shouted, and the children and hangers-on scattered.

The woman opened the rickety wooden door and stepped

inside. Within minutes, a pretty young woman with coal-black hair peeking out from under her red scarf stepped out hurriedly, pushing back stray tendrils as she walked. "Nick," she said softly, her eyes darting nervously. "I only speak in tent, *acha*?"

Nick nodded. "Sorry, Zara. I hope my coming here won't cause you any trouble."

"No, no trouble. My mother like you and your friend, but it's best to speak in tent." She smiled at Abby. "Tomorrow, yes?"

"Yes, thank you, Zara." He turned and placed his hand on Abby's back guiding her along the path.

Abby peered closely at the people as she walked, and once back in the car she turned to Nick. "I see what you mean. These people seem really beaten down, don't they?"

"They do. It's good that you see that, that you see *them*. At home, you've probably seen places and people not so different from this, but your eyes glaze over. You just don't notice, but here, everything's new, everything's different. You're the perfect observer here, no biases."

"Does Hana live here?"

The question seemed to catch Nick off guard and he winced, hesitating before he answered. "I don't know. Why ask me?"

"Jeez, don't take offense. I just meant she's a housekeeper, probably doesn't make much money, and if she lived here, it might explain her hostility."

Nick raised his brows. "Hostility?"

"Not to you, to me. You must have noticed. She ignores me, though she seemed almost kind the other day."

"You're too sensitive. You read into things."

"Forget I asked."

"Well, since you did ask, the answer is she probably comes from a place not so different from this."

Abby peered through the window and took a good long look

around. "Just when you think you've seen all the misery the world has to offer, you step into something else."

Nick chuckled and looked down at her feet, her shoes still covered in reeking bits of garbage. "You, literally, stepped into something else." His smile quickly turned to laughter, and Abby, unable to help herself, despite her attempts to look serious and irritated, felt herself collapse into laughter as well. She leaned into Nick. "I have to agree with you, but don't get used to that. It's a onetime deal only."

"I think you agree with me more than you care to admit."

Abby smirked in reply. "In your dreams, buddy."

Nick winked. "In my dreams, now that's a thought. Come on, let's get lunch."

Nick turned the car toward the American Club, and when they arrived, he opened the front door for Abby. "Even I can rise to the occasion."

Nick led the way up the familiar narrow staircase. The bar was packed, the hum of voices competing with a jukebox blaring out oldies. "Over there." Nick shouted to be heard as he steered Abby to a table in the farthest corner. Once there, the noise seemed muted. "At least here we can speak. What's your pleasure? I'll put the order in at the bar."

They both ordered cheeseburgers and beer, and Nick returned with two frosty bottles. "Food's coming." He smiled and raised his beer, tapping it against Abby's bottle. "Here's looking at you, kid."

"*Casablanca*, right?"

"Great movie." Nick leaned back and settled in.

"Fairy tale." She took a long sip of her beer.

"You don't believe in fairy tales?" Nick asked incredulously.

"Not me. I used to"—she set the bottle back down—"but not these days."

Nick whistled low. "You are an enigma, Abby, a real enigma. I would have bet you were a happy-ending kind of woman."

"Jeez, *happy endings* again—the favorite topic around here it seems. Well, *Casablanca* doesn't exactly have a happy ending, does it?" She raised the beer to her lips. "I'm still hoping for my happy ending, but I'm not gonna get it believing in fairy tales. I *will* get it if I believe in myself."

Nick raised his bottle. "To you, Abby, and your happy ending."

Chapter 12

That night, Abby dreamed, not of the shimmering bracelet or the woman's fall to her death. Instead, she dreamed of Nick, of leaning in to kiss him. But just before their lips could touch, she woke with a start, and rubbed the sleep from her eyes. Shaking the cobwebs from her head, she sat up. She couldn't blame this one on the Lariam.

Later that morning, Nick appeared at the house. "Sleep well?"

Afraid he'd somehow known what she'd dreamed, Abby mumbled and looked away from his face.

"Shit, you still having those dreams?" he asked, concern etched on his face.

"Sometimes, but I took your advice and threw the Lariam out."

"Smart girl, and speaking of smart . . ."

Abby laughed. "You are a charmer, Nick. You're going to the camp to see Zara, and you need me, right?"

"You got me."

"I might as well. I want to hear the stories. Buy me lunch again and you've got yourself a deal."

"That was easy," Nick said. "My kind of girl."

Abby grabbed her bag and settled into Nick's now familiar old sedan. She watched as he eased the car into the streets already bursting with vehicles, bicycles, donkeys, and bony horses decorated with tiny bells and garish flowers. Peshawar was filled with old traditions and modern chaos—always crowded and noisy and exciting.

Abby craned her neck and watched as an old woman hoisted a heavy bundle onto her hunched back. The woman adjusted her veil and staggered back for a minute before she adapted to the weight and shuffled off. As the traffic slowed and then stopped, a young boy approached the car, his hand outstretched, his eyes pleading. Abby reached into her pocket searching for money, but before she could find any, Nick handed her a $5 bill. He nodded. "Go on. And hurry, this traffic's going to be moving again in a minute." Abby passed the bill to the boy, whose eyes grew wide. *"Shukria,"* he shouted as he ran off, swallowed up by the crowds and the cars.

"You made his day, Nick. That was nice."

"It was only five bucks."

"That five was a fortune to that boy." She wondered if Nick did that often. "You know, some people say it creates more problems to give them money."

"The only ones who say that are people who were never

hungry. My philosophy is help when you can, but don't pat yourself on the back for doing what you should do."

Abby whistled. "You're a nice guy, Nick. Why do you hide it?"

"I don't hide it. I'd just rather people find that out for themselves. Enough of this."

The traffic eased and the road opened up before them.

At the camp, Abby and Nick headed straight for the Protection Tent. Inside, Nick pointed and smiled. "She's here," he said to Abby, who turned and recognized Zara.

Abby held out her hand. "Nice to see you, Zara. I'm Abby."

"Sit, please." Zara motioned to chairs in front of her desk.

Zara leaned forward, folding her arms on the desk. "I went to the rescue house, Nick, to ask if any of the girls there would speak with you."

Nick searched through his bag and pulled out a pen and a notebook and started writing. "And?"

Zara nodded. "There is one, a young woman, very young. She was only thirteen when she was trafficked, and just seventeen now. And though she works a few days a week here in the camp, she is a child still in many ways, but she has agreed to share her story, and I must tell you, it is heartbreaking. And, not the least of it is that she was sold by her family."

Sold, Abby thought, and by her own family, just as Nick had described. "How awful," she said.

"Her family is very poor, but they are not bad, at least that is what this woman, and what most of the women, say, and it's true. Many families are tricked into believing they are selling their girls to a better life, and this girl too thought she was going to a good job in India."

Nick wrote furiously. "What happened?" he asked, his head bent to his notebook.

"After the floods in the north, her family was destitute and starving, and she was sold," Zara said, "to a brothel in India. She was beaten and forced to have sex with strange men. She was trapped there for almost three years, and one day, she just fought back. Her owner cut her to teach her and the other girls a lesson."

"Did she escape?"

"Not for another year, and then she jumped," Zara said. "She saw an open window, and before anyone knew what was happening, she had jumped clear through it."

Abby shivered at the image of a woman jumping, and she pictured the woman in Geneva plunging through the air. Maybe she had jumped, Abby thought. Maybe it had just been a tragic accident. A dull pounding started up in her head, and she rubbed at her temples before turning back to Zara, who was still speaking.

"Her leg was broken, but her spirit was not, and she managed to run. She ran until she collapsed in the street. Someone picked her up and took her to a hospital. There the nuns took care of her."

Abby felt her eyes well up, and she turned to look at Nick. He had stopped writing, his pen gripped tightly in his fist. "Were the traffickers arrested?" he asked.

"No. They are still there, preying on the innocents."

Nick slipped his pen into his front pocket. "And we're going to meet this woman today?"

"We are. She works here in the camp two days a week, but she's off today, and she's agreed to speak with you this morning. She's on her way here now, and while we wait, I'll tell you about the rescue house, and about our program." Zara's voice was soft, and Abby strained to hear. "You know this woman and others like her live in a rescue house, the first stop in the rescue process for victims who are not so different from those in the photos in this tent." Zara turned and gestured to the photos that covered every inch of space.

"When we find someone who's been trafficked or lost, or when they find us, as wonderful as that moment is, it is only the beginning of their long journey. For as much as they've suffered, there is more to come, and often they cannot go home. Their own family may have sold them, and beyond that, there is the shame and stigma, and no understanding or compassion for what they've suffered. They are often not thought to be victims; they are thought to be . . ." She paused. "What is the word, Nick?"

Nick sat forward. "*Complicit*. People will think they had a hand in their own trouble."

"Complicit," Zara said, repeating the word. "Ah, that's it. In their home villages, people will believe they have been complicit, and there will be no sympathy for them. They will be outcasts, treated as whores or worse, and they would likely be killed to maintain the family's honor. You understand? Honor is very important, more important than life. But if the family has sold them, and they return home, they will sell them again."

Nick nodded. "As awful as it sounds, it's a complicated, miserable process. I've covered honor killings around the world, and I can tell you there's nothing even remotely honorable about them. It's a repulsive tradition that tyrannizes these women." He turned to Abby. "And it happens everywhere, not just Pakistan and India and Saudi Arabia, but in the US. Not so long ago, I did a story on a young Iraqi woman in Arizona who was killed by her father for bringing shame on the family by forgetting who she was, and where she came from. He wanted to hold tight to his traditions and the ways of his country, and the poor kid just wanted to fit in."

"Oh my God," Abby said, her throat tight. "It's sick, it's disgusting."

Nick nodded, his jaw firm. He turned to Zara. "So this house is a kind of halfway house for victims?"

"That's it exactly."

Nick looked around. "Which leads me to a whole new round of questions. Who came up with the idea?"

"The Red Crescent and one or two of the international aid groups talked about it a few years back, but it fell through. So, the Pakistan Women's Group, a small local organization, stepped in and opened the house just six months ago, and today we have three women living there." A wide smile covered Zara's face. "And it was the women here in Pakistan, the same women the world sees as powerless under their veils, who came to the rescue. The house was donated by a Pakistani family and furnished by local women. And now the victims have a safe place to learn new skills and to cope with what's happened to them. The UN provides financial support and staff"—Zara pointed to herself—"to help. I teach English, and I'll try to connect women with families who *will* take them back."

Nick scribbled furiously as Zara spoke. "The house must cost some serious money. Is there a bankroll?"

"A bankroll? I'm not sure what that is, but there is a wealthy European donor, a very generous man, who supports the house."

Nick's ears perked up. "Do you have a name?"

"No. We have been told he prefers to be anonymous."

"Zara," a soft voice called from the doorway.

All eyes turned and watched as a woman wearing a bright yellow *shalwar kameez* and a yellow scarf draped around her head appeared in the entryway, the sun at her back. She held her head down, and Abby sat up straighter. Something about the woman was vaguely familiar, and Abby looked closer. The woman stepped into the tent, a limp slowing her progress, and Abby narrowed her gaze. She was certain she'd met this woman, that bright yellow scarf, that slight limp. As the woman moved out of the sun's glare, Abby tried to place her, and then she knew.

Mariyah.

Chapter 13

When the woman raised her head, Abby's hunch was confirmed. Mariyah blinked when she saw Abby, and she looked anxiously at Zara. Abby rose quickly to dispel any fears Mariyah might have. She kissed Mariyah on each of her scarred cheeks. "*Salaam aleikum,* Mariyah," she said, gripping her hands. Abby turned to Nick. "This is my friend Mariyah. She works at my clinic. Mariyah, this is my friend Nick, a journalist."

Nick, who'd sat quietly as Abby greeted the newcomer, stood quickly. "I'm grateful that you'll speak with me, with us. Thank you."

"Mariyah was worried," Zara said, "about coming, about telling you her story. I didn't realize that she worked with you, Abby. It is good that you are here."

Smiling, Abby squeezed Mariyah's shoulder and felt the tightness there ease.

Mariyah nodded and sat in a hard wooden chair, her back straight against the rigid frame.

"Wouldn't you like to sit here?" Abby said, motioning to the cushioned chair on which she sat.

Mariyah shook her head, and Zara answered for her. "She has scars on her back, and she needs support. That is why she sits in the hard chair."

"I'd like to tape this." Nick pulled a small recorder from his pack. "Okay?"

Mariyah looked at Abby, who nodded. "*Acha,* okay," Mariyah whispered.

"Do you speak English?" Nick asked as he fumbled with the buttons.

"Little." Mariyah demonstrated with her hand.

"She speaks English, but she's nervous, and she may need a little help," Zara said. Wrapping her arms around Mariyah's shoulders, she whispered in her ear. Mariyah nodded and seemed to sit straighter. Abby sat forward, cupping her chin in her hand.

A lone tear trickled from Mariyah's eyes, and she took a long, deep breath. She looked right at Abby. "I nervous," she said slowly, "but will speak."

Abby smiled in reply and moved forward to the edge of her seat. Only days ago, she'd wondered if Mariyah could speak at all, and here she was ready to share her voice, her life.

"I from small village in North-West Frontier," Mariyah continued. "First daughter of small rice farmer. When big waters come . . ." She paused as if searching for words.

Zara touched Mariyah's hands and nodded. "I will say the beginning for her," Zara said softly. She took a deep breath. "Mariyah is the eldest child of six daughters, a poor farm family in a very poor region in the north. They had no electricity, and no water taps like we have here in Peshawar. In the best of times, it is a very hard life, and when the floods came, the little they had was lost. Mariyah's youngest sister and her mother were washed away in the waters that surged through the town. They have never been seen again."

Abby looked at Mariyah, whose eyes were wet with tears.

Zara paused to run her tongue over her lips. "Their house, their animals, their small rice paddies, all of it swept away, gone. The family was starving, they were homeless, and it seemed they were about to die." Zara glanced at Mariyah, who sat picking at the ends of her scarf. "A man came to the village one day and offered money to Mariyah's father if he could take Mariyah away. He told Mariyah there was a position as a housekeeper with a wealthy family in Mumbai, in India. It seemed a miracle, a job, money, and the hope that comes with that, and her father didn't hesitate—he sold her. But Mariyah and her father believed it was for a better life, a chance to support her family, and they rejoiced in their great luck, and though they didn't know it then, the day Mariyah left with the man, her simple life was ended forever."

Zara took Mariyah's hand and nodded. "Now, you," she said.

Mariyah ran her finger over the jagged scar that crossed her face. She wiped at her eyes before finally taking a deep breath and sitting forward. "Man who take me has another girl with him, and she is quiet like me, but I ask her, 'Are you happy about India?' And she looked at me like I crazy. I think she is the crazy one. I am happy. I sit in big car. I feel important. I have job. I am smiling. After long day in car, man stops and buys us food. We stay in hut on the road. No beds, no chairs, just empty place like stall for animals, I think. The man, he locks the door, and I am too tired to be afraid. I fall asleep on the floor, but the other girl stay awake. She wailing all night that he is bad man, and we are in big trouble."

Mariyah's words were slow and halting, and her hands trembled as she spoke. She paused and murmured in Urdu to Zara.

Abby glanced quickly at Nick, who was hunched over his notebook. He looked up and Abby caught his eye. "Terrible," she whispered, her eyes wide. Nick shook his head before bending back to his work.

Mariyah pressed her back into the chair and clasped her hands together. She looked at Zara, who smiled and said, "Mariyah is afraid she won't know the words. She would like me to help."

Nick nodded and continued to write.

Mariyah listened quietly.

"They stayed that first night in the hut, and in the morning the man got them tea and bread, and Mariyah thought that he was a good man. They drove again all day. . . ."

Mariyah tried to smile, her scar stretching as she spoke. "I see so many places, but they fly away quickly in the car window. Villages, cities, big cars, and crowds of people, more than I have ever seen in my life." Her smile quickly faded. "But, girl with me, she still crying. She say we going so far, we never get home. I tell her to shush. We going to India, and she should be happy, but she not. She cry and cry, and I want her to stop."

Mariyah turned and motioned to Zara, who picked up the thread of the story. "They drove south to Lahore, and Mariyah thought she was in heaven. The beautiful mosque, the gardens, the paved streets. Have you seen it? Lahore is the jewel of Pakistan, and if you see it, you will understand why a poor girl was happy. When the man stopped the car and got out, Mariyah was sure they had arrived in India, her new home, and she was glad, but only for an instant." Zara's voice turned grave, and Mariyah wiped at her face with her scarf.

"Mariyah had no way to know that she was still in Pakistan. Another man, fat and oily looking, and wearing a long frown, joined them. He leaned into the backseat and pulled Mariyah out. He put his hands all over her, and he smiled. Mariyah tried to pull away, but the man held tight, and she was finally afraid. She knew that something was wrong. The two men pulled the other girl from the car, and when she screamed, they hit her so hard, she fell to the ground. Mariyah heard her skull crack. The fat man kicked the girl as she lay on the ground. Mariyah wanted to scream too, but she kept her scream inside. And the girl was finally silenced. She didn't scream again."

Abby studied Mariyah, who held tight to Zara's hand.

"The fat man gave the man who had driven them a roll of money, more rupees Mariyah thought than even a bank might have. And then, Mariyah and the girl were thrown into the back of a truck. A blanket was thrown over them, and they huddled together, afraid. The girl began to cry, but her cries were softer."

Nick looked up. "Does she remember this girl's name? Or anything about her?"

"No," Zara said, and Mariyah shook her head sadly in agreement.

"We lay on floor," Mariyah continued, "banging and bumping as truck move very fast along road. No windows, no sunshine, no air to breathe. I think maybe something wrong, maybe girl was right. We stop at next town, called Wagah, and man pull over at side of road and tell us to get out. I breathe in the air and the sun and think *acha*, it okay now, but then man point to another truck with two men and he push us to them. One man kiss me and pull my dress and pants away, and then he put his hands up inside me. He make me sick with shame, but I not scream. I not want to be hit like girl."

Abby shifted uncomfortably in her seat, the soft cushion suddenly more confining than cozy.

Across from her, Mariyah pulled her legs up on the chair and hugged them in close. She was so tiny, her whole body fit on the small chair. She rocked herself for a minute before turning to Zara. Mariyah shook her head.

"I'll fill in the next part," Zara said. "The men at Wagah handed over money to the fat man and then bundled Mariyah and the girl into the back of their truck. Somehow, they passed through the border station to India and arrived in Amritsar. You know it, Nick? The tourist city?"

Nick put down his pen and nodded. "I do. It's a straight shot from Peshawar on the Grand Trunk Road. It's filled with Sikh temples and shrines and watering gardens. Beautiful place, but with a seamy underside. Anyplace tourists flock attracts the sex trade, and Amritsar is no different."

Zara nodded her head vigorously. "Yes, yes, that's it. Mariyah and the girl were taken to the Good Luck Hotel, but the only luck they found there was bad. The owner or maybe she was just the manager was an Indian woman with bright red lips, and a bright red spot on her forehead. The place, Mariyah says, was filthy, long hallways with small, dark rooms along each side. In each room, the only furniture was a stained mattress, no sheets, no tables, nothing, and that first night Mariyah and the girl were thrown into a room. The door was locked, but at least they were together."

"I talk a little," Mariyah said. Zara smiled and held her hand out to Mariyah. "Good Luck Hotel, not good—bad, bad smells, bad sounds, bad place. But girl and I sleep that night. Girl quiet, no crying. Next morning, skin of girl blue, and she cold, not moving. She dead. I screaming, and big man come in. He hit me, say I kill girl. I not." Tears slipped from Mariyah's eyes. "She my only friend. I not kill her, but I think girl is lucky to have escaped. She not be hit again." Mariyah wiped at her eyes. "I not know her name or her village. Her family never know she dead. They happy for her big, important job."

Nick turned to Abby. "The fall?"

"Head injury, bad enough to cause a subdural, I'd guess," Abby said. "Poor thing, she must have really hit her head when she was hit."

"Man hit me hard after they take girl away. He hit my face, my head, my back. He pull my clothes off and pull his pants down, and then . . ." Mariyah grimaced and covered her mouth with her hand. "He push his man part in my mouth. I gag, he choking me, he killing me. Now I know I dying."

Mariyah closed her eyes, and a sudden chill rippled through the tent.

"He say he teaching me, and he hold my head and that thing stays in my mouth until he push me down on the floor. He get on top of me, and he put that thing inside me down there. He give me big pain, and he make me sick, and I wish I dead like girl." Mariyah started to cry, and her scar curled downward as soft sobs escaped from her lips. "He say I still virgin and to keep my mouth shut or I in big trouble. I already in big trouble, I think, but I not want more trouble so I do keep my mouth shut, but I feel such shame," Mariyah said through her tears.

Nick had stopped writing, and Abby wrapped her arms around herself to ward off the sudden chill in the air. She wanted to throw up, but instead, she took a deep breath. "Mariyah, you have nothing to be ashamed about, and you don't have to continue or tell us more if it's too hard for you."

"No," Mariyah said. "I must to tell story, and you must to tell people so girl with no name will be remembered."

Nick put his pen down. "You are very brave. It's telling your story to me that will save others. You understand?"

Mariyah bit her lip and nodded. "That first night, the Indian woman, she color my face and lips and give me red sari, but nothing to wear under. I look like whore, and then men come, and I know I am whore. I want to cry, but I afraid so I keep my cries inside. Every night after that, the same. Red color on my lips and face, and loud men with rupees, and my job is to give the men big pleasure. I pray to God to get out, but I always locked in. When I ask other women there, they say if I ask too much, I disappear, so I shut up like they say."

"What about the other women? Were you allowed to speak with them, maybe get to know them?" Nick asked.

"We talk, but they not like me. They are from India and Nepal and Bangladesh. I from Pakistan—they say I dirty." Mariyah ran her hands over her dress. She cast her glance downward, and a single tear fell onto her lap.

"Are you *acha*?" Zara asked, caressing her back.

Mariyah nodded and raised her head. "It give me shame to talk, to tell this."

"Do you want to finish another time?" Nick asked gently.

"No, I try to finish." She smoothed her dress and ran her head scarf through her fingers. She closed her eyes as if to gather her strength. "At house, we have to work all the time. At night with men we do that work; in daylight, we clean." Something in her comment made a small tinkling laugh escape from her lips. "For such dirty house, we clean all time." Her scar stretched with the hint of a smile that blossomed on her face.

Mariyah's laugh created a momentary lull in the tension that hung low in the room, and Abby smiled with relief.

Mariyah shifted uncomfortably in her chair. "I stand." She pulled herself from her chair. "Back of me give pain. Scars." She twisted this way and that as her mouth curled down.

Zara stood and rubbed gently at Mariyah's back. "Do you need to rest?"

Mariyah shook her head and turned to Zara. "Too much pain. Some days, my skin feels as though it is tearing apart."

"Can you continue?" Zara asked.

Mariyah stretched and walked around the periphery of the tent, nodding as she took her seat. *"Inshallah."*

Nick prompted her gently, "Cleaning, you were telling us you had to clean the house."

Mariyah nodded. "Clothes washing too. Boss woman take in laundry. She get the money, but we do the work. Scrub clothes and press wrinkles away. Clothes for rich women who no do own laundry. At night, husbands of rich women come to us. Rich women do nothing."

Zara suppressed a giggle. "You were taking care of the whole family."

Mariyah nodded, a half smile at her lips. "Night come, boss paint my face and give me whore's clothes. The men come after that, and all night, every night, it the same. Men groaning and pulling at me. They make me sick, but I make believe I not there. One night, man complain to boss. He say I no good. He want money back. Boss beat me—I think now I die and that okay, *acha,* but I not die. She use leg of chair and her bundle of keys to hit me and cut my skin. She cut my back. She no want mens to complain about girl with scar."

"Mariyah," Nick said, "do you know her name, this woman who ran the house?"

Mariyah shook her head. "She say we must call her *maa,* she our mother, but we call her *bandar,* monkey."

Abby laughed nervously, and Mariyah smiled in reply, though her good humor was fleeting.

"We the real *bandar*," she said, her manner subdued. "We do what she say, we never fight, but one day I tired and say no mens no more. Big man come and beat me, he hit me all over and lock me in room. But I alone, no mens, no washing. I think *acha*, this okay. But it not last. Big man come back, he do sex to me, and then beat me with stick. I bleeding all over, back, front, everywhere. I hurt too much. He leave, and I hear key turn in door. I locked in."

Abby watched, expecting Mariyah to crumple at the memory but she seemed to gather strength instead.

"I no care. I finish with that place. I want to leave, and when man come back, I tell him. He hit me again and again, and then he laugh and tell me I stupid whore. That night, they bring men in, they have bad sex with me, front, back, all over. I hurt, I bleeding. No one care. No one help."

"Did you talk to the other girls about what was happening?" Nick asked.

Mariyah shook her head. "No, they have trouble too, I alone there. They alone too. But I make plan. Men stupid when they in room with me, and I see coins fall from pockets. Twenty-five-, fifty-paisa coins, once a ten-rupee note. I take them all and hide in hole in mattress. Every night, I have more. I know someday I rich and I run."

"How much in US dollars is that?" Abby asked.

Nick looked up. "Not much. One hundred paisa equals one rupee, and one rupee equals two cents."

"To me," Mariyah said, "it is money, *my* money, but not for long. The mattress spill my secret. One day, fat man fall down on mattress and hole grow. Coins tumble out and onto floor, making *ping* noise. Man jump up and point to tear in mattress.

He yelling. Say I steal from him, but *he* steal from me. He take it, he take *my* money, and leave room shouting in big voice. I know what coming. He tell boss, she come and hit me, and lock me in again. Next day, beatings start. I never get out, I think, but I not cry. I not cry again I say to myself."

Nick looked up. "How long had you been there by then?"

Mariyah's brow furrowed, and she shook her head. "Maybe one year, maybe two. I know for sure I miss two, maybe three, planting seasons. I gone long time, and I think my family forget me."

"What happened after the money incident?" Nick asked. "Did things get better?"

"No. Boss lady tell me I stupid one. She say my family not want me—they have sell me to her. She laughing when she tell me. She say no one want me now—I whore. Lies, I think, but she right—I am whore. I never get escape." Mariyah looked away for a minute, seeming to compose herself for what lay ahead.

"I going to Mumbai, they say. That the city I going to when I leave my father's house. I think, *acha,* this good. I and other girl put in crate. You know—big packing crate? They nail it shut. We locked in good. Other girl—well, I see her sometimes at house. She big." Mariyah held her arms wide to indicate the girth of the woman. "Her name I know. She called Zeinab, and she work in kitchen, but something not right with Zeinab. She have eyes so far apart, it look like she seeing things sideways. She just not right and I know *she* not whore. No man buy that. I think this good for me. Maybe, we both work in kitchen."

Mariyah looked straight at Nick, her coal-black eyes flashing. "But it not good. Not good at all. Mumbai more dirty. I smell city through holes in crate. Bad smells—people and animals and *tutty.*"

"*Tutty?*" Abby asked.

"Slang for 'shit,'" Nick said, his eyes on Mariyah. "Right?"

Mariyah nodded. "Shit smell everywhere, even at new house. I want to cry. House big, and dark, and dirty. Man there say he know I bad in past, and if I not good, he cut me." She lifted her chin and made a cutting motion to her throat. Abby saw then the long scar that ran along the crease in Mariyah's neck, and Abby held back the gasp that hovered at her lips.

"I in dirty room, but they give me pretty dress and tell me clean myself for mens. I not want cuts so I do it. That night, mens come. They rough and mean, and I cry. I get beat for crying. Every day the same. I see big girl, but she no talk to me. No smile, she dead in her eyes like she not in there. I not sorry for her. I sorry for me. My eyes not dead yet."

Abby swallowed the knot in her throat.

"More time go by, more mens complain. I bad at sex. I get beaten. One night, man say I bit his man part." She covered her mouth, but her smile peeked out from behind her hand. "It true. I bite him, and I know what coming. I be locked in, but I be alone and that better than dirty mens. But this time, they beat me on back with chains, and man cut my neck. Here." She pointed to the scar at her throat. "My neck, my back bleeding, I sick with fever. I have bad scars here and on my back now." She shifted uncomfortably in her seat as if to soothe the scars on her back.

"She never received medical care for the infections, and she still has trouble," Zara said. "*Inshallah,* with the antibiotics she takes now, she will get well."

"Cuts on back give me pain every day, and when mens get on top of me, I want to scream with pain in my back, but I not. I keep my mouth shut, until one day, man scratch at my back to give me more pain. He crazy and mean, and I scratch his face. He take out knife and cut me here." She pointed to the long, winding scar that slashed across her face. "I think my face fall off, and I try to hold it in. I screaming. Boss come in, and this time, he not mad at me. He go after man with knife and hurt him. I on floor afraid to scream now, afraid my face will fall away, afraid boss will hurt me too, but boss have midwife wallah come. She nice to me, she sew my face back so it not fall off, but it look bad. I cry when I see in mirror, but boss say, keep your veil over your face, and no let mens see. And there I am—back to work."

"What happened to the man?" Nick asked.

Mariyah shrugged. "I not see, I only think about my face."

"Did you know that man? Did he have a name?" Nick scribbled as he spoke.

"No name, all mens—no names. We told to call them *honey*, so they all *honey* to me." She giggled. "They not sweet like honey, them mens mean. They see my face, they want their money back. Boss mad at me and hitting me all time. I know I have to get away, and one day, I see window open. I look out and see we are on second level. I think I can climb down and run. I looking and trying to be brave when boss man see me. He shout and come running, and I know this my only chance, so I close my eyes and I hold my breath and I pull myself through window opening, and then before he can pull me back, I jump. I free, I feel air and sunshine on my face for first time in long time. I flying, but then I land. Hard, and I see man looking out window. I know he coming after me so I pull myself up and I run. I feel pain like fire shoot through my leg." Mariyah bent and massaged her leg while she spoke.

"Finally, I just fall. I have no more run in me. I fall to street, and holy women, nuns, find me. They bring me to their hospital and they so good." Mariyah began to cry. "I think in my whole life, no one else that good to me."

A car horn beeped loudly somewhere outside, startling Abby, who'd been so absorbed in Mariyah's words. She glanced sideways at Nick and saw that he too seemed to flinch at the sound. He placed his notebook down. "What about your leg, your other injuries?" he asked.

"I have broke leg and bad infection in my face and back cuts. But at hospital, I have doctor nun who take care of me, who make my leg so I can walk." She stood and took a few steps, walking slowly to ease her limp. "See?" she proclaimed proudly before taking her seat.

"Did the nuns send you here?" Nick asked.

"Nuns want for me stay in India, want me to learn trade, but I want come home. In India, I alone, I a tree without leaves, a night without stars, a house without windows. You understand?" She nodded toward Nick and Abby. "You know?"

"Yes," Abby murmured, though she knew she'd never understand that kind of aloneness.

"I belong here, in my country." Mariyah's eyes lit up. "And so the nuns searched and searched and found this house, and then send me here."

"But, can't you return home?" Abby asked.

"No, my family would be shamed. I am dirty now, and my face full of scars. No one want me now, and what would they tell people? No, it is best if I stay lost."

"Mariyah, you are not dirty. There is nothing unclean about you. I hope you know that," Abby said, struggling to keep her voice from breaking.

"And we are happy to have Mariyah with us," Zara said. "She is learning how to keep records in the clinic with you, Abby, so that she will have a trade and the means to support herself someday."

"Do you have the contact information for the nuns?" Nick

asked. "I'd like to see where they work, get them some attention with an article, and maybe that attention will raise some money."

"They would appreciate that, Nick." Zara rose from her seat. "I'll see if I can get it for you."

"And you," Nick said, turning to Mariyah, "you've shared an incredibly difficult story. You're very courageous. Don't lose sight of that."

Mariyah smiled, her scar pulling at her skin. *"Shukria."*

Abby blinked back the tears that lined her eyes. "You have a beautiful smile," she said, her voice trembling. "Your scars can't change that." She leaned in and planted a kiss on Mariyah's cheek.

"I learning to smile, to be happy," Mariyah said. "Someday, *inshallah,* I go all the way home, and then I really smile."

Chapter 14

Nick and Abby drove to the American Club in silence. The hideous images of Mariyah's life stuck in Abby's mind, and not until they'd trudged upstairs and collapsed into seats in a dark corner of the bar did they finally speak.

"I just feel sick," Abby said, breaking the long silence.

"It was pretty awful, and it's probably not the worst story there is, you know?"

Abby nodded.

"Cheeseburger and beer?" Nick asked, rising from his seat.

"No. Today, I'll have what you're having. I want a drink that will burn the back of my throat and slam into my gut before numbing my brain."

"Whoa. You sure?"

"I am very sure. I need something strong to clear the misery from my head."

"What I'm ordering may not clear your misery. In fact, by tomorrow, it'll provide you with more misery than you know what to do with. Do you at least want food?"

"Peanuts will be fine. That's all the protein I need today."

Nick shook his head. "You got it. Be right back." He strode quickly to the bar.

Abby fought the urge to bury her head in her arms and just cry. She didn't know what the hell she was doing here. She'd come here to run away from things, but instead she'd run right into utter agony, and she knew that after today, she'd never be the same. For starters, there'd be no more whining about Eric or her shitty decisions, and she'd throw out his damned e-mail when she got home. God, there was so much sadness in the world. Why hadn't she ever noticed? Well, she knew why. She'd been busy working, and planning her perfect life, which turned out to be not so perfect after all. But it was bliss compared to what she'd heard today.

Nick slid a glass full of amber-colored liquid under her nose and set a bowl of peanuts between them. "I was going to order a double, but I nixed that idea and decided to start with a simple scotch on the rocks. Okay with you?"

Abby nodded and raised the glass. "To saving the world." She threw back the scotch and, in one long swig, swallowed it all.

Nick's eyes grew wide. "Jesus, Abby, take it easy, will ya? I know Mariyah's story was hard to hear, but just take it slow."

Abby felt her eyes well up, and she gripped her lower lip between her teeth to stop the flood of tears she could feel forming behind her eyes. She took a handful of peanuts and licked the salt clean off before swallowing them. She could feel Nick's eyes on her, and she took a deep breath and looked straight at him. "It's not fair. Mariyah, who is quite literally scarred, is struggling to make some kind of life for herself, while I sit here with a relatively good life, struggling to drown my sympathies for her in scotch. Tell me, where is the justice in that?"

"I don't have any answers for you, Abby. It seems late in the game to remind you that life's not fair. Hell, at any given moment, there are people living the hardest of hardscrabble lives. It doesn't do them any good for you to drown your sorrows."

"Are you reminding me that I'm not just naive, but I'm a shallow, self-centered bitch as well?"

A look of concern flickered in Nick's eyes as he reached across the table and took Abby's hand. "No, Abby. You're none of those things," he said, his voice calming. "You've just heard a story and seen scars that would make most people weak in the knees, and yet you stayed and listened and soothed Mariyah, and you treated her with respect and dignity. You're inherently good, Abby, and you're here for all the right reasons. You can't change that."

A tear fell from Abby's eyes, and she wiped it away. "I'm not as good as you think I am."

"Sure you are. Believe me, I know plenty of self-centered clowns, and *you* aren't one of them. Far from it. As a matter of fact, I think you're one hell of a dame."

For the first time all day, Abby felt a ripple of laughter surge to her lips, and suddenly she was chuckling. "Thanks, Nick. For the laugh too. *Dame*, huh? What a vocabulary."

"I'm sure you mean that in the best way possible. As you're so keen to remind me, I am a Pulitzer Prize winner."

"That you are, Nick. That you are." He lifted his drink, and the fading tattoo she'd noticed when she'd first met him shimmered in the glass. "What's . . . ," she started to ask him about it, but caught herself. He'd think she cared, and she didn't, or at least she didn't want to.

"What?" he asked.

"Nothing."

"Okay, so here's the plan." Nick pushed away from the table and stood. "I'm willing to get another round, but only if you'll agree to a cheeseburger as a chaser."

Abby nodded and nestled into her chair as Nick headed back to the bar to put in their order. Her thoughts wandered to Mariyah, to her scars, her pain, and her quiet grace in seeming to accept it all. By the time Nick returned with the food and another round, Abby knew she had more to learn, and between bites, she peppered him with questions.

"What did you think of Mariyah's story? Is that the usual kind of trafficking?"

"There's no *usual* way, but I guess her story's not so far off, though I'll tell you I think it's more likely a woman will be thrown to her death, and then the cover is 'Oh, she jumped.'"

"*Thrown* to her death?" Abby asked.

"When the rapes and beatings are too much to bear, a girl might suddenly become bold—decide to go to the authorities or run away. What does she have to lose anyway? It's pretty unpleasant—some are beaten so badly, they die, or they're thrown into swimming pools where they drown, or they're thrown from balconies and their employers—and I use that term loosely—say they jumped."

Abby's jaw went slack. "Thrown? They're *thrown* from balconies?"

"More often than you might think." Nick bit into his cheeseburger.

Images of Geneva flickered in Abby's head—the struggle

on the balcony, the woman's hideous fall, the sickening thud, the sparkling bracelet, and the shadowy figure of the man who just might have thrown that woman—all of it replayed in Abby's mind, and she felt the room sway around her. She could see the woman so clearly, her broken body lying splayed on the street, the bracelet sparkling. *Maybe* she had been thrown. Should she tell Nick? She watched him out of the corner of her eye. He had turned to greet an acquaintance, and he laughed at something the man said.

"What is it?" Nick asked, turning back to Abby. "You look as if you've seen a ghost. No more scotch for you, I think."

"Nick, do you remember the nightmares I mentioned?"

"Your nightmares? From the Lariam? Didn't you stop that stuff?"

"I did. But my nightmares never stopped, and, well, they're not just nightmares. Something happened in Geneva, and I see it over and over in my dreams. I'd like to tell you about it. Not now, but sometime."

Nick looked up from his meal. "Yeah, yeah, sure," he said absentmindedly, pulling his notebook out. "Don't mind me. I just want to write my opening while those images are still fresh in my mind." He motioned to her burger. "Eat, will ya? You're still pale."

Abby picked at her cheeseburger and stared into her tumbler of scotch, twirling it in her hand. She saw the woman from Geneva, her glittering bracelet, and when she looked deeper, she saw Mariyah's scars. She could almost hear their screams, and she felt sick to her stomach. She pushed the drink and the cheeseburger away.

"What about Hana and her boy? Was he taken as part of this?" The very idea was sickening, but Abby had to ask. "Would someone take a child?"

The questions seemed to catch Nick off guard. "Well, yeah. Anything's possible."

Abby felt defeated. Nick seemed somehow unaffected by it all, but perhaps he'd just seen it all before. "Anytime you're ready."

Nick looked up. "You're not eating?" He reached over and snatched the pickle from her plate.

"I'm just not hungry, but don't worry—I don't want this either." She handed him the tumbler of scotch.

Nick took the glass and leaned his head back. "You're the perfect woman, Abby. I get my food and liquor, and yours too."

Abby smiled despite herself. He did have a way of making her feel less terrible, and today that seemed like a gift.

"You sure about leaving? You want to stay and talk about Geneva?"

"Another time definitely, just not today. I want to see if I can speak with Najeela, if she's at the house, that is, and ask about helping out at the rescue house, maybe do some health programs there. What do you think?"

A broad smile broke out on Nick's face. "I think you're a damn fine woman, Abby, that's what I think. Come on." He slid from his chair. "Let's go."

The house was quiet when Abby arrived home, and when she opened the door to her room, she sensed right away that something was amiss. Sunlight streamed in, bathing the room in soft shadows, and she saw that the drawer to her nightstand was ajar, her notebook lying open on the floor. She picked it up and watched as Eric's e-mail fluttered out. Had she left her drawer open, knocked the notebook to the floor in her hurry to leave this morning? Maybe, she thought, maybe she had.

Abby exhaled and went in search of Najeela. When she stepped into the hallway, a smiling Najeela appeared.

"Well," Najeela said, a sly grin on her face, "where have you been?"

"Working," Abby replied tersely. She was in no mood for Najeela's whims today.

"You work too hard. You need a social life, my friend. Any word from Eric? Does he want you back after all?"

The question caught Abby off guard. They hadn't spoken about Eric in weeks. At least it seemed that way. Had she mentioned his e-mail to Najeela? Her mind was a jumble, maybe she *had* told Najeela. "Why would you ask that?" she finally said.

"Why not? He must miss you."

Abby hesitated again. Had Najeela read the e-mail? Had she been in Abby's room? There was that one time . . .

"Najeela?"

"Darling," Najeela said, interrupting her, "we are all sad when you are not here. Even my dear uncle Imtiaz pines for you."

Abby rolled her eyes and tried to change the subject. She wanted to talk about the trafficking victims. "Najeela, I'd like to speak with you about doing some extra work outside of the vaccination program."

"I'd love to chat, Abby, you know I would, but I have dinner plans, so it will have to wait. Tomorrow," Najeela said, patting Abby's hair. "Tomorrow, I promise."

Chapter 15

Mariyah's screams sliced through the morning quiet, and Abby froze. She watched helplessly as Mariyah, her yellow scarf billowing out into the wind, clung desperately to the railing. The man stood over her, then inexplicably, he pulled away and walked back into the room. Mariyah leaned over the balcony and pulled herself up and over the railing. As she stood on the thin ledge holding tight, Abby saw the diamond cuff bracelet twinkling on Mariyah's wrist. Abby opened her mouth to shout, but the sound wouldn't come. Suddenly, Mariyah let go of the railing and jumped, soaring through the air, the bracelet catching the light as she fell. Her screams echoed and bounced off the build-

ings as she fell to the street, where she landed with a thud that made Abby's heart stop.

A scream filled Abby's throat.

And she sat upright. Her skin was damp with sweat again, her hair plastered against her forehead. Her sheets were drenched. Her hands trembled as she yanked the sheets away and pushed herself up and out of bed. She opened the blinds and let the morning sun stream in, but the sunlight did nothing to dissipate the terror and helplessness she felt. Her head began to pound and she sat back down on the bed and tried to rub the pain away, but the pain was immovable, and when her tears started up, she gave in helplessly to her misery. She understood how Mariyah's story could haunt her, but to weave it into that same goddamn nightmare? Maybe it was that damn scotch.

She had to talk to Nick.

By the time Abby stepped from the shower, her headache and the haunting images from her dream had faded, leaving her with only a vague feeling of discomfort. She shimmied into a long cotton dress, and almost immediately the heat of the day seeped through to her skin. She piled her hair on top of her head, fanning herself with her hand. When she stepped into the dining room for coffee, a smiling Nick sat as though he'd been waiting. Abby smiled, relieved to see him.

"Good morning," he said. "I was heading to the Protection Tent to see Zara, but thought I'd stop and see how you were feeling, maybe scrounge some coffee." His brow wrinkled. "You okay today?"

"I . . ." Abby started to tell him about her dream, but she held back. Mariyah had just shared a horrific real-life story, and it somehow didn't seem right to whine about Geneva and her miserable dreams just yet. "I'm fine. Have you seen Hana this morning? I'm starving."

"Haven't seen her, but I did turn on the stove to heat water."

"I'll grab toast." Abby headed to the kitchen. She returned within minutes bearing a plastic tray with coffee, cups, toast, and jam. "Help yourself, but next time, you're cooking."

Nick laughed. "You're on."

Once they'd finished eating, Abby stood. "Can I tag along? I never know if I'll have a car, and the clinic's open today. I'd like to be there for Mariyah."

"Sounds good. I'd like the company."

"Will you clear the dishes?" she asked. "I just want to get online before we leave."

"Okay," Nick said obligingly as he reached for the cups and scooped them up. "I'll find you when I'm done."

Abby headed to the office, and within minutes she'd logged in to her e-mail account and dashed off quick messages to her mother and Emily. Almost as an afterthought, she clicked on Eric's e-mail and read it one more time, lingering over his words.

I hope you'll take me back. My life is dreary without you.

He loved her and missed her, he'd written. A sigh escaped from her lips. A couple of months ago he'd broken her heart, and now he wanted her back. Too late, she thought, her finger floating over the DELETE button.

"Well, are you going to take the boyfriend back?" Abby turned to see a frowning Nick standing behind her, his hands in his pockets.

"Wh . . . what?" Abby heard the stutter in her voice. Had he been standing there reading the e-mail over her shoulder?

Nick shrugged. "Sorry, I couldn't help it," he said sheepishly. "My reporter's instinct to snoop got the better of me. But, now that I've read it, the question is—will you take him back?"

Abby shook her head. "None of your damn business, Nick."

"I hope that means no." He smiled. "I mean, come on, give the rest of us a chance, will ya?"

Abby fought the smile that threatened to erupt on her face. Nick had a way of totally disarming her, of making her forget why he aggravated her. She sighed and clicked DELETE. "Let's just go." She signed out of her e-mail.

Abby slid into Nick's old sedan and felt the beginning twitches of tension in the back of her neck. She rubbed at the spot to relieve the stiffness.

"You okay? My snooping bothering you?"

"It's not you. It's not even the damn e-mail. It's Mariyah. Her story affected me more than I imagined." Abby turned and peered at the passing scenery, all of it seeming quiet this morning. The traffic was light too, and even the beggars must have slept in. "What time is it?"

"Nine thirty. You thinking what I'm thinking?"

"I'm wondering where everyone is. It's just too quiet, the calm before the storm almost. Oh, hell, is there going to be some kind of demonstration today?"

Nick shook his head. "I haven't heard anything, and there's usually some warning." He eased the car onto the camp road and parked there. "But, nothing we can do about that now. I'm gonna head to the tent to have a look. Maybe Zara will be there. I'll find you at the clinic later, okay?"

Abby nodded, and looping her bag over her shoulder, she turned for the clinic. When she caught sight of the small building, she saw that there too things were quiet. A small group of women and babies huddled at the entrance. No long lines today it seemed. She poked her head into the clinic, and a flash of sudden movement caught her eye. Abby stepped back nervously, the sun's glare impeding her view.

"Abby," a familiar voice called.

"Mariyah?"

"Yes." She stepped outside, a smile pulling at the corners of her mouth. "I wait for you."

Abby reached out and caught Mariyah's thin shoulders in a quick embrace. "How are you?" she whispered.

"I good. I tell story, and I not die of shame, and no one look at me like I bad, so today I good, I very good."

"I'm glad, Mariyah." Abby stepped into the clinic. A quick glance revealed that the small space was as empty inside as out. "Where is everyone?"

"Today, only you and me. Simi and the nurses at distribution today."

"Distribution?"

"UN give out food and supply rations. No lines today. Womens getting food, and nurses getting supplies."

Abby smiled. "Let's get started then." She stepped to the far corner and pulled out the syringes and vials she'd need. By the time she'd drawn up the first vaccine, a veiled woman appeared, holding out the frail arm of her baby. Abby checked the vaccine card and plucked a full syringe from her supply before turning to the baby. Abby moved so swiftly, the baby could only whimper in protest. She checked off the card and called her next patient. Engrossed in the work, she lost track of the time until Mariyah appeared before her.

"All finish now. We talk?"

Abby cleared her supplies from the seat and motioned for Mariyah to sit. "We're a good team, you and I. Today went well."

"You good. You good to me, Abby. You my friend."

"I am."

"Yesterday, I tell women at my house about telling my bad

things to you, how good it make me feel. They say, bring you to house. You come?"

"I'd be honored. I'm not sure I should ask, but can Nick come as well? You know he's writing the story?"

"*Acha.*"

Abby smiled. "He'll be very pleased. He's here in the camp. He went to the Protection Tent this morning looking for Zara. Is she there?"

Mariyah shook her head. "She at distribution, but she come here after."

Out of the corner of her eye, Abby saw Nick striding toward her, and she smiled as he arrived at her side.

He nodded at Mariyah. "Hello, Mariyah, how are you?"

"I tell Abby"—she nodded at her—"I good."

"Glad to hear it." Nick turned back to Abby. "You finished here?"

"We are. Today's a distribution day so it was quiet, but"—Abby glanced at Mariyah—"we have some good news for you."

"I could use some good news. I haven't been able to connect with anyone today."

"Well, you're about to connect big-time. Mariyah's friends, the other women at the house, want to tell their stories."

"For my article?"

"For Abby," Mariyah said. "They want to be friend too. Understand?"

Nick nodded and turned to Abby. "Thank you," he whispered.

"*Acha,*" Mariyah said softly.

"Today?" Nick asked. "Can we do it today?"

Before Mariyah could answer, Zara appeared. "Good morning. Has Mariyah told you the news?"

Nick pulled a small notebook from his pocket. "She has. I was just asking if we can do it today."

"Sorry, Nick. Not today. We can do it tomorrow at the house, but if you have a car, you could bring us back there today, and you'll know where we are."

"I'll do that." Nick turned and pointed to the parking area. "Shall we just go?"

Abby took Mariyah's hand and led the way, and suddenly a low rumbling filled the air, followed by bursts of gunfire and shouts. "Back to the clinic," Abby shouted, struggling to be heard over the approaching din.

The four raced back to the safety of the clinic, forming a small knot there at the doorway.

"Riot," Abby said as Nick turned to face her. "Ignore your reporter's instinct and just stay put. It'll pass quickly, and then we can go."

Nick's mouth fell open. "You seem pretty relaxed. How do you know that's what it is?"

"I've been through this once already." She felt curiously calm.

"I'm impressed," he said with a definite hint of admiration.

They huddled there and listened as the gunfire and shouts increased in intensity and seemed to move closer. "We should step back inside," Abby said. "We need to be out of sight. To quote you, the last thing they need to see is a couple of Americans."

They stepped back into the clinic's shadows and waited. Pulling out his notebook, Nick squinted in the dim light that seeped in.

"Too dark to write, but my recorder will catch it." He rummaged through his bag and pulled out his tape recorder, snapping it on and holding it up to the entryway.

They stood in silence and listened as the noise swelled and dimmed before disappearing altogether.

Zara stepped outside. "I think it's all over now. Ready?"

Nick packed up his recorder and fished in his pocket for his keys. "Ready," he said, striding back into the harsh sunlight.

Once at the car, Zara reached for the rear door handles. "Mariyah and I will sit in back. It would not look right if either of us sat next to a man, especially a foreign man." Zara pulled open the rear door and Mariyah slipped in.

Abby settled into the front seat, and Zara leaned forward and directed Nick along a serpentine route that seemed to wind and circle through the same narrow streets before they finally reached their destination, a quiet road filled with small nondescript houses on the outskirts of University Town.

"Not bad," Nick said, surveying the area as he parked by a high, white fence.

"It is safer for the house to be here, away from the slums that most of the women know so well."

"Makes sense," Nick said as Zara and Mariyah slid from the backseat.

"Tomorrow at ten?" Zara asked.

Abby nodded and watched as the two disappeared through the front gate. Abby sat back, lost in her thoughts as Nick drove. She'd not only just lived through her second perilously close riot, she'd taken charge. And Mariyah had liked her enough to invite her to meet her friends. The clinic, though quiet, had gone well. Abby smiled to herself. As if that weren't enough, she'd even managed to get Nick more interviews.

As the car took the last corner before Abby's house, Nick broke the silence. "To say I've underestimated you is a major understatement."

"Glad you figured that out, Nick. Doesn't this occasion call for scotch?"

"It does." Nick maneuvered the car into a spot by Abby's

house. "But, believe it or not, I'm going to ask for a rain check and see if I can chase down those rioters."

Feeling oddly disappointed, Abby grimaced. "Keep your head down," she said softly. "I'd hate for anything to happen to you."

"Hell, Abby, that might be the nicest thing you've ever said to me." He reached over and touched her shoulder.

A small bit of inexplicable joy rippled through her skin, and Abby, caught off guard, jerked back. Smiling uncomfortably, she slipped from the car. "See you tomorrow," she said, hurrying to the gate.

Chapter 16

The following morning, Nick arrived early. "You ready?" he asked brusquely.

"Good morning to you too," Abby said, more than a hint of sarcasm in her voice. Things were back to normal, she thought. They were probably better this way, sticking to banter and baiting. Whatever she'd felt yesterday, her common sense told her she should just ignore it. Her life was complicated enough.

"Help yourself to coffee." She pointed to the full pot.

Nick threw himself dramatically into a chair. "Can we just drink on the way? I want to get going."

"After my second cup of coffee, I'll be ready." Abby refilled her cup. "Relax, Nick. Zara said ten. It's just nine. Have some coffee while I jump on the computer for a bit."

Nick groaned. "You're killing me, Abby."

Abby raised her brows and headed to the office, where she finished up her most recent vaccine report and e-mailed it to the UN vaccine office in Geneva. She hadn't had any feedback yet on her refugee stories, but she expected that sooner or later someone would actually read them and maybe even comment.

At nine thirty they set off for the rescue house, Nick's foot bearing down on the gas pedal the whole way. "We're too early," Abby lamented as Nick stepped from the car.

"They won't mind, bet they're waiting for us." He knocked on the gate.

As the gate opened, a stocky man appeared, blocking the entrance. He opened his mouth to speak, but relaxed his frown and smiled instead. "You here for Miss Zara?"

Abby nodded, and the man stood to the side, motioning for them to enter.

The two-story stucco house was surrounded by flowering plants and trees, not unlike Abby's own UN staff house. She glanced at the windows and wondered if the women were peering out, watching them. They stepped into the house, and a small flurry of activity greeted them. Women scurried down the hall, colorful veils and head scarves flying out behind them like so many butterflies in flight.

"I think they were not quite ready to be seen," Zara said, appearing in the hallway and guiding Abby and Nick into the front room. "Sit. I will see if they are ready now."

Nick nodded and sank down onto a thickly cushioned couch. Abby sat next to him and watched as he pulled a notebook and pen from his bag. He set the notebook on his lap and began to click his pen up and down. Abby raised her brows.

"What?" he whispered.

Abby placed her hand over his pen. "Relax. They're coming, and they must be terrified to speak with a stranger. Don't let them see you're impatient."

Nick nodded and, slipping his pen into his front pocket, turned suddenly quiet.

"Nick," she said, intending to say something supportive, "I . . ." Before she could finish, Zara returned to the room and sat across from them.

"They are coming," she said as Mariyah entered the room.

"Hello," she said, taking a seat by Zara.

A sudden flash of color at the doorway caught Abby's eye, and she looked up to see a young woman clad in a red-and-gold sari peeking in.

Zara turned and stood. "Here we are. Come, Bina. Sit with us." The woman entered the room and walked to Mariyah. "This is Bina," Zara said.

Bina's gaze fell to the floor. Her red sari was woven with flecks of gold and silver, and the colors danced in the morning light. Bina's skin, Abby saw, was the color of creamy caramel, and her long, thick braid was coal black. She was thin as a reed, and like Mariyah she sat perfectly still.

Nick stood and motioned to the couch. "Please," he said to the women, "sit here."

Bina shook her head and nestled closer to Mariyah.

A third woman slipped into the room and took the final chair. She was tiny, almost lost in the voluminous yards of green fabric that covered her frame. Her black hair was pulled tight, showing off clear, chocolate-colored skin and brown eyes so large they seemed to take up half her face. She was, Abby thought, just beautiful.

And absolutely terrified.

"Anyu, Bina," Zara said quietly, "please say hello to Abby and Nick."

Bina smiled, but Anyu seemed to wither at the invitation to speak. "Hello," she whispered, pushing back into her seat.

Nick reached into his bag and retrieved his tape recorder before turning to Zara. "I'd like to record today's interview too, if that's all right with everyone?"

Bina reached out and touched the tiny machine. "Music?"

"No, but watch this." Nick held out the recorder to Bina. "Can you tell me your name?"

Bina leaned in and said, "I Bina," a hint of irritation in her voice. "You not remember?"

Nick smiled and pressed PLAY. Bina's voice filled the room, and the women howled with delight. "Me," cried Anyu, sitting forward, her wariness suddenly vanishing. Nick recorded each of the women in turn, and each time one heard her own voice, she giggled and chattered.

"All right," Zara finally said. "Let's get started. Nick, you know that today Bina and, *inshallah,* Anyu will be sharing their stories."

Abby sat forward, determined not to miss a word.

"Bina will speak first. Our Anyu is not yet sure if she is ready. Understand?" Zara asked.

Nick and Abby both nodded.

"Bina," Zara continued, "is from Nepal and she speaks Nepali and a little Urdu. She is learning English, so I will tell her story." Zara turned and looked at Bina. *"Acha?"* she asked softly.

Bina nodded and pulled at her head scarf. She folded her arms and glanced at Zara, who began.

"Bina is from a small village in eastern Nepal, a place where people live in straw huts and where many are of the lowest caste, the Dalits, the untouchables. You understand, you know untouchable, Nick?"

Nick, still fiddling with his tape recorder, looked up only long enough to nod. Abby sat forward, her eyes on Bina, who sat nervously twirling the tin bangles on her wrist.

"Bina and her family worked at breaking up heavy rocks, that was how they earned their living, but it was a poor life, very poor, and for a girl, it was very bad. You see how thin she is." Zara glanced at Bina. "Girls in Nepal are considered worthless, less than nothing. They work the hardest and they are always the last to eat. It is not a good life, but even untouchables, even girls, have dreams for a better life, and one day, a rich tourist, or so they thought, came through the village. He seemed not to care that this village was filled with untouchables, and more important, he told the villagers the girls had real value. He was a businessman, he said, and he would give money to the families, and in exchange, he would take the girls with him. He told the girls that they would work in nice houses in Kathmandu, and they could save money to go to school. Who wouldn't be happy to hear that?"

Bina seemed to understand Zara's words and she smiled. "I be nurse," she said, motioning toward Abby.

"Bina had hoped to study nursing," Zara said. "Nursing is an honored profession in Nepal, a difficult university course, and only the very smart and the very lucky are accepted there. For an untouchable, there is no chance for school, so when this tourist said he would bring the girls to Kathmandu, where they would work in fancy houses and have a chance to enroll in the university, the girls were excited to go. What an opportunity for these poor girls, and their families were given money. It was good for everyone. You agree?"

Nick nodded.

Abby sighed heavily. She knew this story was about to break her heart.

"Bina and three others packed up their clothes and left with the man, but when they got to Kathmandu, there were no lessons, no fancy houses, no jobs. Instead, the man went to a slum, a bad section, and turned them over to another man. This new man was angry, and he grew angrier when he took money from his fat wallet and handed it to the tourist, who stood and counted the bills. The two men argued over the money, and finally they parted, the angry man scowling and pushing the four girls roughly along until they reached a small house. There the four were locked in a small, windowless room." Zara looked sadly at Bina. "Her story is not so different from Mariyah's, except that she wasn't beaten, she was starved. Starvation will make a person desperate. For three days, the girls didn't eat. They had water and nothing else. On the third night, when they were too weak to fight, they were separated, and Bina was taken from the house and brought to Pakistan, to a brothel in Lahore."

Zara turned to Bina and spoke in Urdu. Bina nodded her head and spoke rapidly, and though Abby couldn't understand a word, she realized that the two were probably discussing the details of Bina's life in Lahore.

Bina turned and looked at Nick, and Zara spoke for her. "Nick, Bina wants you to know that she was a good girl, and when she went to Kathmandu, she was a virgin, and you probably know that virgins are prized and fetch a princely sum in Lahore. On her first night there, she was dressed like a doll in gold and red. They placed flowers in her hair and perfume on her skin, and when she saw her reflection in the large mirror, it took her breath away. She was beautiful, and she thought that surely she was about to be married." Zara paused and exhaled slowly. "It was only when she was brought to a wrinkled old man wearing a stained white pajama suit that Bina understood, and she knew that there were not enough tears in her eyes or prayers to Vishnu to save her from this destiny. She did not scream or cry or fight, and instead she prayed to Shiva and Ganesh to keep her soul safe and apart from that place and that moment. She made it through the night, but even a virgin is only a virgin once, and after that first long night, she was just another whore, there to keep men happy and earn money."

Nick cleared his throat. "Sorry to interrupt"—his tone was apologetic—"but does she know where she was in Lahore, the name of the place maybe?"

Bina seemed to understand Nick's question, and she turned to Zara and shook her head.

"No," Zara said, "but she was there for almost two years, and she wondered if that was to be her karma, her debt to the gods for transgressions in another life. She'd accepted her destiny, and when the police raided the brothel and arrested her and the others, she was sure Krishna had blessed her. The police, however, weren't much of a blessing. They didn't care that these women were trafficking victims, and they probably didn't believe them anyway. In Muslim society, it is always the woman who is to blame, and they charged every one of them with crimes of prostitution and threw them in jail. Even jail might not have been so bad, but it wasn't long before the policemen demanded sex. The women had no rights and no hope until a UN women's group appeared and demanded they be released." Zara smiled as she caught Abby's eye.

"When women work together," Zara said, "anything is possible. The women were released, and Bina, the only woman from Nepal, was sent here to us in the hopes we might work with her and decide if she wants to go home or stay here. Bina is in training as Mariyah is; she helps out two mornings a week in Railway

Hospital, but Bina is also in school, where she is learning to read and write and, *inshallah,* someday she will enter university to study nursing."

"Is there anything else she wants me to know, to write?" Nick asked.

Bina whispered to Zara, who smiled as she listened. "She is still a good girl. She wants you to know that."

"I'll make sure those words are in my story." He turned to Bina. "*Dhanyabaad,* thank you, Bina."

"You speak Nepali?" Zara asked.

Nick shook his head. "I can say hello, thank you, and that's about it."

Bina laughed. "*Dhanyabaad,* Nick."

The room had grown close and stuffy as Bina and Zara spoke, and a line of sweat trickled down Abby's back. She stood and squirmed in her dress. "Water, anyone?"

Mariyah rose from her seat. "I need to move. I get it."

"I'll help." Abby followed Mariyah into the small, tidy kitchen.

Mariyah retrieved a pitcher from the refrigerator. "Please, Abby, you can reach cups?" She pointed to a cabinet over the sink.

Abby reached up and plucked six cups down, placing them on the counter before turning to face Mariyah. "I just want to tell you," she said, taking Mariyah's hand, "how much I admire you."

Mariyah's lower lip quivered. "*Shukria,* Abby. You be my good friend?"

"Forever." Abby squeezed Mariyah's hand.

They returned to the room, and Abby set the tray down. "Help yourselves." She poured out a full cup of water, then swallowed it in one long gulp. Nick and Mariyah poured out cups and sipped, but the others shook their heads and remained huddled in conversation.

Abby and Nick watched as Anyu gestured to Zara, who smiled. "You are sure?" she asked, and Anyu nodded.

Zara turned to Nick. "She will tell you her story."

Nick looked quickly at Anyu. "I'm grateful." He leaned forward to change the battery in his recorder.

The women fell quiet and Zara turned to Anyu, who'd sat meekly as Bina had spoken.

"Anyu?" Zara asked.

Anyu folded her hands together in her lap and nodded. "Yes, I ready." Her voice was soft, her English clear.

"You speak English?" Abby asked.

"Little, little, but some Urdu also," Anyu said. "Zara talk for me, *acha*?" Nick nodded, and Anyu pulled herself forward on her chair.

"Anyu is from Uttar Pradesh in northern India," Zara said, "and in her small district, there was a school, and everyone, even the girls, attended for a time. Anyu can read and write a little, and though she would like to go home, she has a big problem in India, and so for now she is here with us."

Anyu's mouth crumpled into a frown when Zara mentioned her "problem." Abby sat on the edge of her seat, and Nick seemed to catch Anyu's reaction as well, and he moved the recorder closer.

"Anyu's father is a farmer, but heavy rains flooded the area just as with Mariyah, but there the similarities end. When the man with money came to her village, Anyu's father sold her straightaway." Zara turned to Anyu. "How old were you then?"

"I had twelve years then. And my bleeding had just . . . you say it." Anyu turned to Zara.

"Anyu's menstrual cycle had begun not long before the

floods, and the coincidence of that timing, the floods following so quickly after Anyu's blood began to flow, fueled her father's superstitions about menstruations and the impurity of women. He blamed her for the floods, and when the family's only ox died, Anyu was forced from the house. She climbed to the roof and hid there until the day she saw the stranger arrive in the village. He was tall, and even from a distance, she could see the roll of money in his pocket, and she scrambled down to join the others who'd gathered to see what he wanted."

Anyu smiled, an unexpected burst of happiness that made her hands tremble in her lap. "It was good day, but I not know what come. I only know it best day in my life."

Abby listened in silence. There wasn't anything to say.

"The man approached several of the village men, Anyu's father among them. The man had come, he told them, to buy some girls to work for him. He couldn't say what the jobs might be and no one asked. Anyu's father was happy to get the money, and happier still to be rid of his worthless daughter. Anyu was one of four girls who left with the man that day, and she was not sad to leave her home, though she'd heard about these men and the lies they told," Zara said. "For Anyu, there was no pretense, no trick to convince her that she was going somewhere better. For Anyu, anywhere else was better. So, she knew where she was going, maybe not the exact location, but she knew what her job would probably be, and she went quietly because women in her village do what they are told."

Anyu bowed her head. "I think that some of the money men give for me will be mine to keep. I think I save money and come back to village rich. Then father of me be happy with Anyu."

Zara patted Anyu's hand and whispered, *"Acha, acha."* Zara turned to Nick. "The man brought Anyu to Delhi, where he turned her and the others over to another man. That first night, she was cleaned up and offered as a virgin. Anyu was not a virgin, but no one had asked her, and if they had, she would have told them that she'd been raped by a cousin when she was nine, and the rapes had continued until she left the village. Now you see why she was happy to go. If you'll be raped no matter where you are, maybe a new place is your only hope.

"When her customer discovered she was not a virgin, he beat her, and when the man in charge heard her screams and then the customer's story, he beat her as well. For Anyu, her nightmare in Delhi grew by the day, or perhaps *night* is a better word."

Anyu sat quietly, her fingers drumming nervously on the chair's edge.

"In Delhi," Zara continued, "Anyu did what she was told. After that first beating, she'd learned her lesson, and she was determined to go unnoticed, but it was not to be. Her customers were always the dirtiest of the men, the ones who ordered her to perform hideous acts for them. It wasn't just the sex, it was the humiliations night after night." Zara paused, seeming to steel herself for the remainder of Anyu's story. "The men beat her, urinated on her, and placed sharp objects inside of her. When she was torn up in there and bleeding, it was then the men would climb on top. The pain was unbearable, and one night, when a regular customer put the sharp end of a knife just inside her, Anyu snapped."

Anyu had been listening impassively, but now a shadow seemed to pass over her face. She pulled herself straight in her seat, and a long frown sprouted on her lips. Gone was the meek, submissive girl—she had been replaced by an angry, scowling young woman.

Zara seemed to notice the change in Anyu as well. "You must understand," Zara said, turning to Abby, "this was very bad time for Anyu. She is a good girl."

"I know she's good." Abby nodded, tilting her head toward Nick. "We can both see that."

"Yeah, absolutely," Nick added.

"I just wanted to be sure you know that before I continue, but I think you understand." Zara glanced at Anyu, who'd begun to chew on her lower lip. "So I continue. When the man rolled his body away from Anyu, he closed his eyes, and she saw her opportunity. She pulled the knife out of herself, her own blood and tissue on the blade, and she took it and plunged it into the chest of the man who'd lain so quietly. His eyes, she's told me, opened for an instant, and he reached up to fight back, but Anyu cut into his hands and face. He reached up to shield his face, and she plunged the knife into his chest again and again. When she was sure he was dead, she emptied his pockets of his money and identification and escaped. She made her way to Lahore, and a women's group there sent her on to us." Zara gripped Anyu's hand. "She is our newest houseguest, and she arrived only last week."

Nick had placed his pen and notebook down. "I have to ask you, Zara, have you confirmed any of this? I mean, do you know who the man was or where the brothel was?" Not waiting for an answer, he turned to Anyu. "Do you have this man's identification? Have you saved it?"

Anyu shook her head and looked away. "I keep money to get away, and I take match to his papers, and when flames rise, I throw it all in street latrine."

"Street latrine?" Abby asked.

"Public toilets, though the word *toilet* makes them sound grander than they are. They're latrines, and they're pretty awful. Must have been quite a sight with the fire," Zara explained.

Anyu glanced at Nick and smiled.

"We don't want this made public. You understand that,

Nick?" Zara sighed. "It is very complicated. Anyu came to us through a women's network, a group of women who work underground, you understand? They work to help women get out of these bad places. We don't want to jeopardize Anyu or them."

Nick nodded. "Right—don't ask for trouble, just keep it quiet."

Anyu seemed to understand what Nick had said, and her eyes blazed as she watched him.

"We want to keep Anyu safe," Zara said, "and we ask that you conceal her identity and location if you tell her story."

Nick nodded and rubbed at his throat, as though his collar were suddenly too tight. "I'd like to follow up though, see if there's any record in Delhi of the murder."

"You won't give Anyu away, will you?"

"No. I'll protect her. I'll try to just get general information, but in Delhi where murder is more sport than crime, that might be difficult. They probably aren't even looking for her. Hell, over sixty-five percent of murders in Delhi go unsolved. It's not just that the police are inept and corrupt, though they probably are, but they're also woefully understaffed. If you're going to murder someone, Delhi might just be the place to do it."

Abby felt numb. The girls' stories were epic in their misery, each more wretched than anything she could have imagined, and she felt powerless to help.

Anyu, who'd sat silently, seemed to understand the effect her story had had on Abby and Nick, and she finally spoke up. "He bad man," she said defiantly. "I only try to save myself. If he not hurt me, if he not bring knife, he not get knife."

Her voice was strong and unwavering and strangely reassuring, Abby thought about Anyu's boldness as she sat here and shared her story. She glanced at Abby and turned away quickly when she realized Abby was looking back at her. "I . . ." Abby started to thank Anyu, but Anyu suddenly stood, tears shimmering in the corners of her eyes. Her lip quivered, and she bit down hard.

"I alone now, understand? I same as Mariyah—a tree without leaves, a night without stars." Anyu draped her sari over her shoulder and stood tall. *"Khoda khafez,"* she said in a whisper as she hurried from the room.

Abby rose from her chair and started for the door.

"No," Zara said. "Leave her. It is difficult to share a story like that. I will speak with her later."

"You'll be sure to tell her how grateful I am?" Abby glanced at Nick, who was packing his notebook and recorder away. "How grateful we both are."

"You will be careful when you look into this, Nick?" Zara asked. "It is a very delicate situation, I think."

"Murder," he said, "is anything but delicate."

Abby caught a sudden movement at the doorway. She turned and saw Anyu, her eyes wide, listening.

Chapter 17

Once in the car, Abby could only sigh.

"Jesus," Nick said, "sorry you had to hear that. Truth is, aside from the murder, it wasn't so far off what I expected to hear."

Abby shook her head sadly. "It was pure misery though, wasn't it? Just listening was misery. I can't even imagine how these girls lived through this. Jesus, when I was thirteen, I'd just begun to notice boys. At seventeen, I was applying to college."

"Big difference for girls living in these hellholes, huh? Fighting for their lives."

Even Hurricane Katrina, Abby remembered, hadn't affected her the way it had so many others. Although her hospital had closed, and New Orleans had been devastated, her little town just outside New Orleans had remained unscathed by the storm, and she'd only had to kiss her parents good-bye before heading north to Boston. Life was damned unfair.

Abby exhaled, and her thoughts wandered to the woman in Geneva. Fragments of the vivid images floated before her eyes—the scream, the struggle, the body flying through the air, the sparkling bracelet. Could *that* woman have been tormented and then finally jumped as Mariyah did? Abby closed her eyes and saw the stark image clearly. She couldn't let go of that nagging feeling that she'd witnessed more than an accident. Abby felt a hand on her arm, and she looked up to see Nick, his brows furrowed, his eyes on her.

"You okay?" he asked softly.

"I don't know," Abby said, turning her gaze to the window.

"Club?" Turning his attention from the road, he focused his gaze on Abby. "Tough day, huh?"

"For Anyu and the others, probably, but for me it was just exhausting listening to their stories. I know it sounds selfish, but I feel drained, as though I need to sleep. It's hard to stay so focused when people are sharing such suffering." Abby pushed her hair back from her forehead and wiped away the beads of sweat that had gathered there.

"Come on." Nick guided the car into a parking spot. "Let's drink. We'll both feel better."

Abby smiled. "I'll stick with Diet Coke, thanks."

Once upstairs, and installed at their now familiar table in the farthest corner, Nick headed to the bar, where he ordered their food and his scotch. He carried the drinks back and sat heavily, a sigh escaping his lips. "What's up? You look, well, morose, that's how you look. You want to talk?" he asked between sips.

Abby pursed her lips and hesitated, but only for an instant. She knew she had to talk to someone, and who else was there? "I do, Nick. I do want to talk, and, as selfish as it sounds, not just about Anyu and Bina and Mariyah. I want to tell you about Geneva." She saw the look of cynicism in his eyes, and she held up her hand. "Just listen. It's not entirely a nightmare. If you hear it all and think I'm crazy, so be it, but for now just listen."

Nick settled back in his chair, and Abby launched into the details of the event in Geneva. "I was running, my last run before Pakistan, and I was really into it, you know? Anyway, it was so early it was still almost night, the sky still dark, the streets still quiet, the world empty. That time, not quite day, not quite night, is the perfect time to run, for me at least." She described the sounds that drew her eyes to the struggle on the balcony, and the man who had fought with the screaming woman before she plummeted to her death. She felt her eyes well up, and she paused, looking away. "I can still see her face, and that damn bracelet so clearly. Nick, I didn't stay. I was sure she was dead, and I was so scared, I ran like hell back to my hotel. I called the police, but when we went back, my mind was all foggy." She paused to take a deep breath. "In the full light of morning, I couldn't get my bearings. I was just lost in that confusing maze of streets. And when I couldn't find the body or the building, they thought I was just nuts. They brought me back to the hotel and told me to sleep. What could I do then? No body, no building, so I convinced myself it was an accident, that my imagination had made it more dramatic than it already was. But I just can't shake it—the feeling that she was murdered and dumped somewhere, and I'm the only one who knows."

Abby hesitated and pushed her hair away from her face. "I don't know what to do, but I know I have to do something.

I can't just show up in Geneva and say, 'Hey, you didn't believe me the first time, but let's look again.' If you think I'm nuts, just don't say anything. Okay?" She raised her head and looked into Nick's eyes—where she saw not doubt but genuine interest.

"Wow," he said, sitting straighter, "that is one hell of a story. I have to ask—you're certain she was dead?"

"I am."

"Why didn't you tell me about this before?"

"It's not the kind of thing you just tell people, and until I heard the trafficking stories, I thought it probably was an accident. But, once I heard Mariyah's story and your confirmation that women actually might be thrown from balconies, I knew that's what I'd seen. It's not a coincidence, Nick. I know what I saw, and I saw that woman thrown. I'm sure."

"I think we have to look into it." Nick's brow furrowed. "But, I have to admit, I've never heard of anything like this happening in Geneva. Where exactly did you say you were?"

"On the main business street, I don't know the name, but I was in the business district, maybe four blocks from my hotel, Les Armures Hôtel. I don't know for sure. When I brought the police back and the body wasn't there, I panicked. And I thought maybe it was the next street or the next, but the body was gone, and then they just didn't believe me. Plus, I was on Lariam, and you know what that does—it would have given them even less reason to believe me."

Nick sat forward and planted his arms on the table. "I suppose I can try to check it out. The man, the murderer—can you identify him?"

"I think so—he's tall and thin, graying hair, and distinguished, you know the type. Those men who carry themselves differently from the rest of us—you know?"

Nick nodded.

"But it's not *just* him, it's the bracelet too, and believe me, I don't ordinarily notice jewelry, but I know this bracelet by heart." She looked straight into Nick's eyes, looking for what? she wondered—doubt? But all she saw was concern. "I know how this sounds, I do, but it *did* happen. Do you believe me?"

Nick folded his arms and sighed heavily. "I do, Abby." His eyes locked onto hers. "I do. It's certainly worth looking into."

Abby felt a flood of relief. She let herself sag into her seat. "Thanks, Nick. I mean that."

"Don't thank me yet, but I promise I'll check into it." He took out his notebook and pen. "When were you in Geneva?"

"July third through fifth, and I ran early on the fourth and fifth. God, it's been six weeks already." She watched as he scribbled down the dates. "You're really going to check this out?"

"I am. And since we're spilling secrets, I'll spill mine." He took a long swig of scotch. "The story I came here for has *nothing* to do with you, though the UN would like a sidebar on an aid worker. It's you only because my destination was Peshawar, and believe it or not, right now, you're the only American aid worker with the UN here."

Abby's eyes opened wide, and she felt herself relax. "That's a relief, I think. So why are you really here?"

Nick leaned into his seat. "I'm doing an investigative series on human trafficking."

"But why all the secrecy?"

"It's a reasonable question. The truth is, I agreed to the aid-worker story to get the UN's blessing, and a visa. That blessing opens a lot of doors, and without it I might miss the very person I need. In this case, it's turning out to be you." He swallowed the last of his scotch, then exhaled slowly. "Trafficking is the focus of my story, but the hows and whos are what I'm looking into. I know now for a fact that Najeela's uncle Imtiaz is involved in trafficking. Two months ago, he was caught up in a sting the Pakistani police had worked. They had him, but money buys freedom and silence in this part of the world, and palms were greased, and the rest is history. He spent maybe an hour at the police station. The official statement said he was found not to be involved in the trafficking ring they closed in on, and they released him. It's only a matter of time until the international authorities just climb over the Pakistani police and actually do get him, but the fact is—he's not in this alone. There's a second key figure, I'm sure of it."

He leaned forward. "You see, men like Imtiaz direct the dirty work locally, and they collect the money, but who's in charge? Who directs *them*? I think someone higher up, in government or the UN, has to be in on it. I mean, how else do these people get trafficked across so many borders? Who's making the money? It's the third-largest illegal business in the world."

His face darkened. "Someone's making money, and I think people are looking the other way. Is that because they're involved or because someone else has assured them there's nothing going on? I think it's someone big, and I think I know who it is, a wealthy European named Rousseau. But he's hard to catch, and maybe it's not just him. That's what I've been looking into. If the UN knew that I was targeting them, they would have squashed my visa, and more importantly, they'd have shut that great big UN door in my face."

"Nick," a voice called from the bar. "Your food." The man motioned to a tray on the bar.

Nick pushed back his chair and stood. "I'm getting another drink. You interested?"

Abby nodded. "Yeah, why not? After everything today, I'll have one."

Nick returned with the food and drinks and bit into his

burger. "So, do you understand now what I'm doing here? I mean, you heard it for yourself today. It's not just about the numbers, which are staggering, but there's real misery behind every trafficking victim. There's a real person who has suffered unimaginably. And the reality is that if Anyu hadn't killed that man, he probably would have killed her. Understand?"

"I guess I do." Abby sipped at her tumbler of scotch. "As horrible as it is, it's kind of confusing too. And you're sure Imtiaz is involved?"

"Absolutely, that's the one thing I'm certain of, and that's why you can't say anything to Najeela."

Abby opened her mouth to defend Najeela once again, but Nick held up his hand. "I know you like her and she's probably just a spoiled rich kid, but I can't take the chance that she'd repeat anything, even innocently. You get that, right?"

Abby nodded. "I do. My lips are sealed, but why do you think there's a government or UN connection?"

"Who better? People with diplomatic immunity travel the world and never stop at customs or immigration. They're always waved through—their bags might be full of money or forged documents, but no one will ever see them, no one questions these people. Even the people who travel with them are waved through. It's the perfect foil—find a diplomat, or better yet, a UN employee or liaison with easy access to the most vulnerable, and you have instant resources and an endless supply of those resources. I mean, think about it—certain groups can be identified and targeted in a millisecond. There are floods in the north, thousands are destitute and homeless, so you direct your locals to swoop in and grab the youngest, prettiest girls, and then you get them out and across borders before the world has even blinked." Nick heaved a sigh. "Think about it. Isn't that what happened to Mariyah and Anyu?"

Abby swallowed the hard lump in her throat and nodded. It might also be, she thought, what happened to the woman in Geneva.

"And that's where the real evil comes in. Someone has to have the money and the means to profit from those tragedies as they unfold, before there's a response from rescue organizations. And it wouldn't be the first time the UN—well, its employees at least—have had a hand in exploiting the most vulnerable." Nick washed down a mouthful of fries with his scotch.

"What do you mean?" Abby set her own glass down. "The UN are the good guys, aren't they?"

"They are, they are. But in every group there're bad apples, and the UN is no exception. I mean, you've heard of the recurring sexual-exploitation scandals, right?"

Abby shook her head. She didn't have a clue what he was talking about.

"The Oil for Food scandal?"

Abby hesitated. "I guess that rings a bell, but I don't remember the details."

"Not many people do." Nick shook his head in disgust. "It's a scandal that went right to the top, to the secretary-general's inner circle. He wasn't involved, but others were, and that connection made investigators and journalists afraid to ask the tough questions. I mean, if you're wrong, you're screwed professionally. You follow me?"

Abby could barely nod before Nick went on.

"But that's not all. The sexual-exploitation scandal rears its ugly head every few years. Aid workers and even UN peacekeepers have been involved in prostitution, rape, swapping sex for food. Granted, the numbers are small, but remember, these are the world's most vulnerable people, and the accused are sometimes the very people who are charged to protect them." Nick let out a long, slow breath of air. "See what I mean? It's a damn mess."

Abby leaned her arms on the table. "So why isn't the UN looking into this instead of you?"

"This stuff's been going on for years, and there's no direct accusation right now, but the reality is, it's the UN. Everyone's afraid to point the finger or dig a little deeper. That's what I want to do, just dig it all out, see what I can learn." Nick sat back and took a swig from his glass.

Abby could hardly believe what she'd heard, but in a funny kind of way it made sense, and it made her wonder about the woman she'd seen fall to her death. Had she been a trafficking victim as well? "So what's next?"

"Research, try to put some things together. Think I'll head to India first and have a look at the border, the area where Mariyah crossed over, and then try to check out Anyu's story, though that might be a harder nut to crack. The police in Delhi probably don't want an American journalist asking questions about their unsolved murders, which by the way are among the highest in the world. Anyway, maybe I'll head to Geneva after that and look into the UN connection—and see if I can find anything out about your woman on the balcony. I'll check the death records and news reports and see if there was a woman who fell to her death there in early July."

Abby felt conflicted. She was relieved that Nick didn't think she was crazy, but, she was surprised to admit to herself, sorry that he was leaving and troubled that she'd be stuck here by herself, especially now. "Are you coming back?" she asked, disappointment oozing from her words.

"Hell, yes. The story's here. You're here. I'll be back."

He reached out and took her hands, pulling her closer, and

Abby felt a small, unexpected thrill at his touch. This time she didn't pull away. She didn't quite know what was happening between them, but something was.

Don't leave, she wanted to say, but instead she asked, "Any chance I can come along?"

Nick shook his head. "Believe me, nothing would give me greater pleasure, but it's best to keep you out of this. I don't want Najeela or Imtiaz to know what I'm really doing. You're safer here for now. Well, as long as you keep your head down and your mouth shut."

Abby sighed. Without her even noticing, Nick had chipped away at the layer of ice that had grown over her heart. "How long will you be gone?"

Nick sipped his scotch slowly. "Not long. No more than a week."

"Do you have a cell phone? In case I need to reach you?"

Nick shook his head. "I never carry one in places like this, too easy for someone to track me with towers and satellites. I'd rather fly under the radar."

Abby nodded. Suddenly, a week felt like an eternity, and she picked up her own drink. "I never thought I'd be saying this, but I'll miss you, Nick. I'll surely miss you." She touched her glass to his. "To you, and to a safe trip." She took a quick sip of the scotch. Still burned, but the unmistakable burn filled the hollow that she knew Nick would leave behind.

"I'll miss you too, Abby—so promise me you'll be careful, and not a word to Najeela, not about me either. Imtiaz is at the center of this, but he's not alone. I haven't figured out his connection yet, but I will, and Geneva gives me the opportunity to wander through the UN, see who pops up."

Suddenly, he leaned in and planted a quick kiss on her lips. Despite a moment of shock, Abby's lips tingled in response, and a rush of heat filled her head. She closed her eyes to savor the unexpected closeness.

Suddenly, he pulled away. "Gotta go," he said softly.

"Godspeed," she whispered as he turned to leave.

Abby lay awake that night, replaying the images from Mariyah's ordeal and the woman's death in Geneva over and over in her mind. She couldn't shake the feeling that it was all somehow connected. The night air was warm, and she threw off her sheets, tossing and turning for another hour before finally drifting into a restless sleep.

Chapter 18

"There you are, sleepyhead!"

Abby had just stumbled into the dining room in search of coffee, and Najeela's cheery greeting only served to reinforce her morning discomfort. She'd barely slept, and though she'd been spared her usual nightmare, her head felt as though it were swimming in a soupy fog. "Morning, Najeela. You're here early."

"I am early, you're right. You and I never get to chat. I thought today we could have breakfast, and you could tell me about your extra work."

"Extra work?" Abby asked, puzzled.

"Oh, you silly. Just this week, you said you wanted to do something extra, something more than vaccines?"

The fog lifted from Abby's thoughts, and she sat across from Najeela. "Oh, of course. I did want to tell you that I went to a halfway house for trafficking victims." For a fleeting moment she considered sharing that Mariyah was there, that she knew her story, but she remembered Nick's advice and stopped herself. The less she said the better, but she would have to tell Najeela something if she wanted to spend time there.

Abby took a deep breath. "You can't even imagine the stories. I mean, you just wouldn't believe what these women, girls really, have been through, and I want to do something to help. I thought maybe I could start some kind of health program. The UN clinic is only open two days, and I'm sure I can keep up with my responsibilities there, but this is something I'd really like to do. I wanted to know if you think it's okay or maybe I should ask someone at the UN office?"

"Oh, Abby, that's a marvelous idea. Did I tell you that my Lars is involved in helping those poor victims? You'll just have to meet him. Now I'm sure you'll be friends." She clasped her hands together. "Maybe I can come along with you sometime."

Mariyah, Bina, and Anyu flashed before Abby's eyes. She wanted to protect them, not make them dinner topics. "I, well, I guess I could ask."

"This is just wonderful. Let me just get Hana and tell her we're ready for breakfast."

Najeela breezed into the kitchen, and a scowling Hana then appeared with a tray of coffee and eggs. Abby tried to catch her eye, but Hana was as unfriendly as ever this morning. Abby inhaled the sweet scent of the eggs and coffee and remembered that she'd only picked at her cheeseburger the day before. She almost pounced on the food, washing down a large serving of eggs with a cup of steaming coffee. She glanced quickly at her watch. Nine! She pushed her chair back and threw her napkin down. "Sorry to be in a hurry," she said to Najeela. "I want to ask Mohammed to bring me to the camp, and then to the halfway house."

"No Nick today?"

"No, he's away," Abby said, right before Nick's words of caution ran through her mind. She closed her eyes. Just don't say anything else and it'll be fine, she chided herself silently.

"Oh? Where is he?"

"I don't have a clue. I mean, you know him as well as I do. He sure doesn't answer to either one of us."

Najeela giggled. "That's true enough. But where . . ."

Abby grabbed her bag and dashed out before Najeela could finish. "See you later," Abby shouted over her shoulder as she pulled the door shut behind her. She stood on the front steps and heaved a sigh of relief. It wasn't going to be easy, but she was going to do her best to follow Nick's advice and just keep quiet.

Mohammed was busy wiping down the car's gleaming surface with a threadbare rag, and Abby walked to his side. "Good morning, Mohammed."

He looked up and nodded, quickly stuffing the rag into his pocket. "Morning, miss. To the camp?"

"Yes. But only for the time it takes me to get directions to a house in Peshawar. I should know the way, but I don't. *Acha*, it's okay?"

Abby loved the Urdu word for "okay." People drew out the sound—*aacha*—and said it almost breathlessly. "*Acha?*" she asked again, savoring the feel of the word as it slipped through her lips.

Mohammed smiled, and they set off for Safar. Abby sat in

the back feeling almost breezy. She'd definitely found her purpose, and she was eager to get to the house. She watched as the streets of Peshawar slipped by, and when she saw a young girl kicking an older man in the legs before running off, Abby twisted in her seat to see where the girl had gone. But there was no sight of her, she'd disappeared down a long, dark alley. Abby turned to look for the man the girl had kicked, but he was gone as well, swallowed up in the mobs and chaos that filled the city's streets. She sat back. Last week, she would barely have noticed that scene, yet today, she wondered if the girl had been trafficked. Abby folded her arms. The world would never be as simple again.

Mohammed glided the car into the parking area in the refugee camp. "Be right back," Abby said, hurrying to the Protection Tent, where she quickly found Zara.

"Oh, Abby, lovely to see you again," Zara said, pulling her head scarf closer. "But, well, I'm sorry to be rude, but I'm just heading back to the house. I don't have time to speak. You see, two young girls arrived last evening. They've only just been pulled from a *kharabat*, a brothel, in Islamabad, and there was nowhere else for them to go. They've had quite a bad time, I'm afraid." Zara sighed and brushed back a stray hair. "We're not even sure where they're from—their passports and visas were forged, used just to get them across the border—maybe from India, but the girls have been sleeping since they arrived to us. The police think they've probably been drugged to get them wherever they were being sent, so we don't know anything about them. Though we do think the plan was to send them on to Kuwait or Saudi Arabia, where a young virgin will bring a high price."

"Oh, God, poor things." Abby wished Nick were with her. "I hope my being here isn't bad timing, but maybe I can help. You know I'm a nurse?"

Zara nodded.

"I can have a look at them at least. I came today to ask you if I could go to the house to help out somehow. There must be something I can do. I mean, these are really vulnerable women, but, with these two new girls, maybe I can, well—have a look, make sure they're really just sleeping, make sure it's not something more sinister. I want to be involved with what you're doing, and these girls have probably been through a lot." Abby paused. "What do you think?"

"I think we need all the help we can get." Zara smiled. "We're especially happy to have yours. Anyu and the others will be delighted to see you." Zara gathered her papers and her bag. "Do you have a car today?"

"I do. And a driver."

"Wonderful. I was going to the Administration Tent to arrange a car, but if you'll take me, we can go." Zara reached back and pulled out a large bag. "Is Nick with you?"

"No, he's off doing research."

"Oh, the women will be sad. They all liked him very much and thought he was very kind, and coming from three women who've been so abused by men, that's quite a compliment."

Perspective, Abby thought, was everything. Until recently, she'd never given Nick much of a chance. She'd just lumped him in with Eric and countless other jerks, yet here were women who'd seen the absolute worst of men, and they liked Nick. She sighed. She was no judge of men, that was for sure.

When they arrived at the house, Abby suddenly felt nervous. Should she be here, especially with two new young victims? She had no experience with trafficking victims. She wanted to help, but what could she really do? These poor girls, did they really need her, or did she need them? She hesitated at the doorway, doubt like lead in her legs.

"Zara," she asked, "you're sure it's all right? I mean, I don't want to intrude."

Zara turned, and seeing the uncertainty in Abby's eyes, she took her hand. "It is good for these women and the girls to see that not everyone will hurt them. Come." She tugged on Abby's arm. "Have a look at the girls for us, make sure they are all right. *Acha?*"

Abby's shoulders relaxed, and they entered the house together. The house was bustling this morning, the air filled with the hum of conversation and ripples of laughter. Abby smiled to hear the sounds of ordinary life in such an extraordinary place. She smiled. Boston, Eric, and everything else were a million miles away.

Mariyah appeared in the hallway, and Abby watched as her thick scar stretched, allowing a faint smile to seep onto her face. "*Khush amdeed,* welcome," she said softly.

"*Salaam,*" Abby replied. "*Salaam,* Mariyah."

"Are the girls awake?" Zara asked.

Mariyah's smile faded as she nodded toward the back of the house. "No," she whispered. "Girls still sleep."

Abby followed Zara along the hall to a room near the end. She opened the door and motioned for Abby to enter. Zara closed the door softly and tiptoed to the bed. She leaned in, then turned back to Abby. "Still asleep," she whispered. "They've slept too long." Worry lines creased Zara's face.

The room was stale, the windows closed tight against the day. Abby moved to the bed and bent toward its sleeping occupants. Even through the sheets, she could see that the two were young, maybe six or seven years old, and they were small and stick-thin, covered with layers of grime. Their hair, greasy and matted, was plastered to their shiny scalps. Two pitiful little things, Abby thought sadly. "How long have they been sleeping?"

"The police brought them to us last night, and they were asleep when they were found, so for at least twelve hours." Zara adjusted the sheets over the girls.

"Too long. We'll have to wake them." Abby leaned in and placed a hand on the backs of the girls, then leaned her head in close. "Well, their breathing is okay." She pinched one girl's skin between her fingers. "Her skin still looks good, but they'll both need fluids soon. Have they peed?" She lifted the sheet to see for herself. The sheet was dry.

Abby turned to Zara. "We have to wake them, make sure we *can* wake them, understand?"

"Yes, yes, whatever you say." Zara pulled up the shades and pushed the windows open. Bright daylight and fresh air filled the room.

Abby sat on the side of the bed, and with her fingers she rubbed one girl's arms. "Wake up," she said, more loudly than she'd intended. The girl's eyelids fluttered open, then, unseeing, closed again. Abby leaned in and pinched the girl's ear tight between her fingers.

The girl's eyes opened wide, and she looked at Abby, then Zara, then the room, and she screamed. With her little hands balled into fists, she hit out at Abby.

"*Acha,*" Abby said softly. "You are okay." The little girl elbowed her companion roughly, and suddenly she was awake too, her eyes wide with fright. The two huddled together and pushed away from Abby.

Disheveled seemed a funny word to describe little girls, but that's what they were, disheveled and dirty with tangled, matted hair, and large, angry eyes that bore right through Abby. Their dresses were stained and threadbare, and their faces were smudged with dirt.

"*Salaam,*" Abby said, squatting by the bed. The thinner of

the two sat up straight and spit right into Abby's face. Abby quickly pulled away and wiped the spittle from her face. From the corner of her eye, she saw Zara move toward the girl, and Abby put out her hand to stop her. "It's okay." Abby's eyes were on the girl. "I'd probably spit too if I was in a strange place."

The girl drew her knees in, and Abby saw that her bony knees and legs were covered with scrapes and bruises. Abby reached her hand out to touch the cuts, and the girl winced and pulled away.

Zara leaned in and stroked the head of the second girl. "*Amma,*" she said softly, nodding toward Abby. The girls looked warily at Abby, and Zara tried again, speaking slowly. "This lady is a nurse. Her name is Abby, and I am Zara. Understand?"

The girls turned their gaze back to Abby, their eyes wide. "You understand some English, maybe?" she said softly. "So you know that no matter what, you are safe here." She turned to Zara. "And you know too that Zara and I are your friends."

The smaller one sniffled and wiped her arm across her face. She seemed to be letting her guard down, and Abby turned to her. "What's your name?" she asked softly.

"Geeta," the girl replied in a tiny, singsong voice that made her seem all the more vulnerable. Geeta's eyes grew wide as she watched Abby, and a tiny trace of a smile sprouted like an unexpected wildflower. The other girl jerked at Geeta's arm, and Geeta looked away from Abby.

"*Salaam,* Geeta," Abby said. "And *salaam,* Geeta's friend."

The other girl looked suspiciously at Abby. "Pari," she said, her voice tiny despite her hard glare. She pointed to herself. "Name Pari."

Abby leaned forward and held out her hand. "My name is Abby, and I'm happy to meet you, Pari."

A long frown draped Pari's smudged face, and she held tight to Geeta's hand.

Abby smiled and let her hand fall. "Can we get them some water? Something to eat?"

Zara opened the door and called for Bina. "Will you bring food, some chapatis or naan, whatever we have, and some water?" Through the slit in the open door, Abby saw Bina's bobbing back as she scurried down the hall.

Abby turned back to the girls. "English?"

The girls just stared in stony silence.

"What do you think?" Abby asked Zara. "Maybe Hindi? Maybe Urdu?"

"Could be, or maybe Marathi, the language of Mumbai, but I think they know some English too." Zara looked at the girls. *"Inglisi?"*

The girls looked away.

Abby stood. "If they were sleeping when the police took them, they probably think we're the people who were buying them. Right? Think about it. They don't even know where they are. They must be terrified." Abby exhaled slowly and tried to think what to do. "We have to get through to them. Can we ask Bina and Mariyah and Anyu to come in and speak with them? We can step outside when they do, so the girls feel free to speak. What do you say?"

"I'll get the others," Zara offered.

Mariyah slipped quietly into the room. *"Salaam,"* she said softly, bowing her head toward the girls. "I am Mariyah." The girls stared.

Bina approached the bed where the girls still crouched together. *"Salaam.* I Bina."

Still there was no response.

Zara returned with Anyu, who carried a basin filled with soapy water. She leaned down and placed the basin on the floor, and Zara laid two clean, fluffy towels and a bar of soap on the bed.

Anyu put her two hands together as if in prayer. *"Namaste."* She nodded her head. The girls did not respond. *"Namaskar, ullo,"* Anyu said, her voice louder, and the girls looked up and nodded. "Marathi, language of Mumbai."

"Marathi it is then," Zara exclaimed. She looked at the girls. "I am Zara." She introduced each of the women in turn. "You are in Peshawar in Pakistan. Understand?"

The girls sat quietly, watching everything. Abby pulled over the basin of water. "We thought you might want to wash up." She pushed a bar of soap and the towels toward the girls. "We'll leave so you can wash." Abby motioned with her hands to mimic washing.

The eyes of the taller girl seemed to light up in response, and she climbed out of the bed and, in one swift and sudden movement, she kicked her foot out, knocking over the basin, splashing water onto Abby.

Abby rose and dabbed at the wetness with one of the towels. Zara stepped forward, her eyes flashing. "No more, understand? No more."

The smaller girl began to cry, and the larger one took her in her arms and rocked her. Though she comforted Geeta, Pari kept a watchful eye on Abby.

"No," Abby said, "they're still unsure. They have no idea who we are. You said yourself that they've only recently been sold. A few weeks ago, maybe a few days even, they were in their own homes. However desperate that may have been, it was home. And now they're here surrounded by strangers."

Zara bent to retrieve the basin and passed it to Bina. "Come, ladies, let's get them food."

Mariyah, Bina, and Anyu left the room with Zara, leaving Abby with the girls.

"Hungry? *Naan?*" asked Abby, pretending she was eating.

The girls bobbed their heads up and down, and Abby turned to Zara, who'd returned, a small loaf of bread and a cup filled with water in her hands. She handed both to Abby, who passed the bread to the girls.

They pounced on the bread, tearing at it with their hands and teeth.

"Oh, God, they're starving. Is there more?" Abby said, handing the cup to Pari. The girls drained the cup.

"Mariyah and Bina are cooking. Soon," Zara said, "lunch is soon. *Khaana,* lunch. Understand?"

Abby turned to the girls. "I'm going to help in the kitchen." She held out her hand. "Will you come with me? Understand?"

Pari nodded, but she and Geeta stayed where they were.

Abby moved toward the door. "I'm going, but I'll call you when it's ready, yes?" The girls' eyes grew wide, and Abby stepped into the hall, where Zara was waiting.

"Heartbreaking, isn't it?" Abby asked.

Zara nodded. "But for me, it is something that makes me angry, that someone could hurt small girls like this."

"There's no information?" Abby asked.

Zara shook her head. "Very little. The police in Islamabad brought them to us late last night. A UN social worker told them about the house we have here, and though we've never had little girls, there was no place else for them to go. The police raided a *kharabat* just outside the city center. It was filled with women and girls who'd been sold and trafficked and were held there. Some were in the process of being moved to other countries. The police found money and false documents and twenty-eight girls, who were just terrified. These two hadn't been in the house long, and the police were good men. They were determined to get them away from Islamabad, away from whoever intended to buy them."

Zara turned into the kitchen. "At least now we know they understand English a little. It's going to be slow progress, one small step at a time."

The women had gathered in the kitchen, where Bina sifted through rice and Mariyah pounded slices of chicken into thin strips. "You can help here if you'd like," Zara said. "I'm going to get some work done." She turned and headed back down the hall.

"Can I help?" Abby asked.

"No, you guest," Mariyah said, motioning for Abby to sit.

"You like Nepali food?" Bina asked.

"I'm not sure I've ever had any," Abby replied.

"Food of Pakistan not so different from Nepal," Mariyah said. "Maybe better."

Bina laughed and threw a handful of rice at Mariyah. The shrieks of laughter finally caught the attention of Geeta and Pari, who suddenly appeared in the doorway. Geeta's eyes grew wide at the sight of the food.

"Hungry?" Abby asked, knowing the two were starving.

Geeta nodded.

"Come in, then. Sit with me." Abby patted the chair next to her, and though Pari moved warily, she hauled herself onto the seat, lifting Geeta onto her lap where they sat in silence.

Bina smiled at the girls. "*Salaam,*" she said softly. Pari nodded, and Geeta smiled shyly.

Mariyah and Bina worked their magic with the food, and when Anyu appeared carrying fresh warm bread and cold Coca-Cola, the meal was served. The aroma of the dishes, a spicy lamb served on a bed of curried rice, made even Abby's mouth water, and she went in search of Zara.

"Lunch is ready," she said when she spied Zara hunched over a computer in the long hallway. "The girls are in there. We're just waiting for you."

Zara stood slowly, rubbing her back. "There's so much to do, Abby, so much."

"I can help. Even if it's paperwork, I'll help, Zara. I want to be a part of what you're doing here."

Zara took Abby's hand and smiled. "There is a lot to be done. I'm worried that the men who spent a lot of rupees for these girls will come looking for them. It must be our secret, understand?"

Abby nodded.

"Even the local police," Zara said, her brows furrowed, "are not always so honest. They are not paid very well, and for the right amount of money, well, anything can happen. The girls could be snatched away."

Abby gasped. "I hadn't even thought of that. Should there be a guard?"

"There is, the big man who lets you in, but if the authorities come, there'd be nothing he could do."

"Is that what happens? The authorities take girls too?" And, Abby thought, wasn't that precisely what Nick had said?

"I don't know anything for certain. I just want to be ready."

Abby exhaled slowly. "I won't say a word. Not a word."

"Our new friend. *Shukria.*"

They headed into the kitchen and sat to eat. Abby watched as Pari and Geeta shoveled the food into their mouths with their fingers and washed it down with Coca-Cola. "Good?" Abby asked. Pari grunted through a mouthful of rice.

Bina laughed. "Yes, good." She heaped Abby's plate high.

"It is good," Abby said. "But that's enough for me." She reached for an empty plate and filled it with food. "For Mohammed." She turned for the door. "He's outside. I want to be sure he gets lunch too."

Mohammed was sitting under a tree when Abby spied him. He stood quickly when he saw Abby.

"No, Mohammed, please sit. I have lunch for you." She handed him the plate.

"*Shukria,*" he said, then began to eat.

"Mohammed, can we go to the bazaar on the way home? I want to buy some shoes and clothes for little girls. Do you know a shop that will have those things?"

Mohammed smiled. "Yes, miss, very good shop. I bring you."

Abby went back inside and took her seat by the girls. "Mohammed says *shukria*." The girls had just finished eating, and Abby watched as Geeta patted her own belly in satisfaction.

"I'm going to head out," Abby said, rising. "Thank you all for lunch and for a wonderful day. Mariyah, I'll see you tomorrow at the clinic."

Mariyah grinned, her scar almost receding behind her look of happiness.

"Zara, do you need a ride?"

"No, Abby, I'm not ready yet. I'll see you tomorrow?"

"You will, I'll stop by." Abby turned back to the others. "I'll try to see you tomorrow or the day after."

"*Khoda khafez,*" the women said in unison.

Pari and Geeta looked up for an instant before looking away, and Abby bent down to them. "I will see you soon. *Acha?*"

"*Acha,*" Geeta whispered, and Abby felt her heart leap in her chest. She'd do anything she could to protect these girls.

Once on the road, Mohammed guided the car to a small children's shop in the thick of the central bazaar. This was Abby's first visit to the bazaar, a place Najeela thought beneath her. Their shopping trips had been to overpriced boutiques and fancy specialty shops, and though the bazaar was as unlike the mall at home as was possible, Abby felt comfortable here among the narrow, crowded alleys that blocked out all hint of daylight. Chickens squawked, children shouted, merchants bartered—it was as exciting as a shopping center could be.

Mohammed directed Abby along the narrow lane to a small shop set back from the street. Bolts of colorful cloth lined the entryway, and Mohammed ushered Abby inside, where he spoke with the merchant. With gestures and smiles, Abby communicated with the shopkeeper and found sandals and dresses for the girls. "Veils?" she asked, pointing to the colorful head scarves on display.

"Yes, miss," Mohammed said. "Good for girls."

Abby chose two colorfully embroidered head scarves and watched as her packages were wrapped with brown paper and tied with string. Perfect, she thought. No one at the staff house would know what was inside.

She wanted to linger here in the bazaar, but Mohammed tapped his feet as she glanced into another shop, and she turned to him. "Do you have to be somewhere?"

Mohammed seemed to be caught off guard. "No, miss," he said a little too deferentially. "You are the boss."

"Not me, Mohammed, but let's go."

"Whatever you say, miss."

Something in his suddenly fawning voice bothered Abby. Nick is definitely rubbing off on me, she thought, unsure if that was good or bad.

Chapter 19

The next morning dawned hotter than usual, and Abby woke with her nightgown clinging to her damp skin. She exhaled and pushed her sweaty hair back from her face.

An image of Nick flashed through her mind, and she smiled. She wished he were in town, but he had probably at least a week left on his trip. He'd definitely grown on her, but it was more than that. He'd barely left and she missed him already. She swung her legs over the side of the bed and pushed herself up. She headed to the bathroom and stepped into the shower, feeling the warm spray wash away the tension that built up each night.

By the time she stepped from the shower, she was looking

forward to the day ahead. She'd stop at the Protection Tent and give Zara the package for the girls, then she'd spend the day at the Immunization Clinic. She wanted to check the numbers. Maybe the clinic should be open more than twice a week, she thought. She'd have to go over their visit statistics and speak with Simi and Najeela.

She pulled on a long, blue skirt and topped that with a white blouse. She drew a line of black kohl around her eyes and swiped clear gloss over her lips, smiling at her reflection. She was feeling pretty good about herself and her life these days, and it showed. She had some color in her cheeks again, and an unmistakable sparkle in her brown eyes. She pulled her hair back, braiding it before tucking in the loose ends.

She sighed. She hadn't expected to find such purpose in a place called Peshawar. She pulled open her bedroom door and stepped into the hallway. The house was quiet, but a low hum came from the kitchen, where she found Hana tending to a pan that sizzled with butter and eggs.

"Good morning, Hana." Abby steeled herself for the usual curt reply. Instead, Hana turned and *smiled*. Abby almost fainted with surprise.

"Go, have a seat," Hana said, the smile disappearing as quickly as it had sprouted. "I'll be right in."

"Thanks, Hana." Abby stepped into the kitchen. "Can I help?"

"You can take the coffee with you."

Abby lifted the pot and went into the dining room. She poured herself a cup and, bringing it to her lips, wondered if she could bring herself to ask Hana about her son. But when Hana bustled in and deposited the food, Abby paused for a moment too long, and Hana hurried out. Abby sat and ate in silence and wondered where Nick was at that moment. She was lost in thought when the front door slammed, and when it was followed by heavy footsteps, she rose, a smile on her face. Maybe he was back.

She looked up expectantly, and suddenly Uncle Imtiaz appeared in the doorway. Abby gasped. Nick's words rang in her ears: *Imtiaz is at the center of things.*

"Good morning, dear Abby," he said, a hint of scorn in his voice. Or was she only reading that into an innocent hello?

She felt the color rise to her cheeks, and she paused before she spoke. "Good morning," she said, her voice intentionally icy. "Najeela's not here." Oh, God, let him just leave, she prayed.

But he didn't. Instead, he moved into the room and sat across from Abby. "Oh my dear, it's you I've come to see."

Abby looked away. "I'm busy today, Imtiaz. I just don't have time for visitors. Sorry." She rose from the table.

Imtiaz leaned back in his chair. "Where is your friend, the writer?"

Abby felt her heart seize. Why was he asking about Nick? Her mind raced with worry. Jesus, did Najeela tell him about the rescue house? Was he trying to get information? Did he know about the girls? Abby held her breath. She couldn't give anything away.

"I don't know," she finally answered, an unintended tremor in her voice. "He's not my *friend.*"

Imtiaz brushed his beard with his fingers and looked around the room. "Ah, interesting. But he's away?"

Abby shrugged, hoping she appeared truly ignorant of Nick's whereabouts.

"Well, it's good news for me. You are alone, yes?"

He leaned toward Abby, and she took a step toward the door, her eyes on Imtiaz, but he was on his feet in an instant, and he reached out and grabbed her arm. A wave of revulsion shot through her veins.

"Don't go. Don't leave me all alone," he pleaded, leaning in to her.

Abby inhaled the sharp scent of his beard and skin, and the taste of bile filled the back of her throat. The room was closing in on her, and Abby was afraid she was about to faint. With her free hand, she held on to the back of a chair and tried to steady herself, but Imtiaz leaned in closer, and the sour smell of his breath on her face threatened to make her sick.

"What do you think you're doing?" an angry voice suddenly called, and Abby turned to see Hana push her way into the room. Imtiaz dropped Abby's arm, and in that instant she backed away.

"The little miss and I are just making plans for the day," he said in a voice filled with barely concealed irritation.

Abby stood slightly behind him and shook her head only faintly, hoping that Hana would get her message.

"Plans? Well," Hana said with hostility, "I'm sure she's told you about her appointment this morning with the head of the UN Immunization Program. He's on his way here now."

Abby's jaw fell open in surprise at Hana's announcement. UN? Was there an appointment or was Hana bluffing to protect her?

"I—" Imtiaz began, but Hana interrupted him, and turned to Abby.

"So, off with you. You'll need your reports. I believe the UN will be here within the hour, correct?"

Abby nodded slightly.

Imtiaz glared at Hana and poked his finger in the air. "You," his voice boomed, "are a servant. Kindly remember that." He turned to Abby. "I'll see *you* again soon, my dear."

His footsteps pounded angrily down the hall, and Abby, who hadn't even realized she'd been holding her breath, exhaled loudly when she heard the front door slam shut. She collapsed into a chair.

Hana sighed noisily. "What was that all about?"

"That unpleasant man was Najeela's uncle Imtiaz, and you've just saved me from him. Thank you."

Hana leaned over the table and collected the dirty dishes. "You're welcome. What was he doing here?"

"I don't know, but he seemed to know that Nick was away."

"Hmm," Hana muttered, seeming to ponder that news.

"Anyway, I don't actually have an appointment with the UN this morning, do I?"

A trace of a smile swept over Hana's face. "No, you don't. I just wanted to get him out."

"Hana, you're my hero. You were great, and so convincing, I almost believed you."

Hana smiled, picked up the dishes, and headed back to the kitchen.

Abby followed her. She wanted to tell her she knew about her son, about the sadness in her life. She just wanted to say she understood. "Hana." She watched as Hana turned to face her. "I just want to thank you again, seriously, thank you. I know you have a lot on your mind, with your son and all, so I just want to say if I can return the favor, if I can do anything for you, I will."

Hana turned, a puzzled look on her face.

Oh, God, Abby thought, she doesn't know that I know about her son. "Your son?" Abby said softly.

Hana seemed to gather herself, and the familiar disgruntled mask she'd always worn slid back over her face. She nodded and turned back to her dishes.

"I'm going to see if Mohammed's here and head to the camp," Abby said to Hana's back. Hana shrugged in reply, and Abby wished she hadn't said anything. She sighed and picked up her bag and package for the girls and headed to the door.

"See you later, Hana," Abby called over her shoulder, but there was no reply. Abby shut the door softly behind her.

At the camp, she stopped first at the Protection Tent and caught Zara just as she was leaving. "Zara," she said, handing over the small, wrapped bundle, "this is for the girls. Just some sandals and clothes."

Zara took the package and looked it over. "*Shukria,* Abby. Will you come by today to see them?"

"I think I'll catch up on my clinic work and see you all tomorrow, if that's all right? There are all of you at the house with them, and I don't want to wear out my welcome."

"Ah, you will always be welcome, Abby."

"*Shukria* to you. I've got to run, Zara. See you later."

Abby headed to the clinic and stood outside for a minute, searching the faces of the women waiting in line. They all seemed to have desperate, haunted eyes and stick-thin, malnourished babies. These were the women Nick had talked about—invisible and ready to do just about anything to survive. Easy pickings for traffickers. Abby heaved a sigh, stepped around the line of waiting patients, and went into the clinic.

Away from the sharp glare of the sun, it took Abby a moment to see that Mariyah was sitting at the registration desk.

"Good morning."

Mariyah looked up and nodded. "Hello, Abby," she said, then turned back to her work. Abby stepped into the vaccine room and saw that Shoma and Nasreen were busy already with vaccines. Babies shrieked and mothers cooed, and the little room hummed the way a clinic should. Abby smiled. At least she was doing something, she thought, as she settled in to help with the vaccines.

Imtiaz and her nightmare seemed a world away.

Chapter 20

Abby's legs jerked wildly as she tried to break her fall, and she woke with a start, her eyes slamming open. She sat up and took a deep breath, wiping away the film of sweat that had formed on her brow, but she could see him still—the shadowy figure of the man who'd haunted her since Geneva. With his tapered fingers, patrician nose, and silver eyeglasses, there was something almost elegant about him. A man of substance and importance, that's what he was, Abby thought—a man who mattered. She stood and opened the curtains, the flood of sunlight hurting her eyes. She swallowed two Motrin to head off the pounding she was sure was about to start.

At least she wasn't in this nightmare alone anymore. With

Nick to listen and investigate, she knew she had an ally. An image of him drifted through her thoughts, and she wondered when he'd be back. She missed him, she missed the inevitability of his visits, and he'd only been gone a few days. She wondered where he was, and what he was doing, and if just maybe he was thinking about her too.

Stop analyzing this, she chided herself. She took a slow, deep breath and finished up her morning routine before slipping her feet into her worn sandals and stepping out of her room in search of coffee and perhaps the company of Hana.

She poked her head into the kitchen and saw the housekeeper at the sink. "Good morning, Hana."

Hana turned, a look of defeat on her face. She nodded and turned away.

Had she heard something about her son? Abby wondered. She moved closer. "Is everything all right?"

Hana pulled her hands from the soapy water. "Najeela's here. In there." She nodded toward the dining room. "Coffee's in there too."

"Thanks, Hana." Abby took a long, deep breath and headed to the dining room.

"Oh, good morning," Najeela said, her tone as frosty as a Boston winter.

Abby felt the unmistakable chill in the room, but decided to ignore it. "Morning," she said, sliding into a seat and pouring a cup of coffee.

"Uncle Imtiaz told me he stopped by yesterday."

"That's something we should talk about." Abby sipped her coffee, feeling her face flush with anger at the memory.

"He was very disappointed in you." Najeela pouted. "He thought, well, he thought you were rude. I'm sorry to say that, but he felt very badly, and I was surprised to hear it."

"Oh, Najeela, are you kidding me? He shouldn't even be

here! It's not really proper for him to visit me if you're not here, is it?"

Najeela's pout grew thicker, but she was silent.

"And he was aggressive. He has no business touching me or coming here to see me. And you know that."

Najeela's eyes grew wide. "I . . . I, no, he shouldn't be here, you're right. I don't want him to come between us. We are still friends, you and I, aren't we?" Her voice cracked at the question.

"We are, Najeela, we are," Abby said, trying to soothe her friend's hurt feelings. "But I'm not your uncle's friend. Understand?" She reached across the table and took Najeela's hands in her own. "Friends, you and I?"

Najeela nodded. "And, of course, he should never come here if I'm not here. I'll make sure he knows that in the future."

Hana bustled in carrying a tray filled with eggs and toast. The morning menu had certainly improved around here, Abby thought.

"*Shukria,* Hana," Najeela said, reaching for a slice of toast. Her sleeve slipped back from her outstretched arm, revealing a shimmering diamond cuff bracelet.

When Abby caught sight of the glitter, her mouth opened wide in surprise, and she almost choked on the coffee she'd been swallowing.

"Be careful, Abby," Najeela warned. "Don't drink hot coffee too quickly."

Abby sputtered and fought to regain her composure. "Your bracelet is stunning. Is it new?"

Najeela twisted the bangle on her wrist and admired the encrusted gems. The bangle was slim, not the thick cuff of Abby's dream, but the similarity was unmistakable. "I don't think I've ever seen you wear a bracelet," Abby said, trying to keep her tone breezy.

"You haven't? Oh my, I have bracelets, but perhaps I don't wear them often. I think I'm afraid that I'll forget to take them off before I leave for home." She rubbed at the bracelet with her sleeve and held her arm up to Abby. "See how it glitters. I just love it, but if my father saw it, he'd kill me. I know he would."

Abby relaxed. Lots of people had bracelets, for Christ's sake. She was seeing deception and intrigue everywhere. Maybe she'd been listening to Nick's stories a little too much. She decided to change the subject.

"You haven't spoken to your father yet about . . ." Abby paused. She'd forgotten his name. Oh, jeez, what was it?

"Lars," Najeela said quickly. "No, I haven't. There's just so much going on with the government here in Pakistan, the riots and tension. It's just not a good time." Her eyes filled with tears.

"Oh, Najeela, I'm sorry. I haven't even thought to ask how things were. But, don't lose hope. If you're in love, it will work out. You must have faith in that, in him."

Najeela sniffled and wiped her eyes. "Abby, you make me feel better every time we speak. Can we spend the day together? Maybe shop?"

"Oh, sorry. I'm going to that rescue house I told you about. I'm going to help out there."

Najeela's eyes sparkled. "May I come along? Lars would be so proud to know that I'm helping."

"I . . . I, well, I'll ask, but I think since the house is new and people are just getting to know one another, it may be too soon to introduce another new person."

Disappointment etched itself into Najeela's frown. "Don't forget your other duties."

"I won't. And about today, it's just that I'm so new to them, it's not right for me to bring a visitor. You understand?"

Najeela seemed satisfied with Abby's answer. *"Acha."*

"And we'll go out again soon. The Pearl Continental, for lunch?" Abby asked.

Najeela smiled, and they finished breakfast in silence.

Abby rose to leave. "I'll see you later?" she asked, careful not to upset Najeela.

Najeela nodded, and once Abby had gathered her bag, she hurried through the door and to the waiting car.

"Morning, Mohammed. Do you remember the house we went to with Zara?"

He nodded. "Go today?"

Abby smiled in reply. "You remember where it is?"

Mohammed opened the rear door, and Abby slid into the backseat of the car. Her skin was damp with perspiration and she sat uneasily on the vinyl seats. Already, at this early hour, the heat of the day had settled into Peshawar, sucking the air, the life, out of everything. The people and the flowers, she saw as they drove, had gone limp, and even the city's stray dogs were quiet.

The house was quiet too when Abby arrived. *"Salaam,"* she called out, her voice echoing in the empty hallway. "Hello?" she asked into the silence. A patter of feet approached from behind, and Abby, still wary from her dream, spun around anxiously.

Mariyah stood there, a worried look on her face. "We waiting on you," she said slowly, her scar forming a deep frown on her face.

"What is it?" Abby asked.

"Girls gone," Mariyah said.

Abby felt a knot of worry explode in her head.

Chapter 21

Abby raced along the hall to the small room where she'd first met the girls. She opened the door wide. The room was empty.

Abby turned to Mariyah. "Is Zara here?" Oh, God, Abby thought, did someone take them? Imtiaz? Did he know about this house?

"Where is everyone?" she asked too abruptly. Mariyah's face crumpled into fear, and Abby took a deep breath and reached for Mariyah. "I'm sorry. I know that you're afraid for the girls too."

"I afraid, yes. Anyu gone too, and Zara go to Peshawar police station to file report. We not know anything." Mariyah's eyes filled with tears, and she wiped her hand across her face.

The unrelenting fear that until this moment Abby had felt only in her dreams was suddenly real, and she felt acid churning in the pit of her stomach. Her gaze swept the room for anything that would give her a clue, and her eyes fixed on a piece of brown paper tangled in the sheets. The wrapping from her package, she thought, snatching it up like some precious stone. She turned to Mariyah.

A faint smile dotted Mariyah's scarred lips. "Girls receive new things yesterday. Very happy, but not take off other clothes. Put new things on over old smelly clothes." Mariyah held her own nose to demonstrate. "Zara say it because girls afraid. Old things from home—not want to leave behind. Understand?"

Abby nodded and closed her eyes. She felt sick to her stomach at the thought that they were somewhere out there with Anyu. Please, God, she prayed, keep them safe. Find them for us. She stepped outside the room and pulled the door closed behind her. "There's nothing left to do but worry, so let's sit and have some tea until Zara comes."

Mariyah nodded, and Abby followed her into the kitchen, where Bina sat sipping tea. She nodded in silence when Abby entered the room.

Abby swallowed her own fears and tried to smile. "They'll be all right. We have to believe that. Once Zara returns from the police, we'll have an idea of what we can do."

"We have had look around house," Mariyah said. "Money from drawer and a little food from cupboard gone too. Anyu took, we think, to help them run." Mariyah scratched her head. "We would have helped them if they'd asked. Now, we worry."

"What about the guard?" Abby asked. "Didn't he see anything?"

"He asleep. He here but asleep, not see anything. He feel very bad, understand?"

Abby nodded. "But why would Anyu leave? Isn't she safest here?"

Mariyah shrugged. "She afraid she in big trouble because of man in Delhi. She afraid Nick will tell police she here."

"Oh, shit," Abby groaned. "But Nick wouldn't say a word. Ever."

Mariyah nodded, and Bina rose, collecting cups and bowls and spoons. She lit the stove and set the kettle on to boil. She spooned a serving of yogurt into each bowl and passed the first one to Abby, who spooned the creamy blend into her mouth. Her lips puckered instantly at the unexpected sour taste. She tried to smile to prevent the wrinkle in her lips from spreading and looked up to see Mariyah holding back a laugh.

"Sorry, Abby," she said, covering her mouth with her veil, but unable to cover the laugh that escaped from her lips. "We make this. But maybe we need more practice."

Abby let the pucker on her lips fill her mouth and nodded her agreement. The women laughed, then turned as the front door opened and then banged shut. Zara entered the room in a rush of air and threw herself into a chair.

"The police were not much help. They said Pari and Geeta weren't being sold after all. They were headed to Kuwait to be married, and the money that had changed hands was for the dowry. Can you believe that?" Zara dabbed at her eyes. "They said Anyu and the girls have run away from *us,* but since they took our money and food, if we press charges, they will look for them, but if not, they won't help us. They said if they happen to see the girls on the street, they will pick them up, but they are too busy to look for every runaway in Peshawar, and they won't search." A sob escaped Zara's lips. "The girls are just babies, and poor Anyu is broken, and the police won't help. They told me to place their pictures in the Protection Tent. They said it is *my* job to find them, not theirs." Silent tears trickled from Zara's eyes and she wiped at them with her veil. "But we don't even have pictures of them. We don't even have that."

"But we have each other, and we have pictures of all of them in our heads," Abby said. "We can search. They can't have gotten very far."

Zara slumped in her chair. "Abby, how can we look? Where would we even begin?"

"We start here, with you and me, and with Mariyah and Bina, all of us together." Abby looked at each of the women in turn. "Think back to when you were first taken. Bina, you said you'd wanted only to escape. Where did you want to escape to?"

"Home," Bina said sadly and without hesitation. "Same today. For me, home."

Abby motioned to Mariyah, who nodded. "Home," she whispered.

"What about Anyu? Where would she go? Home or Delhi? Which makes sense for her?"

"Maybe home or maybe she'll take the girls to Mumbai," Zara answered. "She was so sad after she shared her story, and I think a part of her was afraid that the police would come and take her away."

"Is Mumbai the best place to look then? Does everyone agree?"

The women nodded, and Abby turned back to Zara. "The police confirmed the girls are from Mumbai?"

"They did. They said the girls were from the slums there."

"Okay," Abby said, "Mumbai. We need a map. I can check on the Internet and look at the route they might take. The train tracks that run through University Town, where do they go?"

"Through Islamabad and on to the border with India," Zara replied.

"Did they take enough money for train fare?"

"Probably it's enough," Zara said.

"Is there an Internet connection here in the house?" Abby asked.

Zara shook her head. "No. We hoped to do that, but not yet."

Abby sighed. "That's a problem. We need to know the roads and train routes before we search. I'm going to have to leave, go back to my house for a bit and research the roads and train routes, and I'll be back. Okay?"

Zara's frown eased. "We can have another look here. See if they left anything behind or maybe there's a hint of their plans. We haven't really looked in Anyu's room. We were just so worried about the girls, we kind of forgot Anyu. We just have to look."

For the first time since she'd learned of the girls' disappearance, Abby felt a tinge of hope, and she smiled. "We can do this. As soon as I can print out some maps and information, I'll be back and we can start looking."

"Nick?" Zara asked. "Has he come back yet?"

Abby shook her head. "Not yet," she said, wishing he were here helping in the search.

Abby and Mohammed pulled into the drive at home at the same moment that a long, black limousine was pulling out. The car stopped abruptly, and Abby, anxious that it might be Imtiaz, watched nervously as a window rolled open. A smiling Najeela leaned out, and Abby, relieved to see it was *her*, waved.

"Abby, I've got to run. I'll see you tomorrow." A sudden breeze ruffled Najeela's hair, and her hands shot up to smooth her waves into place. She sat back quickly, one hand waving as the car pulled away.

Abby was relieved. She could check the routes on the Internet and get back to the rescue house without explaining herself. She raced to the office and tried to connect, but the Internet was down. "Damn it," she shouted, her frustration bubbling over.

Suddenly she heard soft, hurried footsteps, and Hana appeared at the door, worry etched on her face. "What is it?"

"Sorry, Hana. I didn't realize you were here. I just needed to do some work on the Internet and it's down. I'm just frustrated."

A smile twitched at the corners of Hana's mouth. "Your friend the reporter was here."

"Nick?" Abby almost shouted his name. "He's back?"

Hana nodded and handed Abby a business card. "He said to call."

Abby took the card and saw a number scrawled on the back. Abby headed to the hallway. "Hana, I've never asked—does the phone work?"

"It does. Well, it does most days."

Abby picked up the heavy, black phone and dialed the number on the card.

"Green's Hotel," a woman answered softly.

"Nick Sinclair's room, please."

The phone rang, and after what seemed an eternity, Nick finally answered, his voice heavy with sleep. "Hello."

"Nick, it's Abby—"

"I'll see you later."

Abby knew that he was about to hang up, that she had exactly one second to get his attention. "No," she shouted, her voice a little too shrill. "Don't hang up, and don't go back to sleep. It's important."

Nick cleared his throat, and Abby could almost feel that he had snapped to attention. "What is it?"

"I can't tell you over the phone, but can you just get here?"

"Jesus, are you all right?"

"I am, but just get here. Okay?"

"Okay. Give me a few minutes and I'm on my way."

Abby sighed heavily and replaced the phone on its old cradle. When she turned, Hana was standing there, her arms folded, her eyes intent on Abby.

"Is everything all right?"

"I'm not sure. I'm worried about a friend. Do you know anything about these railroad tracks that run along this road out front?"

"I know the trains come by once, sometimes twice, a day to Islamabad, and you can change there to India. Are you traveling?"

Abby shook her head. "Is it expensive?"

"No, you can travel for eight hundred rupees."

Abby's brain jammed as she tried to calculate the dollar equivalent. It was one hundred rupees to a dollar so . . .

"About eight US dollars," Hana said, sensing Abby's confusion.

"Thanks, Hana. How do you know all this?"

"I wasn't always a housekeeper," she snapped, scurrying off down the hall.

Anyu and the girls could be on a train, and if they were, if they were already traveling, there'd be no way to find them. Abby fell into her chair and sighed.

When Nick arrived, he was as scraggly and unkempt as the first day Abby had met him. His hair was tousled, his face was rough with a new growth of beard, but his eyes still sparkled with the same intensity, and this time she felt her heart race at the sight of him. It was just the scare with the girls, she chided herself, nothing more. Still, she couldn't hold back the smile that spread across her face.

"Nick"—she wrapped her arms around his neck—"I'm so glad you're here."

He leaned in and kissed her, and Abby inhaled the familiar scent of stale cigarettes and old whiskey. She touched his face, the beard stubble scratching her fingertips. She couldn't explain it, but she felt safe with him, and more than that, she felt cared for in a way she never had with Eric. Nick, she knew, would look out for her no matter what.

He took her hand, concern in his eyes. "What the hell is it? What's happened?"

"There's been trouble, Nick. I need your help. I told you I was going back to the rescue house, right?"

Nick nodded and sat.

Abby pulled a second chair close. She told him the story of the girls who'd been trafficked and sold and had maybe been headed to Kuwait, and their sudden disappearance. "Nick, they're just kids—even Anyu is still a kid, maybe a little rough around the edges, but kids, and they're out there alone. It scares me senseless."

"Shit." Nick sat forward and leaned on the desk. "Any idea where they'd go?"

"Well, home seems the most likely destination, but home for Anyu is northern India, and Mumbai for the girls. And I'm not sure what Anyu is thinking. Is she trying to help the girls or are they a cover for her own escape?" Abby tried to sort out her own thoughts. "Did you make it to Delhi?"

"I did, and no surprise, the police weren't very forthcoming. An American journalist asking about their unsolved murders rankled a few of them, but I did get some information. This year already, they've had almost four hundred murders, and two-thirds of those are still unsolved. There were thirty-two murder victims found in the red-light district around G. B. Road, and eighteen of those cases are still open. A few could have been Anyu's, but the more I think about it, I think it's likely her brothel dumped the body somewhere else to avoid questions and trouble," Nick said, rubbing his eyes.

"I hadn't even thought of that, but it makes sense, doesn't it? What does it mean for Anyu?"

"It means she should stay out of Delhi, and she probably shouldn't go home, but people never do what they should."

A frown crept across Abby's face. "Where do we start? Jesus, this is harder than I thought it would be."

"Just think. They all want to get out of Pakistan, right?"

Abby nodded. "That was our theory, and we thought maybe they'd take the train. They all speak a little English, but I'm willing to bet they don't know enough Urdu to manage on their own." Abby pointed to her computer. "I was trying to get online to get some maps, figure out where these train tracks just outside go."

"To Islamabad, and from there, you can get to Delhi, but Mumbai's a long way off."

"Will you help? I want to look for them. They're so little, and even Anyu is still a girl. They could all be in way more trouble than they were before."

Nick sighed. "You didn't tell Najeela about the girls?"

"No, not about *them,* but I had to tell her about the house." Abby caught the look of reproach in Nick's eyes. "I can't just disappear for hours. I didn't tell her anything else. That's not all—Imtiaz showed up here right before the girls disappeared. He somehow knew that you were away, and he hoped I'd, well, never mind what he hoped."

Suddenly, Nick was wide-awake, all traces of sleepiness gone from his eyes. "Jesus, what the hell did he want? Are you okay?"

Abby nodded. "I'm fine. Hana scared him off."

"Hana? Well, I'll be damned." His eyes locked onto hers. "I won't leave again, Abby. At least not without you."

Inexplicable relief surged through Abby, and she turned away, avoiding his gaze.

"Did Imtiaz know about the girls? Or even the house? Could Najeela have told him? Jesus," he said, scratching his head, "there's a damn tangled web here. We're going to have to unravel the whole mess."

"I know," Abby said impatiently. "Can we get going?"

Nick stood and stretched. "Where to first?" he asked, walking toward the front door.

"The rescue house first. I promised I'd be back. I only came here to print out some maps and train schedules, but the Internet's down."

They stopped first at the women's house long enough to let them know that Nick was back and he was going to help with the search.

"Zara," Abby asked, "do you want to come? Maybe just to be safe we should have you with us. Two Americans looking for three girls equals trouble."

Zara hesitated. "We are grateful for your help, Nick, and I will come to the train station to help, but then I must get to the tent. That's my job. I have responsibilities there."

"That's okay, that's enough, Zara. If you can get us through the maze of the Peshawar train station, we'll be all set," Nick said.

The three headed to the car. Nick sped through the streets, somehow maneuvering the car in and out of traffic and between people and buildings before gliding into a parking spot at the Peshawar railway station. The building was nice—two stories, white and blue—peaceful almost in this bustling place where the crowds hurried, shoving, elbowing, and shouting their way to the ticket booths. Soldiers and police, guns at the ready, stood off to the side, occasionally growling orders to the mob.

Zara looked around and shook her head. "I think this place would scare them off. Even Anyu—too many people, too much noise, a scary place for girls who don't want to be seen. If they did take the train, they didn't get tickets, I think. I suppose they may have slipped aboard somewhere."

"But you said they're from Mumbai, and Anyu's been in Delhi. If they live in the slums in those spots, the chaos here might feel familiar, comfortable," Nick said, shoving his hands into his pockets.

They headed out to the platform, a wide concrete slab with trains running in a pit in the center. The chaos of the station had spread out here, and the noise of the crowd, the animals, and the thundering trains was deafening. Even the sky was somehow changed and the sun was almost lost in the haze of smoke and smog and steam. The web of wires and cables that ran overhead only added to the frenzied feel of the place. Tea and trinket sellers hawked their wares, and screaming children jostled old women. Scrawny boys lugged heavy bundles on their backs and pulled rickety wooden carts loaded with boxes and bags. The place was too crowded to even keep your eye on one person for long. There was too much movement and activity. Even the soldiers and police seemed at a disadvantage and stood back, looking around aimlessly, occasionally snarling at people to keep moving.

A long train, its engine heaving, groaned to a stop, spewing steam and dirt and heat into the crowd, which surged forward. Abby and the others held back, afraid of being swept up in the crush of people.

In this place, someone, a child maybe, could hide, even live, for a few days. If Pari and Geeta and Anyu had been here, they might be here still. A lone tree on the other side of the tracks caught Abby's eye. That might be a place the three would wander, a place to nap or just watch for an opportunity to jump a train.

"They might be here," Abby said, her gaze drawn to a band of grimy children running along the platform.

Nick shrugged. "I guess it's possible."

"I don't think they'd stay here. I think if they didn't get on a train, they are on the roads. For me, that makes the most sense," Zara said so quietly Abby had to strain to hear. Zara looked quickly at her watch. "It is late, and time for me to go, I am sorry to say. Will you drive me to the camp, Nick?"

Abby took one last look around and saw again the group of disheveled children running roughly through the crowd. She watched as one reached out and grabbed a packet of cookies as he ran, and she smiled. Survival of the fittest, she thought, narrowing her gaze, hoping that the girls might be among them. But the group scurried off before she could get a closer look.

The three headed out and sat in silence in the car. Disappointment hung in the small, airless space like a heavy fog. In the front, Nick yawned and Abby watched as his shoulders sagged. He drove recklessly, weaving in and out of traffic, and Zara breathed an audible sigh of relief when they arrived at Safar. She opened the rear door quickly and almost jumped out.

"I will see you later today or perhaps tomorrow. But, please, if you learn anything, find me here or at the rescue house. *Acha?*"

Abby stepped into the searing glare of the sun and squinted. "*Acha,* Zara. We will find you if there is any news, and *inshallah,* there will be some."

"*Khoda khafez,*" Zara said, waving as she stepped into the Protection Tent.

Abby slipped into the front passenger seat. "I know you're exhausted, but can we look once more and then call it a day?"

Nick rubbed at his eyes. "Why not? I'm awake now anyway."

"Can we go back to the train station?"

"I knew you were going to ask that, but not now, and here's why. That place is too crowded and too dangerous for us. If the girls are there, we'll never see them, and if they've seen us, they're either hiding or on the run. Not to mention, we're two Americans in the terrorism capital of the world." The creases in his forehead deepened as he spoke. "So—imagine this. We actually see them, and no surprise, they run. What do we do? We run like hell after them," he said, looking into Abby's eyes. "And what do you think will happen next?"

Abby returned his stare. "I know you're going to tell me."

"The locals spy us, two foreigners chasing after three young girls. Not a pretty sight, is it? I think it would take them about ten seconds to load their weapons and aim them at us. And while I'm pretty confident that I carry the right ammunition to win a battle of wits anywhere in the world, I'm at a distinct disadvantage in a gun battle, and I'm going to do my best to avoid one."

Abby exhaled, whistling as she did. "Hard to argue with that, but I have to say, I'm not ready to give up. You wouldn't be either if you'd seen them, Nick." She turned her gaze back to the road, and she felt the car accelerate.

"I've met Anyu, so I do understand." His foot bore down on the gas. "So for now, let's drive along the tracks, have a look, and consider all of the possibilities. First, did anyone else know about them?"

Abby shook her head. "No, Nick. I didn't tell a soul."

"How'd you get to the house, then?"

"Mohammed, the driver," she said, her voice tinged with surprise. "You don't think . . . ?"

"We have to think of everything and everyone. Did he know about the girls?"

Abby looked away, her voice soft. "He did. He took me to a shop in the bazaar to get new clothes for them, but that still doesn't mean anything."

"Probably not, but we can't let anything slide."

He drove alongside the tracks, crisscrossing the rutted roads until the tracks ran along Railway Road not far from Abby's house. From there he caught Saddar Road before turning onto Grand Trunk Road. Abby peered through the grimy windshield scanning the landscape and the faces of the children they passed. Once they'd left the city center, the smooth surface gave way to dirt and dust and sleepy villages—too sleepy, too small, Abby thought, not a place where strangers could hide, especially girls on their own. The futility of their search suddenly struck Abby and she turned to Nick.

"I know you're helping and I'm grateful, really I am, but they're not here. I still think they're in the city, in the train station probably."

"Maybe," Nick said, "but I think if they were there, they're long gone by now. These are smart kids who don't want to be found. You said they took money, right?"

Abby nodded.

"Well, they probably had a plan, and in this instance, while that's bad for us and limits our chances of finding them, it's good for them. Means they just might get home."

"But home got them into trouble in the first place. Won't they just be sold again or even punished for getting away?"

Nick sighed. "Probably," he said sadly. "Probably, and the reality is home is a damn long way away, but if that's their dream, they might make it."

Two little girls suddenly darted into the road, and when they spied the car bearing down on them, they turned and ran.

"Stop!" Abby shouted, and Nick ground his foot down on

the brakes. The car skidded in the dirt and Abby opened the door.

"Do *not* leave this car, Abby," Nick said sternly. "You don't know who those two kids you're so keen on chasing are. You're running on nerves, and you've forgotten everything I just told you. You step out and run after those two, and you'll be dead in a New York minute. Just slow down and shut that damn door."

Abby reached out and closed the door. "Sorry, Nick, it's just they're about the right size."

"Abby, even if those two kids you were just so desperate to chase *were* your victims, you can't just go running off to rescue people who are probably more afraid to go with *you* than to stay where they are. For them, the devil they know is better than the devil they don't."

Abby rolled up her window and, exhaling noisily, folded her arms.

"Just relax, will ya?" he said, sensing her anger. "We'll keep trying, but take a deep breath. Rome wasn't built in a day."

"God, for a Pulitzer Prize winner, you sure speak in clichés."

Nick smiled. "I do believe that's the second-nicest thing you've ever said to me."

Abby smiled and relaxed in her seat.

They drove on through countless nameless villages, all with small storefronts boasting COCA-COLA SOLD HERE. Children ran all over the roads and alongside the car once they realized foreigners were inside. Little girls and skinny boys stretched out their grimy hands and shouted, "Gimme, mister." One especially dirty young boy with matted hair, a dirt-stained face, and eyes as black as coal caught up with the car and shouted, "Just gimme, gimme here!" He pointed wildly to his open palm, and Abby hurried to search through her pockets.

Nick shook his head. "Not here, Abby. There's too many of

them and not enough of us. I don't want to start trouble, and way out here, we got no one looking out for us. Matter of fact"—he began turning the car around in the road—"it's just about that time. We should head back. There's nothing out here."

Abby's heart sank. She knew he was right, but she didn't want to give up, not yet. She looked at her watch. It was almost four o'clock already. If Pari and Geeta and Anyu were out here somewhere, they'd probably hide before night fell.

Nick steered the car back onto the dusty road. "Ordinarily, as you well know," he said with a wink, "I'd suggest the club, but today, I gotta get some sleep. Jesus, I'm beat, just beat. You okay?"

"Oh, Nick, thanks, but I know you're tired. It's all right. We can catch up tomorrow—you can tell me all about your trip."

"Oh shit. That's right. I forgot already."

"Nothing noteworthy, then?" Abby asked, unable to hide the disappointment in her voice.

"Just the opposite—I have plenty to tell you, but it can wait till tomorrow. You at the house or the clinic?"

"Tomorrow's Thursday, so both."

"I'll pick you up at the clinic then." Nick parked in front of Abby's house. "In the early afternoon, all right? We can go to the rescue house and then the club."

Abby leaned over and planted a quick kiss on Nick's stubbly cheek. "It's a date." She climbed out and shut the door behind her. "I'm really glad you're back, Nick." She smiled—*glad* was a bit of an understatement, and though she didn't know quite what was going on, she did know Nick Sinclair had stirred something in her.

Nick smiled and ran his hand along the stubble on his chin. "I'm pretty happy about that myself."

Chapter 22

*P*ari and Geeta were running just ahead. "Catch us, Abby," Geeta screeched. Abby sprinted, but the girls seemed to get farther and farther away, and each time Abby was sure she was gaining on them, they slipped from her grasp.

"Wait," Abby shouted. "Wait for me." But the girls were too far away to hear her warning, and when they turned a bend, Abby lost sight of them. She picked up her pace, but the girls were nowhere in sight.

"Geeta, Pari," she shouted, but their names echoed back in the quiet of the day. She ran until she fell to the ground in exhaustion.

"Abby," Geeta called suddenly, and when Abby looked up, she

saw him, the tall, thin, bespectacled man. He was grinning and holding Geeta over his shoulder. Geeta waved wildly, and Abby saw the sparkling bracelet on her wrist. The familiar diamonds, rubies, and sapphires twinkled obscenely on the tiny girl's arm, and Abby pulled herself to her feet.

"Geeta," she shouted, "get away from him!"

But Geeta was tight in his grip, and Pari was at his side, her hand tucked firmly into his. The man turned and looked at Abby and smiled.

A choking sob escaped from Abby's lips. "You bastard!" she shouted, running after them. "Let them go."

But she lost sight of them again, and when they turned the next corner, they were swallowed up by the city's streets.

The girls were gone.

She pulled herself up and looked around. Shit, she thought as the pounding began in the back of her head. She reached for her bottle of Motrin and gulped down two pills. The unrelenting morning sun seeped in through the drawn shade, and already Abby could feel the heat of the day pulsing there. She swung her legs over the side of the bed. Maybe there'd be news today.

When she headed into the dining room, Najeela was there, a smile on her lips. "Good morning, you!"

Abby grunted in reply. She was in no mood for Najeela today. She wanted to get back to the rescue house and the search for the girls, but today was Thursday and she had to get to the clinic first.

"What is it?" Najeela asked. "You look so sad."

"I didn't sleep well. The heat."

"You poor thing, you look terrible. I'll ask Hana to keep the generator on. Here, have something to eat." Najeela pushed the tray of bread to Abby.

Abby pulled her hair back from her face. "Just coffee for me. I have to get going."

"Oh, Abby, you don't have to go to the clinic today, do you?"

Something about Najeela's syrupy tone nettled Abby. "I do, yes," she snapped in reply.

Najeela looked away and dabbed at the beads of sweat that had collected on her face. "The heat is affecting all of us."

Abby sighed. Still, she couldn't afford to ruffle Najeela's feathers. "Sorry, Najeela. I have a lot to do. We'll spend time together later this week, I promise," Abby said, crossing her fingers.

"You should take today off, that's what you should do." Najeela reached up and smoothed the waves in her hair.

"I don't think the UN would like that, do you?"

Najeela frowned. "After clinic?"

"Going to the house," Abby said, a little too quickly.

"Ohh," Najeela cooed. "Really, Abby, aren't you spending a little too much time there?"

"No, Najeela, I'm not, and I'm keeping up with my immunization work." Abby took a sip of coffee. "I don't mean to sound abrupt, but I'm doing my work."

"What do you do at that house anyway?" Najeela asked, a pout playing on her lips.

"Nothing, yet. I'm just meeting the victims, listening. It's all so sad. I mean, these women are so young and they've gone through just unimaginable pain. Najeela, the stories would break your heart. They've been kidnapped or sold or lied to. Some creep tells these poorest of the poor he has a great job for them and then throws them into a brothel." Abby took a deep breath. "I can't even imagine what they've been through."

Najeela rolled her eyes. "Don't be too naive, Abby. Not all the missing are taken against their will. They leave looking for something better, and when things don't work out the way they'd hoped, they cry rape or kidnapping or whatever."

Abby's eyes opened wide in disbelief. "You don't believe that, do you?"

"Well, I guess I'm not sure," Najeela replied nervously. "I told you that my Lars helps these women, didn't I?"

"You did. But you never said exactly what it is he does."

"He works with the UN. Well, he volunteers really, and he helps the women by speaking to them, taking them under his wing. I think he's hired one or two as housekeepers. He's a very good man. He donates a large amount of money to the UN. To tell you the truth," Najeela said conspiratorially, "I think I'll put a stop to that. We'll need the money to get started in married life."

"You must be proud of him, but the problem of trafficking is huge, you must see that." Abby's gaze burned into Najeela's kohl-lined eyes.

Najeela seemed to squirm in her seat. "Suit yourself," she said testily. "I think it is a small problem, not so big as you think." She stood and draped her veil over her head. "Remember, it is the vaccines that should consume your time. Not a silly program for these women."

Abby looked away, afraid that if she spoke again, she'd cross the line. She chewed on her lip and watched as Najeela headed to the door.

"See you later, Abby," she said peevishly.

Abby gulped down her coffee and stewed. She knew her damn job, and she knew she was doing it well. But she knew too that she felt compelled to work at the rescue house. There was no way she'd give that up just to assuage Najeela's feelings.

Abby finished her breakfast and grabbed her bag before heading out to the car.

"Morning, Mohammed," she said, remembering Nick's question from the day before. Did Mohammed know, she wondered, what that house was for, that there were girls there? She eyed him suspiciously before she caught him watching her just as carefully.

"Morning, miss," he said cheerfully. "Are you all right today?"

"I am, Mohammed, thanks for asking. Sorry if I seem out of it. Just tired, I guess." She settled into the rear seat.

She looked up and saw Mohammed watching her through the rearview mirror. "Camp or the house again?"

"Camp," she said, deciding Nick's suspicious view of the world was adversely affecting her behavior. He was right about one thing—she couldn't just race off thinking she could rescue everyone. She sat back and watched the streets, filled this morning with beggar children, and her eyes followed a scruffy girl as she skipped along, darting around a merchant's stacks. She watched as the girl snatched a small chicken. Dodging just out of reach of the bellowing shopkeeper, she disappeared into a long, dark passageway. Abby craned to see, but the girl had made good her escape.

Mohammed guided the car into a shady spot in the Safar parking area. "Thanks, Mohammed." Abby slid from her seat. "I'll be here most of the day, but I have a ride with Nick this afternoon, so you're free unless Najeela or Hana needs you."

"*Khoda khafez,* miss," he said, smiling as he backed the car onto the dusty road and turned for home.

Abby headed into the clinic expecting to see Mariyah, but she was nowhere in sight, and already the registration line snaked out the door. "Morning, Simi," Abby said. "Is Mariyah here?"

Simi shook her head. "No, so it is good we have you. Now that you are here, Shoma can register with me."

Abby hurried to the vaccination area, Mariyah's absence hovering in the back of her mind. Had there been news? Was that what kept Mariyah away? No use dwelling on it right now, she had to get through the day first. "Good morning, Nasreen, Shoma," she said, greeting the two nurses. "I'm going to be in here today, and Shoma can help in registration. *Acha?*"

"Acha," they giggled in unison, and Shoma scurried away.

Abby bent to her work, distracted and anxious, and praying for the day to move quickly. The line of patients was endless, and before long Abby and Nasreen had settled into the smooth and now familiar rhythm of vaccines and check marks. "Next," Abby called again and again, until the line of waiting patients had shrunk. Abby looked at Nasreen. "Finish?" she asked, hoping Nasreen would understand that she was ready to leave. It was one o'clock and she wanted to get to the Protection Tent to see if Zara was in.

Nasreen smiled. *"Acha,* Abby."

"Shukria, Nasreen." Abby ran sanitizer over her hands. "I'll see you all next week." She grabbed her bag and left the clinic. She hurried to the Protection Tent and stepped inside, where she spied Nick off to the side, deep in discussion with Zara. They both turned when Abby entered, and she hurried to join them.

"Any news?" she asked eagerly.

Zara shook her head. "Nothing, and in some ways, that is good news. I think they've made it safely out of Peshawar and probably out of Pakistan. *Inshallah,* they will all arrive safely to the place their hearts call home."

"But will they be safe there?"

"We cannot know that, Abby, but if the girls find peace there, then they must try. Understand?"

Abby nodded, though she wasn't sure she understood why any of them would return to the places and people that had deceived them. She wouldn't go back, and she didn't think Anyu would either, but it wasn't her choice, it was theirs. She sighed. "Is Mariyah all right?" she asked. "She wasn't in today."

"She is fine, but we've decided that someone should always be at the house."

"Good idea," Abby muttered, turning to Nick, who was now clean shaven, with clear eyes and even combed hair. He looked handsome, she thought, and caught herself before she stared right through him.

"Lunch?" he asked.

"Yeah, I guess there's nothing else to do right now." Abby turned to Zara.

"There is nothing right now for either of you to do. I think they are gone, but I will keep you informed, I promise. *Acha?*" Zara said.

"*Acha,*" Abby replied, disappointed that there would be no search today.

"Okay then," Nick said. "Let's go." He nodded at Zara and guided Abby through the wall of pictures.

She hesitated. "Can I check for Hana's son? I know he's still missing too."

Nick shuffled his feet, and she glanced quickly toward him, but a mask of indifference had slipped over his face. Abby scanned the rows of pictures, but Hana's boy was nowhere to be found. Abby felt a tiny bubble of panic welling up and turned to Nick. "I don't see his picture," she said, worried. "Could something have happened?"

Nick shrugged. "I don't know, Abby, maybe his picture's been moved, maybe she found him."

"Not with her moods, she hasn't." Abby thought for a

minute. Wasn't Hana friendlier, less angry, at least a little, or was she just imagining that? "Should I ask her?"

"I wouldn't. Just leave her alone. If she wants to share stuff with you, she will."

The sudden impatience in his tone made Abby wince. She'd thought they were past that antagonism by now.

"Let's go," he said, "the club is calling my name, and there's a medium-rare steak and tumbler full of expensive scotch waiting for me."

"The club has expensive scotch?"

Nick shook his head. "Probably not, but any scotch is good scotch."

Abby smiled. "You're either a raving alcoholic or a comedian, and I'm not sure which."

"I'm neither, Abby. I aspire to hard living and hard drinking. Isn't that what all the best writers do?"

Abby couldn't hold back the smile that burst through her lips. "Could be. But it makes me glad I'm a nurse."

"And I bet you're a damn fine nurse." He opened the car door for her. "But you're more than a nurse these days. You're a bit of an investigator, aren't you?" He slid his key into the ignition and groaned as the car rumbled to life. "Here's another thing to be glad for—I'm grateful every time this old jalopy starts."

Chapter 23

The old sedan grunted and squealed as they made their way to the club. Once they arrived, a smiling guard greeted Abby. "Good to have you back, miss. Nice to see you too, Nick."

"Looks like I have competition for favorite guest." Nick steered her past the club's dining room, to the stairway and their table in the corner, where Nick collapsed into a chair. "For once, I wish they had waiters." He sighed noisily.

Abby stood. "Steak, medium rare, and their finest scotch, right?" She turned and headed to the bar, returning with two glasses of scotch. She slid into her seat. "Food's coming, but in the meantime"—she clinked her glass against his—"I'm glad you're back. You're a colossal pain in the ass, but I missed you, and I'm glad you're here."

"I missed you too, Abby. Didn't I tell you I'd win you over?" He threw back the scotch in one quick gulp.

"Slow down. We have business, you and I. Tell me everything, and start at the beginning."

"There is a lot to tell." Nick was suddenly serious. He leaned across the table. "Trafficking is a big business. It's a damned bonanza—third-biggest illegal business in the world behind arms and drugs, and it has an endless supply of resources. While the supply of drugs and arms could dry up, there'll always be girls and women to exploit. It's a thirty-two-billion-dollar-a-year business."

"Thirty-two billion? Why the hell hasn't it been stopped?"

"Thirty-two billion reasons, I'd say. Let's face it—that's more than enough money to grease plenty of palms. Easy enough to look the other way if it doesn't affect you directly."

"Tell me about India." Abby took a slow sip of her scotch. Her mouth puckered into a frown, and she slid the glass to Nick. "God, I hate the taste of this stuff. I just like the way I sound when I order it—*scotch straight up*—makes me feel sophisticated."

Nick took the glass and raised it toward Abby. "You're plenty sophisticated, young lady. Don't forget that." He settled back into his seat and looked around. "I missed this place, which I suppose doesn't say much for my own sense of sophistication."

"Okay, okay, let's move on, shall we? India?"

"Incredibly easy to slip in and out. That border is porous as hell. No real oversight, and so few manned checkpoints you can just stroll across. The Pakistanis and Indians spend all their energy on the Kashmir border, each side convinced the other is going to steal some bit of land or power, and unfortunately, the result is that stolen people, our trafficking victims, can be slipped right through."

"Did you have a visa?"

Nick shook his head. "Not for India. I wanted to check the borders, and I figured the best way to do that was to test them for myself. I slipped through, in *and* out, so if those girls are heading back, they can do it too."

Abby felt the ache in her heart throb at the mention of the three girls. "What's it like there?"

"It's a tough place, Abby. It's beautiful and desperate and packed with starving people. Not an easy place to make a life."

"Delhi?"

"No more than I told you yesterday. Delhi is the crime capital of India, and two-thirds of those crimes are unsolved, but you can't blame the police. It's just, well, it's an easy place to hide a murder." He took a slow sip of his drink. "That's good for Anyu. She's probably safe as long as she stays out of Delhi."

"What about the brothels? Did you check them out?"

"I thought you'd never ask," he said with a wink. "I went to two in Delhi. I got into rooms in both under the guise of, well, business as usual. As soon as I started asking questions and looking around, the girls went screaming, convinced I was some kind of new Delhi policeman."

"What did you do?"

"I ran like hell. No visa, and no business there either. Best just to get the hell out. If the police ever came, they'd realize I was the foreigner who'd been asking them questions about murder, and I'd be in the slammer. So I ran, and here I am."

"You didn't go to Geneva?"

"I did. I flew from Islamabad and stayed at your hotel, Les Armures Hôtel. Nice place, huh?"

"It was nice, but I can't take credit. The UN booked me there."

"So I walked all over the city—found the business district. And you're right, it's not far from the hotel. Anyway, I spent most of my time wandering through the UN offices. Quite a place. It's big, too big almost to break through the bureaucracy."

"You didn't get anything?"

"I didn't say that, but it wasn't easy. There's one guy, this Rousseau I told you about, a big-shot ex-diplomat and philanthropist. His virtual fingerprints and sponsorship are on so many forged documents it's staggering, but when I tried to ask, I was rebuffed. The guy is some kind of god there."

Abby groaned. "So we're at a roadblock?"

"I don't know. There's no connection that I could find from Rousseau to Imtiaz or anyone else even remotely shady. Who knows? Maybe this guy's a dupe, the unwitting front for the operation, but I have a hunch about him. I just couldn't break through the UN's barriers."

The scowling barman appeared with their food. "Didn't ya hear me? Your food's gonna be cold, for Christ's sake."

"Sorry, Al," Nick said. "How about another round?"

"Diet Coke for me," Abby said, picking up her burger. "The UN, Nick. Don't lose your train of thought."

"I won't," he said through a mouthful of steak. "Perfection," he murmured.

"Geneva, Nick, Geneva."

"Right. Do you know how many people work for the UN and its umbrella organizations? Well over a hundred thousand, and that doesn't even include the consultants, the volunteers, the hangers-on, the visitors, the donors; the list is endless. The potential for corruption at every level is limitless, and it's damn near impossible to investigate everyone. It's the perfect place to hide—under the cover of UN staff. And I can't find a single connection between Rousseau and Imtiaz. So who knows, maybe I'm looking in the wrong direction."

"Any chance Najeela's father is the connection? He works for the UN."

"He does, but he's squeaky-clean, and it looks like he's planning a run for the presidency once Karzai's out. I don't think he's my guy."

Abby wrinkled her brow. "What about the woman, the murder? Did you check it out?"

"Ah, that's where it gets very interesting, and very dicey. Turns out the body of a foreign woman *was* found in a Dumpster near *my* suspect's office. The Dumpster explains why you couldn't find the body when you went back with the police."

Abby's jaw dropped. "Who was she?"

"Not a clue, literally. No identification on her, and the police couldn't find anyone who knew her. But her injuries were consistent with a fall, and they did find defensive wounds on her hands and arms. Whoever she was, she fought like hell. There's no way she jumped, and the police have scrapings from under her fingernails—probably her attacker's skin and DNA. They've left the case open, a questionable homicide, they said. But as of now, they have no suspects, no victim ID, and no witness, unless you come forward. I asked about you, not by name, but I asked if they'd connected it to the tourist who'd claimed she'd seen a woman fall. Know what they told me?"

"They told you they had no record, right? No surprise, the police never wrote anything down that day, and they never did a report once they decided I was crazy."

Nick nodded. "We'll go back and rectify that. Make sure there's a record this time."

"Poor woman. But she was murdered, right, Nick? It really happened, it wasn't my imagination?"

"Looks like it. I asked the police for a photo of the woman, said I thought I might know her from India."

"Did you get it? Do you have it?"

"Not yet, I had to put in my request and I'm waiting for the police to approve that, and then they'll e-mail it. That could take weeks. You never said what she looked like. Do you remember?"

"I remember, and the eerie thing is, to me she looks like every woman here—long black hair, olive skin, delicate almost. I think I'd know her if I saw a photo."

Nick nodded. "I don't know how we can connect her to my guy, but it's worth a look."

"So what is this guy Rousseau like?"

"For starters, he's got quite a pedigree. Swiss businessman and philanthropist on the surface, but he's got quite a past— an international financier and likely crook who has somehow evaded the authorities all these years through his philanthropic work. Every time it seems the jig is up, he donates a fortune and his troubles are over." Nick shook his head and paused for effect. "Interestingly, on the side, he's a diamond broker involved in the sale of blood diamonds, so we know ethics aren't an issue for him."

"And the body was found near *his* office?" Abby could barely hold back the rush of excitement she felt at having a likely suspect for the murder.

Nick held up his hand. "I know what you're thinking, but hold your horses. I checked with his office and he wasn't in town. He was in Paris brokering some big-money deal, but there's no real proof of that. The police in Geneva never questioned him." Nick threw up his hands in mock resignation. "So who knows? Maybe someone in his office is the real culprit—you know, a murderer and a connection to Imtiaz. On the other hand, it may be just a pack of lies. Rousseau's office releases what he tells them to release." Nick sipped at his drink. "In a perfect world, we'd wrap it up just like that, but this is a veritable web of lies, and snaring the spider is no easy task."

"And you're absolutely certain Imtiaz is involved?" Abby picked at her sandwich.

"No doubt. I've had him in my sights for more than a year."

"A year? You've been working on this for a year?"

Nick nodded. "In between my other stuff. And the buzz on Imtiaz is that he replaced Hamid Karzai's brother on the CIA payroll."

"The CIA? So, doesn't that put him in the good column?"

Nick shook his head. "Not this time it doesn't. The rumors swirled that President Karzai's half brother was into drug trafficking, and that he got away with it courtesy of the CIA. When he was assassinated, Imtiaz stepped into the void."

Abby's mouth fell open.

"Exactly," Nick said. "But I don't think the CIA will stand by if they catch him trafficking people. Shit, they have to draw the line somewhere."

"But that actually fits. I thought it was crazy when Najeela told me that Imtiaz wanted her father to replace Karzai once he steps down from the presidency, but that kind of makes sense now. Jesus, that web of yours just grows and grows."

"It does, and now you know why I'm so intent on getting him. It's taken a year of background work, and when I finally had enough to take to my editor, I got the green light for Peshawar. And the rest, as they say, is history." Nick lifted his drink to his lips and took a long, slow sip. "Let me tell you, I had no idea my aid-worker assignment would bring me to you."

Abby smiled. "You should be paying me."

"I should—but I won't. Although I could try to slip you in on my expense voucher as a consultant. But, for now"—he gestured to the food—"consider this an installment."

"Are you going to speak with Imtiaz?"

"Not alone, I'm not. I'm not sure what to do. I'd like to catch him in a crowd in the full light of day, but that's probably a pipe dream."

"What if I speak to him? I mean, he likes me. Maybe he'd let something slip."

Nick put his glass down. "Abby, hear this—stay away from that SOB. Do you hear me? He's dangerous, and I don't want you in his line of fire."

"I know. I just want to do something. What about the girls? Can we look again?"

Nick shook his head. "They're gone. And they're better off than they were just a few weeks ago. I think they'll probably make it home, though I'm not sure about Anyu. And though I hope she stays out of Delhi, and away from her village, I think the only people looking for her are the thugs who ran her brothel."

Abby sat back and wondered what Emily would think if she e-mailed her about everything that was happening. She closed her eyes. It was pretty incredible, the murder in Geneva, the tragedy of trafficking, the intrigue with Uncle Imtiaz, and Nick's suspect. Nick would probably kill her, but Em would be impressed as hell, and she was halfway around the world. It wasn't as if Em would tell people anyway. What could it hurt?

"The murder again?" Nick asked.

Abby's eyes snapped open. "No, just thinking."

"Ah," he sighed. "A thinking woman, the bane of every man's existence."

Abby threw her napkin at him and smiled when it landed in his scotch. "You're a tad out of touch for a hotshot reporter."

Chapter 24

*S*he peered through a tiny gap in the hedge and watched as the man appeared. He stood for a minute in the doorway, squinting and looking this way and that. Finally, he approached the body and knelt over the woman. Abby could see his shoulders and arms moving, pulling at something. The broken eyeglasses! He was pulling them from her hand. He tugged again, and Abby could see the woman's glistening bracelet in the palm of his hand before his fingers curled around it.

He stood and turned, his eyes scanning the street. Abby knew he was looking for her. She scrunched lower and tried to push farther against the wall. He turned toward the hedges and seemed *to hesitate for a minute before he picked up his pace and moved purposefully toward her. Time seemed to stop, and Abby held her breath, the only sounds his footfalls as he approached, and the pounding of her racing heart.*

She watched him—memorizing every detail—the charcoal sweater, slender build, thinning hair, the small eyes lost in pale flesh. When he turned abruptly and dashed back into the building, Abby saw her chance.

She pushed her way out of the hedge and turned, running faster than she had ever before. If he saw her, he would kill her. She knew it. She picked up her pace and wound her way through the streets and back to the area where the UN and government buildings were. She pumped her arms ferociously and moved at what felt like lightning speed.

Her legs jerking wildly, Abby sat upright in her bed. Her mind registered that neither her heart nor her head was pounding, and a swell of relief washed over her. It was real, every bit of it, and that was how it had happened. The woman *had* been murdered, and the man had snatched the only connections to him—the glasses and the bracelet—from her lifeless hand. Abby was absolutely certain of that now.

She was certain too that the woman who had died was Pakistani, or maybe from India. Her olive skin and her clothing indicated that, and though Abby had no proof, she wondered if the woman had been a trafficking victim, forgotten by all but her killer.

Abby sighed and, throwing her covers aside, stood and stretched. She had to talk to Nick about returning to Geneva to tell the police what she'd seen. As miserable as the events had been, she hadn't exaggerated them, and even if they couldn't find Pari and Geeta and Anyu, she would make sure the police knew what had really happened to the woman in Geneva.

A bead of perspiration formed on her brow and she dabbed at it before leaning in to the mirror. She took stock of her appearance and realized that, for the first time since she'd arrived, her eyes were clear, and her skin was flushed with the heat of the morning and not her angst. She pulled her hair into a long braid, drew a thin, brown line around her eyes, and ran clear gloss over her lips. She was renewed. She was no longer some lovesick nurse tormented by nightmares. She was . . . what was Nick's word? A dame. She liked the sound of that—it suggested strength and independence and substance. That's what she was—a woman of substance. She smiled at her reflection and wondered what Nick saw when he looked at her. Oh hell, never mind that. That kind of silliness got her into trouble every time.

She'd e-mail Emily today. That's what she'd do.

She pulled open the door and headed first to the kitchen, poking her head inside, but Hana was nowhere in sight. She strode softly to the dining room, and there sat Najeela, sipping tea. Her face brightened when Abby came into view.

"Good morning, you." Najeela's voice had the sugary, thick tone that Abby had come to expect.

"Morning, Najeela. No Hana?"

"I gave her the day off. She works so hard."

Had Abby heard that right? "The day off? That was nice." And unexpected.

"Well, I thought you and I could spend some time together. It's been so long, Abby, and the clinic's closed today. What do you say?" Najeela pleaded.

"I . . ." Abby wavered. She could go to the rescue house to check on things and come back. Maybe she could even pry some information about Imtiaz from Najeela, who wasn't a bad sort after all. And Abby had been harsh with her. "I guess so," Abby said, the words almost sticking in her throat.

Najeela jumped from her chair and came around to Abby. "You are my true friend." She kissed Abby four times, twice on each cheek.

Abby smiled. It was hard not to like Najeela. Pouty princess that she was, she was nevertheless harmless. And who knew? Today might be just what Abby needed too.

"Okay." Abby pulled herself up. "You're on. I'm going to send a few e-mails, then run out for a bit, and when I come back, we'll go." She didn't mention the rescue house. It might be too late to keep it a secret, but she wouldn't bring it up again. Nick was right, the less Najeela knew, the better it was for everyone.

Najeela clapped her hands together. "Oh, Abby, we'll have a wonderful day!"

"We will." Abby headed to the office. She sat and clicked on the computer, and after an eternity, the screen opened, and she had access to her e-mails. Funny, it seemed so long ago she'd received the e-mail from Eric.

She typed her messages, filling Emily in on the details of the incident in Geneva, and Nick's trafficking story. *I know you won't share this with anyone,* she wrote. *Nick's investigation is still a work in progress.* She typed out another e-mail, a quick *I miss you and love you* to her parents before she logged off and grabbed her bag.

She stopped for a minute by the phone in the hallway. She'd call Nick if she could, but the only number she had was for his hotel. She was halfway out the door when she thought she should probably say good-bye to Najeela.

"Najeela, see you soon," she called out, not waiting for a reply as she pulled the door shut behind her.

Abby squinted as she stepped into the full glare of the morning sun. She and Mohammed exchanged greetings, and Abby paused before deciding that Nick's suspicions were over-the-top where Mohammed was concerned. She smiled and started to slide into the rear seat, then hesitated. "Mohammed, it seems stupid for me to sit back here by myself. Can't I just sit up front with you?"

Mohammed's eyes grew wide. "Oh, no, miss. It would not be proper, and Miss Najeela would not like it." He shook his head. "Not at all," he mumbled, closing the rear door. Abby settled back for the ride to the house, her eyes automatically scanning the streets for signs of the missing girls. A ragtag group of tiny beggars caught her eye, and she sat forward, intending to ask Mohammed to stop the car, but she hesitated a moment too long, and the car glided past the children onto Ring Road. She craned her neck to watch them from the rear window, but they were gone as quickly as they'd appeared, gobbled up by the crowds.

At the house, Mohammed parked the car just outside the gate. "I'll be here, miss," he said softly.

A flash of guilt for her own doubts about Mohammed surged through Abby. "I won't be long. Thank you, Mohammed, thank you."

The house seemed quiet. "Hello?" Abby called.

Bina appeared at the door. "Come," she said, holding the door open. "Come, Abby."

Abby entered the house, and the quiet closed in, heavy and depressing. "*Salaam,*" she said as Mariyah emerged from the kitchen. They exchanged greetings and pleasantries, then Abby asked if there was any news.

"Nothing," Bina said, and Mariyah tilted her head in agreement.

"How are you two doing?" Abby spoke slowly, not sure how

much they'd understand, but realizing they'd been neglected over the last few days.

"*Acha,*" Mariyah whispered, a smile cutting through her scar.

Bina's hand hurried to cover the wide smile that had broken out on her face. "We cooking." She held her hand out to Abby. "Come."

Abby followed the two into the small kitchen, which was covered from ceiling to floor in flour dust and a yellow film. Pots and pans covered the table, and the stovetop was littered with the remnants of their cooking. Mariyah held out a burnt disk for Abby to examine and said, "*Naan.* Pakistani *naan.*"

Abby let slip an unintended laugh. "Oh, I'm sorry. It's just that it looks like something I'd cook. That's why I stick to the microwave."

"We buy *naan,* now," Bina said, looking around the kitchen, surveying the damage. "Today, we clean."

Abby began to roll up her sleeves. "I'll help."

"No, no," Mariyah crowed. "We clean. *Acha?*"

"*Acha,*" Abby said. "Then I'm going, if that's okay? I'll see you tomorrow, maybe later, okay? *Khoda khafez.*"

Bina and Mariyah nodded in agreement and began to sweep up the mess that had claimed the kitchen.

Once outside, Abby slipped into the rear seat of the car. "Home for now, Mohammed." She leaned forward. "But I'm going out with Najeela. Will you be able to take us?"

"Of course."

At home, she found a smiling Najeela poring over a magazine in the dining room. When she saw Abby, she held it up. *Bride,* the cover declared. The magazine had been a staple in Abby's apartment not so long ago, though she'd hidden it from Eric.

"Where did you get that? Surely not here."

Najeela shook her head. "I ordered it from New York. It came just today." The pages slipped through her fingers and Najeela's eyes grew wider. "Come, Abby, have a look. *This* is just what I want."

Abby leaned in and saw that Najeela's finger hovered over a satin Cinderella gown with layers of ruffles and lace and sequins sewn into every available piece of fabric. "It certainly is . . . well, impressive, isn't it?"

"Oh, it is," Najeela purred, and slammed the magazine shut. "Let's hurry. I want to see the dress designer at the Pearl, then we can have lunch. What do you say?"

Abby hurried to keep up with Najeela as she sailed through the front door. Mohammed held the car door open and sat quietly in front as he chauffeured them to the Pearl. He definitely changed around Najeela, Abby thought. Nothing she could do about that, but it still rankled her.

Inside the hotel, Najeela led the way to a small, elegant shop tucked into a long hallway. Inside, she greeted the shopkeeper, Mr. François she called him, though he looked Pakistani to Abby, who watched as Najeela flipped through her magazine until she found the page with the dress.

"This one," she said, her voice quivering with happiness. "Would you be able to order it for me?"

Mr. François lifted the magazine and seemed to study the picture for far longer than was probably necessary. Abby rolled her eyes, but Najeela was too preoccupied with Mr. François and his imminent verdict to notice. Finally, he opined, "Yes, I believe I can order that dress, which by the way, is stunning and so well suited to you, miss. But, you know, it will be, well, it will be very expensive."

Najeela seemed to explode with happiness. "Oh, Mr.

François, price is no object. I don't need it yet, but how long will it take once we've made the order?"

Mr. François scratched at his chin and seemed to be deep in thought. "I would say about three months, maybe less."

A frown settled heavily on Najeela's lips. "Can't you do better?" she asked sadly.

"Well, of course we can. For you. Let me look into it. Come back next week, *acha*?"

His words swept the frown from Najeela's face, and she turned to Abby. "Let's have lunch, and you can look through the magazine and choose your dress."

Najeela's exuberance was infectious, and Abby found herself flipping through the pages as they walked back to the main lobby and into the restaurant. Inside, they settled themselves at the farthest table so that Najeela could see everyone who came and went. Abby chuckled to herself. She'd been in Peshawar for two months, and already she was something of a regular at not one but two restaurants. At home, she was only a regular at the hospital cafeteria and her corner Starbucks. How things had changed. Najeela ordered the lamb korma and curried rice, and a tomato and cucumber *salata,* while Abby looked through the magazine and wistfully glanced at the wedding gowns. Not so long ago . . .

Abby shook herself free of her what-ifs and put down the magazine, looking up in time to see Imtiaz strolling to their table. Her heart began to pound. Relax, she reminded herself. He doesn't know anything, and even if he does, he's not about to do anything in public. Even Nick had said he'd like to speak with him in a public place. Suddenly, she knew that if she worked this moment to her advantage and asked Imtiaz the questions Nick would ask, she might come away with something useful, something Nick could use. She exhaled slowly and forced a smile as Imtiaz pulled up a chair and slid it close to hers.

Najeela's mouth was agape in genuine surprise, Abby thought. "Uncle!" Najeela exclaimed. "What are you doing here?"

"Here for a business meeting, and who do I spy but my favorite niece and her dear friend, thanks be to Allah." He leaned in and kissed Najeela on the cheek, before turning to Abby, who thwarted a kiss by folding her hands in front of her face in a formal *namaste*.

"Nice to see you, Imtiaz," Abby said through her hands, hoping the contempt she felt wasn't obvious.

He leaned in toward Abby, and Najeela said sweetly, "Uncle, none of that now."

Abby could have kissed her for that quick rescue.

"Please join us for lunch, Uncle. Are you hungry?"

Imtiaz shook his head. "Well, perhaps a small bite, and of course I shall be pleased to feast on the beauty before me."

Abby groaned, and Imtiaz and Najeela turned and looked at her. "My stomach is growling," Abby said, hoping that explanation would suffice. "Imtiaz," she hurriedly added, "what is the business you have *here*? The hotel is so grand." She could have vomited at the cloying sound of her voice, but if it inspired Imtiaz to open up, it would be worth it, and Nick would be plenty impressed.

Imtiaz turned to Abby. "My dear, I had no idea you were interested in business."

Abby tried to think fast. "Me either, Imtiaz, but it turns out I am. I'll never get rich as a nurse, so it doesn't hurt to look at other options. Don't you agree?"

"Ah, Abby, you are quite right, and I'd love nothing more than to take you under my wing. I could teach you so much."

I'll bet you could, you old snake, Abby thought, but she smiled as she asked, "Just what is your business?"

"Ah, well." A long pause filled the air. "Here," he said as the food arrived, the fiery fragrance filling the air. "It's impolite to speak of business over lunch, don't you agree?"

Abby reached for the bread. "Actually, no," she said, impressed by her own boldness. "Surely you've heard of the business lunch? Or perhaps that's strictly American." She smiled sweetly through a mouthful of the curried rice. "Please, don't hesitate on our account." She motioned to Najeela. "I'm sure Najeela won't mind."

Abby caught a glimpse of a smiling Najeela. "Not at all," Najeela said. "Please feel free to speak, Uncle. Who knows—maybe someday you and Abby will be partners, and it could all start here."

Abby's stomach churned, but Najeela's words seemed to have the desired effect, and Imtiaz smiled broadly, his dull yellow teeth peeking through his beard. He leaned closer, and the sour smell of his breath filled the space between them. Abby pulled away and reached for her water. "Najeela says you are a farmer, Imtiaz. I've never known a farmer, and I have so many questions."

"As do I," Imtiaz said.

"Guests first." Abby swallowed the lump of unease in her throat. "Tell me about your farm. Where is it? What do you grow? I'm just fascinated."

Imtiaz seemed about to burst at the attention. "Ah, dear Abby, you must accompany me to my glorious fields in Spin Boldak in Kandahar or to my home in Helmand Province." He leaned back and worked a toothpick through his stained teeth. "And you must see my fields for yourself—I grow flowers."

"Flowers? Poppies?"

"Why would you think that?" Imtiaz pulled the splintered toothpick from his mouth.

"Actually, Najeela told me."

Imtiaz lowered his eyes, snaring Najeela with his gaze.

Najeela's eyes grew wide. "You do though, Uncle, yes?" Najeela asked softly.

"I do, but you know how people misinterpret that information. I grow them for medicinal use."

"That's very noble," Abby said, fighting the smile that threatened to spring to her lips. "Is there money in that?"

"Abby, it's very lucrative. You must know too how costly medicine is. And the truth is, I make a fraction of what it's worth," he said solemnly, "but I'm helping those in need, and that makes me happy."

A smile broke out on Abby's face. Nick would love that spin—Imtiaz isn't a crook, he's a humanitarian. She turned back to her food and watched as Imtiaz dipped his fingers into the bowl of rice. He worked his fingers into the center and smiled as he transferred a mound of rice into his mouth. He ate noisily, slapping the food against his tongue. When he reached his stubby fingers into the bowl a second time, Abby, her stomach lurching, set her fork down. She didn't think she'd ever eat rice again.

Abby watched Imtiaz as he ate, his fingers working furiously over the lamb and rice as he stuffed them into his mouth. Finally, he sat back, the toothpick dangling from his lips.

Abby pounced. "So, are the poppies part of your other business, your export business, as well?" She flashed what she hoped was her best guileless grin, hoping to catch Imtiaz off guard. When he began to choke and spit, his toothpick popped out, falling into the rice. He snatched it back, balancing it once again on the edge of his lips, and in a feat of facial contortion, he somehow managed to frown at the same time.

Abby stifled a smile at his reaction and tried to put him at ease again. "Perhaps I misunderstood. Najeela, didn't you tell me Imtiaz was in the export business?"

The smile had faded from Najeela's face, and she glanced at Imtiaz before she finally answered. "Well, I did, yes, but the truth is I have no head for business. I'm not sure what *export* means."

Imtiaz gently removed the now cracked toothpick from his lips, and a small smile replaced his frown. "My sweet niece has no head for anything these days, I would say."

Najeela giggled. "Oh, Uncle," she said sweetly.

Imtiaz poured himself a glass of water and gulped it noisily. And that, Abby thought, puts an end to my questioning.

"And your friend, the reporter," Imtiaz said, his gaze locked on Abby, "he's back, is he?"

A swell of uncertainty broke over Abby.

Najeela spun toward Abby. "Oh my," she asked, her voice tinged with genuine surprise, "is Nick back?"

Think fast, Abby told herself. It seemed clear that Najeela had no idea Nick was back, but somehow Imtiaz knew. How the hell did he know? Maybe he was guessing, bluffing, Abby thought. "I don't know. Is he?" she asked Imtiaz, widening her eyes in feigned surprise. "You seem to know more about him than I do these days."

"Oh, come, my dear," Imtiaz said. "Wasn't he in Geneva recently?"

Abby felt the color drain from her face. He must be watching Nick—or someone was watching for him. Abby sat forward and tried to recover her composure. "I don't know about Nick, but I was in Geneva. That's where I had my UN orientation. Lovely city."

"That's right, Uncle," Najeela said. "Abby came in through Geneva."

Abby could have sworn that Imtiaz froze for an instant, and she watched as he combed his fingers through his beard, bits of rice dropping onto the table.

"Ah, Geneva. You enjoyed it?" He leaned closer, his eyes cold, almost inhuman in their intensity.

A chill ran through Abby's veins. Her mind raced as she tried to find something innocuous to say. Then the waiter miraculously appeared, putting an abrupt and welcome end to the questions. Abby shook her head to the waiter's question about dessert and put her napkin over her plate. "As a matter of fact," she said, looking at her watch, "I think we should go, Najeela, if we're to finish shopping."

"Oh my," she said. "You're right. We're going to run, Uncle, and you'll take care of the bill for us?" Najeela rose and threw her scarf over her head.

Imtiaz grunted an unintelligible reply.

"*Khoda khafez,*" Abby said, relieved to be free of his questions and foul habits.

Now that Abby had used shopping with Najeela as an excuse to get away from Imtiaz, she was stuck. She was desperate to track Nick down, but that would have to wait. She smiled at Najeela. "Where to?" she asked as Mohammed held open the car door.

Najeela clapped her hands together as she slid into the car. "Oh, Abby, the old bazaar. I'll show you the silver shop." Najeela sat forward and directed Mohammed to the bazaar.

Abby sat back. This was going to be a long afternoon.

Chapter 25

Abby slept peacefully that night. Not even her run-in with Imtiaz kept her awake. When she woke, she had only a vague recollection of the night's dream, of the bracelet and the man who'd pulled it from the dead woman. She supposed now that Nick had confirmed the murder, there wasn't any need for her unconscious mind to jolt her memory through nightmares. The facts were all there, safe and just waiting for the final chapter—the identification of the murderer. And *that,* Abby had no doubt, was about to happen.

She looked at her watch. Nine o'clock already. Good thing it was the weekend. Lingering longer than she ordinarily would, she remembered that neither Najeela nor Mohammed would be in today. Maybe she'd call Nick early, see if he'd take her to the rescue house, maybe even go out for another search for the girls. When Abby pulled her door open, she heard Hana's voice in the kitchen, and she headed to see who was here.

She peered around the corner and saw Nick sitting across from Hana, who seemed to be regaling him with a story that had him so absorbed he didn't notice Abby standing there. Hana saw her and stood quickly, almost guiltily, Abby thought, wishing Hana weren't so skittish about being the housekeeper.

Nick caught Hana's sudden move and turned warily. When he spied Abby, he stood and smiled. "Morning, Abby. We were wondering when you'd get up." He glanced back quickly at Hana.

"Go on into the dining room. I'll bring your breakfast in," she said.

Nick and Abby headed to the dining room. "What was that all about? You two seemed deep in conversation."

"We were just chatting about nothing. What about you? Where've you been? I came by yesterday, and no one was here. Not you, not Hana, not even Najeela or that driver."

"Mohammed, his name is Mohammed."

"So, where was everyone?"

"Out," Abby replied. "And I would have called, but aside from calling the hotel, there's no way to reach you."

"Keeps me safe. But back to you. Where were you?"

"I was having lunch with Najeela and Imtiaz."

"Oh, shit, I don't even wanna know."

"Yes, you do, trust me. Imtiaz knows about you, knows you're back, knows you were in Geneva."

Nick sat up straight. "You have my undivided attention. Start with how the hell you wound up having lunch with him."

"I was at the Pearl with Najeela, and we were about to eat when he just showed up."

"Just showed up? You don't think Najeela invited him on the sly? You really don't think it was a setup?" Nick's irritation seeped through his words.

"I don't, Nick. She seemed genuinely surprised to see him. I'm certain she wasn't faking it. And when Imtiaz mentioned that you were back, Najeela had no idea."

"You must have told her, Abby. Just think back. You must've let it slip."

"I didn't let anything slip, at least not to Najeela, and I'm telling you, Nick, she had no idea you were back or where you'd been. But Imtiaz sure did, and he asked about it."

"Jesus, how the hell would he know that unless he has someone watching me, watching us?"

"Maybe he does have someone watching, maybe not—but I may have mentioned to Mohammed that you were back, that you were picking me up from the camp the other day." She caught the look of frustration on Nick's face. "Sorry, Nick, I just told him he didn't have to stay around, that you'd be picking me up. But, Imtiaz definitely didn't know where you were, at least not from me, and I didn't say a word to Najeela either."

Hana bustled in, clearing her throat and banging the tray down. "Breakfast. I'll be in the kitchen."

Nick hesitated for a minute, waiting, Abby thought, for Hana to be out of earshot. "So what else did he know?"

Abby smiled. "Not much. And I think you would've been proud of me. When he showed up, I remembered you said you'd like to question him out in the open, and I thought since I was there, I'd try to do it for you."

Nick leaned forward, his head on his hands, and groaned. "I don't think I want to hear this."

"Oh, come on, you know you do. I asked him about his business and his poppy farms. I even asked if he exported the poppies. You should have seen his face." Abby looked at Nick, his mouth agape. "Jesus, you should see yours. I did pretty well, Nick. He was definitely flustered, and I acted just dumb enough to seem innocent about it all."

"Uh . . ." Nick hesitated.

"What?" Abby asked.

"Nothing, go on."

"Well—you'll love this—he told me he sells the poppies for medicinal use, says he doesn't make what they're worth, but it's for the greater good." Abby chuckled. "He's not a crook, Nick, he's a benevolent old farmer."

"Okay, pretty interesting. But he knows you're not stupid, and now you've really pissed him off."

"I know I have, and up until he turned the tables on me and began to ask about you and Geneva, I thought I really had him."

"Almost hate to say it, but you probably never had him. The old goat's no fool."

"Get your own information then. Christ, why do I even help you?" Abby reached for the coffee, affronted.

"We help each other, don't we?"

"I guess, but why do you have to be such an ass? Jeez, how do you ever get information that way?"

"I've learned that if people are angry with you, they'll let their guard down and tell you more than they intended. If they like you, they clam up. No one wants to share stuff that makes them look bad."

"You have no memory of the day we met, huh?" Abby asked wryly.

"I do, believe me, but it all worked out. I'd never have

learned you possibly witnessed a murder if you liked me from the start, right?"

"Oh, get over yourself, will you?" Abby chided. "I only told you that when I liked and trusted you enough to share that."

Nick's gaze softened. "I concede that I may have to rethink some of my tactics, but did you just say that you liked me?" He winked.

"I did."

Nick leaned in and kissed her quickly. "I like you too, Abby. A lot. And someday soon we'll chat about that, but for now let's head to the rescue house, see if there's any word."

A smile settled on Abby's lips, and she sighed. "Just let me grab my bag and we're out of here," she said, heading to her room. "We're going, Hana," she called from the door.

"Where's Mohammed today?" Nick asked.

"Probably off," Abby said. "He was here yesterday, seems like he's never off, so he's probably due. Najeela always has him running for her."

"But he was here yesterday? Lunch with Imtiaz? A little convenient, don't you think?"

"Jeez, Nick, don't make me suspicious of everyone. He's a nice guy, he works hard."

"But he knew about the house, right? He knew I was away, and he knew you were at the Pearl having lunch. Are you seeing a pattern here?"

"I think there's probably a great explanation. I don't think he's a spy."

"I hope you're right, but for now, do *not* tell him anything, and I mean *anything*. Agreed?"

Abby nodded, and Nick settled in behind the wheel, directing the car into the thick of morning traffic. When they finally broke free, they pulled off Ring Road and through the maze of back streets to the rescue house, where a smiling Bina greeted them.

"*Salaam,*" she said softly.

Abby smiled and kissed her cheeks. "Good morning, Bina. How are you?"

"*Acha.*"

They followed her into the house and into the kitchen. The shades were drawn, the room in shadow. "Why so dark in here?" Abby said, blinking her eyes to adjust to the change in light.

"Because I here," a familiar voice whispered. Abby opened her eyes wide. Anyu was sitting at the table.

Abby's hands flew to her mouth. "Oh my God!" Tears stung her eyes. "Are you okay?" She bent to Anyu and kissed her cheeks. "Are Pari and Geeta with you? Oh, God, I'm so damn happy to see you."

Abby collapsed into a chair across from Anyu, and Nick stood behind her. "We looked all over for you, Anyu. We were all worried."

"Sorry," she murmured.

Abby looked around. "Where is everyone? Where's Zara and Mariyah? And the girls? Where are they?"

"Zara and Mariyah will be back soon. They went to the bazaar for rice and bread," Bina said.

Abby nodded and turned back to Anyu. "Please, Anyu, tell me what happened."

Anyu took a deep breath as if to steel herself and leaned forward. "Girls safe, going home."

"But how?" Nick asked.

"I take them to women who helped me, who brought me here. They good, they keep secrets, so I know girls will be safe with them."

"But what happened? Why didn't you tell anyone you were leaving?"

"I worry for girls when car of you"—Anyu pointed to Abby—"come at night. It park outside, and man walk around. I see him. I know this not good."

"What do you mean 'car of me'? I don't have a car."

Anyu shook her head. "You have car, and you have Pakistani driver, man you brought food to."

"Mohammed?" Nick asked.

Anyu nodded.

Abby gasped. "He was here? At night? Where was that guard?"

"Guard sleep at night, but driver of you here, he wide-awake. And I worry for girls. Why he here? Why he watch house at night?"

"Why couldn't you tell us? Why leave with the girls?"

"I not know if you and Mistah Nick good. Understand? I think, maybe *you* send car. Maybe *you* want girls. Maybe *you* tell police about Delhi. I afraid."

Abby closed her eyes. "I'm sorry, Anyu. I brought Mohammed here. It's my fault."

"It's not anyone's fault, Abby," Nick said in exasperation. "Go on, Anyu."

"I take money only for we need it. I wake girls and say we are leaving. Pari happy, Geeta crying. I shush them, they get dressed in new clothes, and we get to train station when it still dark. Too early for tickets so we hide until ticket man come. I buy tickets to Lahore, but train not leave until afternoon. We hide there in the morning, stay by tree and watch, but no one come."

"Oh my God, we were there, Anyu. I was certain that you'd gone to the station, but I thought you'd head to Islamabad and then into India," Abby said. "We must have just missed you."

Anyu smiled. "But it good that we get away. We go to Lahore and I find my way back to women's house. I know they help, and they do. They send girls to special place outside Mumbai. Pari, Geeta, safe there for now."

"Why did *you* come back?" Nick asked.

"Womens in Lahore have you and Abby looked at. Understand? The women in Lahore know Americans in your State Office."

"State Department?" Nick asked.

"*Department,* that right. Someone there check for womens and say you two not criminals, so I want to come back only to say girls are safe. Then I leave."

"Where will you go?" Abby asked.

"To Lahore to work with womens. We help other girls. I good at helping."

Abby quickly wiped the tears that threatened to spill from her eyes. "I'm so glad you're safe. I don't think I've ever been so happy to see someone in my life."

Nick cleared his throat. "I've been to Delhi."

Suddenly Anyu's smile disappeared. "They look for me?" she fearfully whispered.

"No, no one's looking for you. Well, maybe the brothel owner, but not the police. There's no record of a murder at that brothel. They probably didn't want any trouble and just dumped the body somewhere else. You're safe, Anyu," Nick said. "You should probably stay out of Delhi, but you're safe."

Anyu began to cry, soundless tears spilling from her eyes. She wiped at them with the end of her sari. "I not alone now. There are leaves on my tree and stars in my sky. *Shukria*, Mistah Nick."

Chapter 26

"Jesus, what a day," Nick said as he slid behind the wheel of his car. "Club?"

Abby nodded.

"Why so quiet?" he asked.

Abby sighed. "I screwed up, that's why. I totally trusted Mohammed, and it looks as though he's in the middle of this."

"It sure does, but it's not your fault."

"What about Hana? Could she be part of it?"

"No," Nick said. "She's not involved in this."

Abby shrugged. "You're certain?"

Nick nodded.

"What do we do now?" Abby asked.

"Nothing, literally nothing. We can't arouse Mohammed's suspicions, so go to camp with him as usual and then home, out with Najeela if need be, but nowhere else with him. If he asks you about the rescue house, just say it closed. I'll think of something."

"Think that will work? I mean, he's got to be working for someone."

"Probably Imtiaz. Remember how that bastard showed up when you were alone, and then when I was away? And wasn't it Mohammed who brought you to the Pearl the other day? It adds up. Mohammed is giving Imtiaz the information."

At the club, Nick headed straight for the bar. "What'll it be? Diet Coke or scotch, the breakfast of champions?"

"Funny," she said, looking at her watch. "God, it's one o'clock already, but no scotch for me. My days of feigning sophistication are over. I'll have a Diet Coke and a cheeseburger. Maybe a beer later if I'm feeling wild." She turned and headed for what was now surely their table.

Nick returned, and placing Abby's drink down, he sat across from her, resting his elbows on the table.

Abby slumped in her seat. "This whole mess is depressing." She eyed Nick's scotch. "Maybe I should have ordered something stronger."

Nick held out his drink, but Abby shook her head. "So we can't do anything? We just sit and wait?"

"Well, we wait, but we don't sit. I'll send out a request for information on Mohammed later today, but for now, just be careful, and try not to let on that you suspect him. Keep your head down and your eyes open, and remember Najeela might be in the middle of this too."

Abby sighed noisily. "I don't think so. And now with Mohammed probably involved, it makes me think that even more. Najeela can't stand Mohammed. She goes out of her way to be mean to him."

"Don't be fooled. She could be a great actress."

"I don't think she's capable of pretending like that. She's every bit as self-absorbed as she seems, and that self-absorption would get in the way of her being involved in someone else's intrigue."

"Suit yourself. Just be careful."

"What about the rescue house?" Abby asked. "Can I at least go there with you?"

"Let me think about it. But my instinct is for both of us to stay away—for their safety and our own."

"Food's ready," the bartender called.

Nick stood. "You want a beer with your burger?"

"You never give up." Abby laughed. "No, maybe later. Right now, I want to think."

He returned with the food, and they sat and picked at their burgers.

"What now?" Abby asked.

"I'm going to concentrate on Imtiaz." Nick took a sip of his scotch. "See if I can't put the pressure on, see what he does if he thinks I know something."

"Isn't that dangerous?"

"I'll be careful. Remember, I need proof for my story. The *Times* is not going to publish innuendo and hearsay. I need something solid, so I need to keep at it or hope that Imtiaz thinks I have something on him. That could force his hand."

"Force his hand to do what?"

"I don't know," Nick answered. "I'm just thinking out loud."

"What about Geneva? I know I can identify this guy, and I think he knows that too."

"You can identify him? You're certain?"

"I am. You believe me, right?"

Nick whistled. "I do. We'll get back there. I'm not sure when, but we'll get there."

"Do you think the murder in Geneva is related to all of this, to Imtiaz, to trafficking?" Abby asked.

"I always thought it was pretty damn sinister, and trafficking leads to murder, that's just how it is. If these girls start to talk, you have to shut them up somehow, and what better way?"

Abby shivered. "Evil, Nick, it's evil."

"Abby, you have to promise, no more risks. Understood?"

Abby nodded. "What about you?"

"I really don't take risks. People just assume I do."

"I'll have that beer now."

"I knew you'd come around." Nick headed back to the bar. He returned with a beer and a cup of coffee.

"Coffee?" Abby asked.

"It's going to be a long day. I'll need all the help I can get."

Abby shook her head. "There's just no figuring you out, is there?"

Nick winked. "Why would you want to?"

"You've got a point. So, today, can I come with you? I can help."

Nick shook his head. "I don't want anyone who might be watching me to see you with me today. I want to look into some stuff, and I need to do it alone. Trust me."

"Oh, shit, Nick, don't be so dramatic. Let me come."

"No, Abby. It's for your own good." He looked at his watch and stood. "I'd love to hang out, but I've got to check this stuff out and it's getting late."

Abby drank the last of her beer, and they drove home in silence. Nick pulled up to her gate. "Just stay in, do some work or something. Don't go anywhere, not even with Najeela. Not today. Agreed?"

Abby nodded. "I'll see you tomorrow?"

"You will. Maybe later in the day, but you'll see me."

He leaned over and kissed her lightly, and Abby didn't pull away. Instead, she leaned in and kissed him back. "See you tomorrow," she said. Abby rubbed away the goose bumps that had sprouted on her arms. She had a bad feeling about whatever he was going off to do, but she knew Nick was immovable once he'd set his sights on something. She took a deep breath and tried to smile. "Promise me you'll be careful."

Nick smiled and touched Abby's cheek. "I will. You know I will."

Abby let herself into the house, and right away she sensed the overwhelming quiet, the emptiness. Her footsteps echoed all the way to her room, and when she opened the door, she froze, her eyes riveted on the scene inside. She felt her bag slide from her arm, and she heard the small thump as it landed at her feet.

Her room had been torn apart, drawers pulled out, her clothes thrown on the floor. The old wooden chair had been knocked over so roughly, its legs had splintered. Her notebook, its pages torn to shreds, lay on the bed, the mattress askew. Her suitcase lay open, its contents strewn about. The curtains were drawn, but daylight seeped in, slicing through the debris and disarray.

Abby stood motionless as she tried to make sense of it all. Someone had turned her room upside down.

But why?

Her heart pounding, she stepped back into the hall.

Shit, shit, shit! Oh, God, was someone still here? Abby ran back through the house and, pulling open the front door, ran to the gate, yanking that open as well. She peered out and looked up and down the street, but Nick was gone. She slammed the gate shut, locking it behind her before leaning against it. What if the intruder was still here? *Shit!*

She took a deep breath. If someone was here, he would have come after her already. With that thought in mind, Abby walked slowly back into the house, leaving the front door wide open as an escape route—just in case.

She stood in the hallway and tried to think what to do. She had to check the house, but first she'd need something to protect herself with. A knife, she thought, one of Hana's carving knives. She walked slowly, hoping to calm herself, and when she reached the kitchen, she grabbed a sharp knife from the counter. Her mind registered that Hana's kitchen was spotless.

Something behind her creaked, and she spun around, the knife in her hand. She held her breath and listened, but the house was silent as a tomb. She stood perfectly still and tried to think what the hell someone might be looking for, but she didn't have anything. Maybe it was a robbery. Maybe *she* wasn't the target. She turned then for the dining room, but it was untouched, and as neat as it had been this morning. She ran to the office, but that room too was still tidy. Not even a breeze had disturbed its contents. She checked the two unused bedrooms off the hallway, but they were quiet and still. Only her room, it seemed, had been searched.

Abby walked back to her room and snapped on the light. Her eyes flickering against the sudden flash of brightness, she bent down and went through the clutter. Everything was there. *Everything.* Did someone want to scare her, or was there something else? Maybe they didn't find what they wanted, which could only mean she had it on her, but all she had was her bag. Surely nothing of value was in there.

She picked it up from the floor where it had fallen and emptied the contents onto her bed. Keys, sunscreen, a handful of Pakistani rupees, a $20 bill. Her passport. Would they want to see the dates she was in Geneva? No, they must know that already, or Imtiaz could just ask Najeela. Her makeup; a tiny mirror; sunglasses; a gooey, half-melted peppermint; some pens; a work notebook; a folder with vaccine statistics, and Nick's card. Shit, did they want that? No, they knew where he was. She had nothing that anyone might want.

She reached into the now empty bag, scouring the bottom of the tote. Her hand folded over a sheaf of papers stuck on a zipper, and she yanked them free, holding them up for inspection. An old newspaper? Why did she have this? She unfolded it and remembered. This was the newspaper Najeela had shown her ages ago at the Pearl. It had some story about her boyfriend, Lars. Abby had forgotten about the paper, and apparently Najeela had as well. She'd never mentioned it. Could someone want this old paper?

Abby smoothed out the creases and folds and spread the pages before her. The story was on page three. The picture, at the bottom of the page, was small. "Lars Rousseau, European Philanthropist, Donates to UN," the caption read. Rousseau, Rousseau—where had she heard that name? The photo was grainy and now creased from so much folding. Abby ran her hand over the page to smooth out the wrinkles and looked closely at the image. Something about the man in the photo was familiar. He wore wire-rimmed glasses over drooping eyes, and thinning gray hair framed his face.

Abby held the newspaper closer and squinted to get a better look, the picture seeming to come into sharper focus.

Thinning gray hair, wire-rimmed spectacles, distinguished looking . . . a picture of a man who knows he's important. Suddenly, a vision of the dead woman clutching broken wire-rimmed glasses flashed before her eyes. Abby's mouth went dry. She saw him, the shadowy stranger on the street as he turned toward her hiding place. She could hear his footsteps as he moved closer.

The newspaper photo suddenly seemed to come alive—it was *him*. *Lars Rousseau*. *Rousseau*—the name of Nick's suspect, and the man from the balcony in Geneva.

Abby dropped the paper and stood, the floor swaying beneath her. She sat back down as a wave of dizziness washed over her. Was this newspaper photo what someone was looking for? Damn it, was it Najeela? Was she part of this after all? Was it Hana? Mohammed?

A heavy weight pressed down on her chest blocking her air, and she forced herself to take a slow, deep breath. She had to show Nick. Abby folded up the paper and stuffed it back into her bag. Her head still spinning, she took his card and went to the hall phone to call the hotel. Surely he was back by now. Her fingers trembled as she dialed the numbers, and she heard the first ring. But then it rang again and again, and Abby began to hyperventilate.

"Green's Hotel," a man said lazily.

"Nick Sinclair."

"Not in," the man replied without hesitating.

"Can you check, please?" Abby asked, her voice quivering.

"He hasn't checked back in. He's not here. I don't have to check. I have his keys."

"Can I leave a message?" Tears streaked Abby's face.

"Hmm, go ahead," the man said, exasperated.

"Tell him to see Abby. Tell him it's important."

"Anything else?"

"No, just that." Abby laid the receiver back in its cradle. She sank to the floor, Hana's knife in her hand. She'd have to check the house herself, make sure everything was locked. She pulled herself up and headed back down the hall, snapping on lights as she went.

The rooms were empty, the windows shut tight, the back door secure. She closed the front door and slid the locking bolt into place. There wasn't any sign that someone had broken in— no shattered glass, no splintered doorways.

Nothing.

What the hell was going on? Was someone just trying to scare her? If that was the point, they'd succeeded.

Goddamn it, Nick, get here. Abby sank down onto her bed. She couldn't let her thoughts run wild. If it was just a robbery, and maybe it was, wouldn't someone go through the rest of the house? Steal the computer? Suddenly Abby remembered Najeela's jewelry. Was it there? Abby took a deep breath and walked back to the office. She dropped into the chair in front of Najeela's desk to have a look. The lock seemed to be intact, the desk untouched. She tugged at the handle, expecting resistance, but the drawer slid out easily. The glitter and sparkle were almost blinding, and Abby blinked at the sight of the gaudy stash. The drawer was still filled with Najeela's treasures, and Abby's eyes suddenly locked on a diamond cuff bracelet adorned with rubies and garnets and sapphires.

The bracelet.

Abby's heart pounded hard against her rib cage, and she opened her mouth to gulp in air. She slammed the drawer shut and closed her eyes. Take a deep breath, she commanded herself. Panicking now wouldn't help anything. She steadied her arm, rested her fingers, now sticky with sweat, around the handle, and pulled. And there it was—the bracelet, shining and shimmering, taunting her with its familiar sparkle. Her hand trembled as it hovered over the bracelet, but as though a flame had licked at her fingers, she pulled away.

She knew she had to take the bracelet. It was further proof—the final nail, she thought, in the case against Lars, and a final act of respect for the woman who'd died. She examined the stones and remembered a *CSI* episode where someone had said fingerprints remained on jewelry. She had to remove the bracelet carefully, without touching it, and she had to store it in plastic. Isn't that what they always did to preserve evidence? A Ziploc bag, that's what she needed. She hurried into the kitchen, pulling open cabinets and drawers until she found what she needed, then she returned to the desk. She used a pen to lift the bracelet and guide it into the bag, exhaling loudly as she zipped it shut.

She sat and tried to clear her thoughts, to form a plan, to do something to help herself out of this mess. She turned to the computer. She'd check her e-mails, see if Emily had replied. She logged on, but her e-mails were gone—nothing in the Inbox, nothing in Sent. *Nothing.* Where was everything? She logged out and signed in again—but still—there was nothing. Her account was empty. When she clicked on the Inbox, a tiny dialogue box appeared. *You have no messages,* she read. The same notice appeared in her Sent folder. Pay attention, she told herself, and she logged in yet again. The screen flickered, and the same messages appeared. What the hell, Abby thought. She sat back, confused. She'd had this account for years. Why the trouble now?

Suddenly the fog in her head cleared, and she knew. Her account had been hacked. Someone had read her e-mail to Emily. Someone knew *everything*.

She looked at her watch. Six o'clock. Where was Nick? Abby retraced her steps to the phone and dialed Green's Hotel once again. This time, a woman answered on the second ring.

"Nick Sinclair, please."

"Just a moment," the woman said. "I'll connect you."

Abby swiped her hand at the beads of perspiration that had formed on her forehead and listened to the shrill ringing of the phone. Six rings, no answer; then ten and then twenty, and still no answer; and Abby knew. He wasn't there.

She hung up the phone and closed her eyes, her grip tightening on the bag that held the bracelet. She'd have to get through the night alone. Already, darkness had settled over the house like a shroud. Abby considered turning all the lights on, but decided that might attract attention. She wanted everything to seem normal to any outside observer. She returned to her room and shut the door behind her. She dragged the nightstand to the door and wedged it in between the door and her bed. She pulled on the door to test it, but her makeshift barricade worked. The door wouldn't budge.

She piled her stuff back into her bag, then took out and carefully refolded the newspaper before replacing it in the bag. She took one last look at the bracelet that had haunted her for so long before gently placing it in her bag. She cleared off her bed, laid the knife and the bag at her side, and pulled out her notebook and a pen. They may have torn out the pages that held the story of what she'd seen in Geneva, but she'd rewrite it. It would give her something to do instead of listening to every creak and groan in the house.

Abby bent over her notebook and began to write. Her story flowed easily, and before long, she set her pen aside and looked at her alarm clock. Ten o'clock. Seven long hours before daylight. Abby dimmed the lights and stretched out on the bed. Listening for the slightest creak, she watched the shadows dance on the ceiling.

She wouldn't sleep, but at least she'd rest. She closed her eyes and prayed for morning.

Chapter 27

Asliver of sunlight tickled Abby's eyes and she woke with a start. She hadn't expected to sleep at all, and she sat upright, listening, but everything was quiet. She breathed a sigh of relief.

She had to get to Nick, and she swung her legs over the side of the bed, contemplating her options. She couldn't wait for him. She had to get to Green's, and the sooner the better. She rose quickly, stepping around the debris that still littered the floor. She showered and dressed, pulling on a long cotton dress and winding a scarf around her head and neck. It would, she hoped, make her somehow less conspicuous in the streets of Peshawar. She reached for Nick's card on her bedside table. On the back he'd scribbled *Green's Hotel—Saddar Rd*. She checked her bag one last time. The photo and the bracelet lay safely within.

Abby pulled the nightstand away from the door and took a deep breath. She knew she was about to jump off the cliff, but the time had finally come. She opened the door and immediately sensed the quiet that still lay over the house. She looked at her watch—7:00 a.m. Hana should just be arriving, but Najeela wouldn't be here for hours. Abby stepped into the hallway. From the far end, where her office was, she could see a flood of light streaming down the hall. How could that be? She was sure she'd turned off the light last night. She craned her neck to see if anyone was there, and she gasped as she spied Najeela at her computer, so intent on something she didn't notice Abby. Abby turned and tiptoed through the hall to the front entrance, pulling open the door and willing it not to squeak.

"Where are you off to so early?"

Najeela was right behind her, and Abby spun to meet her. She couldn't think what to say, her mind was a jumble, but Najeela would know soon enough the bracelet was missing.

"We were broken into," Abby said quickly.

"When?" Najeela asked, her eyes wide with fright.

"Sometime yesterday. I came home late in the day, and my room had been ransacked. I don't think there's anything missing, but someone made a mess in there."

"Did you call the police?"

Abby shook her head. "I was afraid. I didn't know what to do, so I cleaned up and went to bed."

"I think we should report it now, Abby. You're probably still upset. Sit. I'll make us some tea."

Abby shook her head.

"I'll have to report this to the UN," Najeela said. "This is a serious breach in security, even worse than that riot. It may mean that you get sent home. For your own safety, you understand. Stay, Abby, let's talk."

"No, Najeela. I want to see Nick. I thought I could finally do that interview. That will relax me. I won't be long. We can talk later."

"You don't want to do the interview here or perhaps later in the day?"

"No. I'd like to just get out of here, and I'll lose my nerve if I don't go now. I'll see you later."

"But wait, there's no car. Mohammed's not here yet. Wait a bit, have some breakfast, and then I'll go with you."

Abby shook her head. "I'll just get a taxi or rickshaw," she said, hurrying into the courtyard. She turned and saw Najeela just standing there, watching. "I'll see you later," Abby called as she pulled open the heavy gate and stepped into the road.

The morning was quiet; no taxis or rickshaws in sight, and Abby knew she'd have to walk to the main road. She pulled her scarf over her head and quickened her pace. Considering the riots and trouble here, she didn't want to be long in the road. A bony old horse clip-clopped by, his weary back covered with an ornate, sparkly blanket, his forehead decorated with flowers and ribbons, and his hooves adorned with tiny bells. He pulled a small carriage, and Abby's heart quickened. A taxi, she thought. "*Maaf karna*, excuse me," she called. The small man sitting atop the carriage pulled on the reins, and the horse stopped. The man turned.

"Green's Hotel on Saddar Road?"

"*Acha*, okay," the old man replied, and Abby pulled herself up to sit in the carriage. The driver turned and offered a greasy old blanket. She shook her head no. This carriage looked just like one of the hansoms that she used to see in Boston, steering tourists around the Common, but this old horse was slow, slower than any she'd seen in Boston. Impatient, she tapped her feet on the footrest, and her fingers on the cushion. She was worried that she'd miss Nick, and there was just too much danger right now. He had to know. The bracelet, the photo. Maybe Hana was involved after all. She spoke perfect English, and she could read despite Najeela's assumption that she was illiterate. Maybe Hana had ransacked Abby's room and hacked into her e-mail account. The very thought gave Abby a chill.

Abby turned her attention back to the road, and she looked up just as the horse made a plodding turn onto Kohat Road. She could have walked faster than this damn horse moved. She drew in a deep breath. There was nothing she could do about it—she couldn't just hop off and walk, not with the trouble here. She watched as the streets, shaking off the night, began to fill with the day's workers and shopkeepers and even a few early-morning beggars.

She reached into her bag and drew out the newspaper, peering for what seemed the hundredth time at the grainy photo of a smiling Lars Rousseau. Why hadn't she looked at this before? How long had it sat crumpled at the bottom of her bag, and was this photo what her intruder had been looking for? How could she not have put it together before? She pulled out the bracelet that she knew so well. It shimmered in the morning light, just as it had the last time she'd seen it. She shook her head at her ineptness, but brightened at the prospect of sharing this with Nick. The bracelet and the newspaper were the final pieces of Nick's puzzle. His Rousseau was Najeela's fiancé, Lars, none other than her uncle's business partner. Collaborators in crime and in love.

The old horseman pulled up tight on the horse's reins, and Abby was thrown forward.

"*Acha*," the old man said, nodding toward the hotel just across the road. Abby replaced the bracelet and the newspaper in her bag and pulled out her purse, holding a fistful of rupees for the driver. He picked through the bills and coins, taking just what he was owed. Abby smiled and poured the remaining coins into his hand before climbing down and peering across the street.

Though the street was filling up now with screeching donkeys, speeding cars, and careening rickshaws, Green's Hotel looked quiet. It was early yet, Abby thought, hurrying across the road. Just in front of the hotel's entrance, she thought she heard Nick's voice. "Hey," he shouted, and she looked up, certain that he was leaning from his window. But there was nothing to see, only the unremarkable front of the hotel.

Abby pulled open the front door and squinted into the darkness before venturing inside. The bitter smells and piercing sounds of the street wafted in behind her, but the lobby was surprisingly bright and welcoming, quiet even once the door closed. Comfortable chairs were scattered around the lobby, and a crystal chandelier hung precariously over the front desk. The building's exterior had been nondescript, but the interior was something else entirely.

A smiling clerk looked up from the breakfast he'd arranged on the remnants of today's *Peshawar Daily News*. He licked the grease from his fingers and rubbed them on the newspaper.

"Yes?" he said, his voice unexpectedly friendly.

"Nick Sinclair?" Abby asked timidly.

The clerk stood and leaned over the counter. "And you are?"

"A friend," she answered, her timidity gone. "Is he here?"

"You just missed him. He is perhaps just outside." The clerk pointed to the door and turned back to his meal. Abby stepped outside and peered up and down the street, but there was no sign of Nick. She hesitated. Maybe she had heard him after all, maybe he was calling to her from a passing taxi. Maybe she should just leave a message, she thought. But no, she'd come this far, and she wasn't going back to the house. She had to catch up with him, wherever he was. She turned right and headed toward the center of town.

Just past the entrance to Green's, she heard Nick's voice raised in anger. Abby stopped and listened and caught the unmistakable sounds of fighting, scuffling feet, grunts, and the distinct echo of fists striking skin. The sounds were coming from the alley that ran alongside Green's. The area was dark and menacing, and Abby hesitated. Just then Nick shouted again.

She turned into the alley. "Nick?" she called into the blackness. The scuffling stopped. A chill passed through Abby, and she paused, unsure what to do. She blinked to adjust to the darkness, and then, her eyes wide-open, she spotted Nick on the ground, unmoving and bleeding. Two men stood above him, and she watched in horror as one delivered a swift kick to his head.

At the sight of him lying helpless, Abby's fear vanished.

"No," she screamed, running to his side. Slipping her bag from her shoulder to her hand, she swung it in a wide arc at the attackers. "Get out," she roared. She swung the bag again, and the men stepped away from Nick. They stared at her, their eyes wide, and she remembered the words of a Boston police officer at a self-defense course she'd attended: *If an attacker thinks you're crazy, he'll run.*

She struck wildly at the air, almost giddy with the possibilities. She shouted at the men, "Get back!" Her voice was firm, assured. She swung again, but this time, one of the men grabbed her bag, yanking it from her hand. Abby stood, helpless, unable to think. The second man pushed her up against the wall, the ragged plaster scraping her back. He seized the ends of her head scarf and pulled her face to his. His eyebrows, thick, heavy lines of black, hooded his eyes in a sinister shadow. Beads of sweat tracked along his cheeks before disappearing into his unkempt beard. Abby closed her eyes and turned away. He pushed closer, smelling of the streets, that unmistakable scent of sweat and misery and hate. She held her breath, and at that moment he spat in her face.

Abby forced herself to remain perfectly still.

A quiet descended on the alley. Everything seemed to stop, then almost as an afterthought, he shoved her roughly to the ground. She heard their footsteps as they ran, and she opened her eyes slowly. Tears stung her eyes as she wiped the spittle from her face. She pulled herself up and leaned over Nick.

"Nick, can you hear me? Are you okay? Oh, God, you're bleeding." She pulled her scarf from her shoulders and wiped at his wounds.

Nick groaned and pulled himself up, pushing her hands away. "Oh, shit," he said, his fingers surveying the squishy softness of his cheek. "I think they broke my ribs, maybe my jaw."

"Come on, we've got to get you to the hospital." She pulled him to his feet and he stumbled, his legs wobbly.

"What the hell are you doing here?" he asked as though he'd suddenly realized she was there.

"I came to . . ." Abby stopped. Her bag, the picture, the bracelet, their proof—gone, all of it gone. She pulled Nick closer. She couldn't think of that right now. The only thing that mattered was Nick, and getting him to the hospital.

"I'll tell you later," she said as they stepped into the street.

Abby hailed a small taxi and they sped off, Nick leaning into her as the car careened around corners and through a herd of goats to the Lady Reading Hospital, a one-story building that from the outside appeared to be a sprawling house surrounded by gardens. The car screeched to a halt just outside the Casualty Ward, and the driver rushed around, helping Nick from the backseat. Abby followed them into the lobby, where they were caught up in the morning crush—crying patients whose bandages were grimy with dried blood and dirt, wailing women, and children who shrieked in fear. The air here, thick and heavy, smelled of defeat.

The driver guided them through the pack of injured waiting to be seen. "Here," he said, pushing his way roughly through the crowd to the registration desk. He spoke rapidly in Urdu, gesturing wildly to make his point. The clerk came around and took Nick by the arm. "Doctor," said the driver as the clerk led Nick away.

Abby counted out the fare from the coins in her pocket and thanked the driver. *"Shukria,"* she said before taking a seat on the lone wooden bench in the corridor. She inhaled the metallic scent of old blood mixed with fresh vomit. Rusty stretchers, many held together with duct tape, and some still covered with the blood of the previous occupants, lined the hall. She felt a twinge of anxiety and hoped they were in the right place.

She exhaled and leaned back against the wall, finally brooding over the loss of her bag with the photo and the bracelet—her proof, she was sure—that Lars Rousseau was the murderer. "Damn it," she swore out loud, her frustration bubbling over. A small Pakistani nurse stopped and stared.

"Sorry," Abby muttered, and closed her eyes to shut out the place.

After an eternity of waiting, the nurse reappeared. "Come," she said, her face a mask, no smile, no frown, nothing. "Your husband is in here."

Abby stood. "He's not my . . ."

The nurse was in front of her and seemed not to care or even know that Abby was speaking. Instead, she pushed open a large door and motioned for Abby to enter before she hurried away.

Through the now open door, Abby saw a row of stretchers, all holding bleeding, half-dressed men. Visitors squatted on the stained floor, and Abby looked around nervously. In the corner she saw Nick lying on a stretcher, looking vulnerable, less sure of himself.

Suddenly he turned, and seeing Abby, he sat up and waved her over. "There you are. I was starting to get worried. Hey, I didn't even ask—are you okay? Did they hurt you?"

Abby shook her head.

"Did you see the men?" he asked, excited. "Could you point them out?" His fingers probed the wounds and stitches on his face.

Abby reached out and pushed his hand away. "Leave those sutures alone," she said firmly.

Unperturbed, he lifted up a mirror to inspect his wounds. "Jeez, what a mess, huh? Doc says broken ribs and a concussion, and these damn cuts. Maybe a few scars will give my face some character. What do you think?" He peered again into the mirror.

Abby smiled. "I guess you're going to live, huh?"

"That's what they tell me, thanks to you. I have a vague recollection of you fighting them off."

"They did seem pretty intent on doing you some serious harm. Were they trying to kill you?" she asked, dropping her voice to a whisper.

"No, I don't think so, but I suppose if they had killed me, my story would have died as well, so maybe that was their plan. But you interrupted that. Killing me's one thing, but killing a pretty young aid worker, well, that's some pretty serious headlines. So, I don't know." He seemed to be trying to convince himself. "Nah, they probably wanted to scare me off. They might have been looking for this"—he pulled out the tiny tape recorder that held all of his interviews—"but I still have it." He kissed the recorder and returned it to his pocket. "Those thugs assumed I'm another thin-skinned journalist who'll take their hint and get the hell outta here. They sure as hell didn't count on you showing up. They must have some serious explaining to do to someone today, huh?" He smiled slyly. "But I'm not going anywhere yet, except out of *here*. You ready?"

"I . . ." Abby started to tell him about her room and the photo and the bracelet, but she stopped herself. It could wait. There wasn't anything else to do. "Do we need to settle your bill or papers?"

"No." He pulled a sheaf of papers from his pocket—discharge instructions and prescriptions. "I told them to send the bill to the *New York Times*."

The absurdity of the situation suddenly struck Abby, and a chuckle escaped her lips. It all seemed so funny now, which meant she'd probably be crying soon.

Chapter 28

Once outside, Abby hailed a taxi, and after they'd piled into the grimy backseat, Nick sat forward. "Khyber Road—the Pearl Continental," he said before leaning back.

Abby looked at him questioningly.

"I think it might be a good idea to move," he said. "The Pearl is bigger, has better security, not to mention the best scotch in Peshawar, which I think I'm going to need."

At the hotel, Abby whistled. "I've been here with Najeela, but today it looks even more imposing, gaudy almost, just out of place here in Peshawar."

"That's because you're with me. Makes everything look bigger."

Abby couldn't stop the laugh that slid from her lips. "Glad to know the attack didn't hurt your enormous ego."

"Not a bit. And speaking of attacks, the Taliban attacked the Pearl a couple of years ago. Since then it's been renovated and fortified against terrorist attacks. It's probably the safest place to be in the least safe place I know."

"The *least* safe place?"

"Abby, you were attacked too. They took your bag, pushed you around, spat in your face! I mean, you get it, right? Finally? This place is dangerous."

"Oh, my bag," Abby said, suddenly remembering. "Oh, shit! Nick, I have so much to tell you. My room was ransacked, but I *had* what they were looking for. It was—"

"Sshh." Nick put a finger to his lips, his eyes on the driver. "Tell me when we're in the room."

Inside the hotel, Nick motioned for Abby to wait by the elevators. "Pull your veil over your head and stay out of sight." He strode to the hotel's main desk and checked himself in, booking a luxurious suite. Without missing a beat, he asked that a bottle of scotch be delivered to his room.

"The *Times*," he explained to Abby in the elevator, "will want me to be comfortable." He winked, and Abby smiled.

They took the elevator to his suite, and once Nick's scotch arrived, he settled in. "Back to you," he said, twirling his glass. "Finish your story."

"That's just it, Nick. My story finally had an ending. When you let me off yesterday, the house was empty, and when I went into my room, it had been ransacked, and I mean *everything* had been torn apart."

Nick sat up. "Jesus, why didn't you call me?"

"I did. I left a message and waited for you."

"I never got a message, Abby. Shit, are you all right?"

Abby nodded. "I decided that whatever someone was looking for must be with me, and I pulled my bag apart, and there it was." Abby paused.

"Cut to the chase, Abby. What was it?"

"It was a newspaper picture, a grainy photo of a man, and I knew him immediately. He's the man I saw in Geneva. He murdered that woman."

"You're sure it's him?"

Abby nodded. "But there's more. The newspaper belonged to Najeela. She'd handed it to me to have a look at a picture of her fiancé. We were rushing at the time so I stuffed the paper into my bag and I just forgot about it. It's been sitting in the bottom of my bag for at least a month. When I did find the paper and had a good look at the photo, I recognized him right away." She leaned in closer. "He's your man too. His name is Lars Rousseau."

Nick's mouth fell open. "Shit, her fiancé is Lars Rousseau? She's engaged? I have to ask—did you know?"

Abby nodded. "I knew she was engaged, but I never connected her rich European fiancé to your Rousseau or the man in Geneva."

Nick's brow creased. "Do you remember the name of the newspaper or the date?"

"I have no idea what the date was, but the newspaper was local."

Nick seemed to stiffen. He set his glass down. "Jesus, Abby. We're in trouble."

"Wait." Abby held up her hand. "Remember the bracelet I told you about? The one the dead woman was wearing? That ornate, unmistakable diamond cuff? Well, I found that too."

"In your bag?"

"No, it was in Najeela's jewelry drawer. She keeps the jewelry this Lars gives her in a desk in the house. Says her father would kill her if he knew about Lars. She has a stash of the stuff."

Nick whistled. "And you're sure about all of this? The bracelet and Lars and Geneva? All of it?"

"I'm one hundred percent certain." She snapped her answer at him and folded her arms across her chest. "That's why I was coming to see you. The photo and the bracelet were in my bag."

"Incredible, there's my connection. I *knew* Imtiaz and Rousseau were in this together, the moneyman and the field crook, but I just couldn't find the link. They've *never* been seen together, and they cover their tracks so well, there's just been no evidence to connect them. But, damn, he's Najeela's fiancé, huh? There it is. *They* are the team. Rousseau is the brains and the UN and diplomatic connection, and Imtiaz is the street guy, knows where the drugs are and the soft borders. Christ, this breaks my story wide open. And even without the bracelet, you're an eyewitness to everything." Nick whistled softly. "My story gets better by the day."

"If Rousseau is so evil, why is he still operating? I mean, if we can dig this stuff up, why can't the authorities?"

"Good question. I think they must know about his other life, but he's a legitimate diplomat and businessman, and they've never had a serious look at him."

"What about the woman he murdered? Why kill her?"

"Who knows—he'd probably been abusing her at the very least, maybe buying her silence with gifts like that bracelet. When she finally figured out he'd never let her go, she decided to run or get help. He couldn't risk exposure, he couldn't take the chance that the world would know who he really is. Killing her was the least risky road for him. Who will miss an unknown woman? He likely kept her isolated in Geneva, and by the time she realized that there was no way out, it was too late."

"But we can't connect her to *him,* can we?"

Nick drew a deep breath. "Actually, we can. Yesterday, I learned the dead woman was identified as Lars's housekeeper. Turns out one of the women who works in the building heard about the body in the Dumpster, and when she hadn't seen her friend, she went to the police and identified her body."

Abby closed her eyes at the image of the poor woman lying alone in the street. "Do we know who she was?"

Nick shook his head. "Only her first name, Amel, and that she'd been seen cleaning Rousseau's office on more than one occasion, but nothing else."

"We can go to the authorities with this though, right?"

Nick reached out and drew Abby closer. "Not yet, Abby, not yet," he said soothingly. "We have other business first. If she was his housekeeper or companion, and if he saw you—and there's a good chance he did—you're in real danger."

"But how would he know me? I was just some unknown runner in the streets of Geneva. It wasn't like I was wearing an ID. And how would he know I'd wind up with his fiancée? It's not like she took a picture of me."

"Somebody knows who you are already, since your room was tossed. Remember, he saw you in Geneva, and he probably got a damn good look at you. He knows there's a good chance you're with the UN. I'm willing to bet he's already searched through the UN database and found you in the UN IDs—a smiling eyewitness." Nick wrinkled his brow. "I hate to say this, but my trip to Geneva was probably the final straw."

"Oh, Nick, there's more. My e-mail account's been hacked, I think. My e-mails just disappeared, all of them. Just gone."

"That's okay. You didn't have anything in there about any

of this, right?" Abby hesitated, and Nick pounced angrily. "You might as well tell me. Stalling won't change anything."

Abby told him about e-mailing Emily. "It seemed exciting, Nick, and I figured, who would she tell?"

Nick exhaled. "Anything else?"

Abby nodded. "One more thing. Najeela was in the house this morning, and she saw me leaving. She was at the desk, at the computer."

Nick groaned. "I knew it."

"I had the bracelet in my bag, and I knew she'd discover it missing sooner or later, so I told her about, well, I called it a break-in. I figured I needed time to decide what to do with the bracelet."

"Did she seem surprised?"

"I'm not sure, but she did want me to report it to the police, said she'd have to make a report to the UN, and they might send me home because of the security situation."

"Right about now," Nick said, "I'm betting home sounds pretty good."

Abby nodded. "So what do we do now?"

"We get the hell out of here. But, before I forget—I haven't thanked you properly for saving my life."

"I didn't save your life—don't make a bigger deal out of it than it was. I'm a nurse. I'm supposed to do that."

Nick chuckled. "You're supposed to go running in and start beating on men twice your size?" He took a long sip of scotch. "Which hospital did you say you work for?"

"Very funny. Those guys meant business. I had to do *something*."

Nick wrapped an arm around her and kissed her cheek. "I never thought a pretty young woman would rescue me. In my mind, it was always the other way around. Thank you, Abby, seriously."

"Just one more question," she whispered. "Do you think Najeela's involved in all of this?"

Nick frowned. "I'm not even going to answer that, but I will say that Imtiaz and perhaps Rousseau are probably behind today's little incident."

"But—"

Nick held up his hand. "Let me finish. Think about it— US soldiers are intent on destroying all of Afghanistan's poppy fields, and that includes Imtiaz's. He needs another line of work, and though he's always had his hand in trafficking, I think now he's going to jump all the way in. He knows why I'm here, and he and Rousseau have to put a stop to my story. On top of that, now they have the photo and the bracelet, and they've put everything together—the murder, the trafficking, and us. All of it." Nick paused and took a long look at Abby.

"What are you thinking?" she asked, feeling uncomfortable.

"That you and I have to get out of Peshawar. It's just not safe, not that it ever was, but now it's the worst place in the world for us to be. Understand?"

Abby nodded.

Her hands began to tremble and Nick took them in his own. "You'll be okay, but you can't go back to the house. You know that, right? Ransacking your room was sloppy, but it was also a sign that they don't care anymore. This whole thing is about to blow up. We're staying right here until I can make arrangements to get us out."

"Are we safe *here*? Can't they track us?"

"Maybe." Nick winked. "But I registered as a single guest, Ali Hussain."

Abby shook her head. "What about my stuff? My clothes, and—oh, shit, my passport. It was in my bag. I can't go anywhere if I don't have that. And I have work here. I can't just disappear."

"I'll make a call, get a new passport for you, and don't worry about the UN. There'll be plenty of time for discussions with them."

"You can get me a passport, *and* I don't have to worry about the UN?"

Nick nodded and raised his glass, taking a slow drink. His skin, Abby noticed, was the color of wallpaper paste, and his hair, slick with sweat, was plastered to his forehead. The bruises and cuts on his face were blossoming into swirling knobs of red and purple and blue. She reached forward and gently touched his face. "Does it hurt?"

"Not just now." Nick reached up and took her hand in his. He drew her in close and kissed her.

Abby cupped the back of his head and responded with a deep kiss of her own. She sat back and smiled. "I think you should lie down. You look like hell."

He lifted his hand, running it along the sutures under his left eye, and a smudge of color on the inside of his wrist caught Abby's attention. It was the tattoo she'd seen the day she'd met him, but now, surrounded by bruises, it seemed somehow shriveled. She peered closer but couldn't make out what it was—a heart maybe? Funny, she wouldn't have figured him for a heart tattoo. "Old girlfriend?"

He held his wrist out as if remembering the tattoo. "Yeah, long ago. I had her name removed—painful as hell. Decided to stick with the heart." He looked at her intently. "But I could always have a name tattooed there again."

Abby rested her head on Nick's chest and stroked his arm. "You should rest. And you have a head injury. Go easy on the scotch."

Nick sipped at his drink. "You know what they say about saving someone's life? That you're tied to that person forever. You might as well get used to me, huh?"

Abby stood and plucked the glass from Nick's hand, placing it on the table. "Come on." She led him into the bedroom. "Lie down." She pushed him gently onto one of the two beds in the room and pulled off his shoes. "Get some sleep. I'm going to lie down right here." She pointed to the other bed.

"Aww, Abby. I'm a sick man. I need you here." He patted the spot beside him.

"In your dreams, Nick, in your dreams." She leaned in and kissed him again. "Sleep tight," she whispered, pulling a sheet over him.

Chapter 29

"Jesus, my head is killing me. Any pain medicine in that bag they gave me?" Nick cradled his head in his hands.

"Whoa, sorry, Nick. I didn't know you were awake." Abby walked back into the bedroom, bathed now in the shadows of late afternoon. She picked up the paper bag that held Nick's discharge instructions and peered inside. "Paracetamol," she said, holding a bottle of pills.

"What the hell is that?" he asked, suspicious.

Abby laughed. "Tylenol, Nick. They gave you Tylenol. Will that do?"

"It'll have to do for now." He reached for the tablets Abby

held out. He swallowed the pills and chased them down with his unfinished glass of scotch.

"Nick, seriously, no more scotch. That stuff can make you bleed or affect your head more than it already has."

"Fair enough, I can follow orders. Besides, I have to get busy making arrangements to get us out of here." He pushed himself up from the bed and pulled on his shoes. "I have to go down to the lobby and make some calls, see if I can get a computer and Internet connection."

"Can't you call from here?"

"No," he answered almost too quickly. "The lobby is more anonymous, harder to trace. So"—he checked for his wallet—"stay here. Don't let anyone in and do not go out. Understand?"

"Can't I come down with you?"

"A pretty young blonde will stand out like a sore thumb, and Imtiaz will be all over us in a flash."

"But why are you going?"

"Dark hair, nondescript male, no one will ever notice me. Plus, I know how to slip in and out of these places."

A laugh broke through Abby's smile. "Sorry, Nick, but maybe you should have a look in the mirror. *Nondescript* is not exactly the word I'd use." His wounds had flared into livid bruises while he slept, and he now sported a swollen fighter's face complete with stitches.

Nick hurried to the bathroom and stood in front of the mirror, surveying the damage to his face. "Ah, shit!" she heard him mutter. He stormed back into the bedroom. "I'll call the concierge and say I have a big business deal going through, ask him to get me a computer and cell phone."

"Will they do that?"

"For Mr. Hussain in the fancy suite? They'll be tripping over themselves. I'll get us some food while I'm at it." He picked up the phone, dialed the desk, and spoke in an uncharacteristically soft voice before turning back to Abby. "Coffee and Diet Coke. My new beverages of choice. You too?"

Abby nodded.

A few minutes later, a soft knock on the door made them both freeze. "Shh," Nick said. "Who is it?" he called.

"Concierge, sir, with the items you requested. Shall I leave them by the door?"

"Yeah, thanks. If I need any help, I'll call you."

"Yes, sir." Footsteps echoed back down the hall.

Nick peered through the peephole and opened the door, quickly pulling in the computer and phone. He set up a workstation at the desk and sat in front of the computer, typing furiously.

"Nick," Abby asked, "do you mind if I turn on the television? I haven't seen the news in ages."

"Great idea. See what's happening in the world."

Abby curled up on the couch and clicked on the television. She ran through the channels until she found the BBC.

"Keep it there," Nick said.

"Room service," a voice called from the hall.

"Just leave it," Nick called. He rose and looked out before opening the door and pulling in the tray. "Didn't know what you might want, so I got steak, cheeseburgers, hot dogs, and fries."

Abby pulled herself up. "I'm starving." She sank into a seat at the table. "How are things coming?" She nodded toward the computer.

"Great." Nick moved to the table to eat. "I'm in touch with someone in Pakistani Intelligence. I can't tell you more than that right now."

"That's okay. Is he going to help us?"

Nick hesitated, smiled, then laughed. "He is."

"What's so funny?"

"Nothing," Nick said almost too quickly. "I have a head injury, remember?"

"Oh, God, are you going to use that excuse now?"

"Maybe, but for now, I just want to devour this steak. You all set? How's the burger?" he asked through a mouthful of food.

"Good, really good."

Nick finished his meal, and picking up the cell phone, he walked into the bedroom. "I'm gonna shut the door. Don't be offended. This call is business."

"I'm not a thin-skinned damsel, Nick. Do what you need to."

Abby turned back to the television and clicked to the local evening news. There on the screen, a smiling Lars appeared. Abby stood and moved closer. "Nick, hurry. You've got to see this."

"What?" he asked, opening the door.

Abby motioned toward the television, and Nick turned, his jaw dropping. A second picture of Lars Rousseau flashed across the screen.

Nick stood and watched.

"Look behind him. There, do you see *him?*" She pointed to a faint but unmistakable image of Imtiaz in the crowd of partyers.

The photos faded and the newsman returned to the screen. *"The UN raised more than one million dollars last night here in Peshawar for its Pakistan programs, and European philanthropist Lars Rousseau hosted the lavish event. Now, on to other stories. . . ."*

Nick snapped off the television. "Shit, they're both in town and not afraid to be seen together. Where does Imtiaz live?"

"He has homes and farms in Afghanistan, and when he's here, he stays with Najeela's family. I don't think Lars would stay there. It's too risky for him and Najeela."

"Shit, he's somewhere in Peshawar, maybe even here at the Pearl. This is the best place, and he sure as hell wouldn't be at Green's."

"What's that mean for us?"

Nick turned and headed back to the bedroom. "I'm gonna be blunt. I think Lars is going to come after you. They tore your room apart yesterday, and today they have the newspaper and bracelet, proof that you've put it together. They may have been interested in me this morning, but now it's you they absolutely have to eliminate if they want to survive. It means we need to get out of here ASAP."

"Can we?" Abby asked, trying to hide the tremor in her voice.

"We can." Nick's brow wrinkled. "I'm still working on it, but we'll get out." He turned and went back to the bedroom, shutting the door as he went.

Abby curled up on the couch and waited. It seemed hours before Nick emerged. "We're all set," he said, smiling.

"When?"

"Early tomorrow. We're on a UN convoy with aid supplies to the north, to Skardu and beyond. That area is still a mess from the floods, and they're resupplying. We'll follow, and then we'll separate from the convoy in Islamabad, where we'll be met by consular officials."

"Tomorrow seems a long way off."

"It'll be here before you know it. Relax." Nick stole a kiss, grinning. "Just trust me on this." He looked at his watch. "Christ, it's eight o'clock. You must be exhausted. Go lie down. I'll be in soon, and remember, dream of me tonight and not the wily Lars."

Abby laughed. "I'll do my best."

Chapter 30

"Wake up, Abby," Nick whispered, his lips brushing her temple. "It's six a.m., time to go."

Abby opened her eyes and smiled. "Best wake-up I've had since I arrived in Pakistan." She sat up and stretched. "Is it too much to ask if there's coffee?"

Nick shook his head. "Sorry, we're leaving quietly and without notice. That means no coffee, no breakfast. We'll get something later."

"Pass me that robe, will you? I'm not decent."

Nick smiled. "Jeez, Abby, I'm still in pain. Have a look at these wounds. You don't really think I'd be ogling you, do you?"

Abby laughed. "Of course not. I just like robes."

He handed her the robe. "You're killing me here, Abby, killing me."

"Do I have time for a shower?" she asked, pulling the robe on.

"If you're quick about it."

Abby headed to the bathroom, and as directed, she took a quick shower and wriggled into the only clothes she had. She ran her fingers through her wet hair and frowned. No comb, no eyeliner, no lipstick. She couldn't remember the last time she'd shown only her fresh-scrubbed face to the world. "I'm as ready as I'm gonna be," she said, stepping back into the room.

"You look beautiful in the morning, Abby."

"Wow, thanks. Seriously."

"You're welcome, but back to business. Here's what we're going to do. We're taking the stairs, and we're not checking out. The car is here, but it's by the garage entrance, so we're going out that way. We don't want anyone to see us. Stay right behind me, and move quickly." He slipped the cell phone into his pocket.

"We're not checking out, *and* we're taking the phone? Won't we be in trouble?"

"You are a refreshingly middle-class girl, Abby. Not to worry—the hotel will be paid, just not today."

"All right, lead the way."

He opened the door and peered into the hallway. "Let's go." Nick held his finger to his mouth. "Remember, quiet."

Abby nodded and followed him to the hallway and the staircase. They jogged down the steps, and at the bottom, Nick opened the door. "Garage. We just have to get through here."

They dashed through the garage, their footfalls echoing in the empty space. A ray of light poked through the dim structure, and they emerged into a full early sun. Abby held her hands up to block the light, already beating down in what would be another scorching day.

"Over there." Nick tilted his head toward a shiny white SUV, the blue UN logo on its door, parked by the garage entrance.

Abby couldn't help the heavy sigh of relief that slipped through her lips.

"This," he said, pulling open the door to the SUV, "is our vehicle, a very generous loan from the UN. Hop in." He turned the key that had been left in the ignition, then eased the car out onto Khyber Road. "We're heading up to Circular Road. The convoy's leaving from the UN suboffice there."

"I just have to ask," Abby said, adjusting the visor against the morning's growing glare. "You're sure the UN office knows I'm leaving my post?"

Nick nodded. "They do. They actually sent a message that they loved you, wanted to offer you a safer posting."

Abby felt a small thrill—the UN loved her! How many people could say that?

Nick frowned. "I told them you'd be busy."

"Nick, are you kidding me? Why would you do that?"

"You're coming to New York with me, right?"

"I guess, at least until we get this stuff straightened out, but I think I'd like to work with the UN again. You better not have messed this up for me."

"I haven't, I promise, but just wait—anything can happen in New York."

Still secretive, she thought, shaking her head. Some things would never change.

They set off, and Abby tried to quiet her nerves. They'd be fine, she reminded herself once again. Lars was probably still sleeping back at the Pearl, and Nick would write his story and put Lars away. Abby sat back and watched as Nick pulled onto

Circular Road to join the line of vehicles parked along the narrow street.

"Stay here," he said as he parked the car and stepped out to speak with a group of men standing by their vehicles.

Abby watched as Nick spoke with the men, mostly Pakistani drivers, she thought. He folded his arms across his chest and nodded intently as the conversation wore on before he turned and headed back, leaning into the window. "Bad news—the UN's decided to join a NATO supply convoy, and they're carrying fuel in their trucks. All that fuel makes me nervous, but the good news is there are armed soldiers in the lead."

Abby peered through the windshield at the line of tanker trucks. "That's even better for us then, right? I mean soldiers. I think it's good news."

Nick smiled. "Ever the optimist. Okay—we're just waiting for two more tankers." He pulled himself into the SUV and squeezed Abby's thigh. "Tomorrow at this time, we'll be in Dubai, or maybe Paris if that strikes your fancy."

Abby smiled. "Just about now, anyplace but here strikes my fancy."

A loud rumbling broke through the hum of the idling vehicles, and all heads turned as the final two trucks, snorting and spewing exhaust, pulled into position behind Abby and Nick. Within minutes, a small, wiry man ran the length of the convoy. "He's doing a final count," Nick said. "As soon as he cross-checks his numbers, we'll be moving out."

"Are you okay to drive? Your eye is really swollen. Can you even see?"

"I'm fine, we're not going too far anyway."

Within minutes, the vehicles pulled out and wound their way along the street before turning onto Kohat Road, and finally onto the Grand Trunk Road. Nick reached over and stroked

Abby's face. "Close your eyes if you want. This will be an hour or so."

The city of Peshawar faded away in the rearview mirror, and Abby let her head fall back, a yawn escaping from her lips. "Well, maybe . . . maybe I'll just close my eyes . . ." With that, Abby was lost in her dreams until a loud explosion jolted her awake. She sat bolt upright. The convoy had ground to a halt.

"What the hell was that?" she asked, her voice hoarse with sleep.

"Stay here," Nick shouted as he bounded from the vehicle and sprinted along the convoy. Abby craned her neck and watched as a large cloud of curling black smoke filled the sky. She could see orange flames leaping over the vehicles, and she watched as the thick, choking black fog began to fill the road. She pushed open her door and stepped onto the tarmac. Once there, she could see it. An enormous fireball up ahead—one of the trucks was on fire.

Oh, God, the fuel trucks! She watched as the fire and explosions spread to the next truck in line, then the next. The sky turned black, and the road seemed consumed with orange balls of fire. She couldn't see Nick through the thick haze of smoke, but she could see the flames spreading. It wouldn't be long before they'd be here, right where she stood. She froze, unsure where to go, what to do. Where the hell was Nick anyway? Just as she began to silently curse him, he emerged from the shroud of smoke. Coughing and covered with a layer of soot, he pulled Abby from the road. "Get over there," he shouted over the thunderous explosions, "but not too far. It was an IED. Someone was waiting for us."

A cold, hard chunk of fear sat heavily in Abby's chest. "*Us?* You and me?"

"No, I don't think we're the targets. Probably NATO and the

fuel trucks, or maybe they thought it was a US military convoy. It doesn't matter right now. The vehicles damn near ran into one another when they all suddenly braked, and now there's too much heat and no damn room to maneuver them away," Nick said, guiding Abby from the road. "They've already radioed for an evacuation. The helicopter will be here shortly. This area here is the clearest, so probably best for a landing. Stay right here and listen. When the chopper arrives, get on."

"No, Nick. I'm not going without you."

"Just get on. Do you hear me? No arguments. I'll be right back. I'm going to check for wounded."

"I'm the nurse, I should go." She shouted to be heard over the roar of the advancing flames.

"I *know* you're the nurse! For Christ's sake, stay here and we'll get the injured to you. If the chopper comes first, just get on it. I'll be right behind you. Do you hear me?"

Before she could reply, Nick turned and sprinted back into the thick blanket of smoke that covered the road. Abby stood alone and watched as the swelling black clouds billowed over the road, orange flames licking at everything in their path. An overwhelming fear washed over her, and she stood perfectly still. She took a deep breath and inhaled a mouthful of acrid smoke. The smoke caught at the back of her throat, and she was seized by a spasm of coughing. Her eyes watered and she tried to blink away the sting. Instinctively, she moved back to where the air seemed not as dense.

She stood waiting, alternately holding her breath and exhaling. She could feel the scorching heat on her skin, and she watched as burning embers filled the sky. The fire was only four vehicles ahead now. In only minutes the inferno would incinerate everything on the road.

Suddenly, over the din of the explosions, she heard the unmistakable whir of helicopter blades. *Rescue*—they were going to be rescued. She stood on her toes and peered down the road, but there was no sign of Nick.

She turned back, and there, hovering just above the cloud of smoke, she spied the sweetest sight imaginable—a shiny helicopter with the blue UN logo on the side, its spinning blades cutting through the smoke and fanning the fire with fury. Abby stood and watched as it descended and landed with a soft thud. She waited, unsure what to do. The lure of safety was great, but she just couldn't leave yet. She'd ask how long they'd wait—how many they could take. Then she'd wait for Nick and the others.

She moved closer and watched as a man appeared in the doorway, furiously waving her over. He poked his head out and looked straight at her—and Abby stiffened. Through the fog of smoke, she could just make out his wire-rimmed glasses and thinning gray hair. Abby felt a chill run down her spine, and slowly, as though time had stopped, it came to her who he was.

It was *him*. It was Lars Rousseau.

Abby was suddenly paralyzed—unable to move, unable to think, unable to breathe.

"Do you remember me?" Lars Rousseau shouted over the roar of the engines.

Smoke filled Abby's throat, and she watched helplessly as Lars jumped to the ground. She coughed, and fueled by a sudden surge of energy, she turned and ran. But Lars was too quick. He was on her in an instant. He grabbed her arm and she fell forward, her face in the dirt.

Lars pulled her up roughly and shouted into her face, "Didn't think I'd find you, did you? You thought you could slip away." His eyes flashed, and Abby tried to pull away, but his grip was too tight. "You're nothing," he spat out, "just like the others—the women who thought they'd get something from me. But I'll always win. The world loves *me,* and your death in this fire will be a sad dot on Pakistan's history—nothing else." His spittle sprayed onto Abby's face, and she watched as he nervously eyed the rapidly approaching fire.

Abby felt the heat sting her eyes, and her nostrils and mouth filled with smoke as the fire spat burning embers everywhere. Lars was suddenly seized by a long, choking cough, and his grip on Abby loosened. She snatched the opportunity and pulled away, preparing to run, but instead Lars turned and sprinted to the helicopter, quickly hoisting himself back inside.

As Abby watched, a second figure appeared in the doorway.

A woman, it was a woman. The shadowy figure embraced Lars, then lifted a delicate hand and waved. Abby froze.

Najeela. It was Najeela.

Oh my God, Najeela was one of *them,* the tightly woven circle of thieves and killers. How could she not have seen it? Abby watched as Lars tenderly smoothed Najeela's hair. They shared a kiss—and suddenly Abby's fear vanished. A sudden burst of anger, of hate, welled up inside, and she froze where she stood, oblivious to the flames inching ever closer.

Suddenly an arm encircled her, pulling her back. She opened her mouth to scream, but then she noticed the tiny, heart-shaped tattoo. Relief swept over her. She turned and followed as Nick led her away from the flames. In a haze of smoke, Abby and Nick stood perfectly still and watched as the helicopter hurtled into the air. Then it was gone, swallowed up by the dense fog of smoke and fire. Only the rumble of the engine and the churning columns of smoke were proof that it still hovered just overhead.

As Abby raised her head to peer through the cloud of smoke, the engine suddenly silenced, the furious spinning of the blades through the smoke ceased. The only sound was the thunder of the raging fire. Despite the sting of the smoke, Abby opened her eyes wide and turned to Nick.

"Where is he?" she shouted.

Before Nick could answer, a thunderous explosion rocked the sky. The helicopter had exploded in midair, a fireball erupting in the sky. Bits and pieces of metal rained down on them and they ran for cover, watching in disbelief.

"Najeela—" Abby broke down, unable to finish.

"I know," Nick said. "I saw her from the road. I know you believed in her for a long time, and I'm sorry."

They huddled, wrapped about one another, watching as the flames inched closer. "NATO radioed for an evacuation *vehicle*," Nick said. "We should be out of here in no time."

Abby nodded, tears and smoke stinging her eyes. She wiped her face on her sleeve, and as she lifted her head, she saw a Pakistani army vehicle pull up nearby. She breathed a long sigh of relief and watched as a small soldier, short and muscular, hoisted himself out of the vehicle, some kind of machine gun in his hand. He turned and strode toward Abby and Nick, pulling off his combat helmet as he walked. When he lifted his head, Abby gasped in recognition.

Hana! The soldier was Hana. Abby turned and looked at Nick, who was smiling broadly at Hana. "Good to see you," he said. "What took you so long?"

Abby remained speechless, her mouth open wide. She could only gape at Hana. Gone was her sullen expression, and gone too was her drab *shalwar kameez*. Instead, she was dressed in fatigues, a bevy of stripes and emblems adorning her lapels.

She smiled confidently, and cradling her gun close to her chest, she reached out and took Abby's hand. "Glad to see you're safe. Come, let's go. I've already ordered the remaining vehicles to set up a perimeter. Let's get you out of here before the press shows."

"Did you see the helicopter go down?" Nick asked. "Lars and Najeela were on board."

Hana nodded. "A rescue team will check for survivors, though I don't think anyone survived the force of that explosion."

Still grappling with the sight of Hana as a soldier, Abby could only gape as Nick pulled her into the rear seat with him. Hana, her gun in hand, rode shotgun. She barked orders at the driver, who turned the vehicle around and headed back to Peshawar.

Abby almost stuttered when she finally asked Nick, "Did you know? Did you know that she's a soldier?"

"Well, strictly speaking, she is a soldier, but she's in the Intelligence branch, the ISI, and she's currently working with the UN and Interpol to break a huge trafficking ring."

Abby's mouth fell open once again. "Hana was your intelligence connection?" Abby looked again at Hana, crisp and professional and definitely a commanding presence. So different from the brooding maid whose face had been such a mask. Abby shook her head and leaned forward. "Hana, it's an honor to finally meet you."

Hana nodded, a smile breaking through the mask of her face. "We'll talk later," she said, her eyes resting on the driver.

Abby sat back into Nick's embrace. "Is it over?"

"Almost," he said, planting a kiss on her head.

Chapter 31

T he Pakistani army SUV flew over the roads, depositing its three weary occupants back at the UN staff house, where a still-stunned Abby was finally able to take a slow, deep breath. Her heart ached in this house where so much had happened.

"I'll make the tea," she said, looking pointedly at Hana. "But we have to talk. There's so much I don't know."

"Seems fair," Nick said, dropping into a chair.

Hana followed suit. "This is the first time I've sat in here. It looks smaller from this vantage point."

"Since this was really your project first, Hana," Nick said, "you should probably start."

Hana folded her hands, resting them demurely on the table. "The problem is—where to start?" She hesitated, pushing a stray tendril of brown hair behind her ear. "Well, as you can see, I'm an officer in the Pakistani army. I trained in London and in Texas"—she turned to Abby—"which accounts for my perfect English."

Abby smiled, remembering that first day, when she'd spoken louder, hoping that might help Hana understand her.

"My name is Hana Rahim, and I'm assigned to the Intelligence unit, the ISI."

Abby sat forward, her eyes wide. Hana was an honest-to-God spy?

"I've worked mainly on Taliban and Al Qaeda issues, but was asked to join Interpol on this assignment, digging into human trafficking. It's a painful subject here in the East, and I was honored—well, until I learned that I would be the housekeeper and cook here." Hana smiled then. "You may have noticed that I wasn't very good at it."

Abby laughed. "Why a housekeeper then?"

"People don't notice housekeepers. They're invisible to so many people."

"Like Lars's housekeeper in Geneva?"

"Exactly. And here, Najeela hardly noticed me. Her eyes glazed over when she saw me. I simply didn't exist, and that made it easy to watch and to listen. But then you came—all cheerful and bubbly and hoping to be my friend, and I thought you might blow my cover. I had to keep you at a distance."

Abby nodded. "But why here? Why this house? Why not the Siddiqui house?"

"I was assigned to this house because of Najeela's relationship with both Imtiaz Siddiqui and Lars Rousseau. You know about their involvement by now, I think?"

Abby nodded.

"They were partners in crime—they ran Afghanistan's largest opium-smuggling project for years, and though they've long been suspected of being involved in trafficking, that was harder to unravel. They leave fewer fingerprints and their victims are afraid to speak up. It's a mess, and Interpol's been working to flush them out for years. It was decided to infiltrate them where they live—quite literally—and Najeela, as the common denominator, was to be our focus. We had no idea you were coming here, and when we learned that the UN was sending an American nurse, we did consider shutting down the operation, but, as you know now, we didn't."

Nick piped in, "My arrival threw a wrench into Interpol's plans. I came to Peshawar to chase after Imtiaz. When the UN heard I was coming here, they chose you as the focus of my sidebar story. Interpol didn't know what I was up to, but they didn't like it, all these Americans in the middle of their investigation. Poor Hana here spent a few weeks trying to figure me out. It was my trip to Geneva that piqued her interest, and when I returned here, she finally opened up to me, and we compared notes. But even then, she wasn't allowed to share the Rousseau and Imtiaz connection with me. I only learned that solid link yesterday when you told me about the newspaper photo of Rousseau." As though Nick just remembered his injuries, he ran his hand along his swollen eyelid.

"Are you okay? Do you need ice?" Abby asked.

"Only if it's in a glass filled with scotch," he said with a wink. "But like so much else, that'll have to wait."

Abby rolled her eyes. "Back to business—you really didn't know each other before all of this?"

Hana glanced at Nick and shook her head. "No, we didn't. And when he first arrived, I was as suspicious of him as you seemed to be. I thought he could blow our whole operation here, and I tried to get to know him, to be nice, but as you may remember, he didn't even notice me in the beginning. It was only after you first met Imtiaz and Nick grilled you about the meeting that I thought he could be a help to me and not a hindrance. But even then, I didn't share much with him until after he returned from his Geneva trip."

Nick smiled sheepishly. "True. The housekeeper ploy worked, at least in the beginning. I didn't pay much attention to her beyond the usual pleasantries. It was your telling me that she scared Imtiaz off when I was away that made me finally take another look. And with you as a witness to Lars's murder of the woman in Geneva, the pieces of the puzzle are falling into place."

"What about Najeela?" Abby asked. "Was she a part of it?"

"We'll never know for sure," Hana answered. "But at Lars's bidding, she was watching you. Lars probably got a good look at you in Geneva and traced you here. He must have been giddy with the luck of you landing here with his girlfriend. He was probably watching you and just biding his time, waiting to see if you knew anything. To cover himself, and not scare Najeela away, he likely told her you'd seen something in Geneva—I don't think she knew just what that was."

"Did she ransack my room?" Abby asked.

Hana shook her head. "I think Imtiaz was behind that, but who knows? Najeela may have been involved in that as well. At the very least, I'd say she was guilty of helping them cover their tracks. She was their money conduit. She made all their money transfers. That's why she was so often gone from the house. It wasn't UN business, it was her own business."

"What about Mohammed, the driver?"

"He did work for Imtiaz. Nick tried to warn you."

"Why couldn't *you* tell me, at least about him?"

"Abby," Hana said, "this was a big operation. We couldn't just let you in on it. We couldn't risk your slipping and somehow tipping him off."

Abby sighed. "He was seen one night at the rescue house. Was it Imtiaz who sent him?"

Hana nodded. "Mohammed's in custody. He told us that he was instructed to have a look at the house and try to see the girls, make sure they didn't belong to Imtiaz."

"What about the rescue house? Will word get out? Will they be in danger?"

Hana smiled. "That house has been relocated. Everyone there is fine."

"Finally, some good news." Abby leaned forward. "But, there's still so much. What about Malik, your son, the picture in the Protection Tent? Is he real? Is he your son?"

Hana's brow wrinkled. "He's the son of my sister," she said with a hint of sadness. "And he *is* missing, sold by his father to a camel jockey or trafficker. I hoped that if I told his story, we might find him, and although there has been no news, the search will go on—for him and the others. That search won't stop."

There was almost too much information for Abby to digest. Her mind was a jumble, but she had to ask about Lars. "I know that Lars was important, but how could he get women out, how could he travel with such impunity?"

"He was a former midlevel Swiss diplomat. That gave him lifelong diplomatic status—no customs checks or searches for him. He slid through every time, never warranting a second look. But it didn't stop there. He donated to the UN for the easy access it afforded him to refugee areas, where he targeted the most vulnerable, the women and children who'd barely be missed, and he passed that information on to Imtiaz, who passed it on to the front men, who made the first contacts and bought or tricked the women. The police in Geneva are looking into all of this, and they've reopened several unsolved cases with similar victims, all, they think now, likely trafficked."

"It's all so heartbreaking." Abby looked away and swallowed the sadness she felt for Amel. "What about Najeela's parents? Were they involved?"

"No, at least as far as we can tell, they're innocent," Hana said, "but the investigation's a long way from over. Who knows where it will lead."

"And Imtiaz?" Abby asked.

"Picked up by Interpol just minutes after your convoy rolled over the IED. He's in custody, sitting in an Islamabad prison awaiting arraignment in the International Court."

"That's a relief, but what about the IED? Was it intended for us?"

"No, it's more likely the NATO fuel convoy was the target, not you and Nick. And as for the UN helicopter with Lars and Najeela, Lars may have known you were on that convoy, but maybe not. He did know his time was up, that we were closing in, and we think he was trying to get out before we arrested him. Because of Lars's position, he was able to arrange for a UN helicopter, and when the explosion occurred, the pilot likely heard the transmission requesting help, and he *had* to respond. Lars had no choice. That pilot was mandated by the UN to help— they had to turn around. When Lars saw you, he may have thought he could grab you, or maybe kill you there, but that fire was too fierce, and when you ran and then struggled, he probably decided to let the fire kill you. He could keep his hands clean, and he probably ordered the pilot to take off, telling him you'd refused rescue. It was his own arrogance that killed him."

Abby shook her head, inhaling deeply. "I'm just not convinced Najeela knew everything. She was spoiled and self-centered, I'll give you that, but I don't think she was evil."

"Maybe not," Hana said, "but it doesn't matter now."

Abby sighed heavily and rose. She had tea to make.

Abby and Nick were booked on a UN flight to Dubai, the spot where Abby's nightmare first surfaced. It felt a bit like coming full circle. Now she could call Emily and tell her the full and final story of her nightmare in Geneva. While she headed for the phones, Nick headed for the Irish pub smack in the center of this flashy Middle East terminal. "You can find me at the Irish Village when you're done," he said, then planted a lingering kiss on Abby's lips. "Don't be long or there'll be a line of willing ladies ahead of you."

"Now that I finally know you, I think you're pretty funny for a pain in the ass, Pulitzer Prize winner."

"Jesus, are we on that again?" Nick winked.

The following day, they arrived in New York, where Nick put the finishing touches on his story, and Abby headed to the UN for wrap-up meetings. She'd moved into his apartment, a third-floor walk-up in Murray Hill, and though the space was tiny, it was perfect for two people still getting to know each other.

Nick submitted his series on trafficking. *It was Abby Monroe's courage,* he wrote, *that exposed the full story of corruption threatening the very foundation of the UN and the people it served and protected. Lars Rousseau was nothing more than a common criminal, but his days of victimizing the world's innocents are over.*

*Human trafficking along the Rousseau/Siddiqui route has ended
forever.*

The series went to press within days, and Abby wasn't surprised when it was mentioned as a Pulitzer Prize candidate. The
series was picked up by the wires and carried in most news-
papers around the world.

"Listen," Nick said one morning not long after they'd settled
in with coffee and the Sunday edition of the *Times*, "what do
you think? You gonna stay here in New York with me?"

Abby closed her eyes for an instant before she answered.
"I'm not sure yet, Nick. How about we just try this—try *us*—on
for a while?" She leaned in and kissed him, a long, slow, deep
kiss, then she nestled into his arms. Her skin tingled as he ran
his fingers through her hair.

"You have to admit, we are good together, aren't we?" Nick
asked.

"Hmm, we are. But you should know I've talked to the UN
about going to India, working with one of the rescue houses the
UN sponsors there. I want to help women like Mariyah and
Bina and Anyu find the leaves on their trees and the stars in
their sky. I want them to know they're not alone."

Nick whistled. "You are something, Abby Monroe." He ran
his fingers through her hair. "But what about the stars in your
sky? I'm not very poetic, but, well, need an assistant? Because it
sounds like a perfect sequel to my trafficking series."

Abby smiled. "Maybe . . . after all, things worked out pretty
well with the last reporter who interviewed me."

Author's Note

When I began to research human trafficking for this novel, I was stunned by the extensive local and global reach of this insidious and cruel business. The harsh reality is almost mind-numbing, for human trafficking may well be the fastest growing industry in the world. And, why not? The UN Population Fund recently reported that it was the third most lucrative illegal trade, surpassed only by drugs and arms trading, and brings in an estimated 32 billion tax-free dollars per year.

The International Office for Migration (IOM) estimates that between 700,000 to 4 million people are trafficked each year, but those numbers may be much higher, and because of the secretive nature of trafficking, the exact numbers will likely never be known.

Human trafficking remains the world's dirty little secret, and it's been easy for us to turn a blind eye because we've believed it happens *somewhere else,* in Cambodia or China or Bangladesh, but that *somewhere else* has come home, and these days, it's happening right where we live.

Here in the United States much of the sex trafficking occurs in massage parlors, which frequently operate in strip malls, office buildings, and, sometimes residential homes in urban, suburban, and rural areas in almost all fifty states. The Polaris Project reports that these storefront massage parlors have sometimes been found to be fronts for these brothels. The common denominator among victims is that, more often than not, they are undocumented, and therefore isolated. It is that isolation that makes them easy prey, invisible to the rest of us, and because they are, their miseries continue unabated.

Potential victims are everywhere. They are the voiceless, the invisible, the throwaway street children in big cities, the long forgotten and the most vulnerable among us.

There is much to be done, but first we must open our eyes to the misery that is too often right in front of us. Only when we finally see them, can we make a difference.

For more information, please visit my website: www.roberta gately.com.

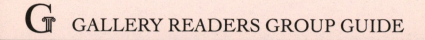

The Bracelet

Roberta Gately

Introduction

Boston nurse Abby Monroe takes a UN position in one of the most dangerous and unstable countries in the world: Pakistan. Nick Sinclair is a *New York Times* reporter on a mission to uncover a human trafficking ring that spreads from the villages of India and Pakistan to major cities in the West—and with Abby's help, he thinks he can finally incriminate the shadowy figure at its heart. As Abby struggles to heal the refugees she works with every day, she also volunteers at a local halfway house, where women who have escaped their captors can recover from the ordeal of being trafficked and work toward a better life. But when a unique piece of jewelry helps Abby realize she's witnessed a murder by a high-ranking official, she and Nick must break the story before she becomes its next casualty.

Questions and Topics for Discussion

1. Abby takes the nursing position with the UN as a way to escape from her past—the ex-boyfriend who dumped her and the job from which she was laid off. How does her desire to run away mirror that of the underprivileged women and girls who voluntarily go off with traffickers in an attempt to have a better life? Is being able to escape one's surroundings a privilege of a particular class?

2. Would you ever do as Abby did and travel to a foreign, dangerous place in order to change your life? What are the risks and what are the rewards?

3. Abby feels guilty that she and her roommate Emily left New Orleans after Hurricane Katrina. How do the atrocities of Katrina compare with what Abby eventually sees in Pakistan? How are they connected?

4. When did you first realize that Najeela is not the trustworthy friend that Abby wanted her to be? What were some red flags? Have you ever been in a similar position with a friend?

5. Abby doesn't have her own car and it's dangerous for her, an American woman, to walk the streets of Peshawar alone.

How does her isolation in the UN house amplify her own fears and put her at risk? Is she more vulnerable there than she would be at Nick's hotel? Are there positive aspects of her seclusion?

6. So much of the secrecy surrounding human trafficking, and so much of the shame for the victims, seems to be related to the patriarchal society of Pakistan and its surrounding areas. How does the subjugation of women in this part of the world allow for these greater atrocities to take place?

7. Abby dislikes Nick when she first meets him, but ultimately he proves to be a great romantic hero. Is there ever any doubt that they might end up together? Did you think she'd ever consider going back to Eric? How does Abby and Nick's love story enhance the novel?

8. On page 166 Zara says, "When women work together, anything is possible." How are women in a unique position to fight against corruption in the Eastern world?

9. One of the refrains that we hear from so many of the women at the safe house is, "I'm still a good girl." Why do you think it's important for them, after their terrible ordeals, to reiterate this phrase? What does this say about their culture, that the victims of sexual crimes are often the ones to be blamed?

10. When the women at the halfway house told their stories, how did you react? Were you able to read the explicit parts? Was it difficult to read?

11. Did you suspect Hana's and Mohammed's true loyalties? Were there hints along the way?

12. *The Bracelet* is a novel, so the events that take place in it are fictional. But human trafficking is a very real and dire problem. How would your understanding of the events of the book change if the book were nonfiction? Does reading a fictional account provide a more accessible window into this world of corruption?

13. What do you think Abby's future has in store for her? What do you think will come of Abby and Nick's relationship?

Enhance Your Book Club

1. The most significant characters in *The Bracelet* are the victims of trafficking—from the women at the halfway house to the missing people whose photos graced the walls of the Protection Tent. Visit the website www.human trafficking.org to learn more about real-life cases and what you and your book club members can do to help.

2. Abby's volunteer work at the refugee camp in Peshawar is enriching and opens her eyes to a new world. Schedule a volunteer day with your book group. Whether it's serving food at a local soup kitchen or delivering meals to the infirm, spend some time helping others. Discuss what you learned with your book club.

3. Although Abby eats plenty of cheeseburgers at the American Club, she also enjoys Pakistani cuisine. Consult a Pakistani cookbook and arrange a potluck dinner with your book group!